CHELSEA TOFFS
AND
FULHAM BARBARIANS

Chelsea Toffs
and
Fulham Barbarians

Harry Turner

eMPIRICUS
BOOKS

London, England

First published in Great Britain 2012
by Empiricus Books,
93–95 Gloucester Place,
London W1U 6JQ

www.januspublishing.co.uk

British Library Cataloguing-in-Publication Data
A catalogue record for this book is available from the British Library

ISBN 978-1-902835-27-3

Cover Design: Baker
www.jackets.moonfruit.com

Printed at AAR VEE Printers Pvt. Ltd.

Dedication

For Carolyn, Gregory and Jane

Contents

Acknowledgements

Grateful thanks are due to the following:

Ackroyd, Peter, *London: The Biography* (London: Chatto & Windus, 2000)
Ackroyd, Peter, *Thames: Sacred River* (London: Chatto & Windus, 2007)
Bone, James, *The London Perambulator* (London: Lombard, 1903)
Denny, Barbara, *Fulham Past* (London: Historical Publications, 1997)
Masters, Brian, *Swinging Sixties* (London: Jonathan Cape, 1985))
Matthews, W., *Cockney, Past and Present* (London: Routledge & Kegan, 1938)
Miles, Barry, *London Calling* (London: Atlantic Books, 2010)
Pérez-Reverte, Arturo, *The Fencing Master* (London: Harcourt Inc., 1975)
Picard, Liza, *Victorian London* (London: Weidenfeld & Nicholson, 2005)
Renshaw, K. T., *Festival of Britain Year* (London: Lyle Press, 1952)
Turner, Harry, *Growing Up in Fulham* (London: Janus Publishing Co. Ltd, 2004)
Wilson, A. N., *Our Times* (London: Hutchinson, 2008)
Wilson, A. N., *The Faber Book of London* (London: Faber & Faber, 2002)

Also

The London Transport Museum, the British Museum, the National Army Museum and the Fulham and Hammersmith Archives.

Foreword

It is 1949 and a rail-thin 15-year-old boy in big grey trousers with a waistband just shy of his sternum, boards a number 14 bus at the beginning of the Fulham Road.

This iconic thoroughfare that knifes through the boroughs of Fulham and Chelsea begins on the curve of a road that leads up from the Bishop of London's Palace not far from distant Putney and the River Thames. Its serpentine journey is a tour of social history, from Mr Shepherd's tiny grocery store, itself no more than a corridor, stacked with sacks of rice and tinned boxes of biscuits, onwards past the Claude Rye Motorcycle Emporium with its jaw-dropping display of gleaming, faintly sinister machines, and still further past the shabby, box-like Laski House, home of the Fulham Labour Party.

Across the lights at the junction of Munster Road, it snakes on inexorably with the faux classical facade of the Fulham Public Library on its left and still further on the right, the fire station with its gigantic red engines poised in mute readiness at the lip of the kerb.

A yard or so beyond, looming on the left, the shadow of The Red Lion with its maned Simba perched gloriously aloft. Then as the road bends right, a glimpse of the Samuel Lewis Trust Buildings before gliding alongside the Granville Theatre, its faded music hall glamour never failing to quicken the pulse of scrofulous Fulham youth with its promise of carnal delights such as "Nudes of all Nations" and "Jane of *The Daily Mirror*" in the flesh.

Now swinging leftwards past the Broadway Gardens Cinema, a pleasure palace of excruciating squalor with its wrecked seats and moth-eaten velvet curtains where, interminably it seems, they are showing Johnny Weissmuller in some *Tarzan* epic.

Still onwards through Walham Green, later renamed Fulham Broadway, past the sporting citadel of the Stamford Bridge home of Chelsea Football Club, The Blues, and finally, with an imaginary roll of drums, over the little brick bridge, the apex of which dissects proletarian Fulham from nostril-flaringly middle-class Chelsea.

The Rubicon has been traversed. We are in another time zone, another planet perhaps. There is no other road or street in London which undergoes such a metamorphosis.

Moments after crossing the bridge, the domed college of St Marks appears on the right, followed immediately by a massive slab of a building which is the Sloane Grammar School, an educational establishment of Bohemian character and reputation where many a teenage sow's ear has been turned into an adult silk purse.

But we are in Chelsea now, where the side streets leading off the Fulham Road offer hints of raffish glamour with names like Beaufort, Hollywood, Hortensia and Park Walk. The pedestrians sauntering along the pavements are noticeably better dressed, whereas in Fulham, cloth caps proliferate together with headscarves for the women. Here in Sir Thomas More's parish, the ubiquitous bowler can be seen accompanied by the nodding feather that decorates the lacy cap worn by the ladies.

It is 1949 and there are not many motor cars about, the main road being dominated by the big red double-decker buses. However, it is not too far into the borough before the occasional Alvis can be seen, in reassuring British racing green or excitingly, an SS Jaguar, blood-red and phallic, parked with careless insouciance on the corner of Elm Park Gardens.

Now we are reaching the end of our journey and the young boy who boarded the number 14 bus outside Mr Shepherd's grocery hole in Fulham is preparing to dismount. Past the gloomy Gothic brownness of the Royal Marsden Hospital and onwards to even more exotic South Kensington.

But before the bus swings left towards the brick-red-tiled facade of the South Ken Underground Station, the Fulham Road stops. Suddenly, as if buried beneath its tarmac surface beats a heart that knows it has to surrender to infinitely superior thoroughfares such as Knightsbridge and Cromwell Road and eventually Piccadilly.

But our boy has alighted. He adjusts the hated waistband on his big grey trousers and sniffs the rarefied Chelsea air. What adventures await? What dramas can unfold now he is in such an alien environment? Will he one day be accepted in this exotic place as one of "them"?

As the bus pulls away, he catches a glimpse of his reflection in its glossy red side and resolves there and then that the first step in his transformation from cockney barbarian to Chelsea swell will be to ditch his big grey trousers and beg, borrow, buy or steal a pair of silver blue slimline trousers, where the waistline no longer chafes his nipples sore. It will be a modest start, but a start nonetheless.

The Fulham Road forty years on in 1989 still begins and ends in the same places it did in 1949. The skyline has changed a little with tall, narrow glass-and-steel buildings sprouting behind the brick-faced villas and sloping rooftops and occasionally in gaps between houses that have lain fallow since being struck by bombs in 1943.

At the Fulham end of the road, the street names are unchanged and we still cruise on the number 14 bus past Clonmel, Rostrevor, Radipole and Munster Roads. The 14 bus, however, is sleeker, shinier and quieter and the lovely coloured cardboard tickets have been replaced by a sort of mini printer which produces rolls of thin paper which carry nothing like the authority of the old ones.

But what has happened to Fulham? The side streets are stuffed with cars, some of them glossy beyond belief, and most of them costing a great deal more than the original price of the houses outside which they are now parked.

On the journey from Mr Shepherd's shop, which is alas no more, replaced by a kebab-type house in the wall, we do not in 1989 encounter a single cloth cap or headscarf. Not one. In 1949, the Fulham Road had few shops and just the occasional cafe, all temples to the culinary art of the "fry-up", their bleak interiors furnished with spindly-legged plastic tables and inevitably wreathed in cigarette smoke.

However, on the very lip of the 1990s, there are shops displaying fancy glassware or smart ladies clothes and a few restaurants with potted ferns outside serving chicken kiev and weird vegetables from Mongolia, which are good for those with high cholesterol. Just like Chelsea.

Indeed, parts of the Fulham Road are now more like Chelsea than Chelsea itself. The labourers' cottages in a small street near Fulham Broadway have been gentrified almost to death, with coaching lamps framing the shiny yellow front doors and multi-paned bow windows replacing the old. Edwardian villas which were once divided into three or four flats are now single family homes with BMWs parked outside.

As the pages of the calendar fall like leaves in autumn, we find ourselves another twenty years on, in the first decade of the twenty-first century – 2009. The 14 bus still ploughs its way from the old Fulham Palace Road, where sixty years earlier trolley buses went gliding silently to Hammersmith. But now the journey through Fulham is punctuated by a proliferation of smart, even exotic, restaurants, glass-fronted boutiques selling ladies' shoes at two hundred quid a pop, health stores offering acupuncture, modernised pubs that can't even pronounce "ploughman's lunch" but offer you mangetout and Japanese beef fillets. There are also antique emporiums where a modest eighteenth-century escritoire can set you back sixteen grand. The 14 bus, though still a double-decker and pillar-box red, now has no conductor, no cheeky chappie with a gap-toothed smile, no ticket-sweetie with blonde curls and Woolworths' drop earrings.

Enough already, as Jack the Demon Barber used to say in 1949. Is this too much information? It may well be, but Jack is dead and his red-and-white barber's pole long gone, both buried side by side in Fulham Cemetery.

The synergy that began slowly in the 1960s between the boroughs of Fulham and Chelsea accelerated in the seventies and eighties until today, well into the first decade of the twenty-first century, it is all but complete.

It was in essence a property-driven synergy that produced this enclave of the two districts, both with access to the River Thames, and made them as desirable a place to live as Kensington, Mayfair, Knightsbridge or even Hampstead.

Yes, Hampstead has its rural aspect, the Heath, but Fulham is but a short step over Putney Bridge to Putney Heath and Wimbledon Common.

Young professionals, like several in the following chapters, found obtaining a desirable residence in Chelsea difficult as demand in the eighties outstripped supply. Clever estate agents, with a combination of guile and hard marketing, persuaded many to leak across the border into hitherto unfashionable SW6.

There are many streets in Fulham with houses as grand as those in Chelsea, though perhaps not quite as iconic as those on Cheyne Walk along the Thames Embankment. The other factor which encouraged this seismic shift in house-buying habits was the change in the nature of work young Londoners now found themselves engaged in.

In the forties and fifties, we had the dwindling remains of a manufacturing industry and this required a ready supply of working-class labour, both skilled and unskilled. Many large Fulham houses were converted into flats after the 1939–1945 war to house these post-war proletarians.

As our society turned its back on manufacturing, actually making anything, it moved stealthily into what is now described as the service industries. In Hestercombe Avenue, where the author grew up, we had as neighbours a kaleidoscope of real working people. Boilermakers. Coalmen. Barbers. Gas fitters. Electricians and unskilled labourers. One such man who eventually became a superb bricklayer worked so much overtime that he was one of the first people in the street to own a motor car. An Austin Seven. This was in the late forties and early fifties, when the economic wounds of war were still healing and people still needed their ration books to acquire their weekly joint of meat.

By the sixties, barbers now became hairdressers, builders became property developers and with the start of ITV on television, the culture of "the consumer" became widespread. All the wonderful products, services, holidays and various trivial but desirable items were on show each night in the living rooms of the nation and all this excitement was accompanied by an explosion of popular music, modes of dress and a sense of sexual and political liberation.

The characters in the chapters of this book were, or are, real people, although names have been changed in all cases. The author has allowed himself a certain artistic licence in the storytelling, but I venture to suggest that almost all writers of history, whether social, military or political, indulge in this, too. History, after all, is just another narrative and a good story is worth embellishing.

The old barrow boys in the North End Road could have taught my clever colleagues in the advertising industry a thing or two. When delivering a "narrative" about the products they were attempting to sell, they denied they were "exaggerating". What they were doing was "giving the apple a bit of a polish".

So there you are.

I've done my best to polish the apple without, I hope, bruising the fruit.

Harry Turner
Born in Fulham, 1935

P.S. Though I was born in Fulham, and educated in Chelsea, both my children were born in Chelsea. The bloodline is secure.

Artistic Licence

The King's Road runs almost parallel to the Fulham Road and its most notorious stretch is in the very heart of Chelsea right up to Sloane Square, where its culmination is marked by the Royal Court Theatre on one side and the excruciatingly fashionable Peter Jones department store on the other. But like its cousin the Fulham Road, the King's Road starts in a decidedly downmarket environment in Fulham close to the famous Fulham Pottery, where a nineteenth-century kiln still stands. Here, however, it is called the New King's Road and remains so until it reaches the curiously named World's End where, as it crosses the invisible line, it becomes the King's Road, Chelsea.

Before reaching this vital junction, it passes Cortayne Road and a number of undistinguished thoroughfares many of which lead, by serpentine twists and turns, to the famous and robustly exclusive Hurlingham Club, home to international polo, pink champagne cocktails and men with suede shoes and no chins to speak of.

Beyond World's End, the King's Road sprouts a plethora of antique emporiums and second-hand shops that draw collectors from the four corners of the universe like moths to a flame.

Leading off the King's Road are dozens of fine streets of eighteenth- and nineteenth-century houses ranging from modest two-storey cottages to grand five-storey mansions.

Since the seventeenth century, possibly earlier, this part of London has attracted artists, writers and poets and in the late twentieth century, "creative" people from London's advertising agencies.

It's combination of elegance, style and raffishness, plus of course its boutiques and pubs and restaurants that line the King's Road, are a magnet for both the rich and those who aspire to be.

1

One such was Dermot Winterbottom, a 22-year-old orphan who, after graduating from the Chelsea College of Art with a barely distinguished degree, had managed to secure two rooms in the top of an old house in Anderson Street but a stone's throw from the bustling King's Road. Here, after his minuscule savings had evaporated, he had obtained a job in a fashionable Mayfair advertising agency in the art department. It was not what he had originally planned for himself as a first step on his career as a painter, but a man had to eat.

What he really wanted, of course, was to become a *real* artist, a painter of explosive talent and cunning observation, a Picasso perhaps or even a Chagall. At a pinch, he even considered being Salvador Dali, a man of immense technical skill and mind-bending creativity.

So during his days at the advertising agency, among men and women who wore expensive shoes and waxed enthusiastic over baked beans, underarm deodorants, washing powders and products in phallic-shaped bottles that expunged under-stains from the knickers of incontinent matrons, he toiled keenly. He turned out black-and-white drawings of double-glazing techniques that would enable simple punters, if they followed the instructions, to assemble and erect their very own insulations and enhance, beyond the dreams of avarice, the value of their pitiful semi-detached slums in Hendon, Tottenham and Slough. The pay he received from his labour was really quite respectable and he noted that some of the senior members of the agency drove Ferraris and Jaguars and lunched, it seemed almost daily, in London's most fashionable restaurants.

Nonetheless, Dermot Winterbottom had no intention of making a career in the glitzy world of publicity and marketing. He was an artist. And it was as an artist he intended to establish himself. The ad-agency job was no more than a potboiler, a source of income while he developed and honed his latent talent as a truly creative person. He had few friends, mostly Bohemian types who hung around the Chelsea Potter pub in King's Road and spoke of art and politics and poetry and drank cheap red wine rather than halves of bitter. In truth, their knowledge of art, poetry and politics was nugatory, but at least they looked the part in their paint-stained denims, fake Afghan fleece jackets and open-toed sandals. They worked, like Dermot, at various day jobs, which ranged from builders and decorators to civil servants and bus conductors on London transport. But at night and at weekends, they toiled at their sculpture or painting or poetry conspicuously without success. All of them, rather touchingly, nursed the belief that a "breakthrough" would eventually come and the 30,000-word poem would at last find a publisher or the twenty-eight hideous canvasses of aubergines in baskets or skinny naked women reclining on tiger-skin rugs would open up the chance for a "West End gallery" to showcase their work.

Dermot, however, knew that he would have to work assiduously at his painting, experimenting with various styles, switching from oils to watercolours, painting still life, portraits, animals, buildings and flowers he had seen at the Chelsea Flower Show.

He also decided, unlike his chums at the Chelsea Potter, to revisit the history of art, a subject he had only skated over in a superficial way at art college. He bought various books from the second-hand shops in the King's Road, covering the history of art in its entire span, from Palaeolithic images, primitive cave art and sculpture through to the development of the Western tradition traced from Egypt, Greece and Rome to medieval art, the Renaissance, the baroque and early-twentieth-century Impressionism.

He studied the art of Islam, Asia and Japan, also becoming fascinated by African art, tribal, primitive and modern. He consumed books about North American Indian art, wall paintings, totem poles, rock carving and paid £50 for a magnificent book of Byzantine icons all created in the seventh century about the lives of Caravaggio, Botticelli and Picasso. He bought prints of Leonardo Da Vinci and stuck them up in his bathroom; collected pamphlets about Bellini when he visited Venice on holiday and marvelled at the monumental works of Titian and Michelangelo; pored over old books on Bruegel and Bronzino; laughed at collections of prints by Salvador Dali and stood slack-jawed in amazement at the romantic landscapes of Constable and Turner.

He loved the work of Delacroix and Ingres, his favourite being the erotic *La Grande Odalisque*, a superb nude commissioned by Napoleon's sister, the Queen of Naples. He was struck by the delicacy of the Degas ballet dancers, Rodin's fabulous sculptures and the ultra-modern work of Swiss artist Paul Klee, with its cube-like shapes and random but exquisite colours. He read of Schrimpf and Schiele and Hepworth and Graham Sutherland and Robert Rauschenberg and Andy Warhol, Jackson Pollock, John Augustus and Lucian Freud. Indeed, his mind was so crammed with the images and words he had digested from his books and gallery visits that he found he had no time for much else in his life.

His work at the agency was not too demanding. He would execute illustrations very quickly and this made him popular with the management. He became a dab hand at creating TV storyboards with a few deft strokes of his pen and the agency gave him a thumping raise in his salary.

But his obsession with art remained unflagging and he never entertained for a moment the desire to spend his life in advertising.

One burning July evening while he was in the Chelsea Potter chatting to his cronies over wine, beer and ham salad with chunky chips, a stranger came gliding into the bar. A most striking fellow clad in a black velvet suit, ruffled shirt front and a red fedora. He looked about forty with long, beautifully groomed hair and aquiline features. He went to the bar and ordered a treble Campari and soda, unusual in the Chelsea Potter, and the barman winced.

One of Dermot's drinking pals nudged him. 'See that chap at the bar?'

Dermot shook his head.

'Owns a fabulous gallery in Mount Street, Mayfair.'

'Really?' said Dermot, antenna twitching.

'Yeah,' said his companion, taking a sip of plonk, 'he often comes in here. And sometimes he asks blokes if they have any work they could show him.'

'Get out of here,' said Dermot.

'God's truth,' said his chum. 'I'll introduce you to him if you like.'

'Do you know him, then?'

His chum shrugged. 'Sort of,' he said and then waved to the tall fellow who had started work on his pint-sized Campari and soda.

'Evening, Jacob,' he said.

The fellow nodded and smiled. 'Good evening to you, Ted,' he said, his accent decidedly mid European.

Ted, Dermot's companion, smiled gratefully at this acknowledgement. 'He came and looked at some of my stuff last month.'

'What?' said Dermot. 'Your paintings?'

'Yeah.'

'And?'

'He said they were biggest heap of crap he'd seen in years.'

'You're joking, Ted.'

'No, Dermot, straight up. He's blunt but honest. I've changed my style. In a year he said he'd look again, see if I've improved. Would you like to meet him?'

Dermot took a sip of Beaujolais and drew a deep breath. 'Oh, I don't know.'

'Go on; let me introduce you – unless you don't fancy an appraisal from a real pro.'

Dermot shrugged. 'OK.'

'Jacob!' called Ted. 'Come and meet a friend of mine.'

Jacob, who was leaning on the bar, turned and smiled. A gold tooth winked in the corner of an otherwise perfect set of gnashers.

'Jacob,' said Ted, 'this is Dermot. Dermot, this is Jacob.'

Jacob took a few paces towards the pair and extended a be-ringed right hand. 'A delight, I'm sure.'

Dermot took his hand and the grip was firm.

'Dermot paints,' explained Ted, unnecessarily.

'Of course he does,' said Jacob, his tone only mildly patronising.

'Actually,' said Dermot, 'I work in an advertising agency.'

Jacob nodded and took a sip of Campari. 'Excellent. I have little time for layabout artists who think a job of work, real work, is somehow below them.'

Ted snorted and disappeared behind his glass of red wine. He'd last worked full time two years previously as a shelf-stacker at Waitrose.

'What sort of thing do you paint?' said Jacob, directing his gaze at Dermot.

'Well,' said Dermot, 'I'm sort of evolving, moving through different styles. At the moment, I'm sort of between abstract and Impressionism. Sounds pretentious, doesn't it?'

Jacob smiled and the gold tooth winked. 'Not necessarily,' he said. 'May I see your work?'

'Well yes, I suppose.'

'Entirely without obligation on either side,' said Jacob.

'Well yes, if you like.'

'Good. Here's my card. I'm in Paris next week, but give me a ring the week after and we can fix a meeting. Are you local?'

Dermot nodded. 'Around the corner. Anderson Street – 16A. It's a basement flat.'

'Much light?' asked Jacob, handing Dermot a glossy embossed card.

'Not much,' said Dermot, 'but I've got additional spots. That helps.'

'Nothing like daylight, though,' said Jacob.

'You bet,' said Ted, anxious not to be completely obliterated.

Jacob downed the remains of his Campari as if it were a pint of bitter, wiped his mouth with a tiny lace handkerchief and nodded at the two young men. 'Just came in to wet my whistle,' he said. 'Must be off now. Boring meeting with an entirely talent-free sculptor in Putney. Duty visit. Son of a friend of mine. Just going through the motions. Ta-ta!' Then he was gone, leaving a hint of some expensive unguent hanging in the air.

Dermot looked at the card and read:

> The Jacob Holstein Gallery,
> Contemporary and traditional works of fine art,
> 22 Mount Street,
> Mayfair,
> London,
> W1.

He tucked the card into his breast pocket. 'Shirtlifter, is he?' he said.

Ted nearly spluttered into his wine. 'Jesus! no, Dermot. He's a bit of a swordsman if you can believe what people say. And he's married to a right stunner.'

'Well that shows what a lousy judge of character I am,' said Dermot.

'Oh, he's very camp. Part of his professional charm,' said Ted. 'You will ring him, won't you?'

Dermot nodded. 'I guess; what have I got to lose?'

'Well certainly not your arse, that's for sure.'

'Oh piss off, Ted. Have another drink.'

A couple of weeks later, Dermot rang the gallery and spoke to a woman with a voice like cut glass. It was clear from her tone that her primary role was to prevent ordinary human beings from ever speaking to her boss, Jacob Holstein, unless they were members of the Saudi Royal family, Henry Kissinger or the Duke of Westminster.

Eventually after a conversation crammed with polite negatives, evasions and sharp requests to 'speak more clearly, please', Dermot left his phone number saying, 'I'm Dermot Winterbottom from the Chelsea Potter.'

'I'll pass on the message,' said the duchess, 'but he is very busy at the moment,'

So it was with some surprise that about a month later Dermot received a call from Jacob Holstein. There was a message on his answer phone.

'Jacob Holstein here, Dermot. I'll be in the Potter tomorrow about six. Any chance of a swift drink and a visit to your sumptuous gallery of delights? No need to ring back. If you can make it, fine; if not, we'll talk again. Bye.'

At six the following evening, Dermot was in the Chelsea Potter with a half-bottle of Pouilly-Fuissé in ice and smoking his twentieth slim cigarillo of the day.

Jacob Holstein sauntered into the bar at about six fifteen with an enormous white hound on a long chain. The creature's massive jaw hung open, revealing a set of gleaming fangs and a great lolling pink tongue from which a thread of saliva dangled.

'Do excuse Nero,' said Jacob, 'he's quite harmless. Had to bring him; my wife's playing bridge tonight and Nero hates being left alone.'

Dermot poured a glass of wine and offered it to Jacob, 'Unless you'd prefer Campari?' he said.

Jacob grinned. 'Well remembered,' he said, 'but no, wine will be just fine. Before we go,' he continued, 'I have to tell you that I think your friend Ted is quite without a shred of talent. But there is an outside chance he might improve, if he takes my advice, which he is unlikely to do.'

'Why are you telling me this?' said Dermot, frowning.

'Because I don't want you to entertain any illusions. I am a professional and entirely without sentiment. I earn a very substantial living by being brutally frank with the artists whose work I display. You OK with that, Dermot?'

Dermot nodded. 'Fine with me.'

'Let's go, then,' said Jacob, upending his glass of Pouilly-Fuissé.

They stopped outside 16A Anderson Street and Jacob tied Nero to the iron railings. Dermot's flat was down a flight of stone stairs to the basement and consisted of two large rooms, a corridor, a bathroom and a pygmy kitchenette. As Jacob stepped over the threshold, he saw a vision of near chaos. The carpet runner in the corridor was covered in newspapers and dozens of canvasses were stacked against the walls.

In the first room there was a sofa covered with a tartan rug, a table stacked high with small canvasses, a bookshelf crammed with what looked like expensive art books and the walls were hung with a dozen canvasses. They had been placed so close to each other that they overlapped.

The second room, Dermot's bedroom, could only be identified as such by the single bed in one corner which was covered with a pile of small canvasses. On a large trestle table was an array of paint pots, jars full of brushes, bottles of white spirit, charcoal pencils, rags and cloths and a couple of dirty mugs decorated with rude slogans and cartoons of naked females. The walls were hung with large paintings, mostly abstract, all of them unframed. Some were watercolours in peachy-pastel hues, most were oils, heavily applied with brush and knife. Some of the application had been so thick that globules of paint hung over the edge of the canvas like miniature stalactites.

Jacob Holstein wandered through the flat with his hands clasped behind his back, Dermot following a pace behind. He riffled through some of the canvasses that were stacked one on top of the other and examined them all with great care. One or two he picked up and put against the wall so that he could view them from a distance.

After trawling through the canvasses in both rooms and the bathroom, he sat on Dermot's bed and lit a fat Cuban cigar. 'Mind if I smoke?' he said, as the first plume of Havana curled upwards.

Dermot shrugged and lit one of his thin cigarillos.

'Well now,' said Jacob, 'just tell me, Dermot, the larger canvasses, the really big ones, they are your latest work?'

Dermot nodded. 'Yes. I just need bigger surfaces for what I'm trying to achieve.'

'So the smaller work, and the miniatures?'

'Oh,' said Dermot, 'early stuff. Years ago. Crap, really.'

'Part of your self-taught learning curve?'

'Yes,' said Dermot.

'And they are *crap*. You are quite right. Not even chocolate box. Jesus Christ! Puppies in slippers.'

'Just an experiment.'

'Quite,' said Jacob. 'Now these big jobs, how many are there, five? Six?'

'Six. Just finished one by the door. It's the biggest I've done.'

Jacob nodded. 'Now they are *almost* good. But not quite.'

'Not quite?' said Dermot. 'How do you mean?'

Jacob stood up and drew hard on his cigar, the exquisite aroma of Cuban tobacco smoke wafting across the room. 'I like my painters to have a narrative attached to their work. Each painting that hangs in my gallery must be part of a story. It should reflect the artist's mood or frame of mind, whether conscious or unconscious, at the time he applied brush to canvas. Your large works are striking. I like the colours, the shapes, the random geometry, the excessive use of thick paint. But there's no passion. No anger. No hint of sex. No contemplative serenity, even in the watercolours. You seem to like orange. Probably the most loathsome colour in the spectrum. Drop it.

'Now forgive me if I speak frankly. Your work as it stands is just not ready for me to hang in Mount Street. Do understand that work that is displayed in my gallery sells for very high prices. Very high prices, indeed. Last month, I shifted six canvasses painted by a young Moroccan artist for £200,000. I should add that the same sale was aided and abetted by my being able to write a narrative for the brochure that described the lady's moods and life cycle; her work showed a whole gamut of emotions and I pinpointed them. In fact, I would guess I'm something like a copywriter in an advertising agency. I give paintings a personality.'

'Or brand image,' said Dermot dubiously.

'If you like,' said Jacob. 'We live in harsh commercial times. So what I suggest you do, Dermot, and you can tell me to fuck off at any time. But what I suggest you do is dump or burn *all* of you small stuff, *all* of it. Concentrate on the bigger canvasses. The *very* biggest. Redo that six ...' He pointed to the half-dozen large abstracts propped along the entire wall of the bedroom. 'Redo them, take out the orange, paint over it, get *cross* with it. Add darker colour. Make it even thicker. Use your hands if necessary. Smack the paint on with your palms. Be angry. Think of what makes you really cross. Get agitated. Get pissed. Paint in the middle of the night with a violent headache. I want a narrative, Dermot. I want a story. I'm just a huckster after all, my dear boy, like you, except I deal in art, not soap powder and Pepsi Cola.'

Dermot stood there for a moment and took a drag on his cigarillo. 'OK. So if I do all that, what then?'

Jacob strolled over to the door and smiled. 'Then you should paint six more to add to those already finished. I may offer some help along the way.'

9

'Six more?'

'Six big ones. Monsters. I need a round dozen for my gallery. In six months' time, I have a gap in my schedule. I need to fill it. I have some rich American collectors coming over in September who stay at The Connaught. They only buy from my gallery.'

'You mean –'

'What I mean, Dermot, is you might just produce work that we can shift. But as I said in the pub, I make no promises. Your work as it stands is no good to me at all. If you can invest it with some real emotion, I will hang your work in Mount Street and sell it for more money than you have ever dreamed of. But if, as is more likely, sorry to be so blunt, if you *can't* achieve the required standard, then tough. You will have just wasted your time and I shall move on to find another young artist to dazzle the Americans. So what I'm suggesting is this. You take a gamble, you have a crack at it and you don't whinge if after I review it I tell you it's a crock of shit and you should take up accountancy.'

Dermot managed a nervous laugh. Was this man crazy or just crazy like a fox? He certainly spoke his mind.

'Well?' said Jacob, licking the end of his cigar. 'What's it to be, Dermot? Fuck off, Jacob, you are a pretentious asshole or yes, Jacob, I'll have at stab at it?'

Dermot grinned. 'Well it's fuck off, Jacob, and yes, I'll have a stab at it.'

Jacob gripped his hand and shook it. 'I'll be in touch, sooner than you think. Goodbye, Dermot. Get stuck in. Who knows, you might discover hidden truths about yourself.'

'Like I'm a gullible prick.'

'Very possibly. Goodbye, Dermot, I'll let myself out.'

A few days later in the Chelsea Potter, Dermot was enjoying a pint and a steak-and-kidney pie when Ted strolled in with a very pretty blonde on his arm. He introduced her as Sylvia, his girlfriend, and Dermot offered to buy them a drink.

'Thanks but no,' said Ted, 'we're here to snatch a quick lunch. By the way,' he continued, 'how did you get on with Jacob?'

'OK I think,' said Dermot, trying to drag his eyes away from Ted's girl's low-cut blouse.

'I bet he told you your work wasn't *quite* up to snuff.'

Dermot nodded. 'More or less, but he thinks my bigger canvasses have potential.'

'Oh yeah. Funny that. Still, you never know, something you do might press the right buttons for old Jacob. He's a bit of a charmer.' Ted then escorted Sylvia to a table at the far side of the pub and Dermot noticed, with a stab of jealousy, that Ted's hand was placed in a proprietorial way over her left buttock.

Dermot finished the remains of his pie, drained his glass and left, still slightly irritated with himself at the emotions Ted's girl had kindled. As it was Saturday, he had no major plans other than to paint and once back in his flat, he stripped down to his vest and began to collect up all of his small canvasses. Jacob's words rang in his ear: 'dump or burn *all* of your small stuff, *all* of it!'

After piling the canvasses up, he carted them into the hallway of his flat. Burning them was out of the question. He'd take them to the city dump instead. That seemed slightly less like the act of a vandal. Then he returned to his sitting room, still littered with paintings, brushes, two easels and other detritus.

He selected a large oblong canvas he had finished about a year ago. It was an abstract, a fairly bold work of blues and golds and slashes of orange. All the brush strokes sweeping up towards the right-hand corner of the canvas as if they were being sucked into a vortex. 'Orange,' Jacob had said, 'probably the most loathsome colour in the spectrum.'

'Oh come on,' said Dermot out loud, 'it's not *that* bad.' Then he turned the big canvas so that it faced the small shaft of daylight coming into the room. Suddenly the orange streaks looked horrible. They jarred against the blues and the golds. Dermot heaved the canvas onto one of his big easels and grabbed an industrial-sized decorator's paintbrush. On the wooden trestle table was a large pot of domestic gloss paint. Dermot prised up the lid, plunged the brush into the paint, stirred it briefly and then drew of slash of black across the canvas, completely obscuring the orange. 'Death to you, you tangerine bastard!' yelled Dermot. He applied a second coat and it ran in globules over the blue streaks. One of the drops formed a protruding blob, standing proudly out of the canvas.

Suddenly, Dermot's mind was filled with images of Ted's girlfriend. Of her magnificent breasts. Her nipples had been clearly protruding through the flimsy blouse she wore. 'Bloody Hell,' cried Dermot, throwing down the big brush. He seized a tin of pastel pink paint and opened it with the aid of a palette knife. This was unprofessional, the pink paint, like the black was domestic decorator's stuff. Then he dipped both hands into the paint and applied his palms to the canvas. He surrounded the protruding black blob with swirls of pink moving his hands in a circular motion. There it was, still wet, still gleaming, a magnificent pink woman's breast with nipple erect.

'Blimey,' said Dermot, realising at once that this was a wholly inadequate response to what he had just done. He staggered off to the kitchen and picked up a rag. Then he unscrewed a bottle of turpentine and began cleaning his hands. What in heaven's name had come over him? Then he recalled Jacob's words about injecting passion into his work, creating a narrative. Complete nonsense, of course, and yet? He had just attacked a canvas in a mood of sexual frustration, goaded into action by the random fall of the black paint and his vivid recollection of Ted's sexy companion. A mixture of jealously, frustration and unfocused anger. Wow! now he needed a drink, or three.

Early the following Monday morning, he took all of his early canvasses to the city dump and, with hardly a twinge of guilt, deposited them in one of the enormous skips provided. A council worker, a rail-thin fellow with unnecessary side whiskers, watched Dermot carefully as he tossed his paintings to recycle to hell or wherever it was they were destined for.

The man drew on his cigarette and exhaled smoke from both nostrils. His eyes met Dermot's and he gave a rueful grin. 'Was they pictures?' he asked in a tobacco-soaked voice.

Dermot nodded, anxious to get away from the graveyard atmosphere of the dump with its stench of rotting vegetation and general decay.

The man shook his head. 'Shoulda taken 'em to the Oxfam shop or that hospice place near South Ken. Shame to chuck away pictures.'

Dermot felt a lance of guilt as he climbed into his Mini, but he didn't look back at the council worker as he drove out of the dump. 'Damn it,' he muttered to himself, 'I'm behaving like a complete prat.'

After a complete day's work at the agency, he returned to his flat and took up a large blank canvas and propped it on an easel. With the words of rebuke from the council worker ringing in his ears, he seized a brush and began poking around his various tins of paint. He was seeking, half consciously, to find a colour or combination of colours that would match his mood of guilt and self-loathing.

Grey, he thought, might suffice, applied across the canvas in huge sweeping stokes, perhaps a little black like his current despair, and some random splashes of red to signify the blood leaking from his selfish, foolish soul.

He had completed less than a fifth of the canvas two hours later, but he was working slowly. At a funereal pace, the greys blending with the darker patches of black, the paint being dragged slowly over the surface of the canvas. Twice he seized a rag and removed a few of the strokes he felt weren't "real". Each movement, each patch of paint had to reflect his sombre mood.

Later, after showering, he drank a quarter bottle of Chivas Regal and went to bed feeling utterly wretched.

In the days that followed, he painted very little. His work at the agency occupied him fully and his moods, at night when he tried to paint under the artificial light of his flat, were flat and dull. He just seemed to be going through the motions of applying paint to canvas. Nearly all the stuff he started, he wiped clean or painted over.

'Bloody Jacob Holstein,' he fumed, 'all his bull about investing emotion in my work; I must be mad to have fallen for it. What pretentious crap.'

He threw down his brush, washed and decided to read instead. *Caravaggio: A Life Sacred and Profane* by Andrew Graham-Dixon. He was already halfway through the book and it was riveting stuff. Caravaggio, an undoubted genius, was a tormented, angry man whose life was a roller-coaster of violence, even murder, brawls, sword fights and whoring. His patrons were nearly all religious leaders, cardinals, wealthy priests and the like, and Caravaggio, whose brief but tumultuous life only spanned the years 1571 to 1610, produced some of the most dramatic paintings of his age.

Then it struck Dermot like a gong. Of course, "dramatic", "dramatic" was the word! The mood swings Caravaggio suffered in his rumbustious life in Milan and Rome, Naples and Malta, were translated into his art. His anger, his lust and his occasional piety were writ large in his work. Each painting, whoever commissioned it, was executed by Caravaggio in either a frenzy of anger or sorrow or sexual longing, but all of them were like mirror images, reflections of reality like twentieth-century photographs.

Dermot put the book down and lit a cigarette. 'So be it,' he mused. 'I have a lot of work to do and, Jacob Bloody Holstein,' he continued, 'I'm going to paint pictures that will blow your damn socks off!'

Weeks passed and Dermot threw himself into his painting with zest. He rose early in the flat, at the first hint of dawn so he could get a few hours' work under natural light before going off to the agency. He was taking huge canvasses, some of them 6 feet by 6, and was experimenting with colour and paint thicknesses, brushes and palette knives and his own bare hands. Each work, or part of work, he tried to inject with his mood of the moment, the narrative of his life translated in oils.

It was grindingly tough work, coupled as it was with his increasing responsibilities at the agency; he was usually quite exhausted at the end of each day. Weekends were devoted to painting and he only dropped in to the Potter for a brief lunch. Ted was usually there with the blonde Sylvia and one day, out of the blue, Ted said, 'Would you like to paint Sylvia?'

Dermot nearly spilt his beer and looked at Ted. 'What, you mean –?'

'Yeah, nude of course. She's posed before.'

Dermot took another swallow of beer and glanced at Sylvia. She winked and smiled. 'Yes,' she said, 'I've done a bit of that. For students and stuff.'

'Well why don't *you* paint her?' said Dermot, feeling strangely uneasy.

'Oh! I'm no good at figures,' said Ted. 'Not my scene. Anyway, Sylvia suggested it.'

'Sylvia?' said Dermot, catching a tantalising whiff of her perfume.

'Yeah,' said Sylvia, 'why not?'

'But I only do abstracts now,' stuttered Dermot.

Sylvia made a pouting face. 'What about Picasso? He had models for a lot of his stuff, even though he painted them with their eyes in their armpits and their elbows up their arses.'

At this subtle quip, Ted burst into a bout of laughter and clapped his hand on Dermot's arm. 'Well, what do you say? Go on, paint her.'

Dermot shrugged; this whole situation was getting dangerously surreal. He looked again at Sylvia.

She ran her fingers through her blonde hair and grinned. 'And I can sit still for hours,' she said, 'when I want to.'

'OK,' said Dermot weakly. 'Maybe next week.'

'Whenever,' Sylvia said and drained her gin and tonic. 'Shall I ring you?'

'Er – yes,' said Dermot, looking back at Ted. He showed no hint of displeasure at Sylvia's boldness. 'You sure you don't mind?' he said to Ted.

Ted laughed again. 'Mind! Don't be so bloody suburban. Course I don't mind. We're Bohemians, aren't we?' Then he laughed again, coarsely, and punched Dermot gently in the chest. 'Just bring her back undamaged,' he said.

When Dermot opened the door of his basement flat to the insistent ringing of the door bell, it was past midnight, a full month after his meeting with Ted and Sylvia in the Chelsea Potter. Sylvia stood there framed in the doorway backlit by the street lamp and she appeared to be wearing a shiny black leather topcoat. For a moment Dermot stood there, slack-jawed, trying to get his mind, still numb from sleep, to compute just what was happening on his own threshold.

'Well, aren't you going to ask me in?' she said, blowing a plume of smoke skywards.

Dermot gulped, drew his open pyjama jacket over his chest and nodded. 'Well yeah, sure, come on in.'

Sylvia swept past him into the hall and down towards his cluttered sitting room. As she walked, she let the leather coat slip from her shoulders and it pooled in a heap on the tiled floor. She was entirely naked underneath, save for the blood-red spiked heels with their gaudy gold ankle straps.

Dermot closed the front door and followed her into the room, carefully stepping over the crumpled leather overcoat.

She turned and smiled at him. 'Well, do you want me sitting down, standing up or draped?'

'Do I what –?' he blurted, his eyes fixed to her truly monumental breasts.

'How would you like me to pose?' she said.

'Ah!' said Dermot. 'Ah!'

Sylvia laughed. 'Dermot, my dear, you look as if you can't make your mind up whether to take a shit or go blind. Where would you like me to pose?'

Dermot shook his head as if trying to clear his brain and waved weakly in the direction of his moth-eaten sofa draped with a tartan rug.

Mechanically, as if propelled by an unseen hand, he moved towards this stack of large, clean canvasses that were leaning against the wall. He turned away from her, trying to gather his thoughts, and made a great business of riffling through the canvasses. Then he felt her breath against the back of his neck and when he swung round, she looped her arms around his shoulders and pressed her mouth against his. Her tongue felt a foot long and he almost gagged.

'Sylvia!' he cried, finding his voice at last.

'Just a hello kiss,' she pouted and wiggled back to the sofa.

Dermot fussed around his big jar of brushes and after a few moments had regained his equilibrium. 'Oils I think,' he muttered, 'yes.'

'That's a big canvas,' said Sylvia, pointing. 'You can do me life size.'

Dermot pulled his pyjama jacket closer over his chest. 'I only do abstracts,' he said, somewhat pompously.

'Yeah, sure,' said Sylvia, crushing out her cheroot in a saucer. She crossed her legs and stretched her arms and the movement made her whole upper body quiver exquisitely.

'You might have phoned first,' said Dermot, propping an enormous canvas on the easel.

Sylvia shook her head, 'Element of surprise. Catch you in a state of mind that could be conducive to real creativity. That's what Jacob Holstein told Ted once.'

'Oh did he?'

Sylvia nodded. 'Yes. But Ted knows, and Jacob knows and you know and I know that Ted is about as talented a painter as I am a professor of quantum physics. But you, my boy, are the business. Potentially at least.'

'What the hell do you mean?'

'Just what Jacob told me himself. He really thinks you have potential. He suggested I pose for you. How about that?'

'You?' said Dermot. 'I thought Ted –'

'Oh! Ted just goes along with it. He knows he's a no-talent bum. But he'll live vicariously through you, if you make it.'

'You're talking nonsense and quite frankly, I think –'

'Oh! sod what you think, Dermot,' Sylvia said. 'It's true. Jacob thinks you could be the next big thing.'

'You know Jacob well?'

'Oh yeah. He took my virginity when I was fifteen. Naughty boy.'

'What?' yelled Dermot.

'Don't look so shocked,' she said. 'That was a long time ago, before I met Ted. Anyway, Ted and I aren't serious.'

'Obviously.'

'Oh don't be such a klutz,' said Sylvia. 'And talking of "obvious", you are pleased to see me.'

'What do you mean?'

Sylvia pointed at him. 'Well *he's* pleased to see me even if you aren't.'

With a gasp, Dermot realised the gap in his pyjama trousers had revealed a most convincing evidence of his pleasure. 'Oh my God,' he said, 'oh my God.'

Sylvia walked over to him and with a deft movement, tugged at the cord of his pyjama pants and the garment slid to the floor. They sank together onto the shabby, old Persian rug and the sex began, but slowly, smoothly, almost calmly. A few minutes later they fell apart, their bodies slick with perspiration.

'Now fucking *paint!*' she said. 'Let's have a post-coital work of spectacular genius ...'

And paint he did. Great swathes of colour drawn across the enormous canvas. Sylvia sat on the old sofa smoking another cheroot as he worked. At first he had felt a little silly painting furiously without any clothes on, but the fact that Sylvia remained naked made it seem almost respectable.

After an hour he stopped and surveyed the canvas. It was a riot of colour, thick and gleaming. But he needed more layers, more overpainting. Sylvia uncurled herself from the sofa and came across to him.

'Paint me,' she said. 'Put paint on me. Then make love to me again.'

Dermot shook his head, but the close proximity of her body and its heat stirred him and he picked up his brush. He drew a streak of blue paint across her breasts, then a line of red that ran from her belly to the "V" between her legs.

Their second coupling was frenetic. They rolled over the floor like Shakespeare's "beast with two backs", and as Sylvia raised her legs, she kicked the easel and Dermot's canvas slid off and dropped on top of them. She rolled Dermot on his back and straddled him, pressing him into the wet paint. He flipped her over like a wrestler until she was sliding on the canvas. Now, both streaked with paint, they heaved and bucked until a mutual climax released them and they rolled apart, breathless.

The canvas bore the imprint of their bodies, Sylvia's buttocks and hips and Dermot's back, elbows and knees.

'Oh shit!' said Sylvia. 'I've ruined your painting.'

Dermot knelt up, a smear of bright red oil running across his chest. 'No,' he said, 'absolutely not. Just look at it. It's fantastic.'

Sylvia pushed herself up on one elbow. 'I suppose that's what they call action painting!'

Dermot grinned and wiped a globule of blue from his chest hair. 'Jackson Pollock, eat your heart out,' he said.

'Jackson who?'

'No matter,' said Dermot. 'Come here and kiss me.'

'Jesus, Dermot, where do you get the energy?'

'I only said kiss me,' said Dermot. 'I'm not planning to take you roughly from behind.'

'I should hope not,' said Sylvia, pressing her paint-smeared lips against his.

The next two weeks passed without major incident, Sylvia showing up at the Chelsea Potter with Ted as if nothing had happened. 'Oh, it worked fine; she's a great model,' said Dermot when Ted asked him how it had gone. Sylvia, who was sipping a gin and tonic, winked at Dermot and gave a sly thumb's up.

A few days later, Jacob Holstein swept into the pub with Nero on a short leash. He made a beeline for Ted, Sylvia and Dermot, ordered Nero to sit, which the beast did, and demanded from the startled barman a Campari and tonic.

'Gone off soda,' said Jacob, 'time to ring the changes. How goes the work, Dermot?'

Dermot glanced at Sylvia and said, 'Well OK, I think. Still a lot to do.'

'I imagine,' said Jacob. 'Can I come and see what you've done? I mean like now. I'm off to Rome tomorrow and won't be back for ten days.'

'Well yes, if you want to,' said Dermot.

'Dermot's been painting Sylvia,' said Ted proudly. 'She's modelled for him.'

Dermot felt himself blush and Sylvia retreated behind a cloud of cheroot smoke.

'Has she now,' said Jacob, looking directly at Dermot. 'How very nice for the both of you, I'm sure. Well, let's go and have a look at your stuff, chop-chop.'

'You haven't even started your drink,' said Ted.

Jacob shrugged. 'You have it. I'm not thirsty.' He tossed a five-pound note onto the bar counter and touched Dermot's arm. 'Come on, come on, I haven't got all day.'

Then they were gone, through the glass doors into the King's Road, Nero straining at the leash. And back at the bar, Ted and Sylvia stood there in mild shock.

'Yes. Good, good, very good. Outstanding. I like it. I like it a lot. It's good, good, good, but we, I mean I, need more. At least four more canvasses. Big buggers like these ...' Jacob waved an arm at the easel on which was propped the kaleidoscope of colour that was the result of Dermot and Sylvia's rumbustious copulation. Jacob went over to the painting and touched it with his forefinger. 'I imagine you had fun doing this one,' he said, turning to Dermot.

'Yeah,' said Dermot, not meeting Jacob's eye.

'Keep up the good work, and I do mean "up"! Now no backsliding, young man. If you can do four more biggies as good as this, then we're in business. So follow your moods. Do as I originally said. Put your emotions on the canvas, along with ... er ... all the other things.'

Dermot felt himself colouring again. Damn Jacob Holstein, he *knew*. He damn well knew. 'OK, Jacob,' said Dermot, 'I'll do my best. But they're big canvasses; it'll take a bit of time.'

'My dear boy, take as much time as you like, as long as it's no more than a month. My Americans are coming over in September.'

The next few weeks passed in a blur. Dermot took a few illicit "sick" days so that he could paint, not just through the night, but all day as well. Each huge canvas reflected his mood at the time he painted it, but this had been the difficult part: how many moods or shades of temperament could be conjured up as he raced towards the deadline Jacob had set him? There had been self-loathing and despair, a symphony of greys and blacks. There had been unrequited lust, prompted by his first view of Sylvia in the Chelsea Potter. This was mostly pink with corny representations of Sylvia's breast, then guilt, more grey with a streak of yellow. Followed by boredom, white mostly with just a dribble of dull purple.

And so on, canvas after canvas, all drinking up a rainbow of colours, mostly in oils. And in each were hints of the earlier works of other artists who had influenced his style, which in itself was constantly changing. In some a tiny whiff of cubism, others the random energy of Pollock; each time he found himself reflecting others in his work. He worried about Jacob scorning him as a plagiarist, but he pressed on, sleeping little, eating less, only twice inviting Sylvia round to the flat for bouts of unsentimental, mutually exhilarating sexual congress.

It was during the night he was finishing his final canvas that the "incident" occurred. In the 1960s it might well have been described as a "happening" and in America as "performance art". Just after midnight on a Thursday, Dermot had stood his last, still-wet, canvas against the wall of his sitting room. He had positioned it at an angle so that the drips of heavy paint would slide down the surface of the canvas as they dried, creating a random cascade like coloured tears – of joy, of course. It would crown his efforts with a clear sense of triumphant satisfaction, or so he assumed in his mood of slightly pretentious euphoria.

He was cleaning his brushes in white spirit over the kitchen sink, when the person burst into the room. He had obviously gained entry through the front door and now stood facing Dermot in the small kitchen. He was a boy, black, slim, crouching like a panther about to spring.

'What the f –?' said Dermot.

But the lad was on him in a single leap and the two of them fell against the side of the sink. The boy was a foot smaller than Dermot, but as lithe as an eel. Dermot easily deflected his first, half-hearted, punch and pushed him towards the door. The boy wriggled free and ran like a startled deer into the sitting room. He dashed towards the line of big canvasses lined up along the wall and to Dermot's horror, stamped his foot through the surface of one of them.

Dermot screamed in fury and leapt at the boy, bringing him down with a perfectly executed rugby tackle. They fell onto the canvas, making another hole in it, and as Dermot tried to pin the lad down by sitting on his head, he kicked out both feet like a mule, sending two other canvasses crashing. Over and over they rolled until Dermot's superior weight and strength finally immobilised the lad and had him face down and spreadeagled, with Dermot kneeling in the small of his back. At that precise moment, the melodious chimes of a mobile phone filled the room. The boy turned his head slightly, blood showing in the corner of his mouth.

'The phone's in my jacket pocket,' he said.

'What in hell's name are you talking about?' yelled Dermot, whose own blood was truly up.

The lad actually grinned and repeated his statement. 'The phone's in my jacket pocket. Please answer it.'

'Are you *crazy?*' screamed Dermot.

'Please,' said the boy.

With a sense of unreality, Dermot put his hand inside the boy's jacket and took out a smart, state-of-the-art mobile phone, pressed a button and placed it against his ear.

'Hello, Dermot,' said a voice. 'You can let the boy go now. And please don't hurt him.'

Dermot took the phone away from his ear and looked at it as if he couldn't believe what he'd heard. The voice had been Jacob Holstein's.

'You're hurting me,' said the boy. 'Please let me up.'

Dermot raised the phone again and yelled into it. 'Jacob, you bastard! What the hell is going on?'

'Just let the boy up,' said Jacob.

'Where the hell are you?' bellowed Dermot, still kneeling on the boy's back.

'I'm outside your flat, Dermot. I'm coming in. Don't hurt the boy. Do you hear?' Then the connection went dead.

Jacob strolled into the room ten seconds later with Nero on a silver chain. He smiled at the tableau before him and indicated that Nero should sit, which the beast did. Dermot noticed that Jacob was immaculate in full evening dress with black tie and a ruffled silk shirt that gave him the appearance of an eighteenth-century dandy.

Dermot climbed off the sprawling boy and stood up, his face purple with fury. 'What kind of damn nonsense is this, Jacob?'

Jacob took a fat cigar from his breast pocket and smiled. 'Do you have any matches by any chance?'

The boy, who had leapt up as nimble as a cat, ran to Jacob and stood beside him facing Dermot. Dermot gave a choking, wordless roar of rage, then seized a large tin of paint and hurled it with all the force he could muster at the pair of them. They ducked in unison like a well-trained dance duo and the paint pot struck one of Dermot's canvasses, burst open and green paint splattered over the canvas, the wall and the floor.

'Excellent,' said Jacob. 'An expression in oils of primeval anger, just what your other work didn't quite catch. And the painting with a hole in, what a masterly touch.'

'I did that,' said the boy, wiping his mouth on his sleeve.

'No matter,' said Jacob, 'I'll still write in the blurb that it was Dermot. It makes a *great* narrative.'

Dermot dropped to his knees, exhausted. 'You bastard,' he said softly, 'you set the whole thing up,' all anger draining from him.

'Well of course,' said Jacob. 'I hope young Sam here didn't frighten you too much. He's really a jolly good lad. Hopes to go to ballet school in due course. He works for me part time, you know. Jack of all trades, really. No parents. Brought up in an orphanage. Like you, Dermot. Just like you. How did we get in? Very simple, I nicked your spare key last time I came here.'

'I hope you pay Sam well,' said Dermot grimly.

'Oh yes,' said Jacob, biting off the end of his cigar. 'He gets a bonus for tonight, fifty?'

'That's all you have to bloody well say?' cried Dermot, looking across at the wreck of paintings scattered on the floor.

'For the moment, yes. Now look, Dermot, your work is complete – ten fine canvasses each with its own special story. Masterpieces I shall call them. I'll have my people at the gallery pick them up tomorrow in my van. It's such a petty van, too. Lilac with gold stripes. My wife thinks it looks like a poof's wagon, but what does she know about art. She's just a woman.'

'Not only mad, but a bloody male chauvinist pig, too,' muttered Dermot, dragging himself to his feet.

'Right now,' said Jacob, 'let's have that drink. Have you any of that Chivas Regal left? It goes down as smooth as silk.'

The Jacob Holstein Gallery on Mount Street, Mayfair is on the ground floor of a fine eighteenth-century town house. The high-ceilinged main room is 40 feet long by 25 feet wide with bright white-painted walls and powerful overhead lighting. On the morning of 16 September, 2000, ten vast canvasses hung along the walls, all unframed, but beneath each of them was a printed narrative describing the work in both flowery language and intimate detail. There was also a large photograph of Dermot Winterbottom smiling modestly at the camera.

The gallery was full of men and women talking in loud American accents. The women in particular seemed mesmerised, not just by the paintings, but also by the narrative that accompanied them. The one titled *Fornication* appeared to cause most interest.

Young Sam darted between guests carrying a tray of drinks, while Jacob stood next to Dermot who was busy signing autographs.

By noon, three hours after the gallery had opened, all ten paintings had been sold. The total paid, before the gallery commission, was £466,000.

Jacob turned to Dermot and patted him on the shoulder. 'Not a bad morning's work,' he said.

Dermot nodded. He felt numb and just a little drunk.

'Oh, did you get an invitation?' said Jacob.

'To what?' said Dermot, draining his glass of champagne.

'Ted and Sylvia's wedding. I think they will be very good for each other, don't you?'

Dermot nodded. 'Absolutely,' he said, 'a match made in heaven.'

'Or at least in the Chelsea Potter,' said Jacob, lighting a large Cohiba cigar.

Not a Lot of People Know This, But ...

In 2012 Chelsea is still regarded as a village, neatly bisected by the King's Road. It includes the seventeenth-century Royal Hospital founded by Charles II in 1682 and designed by Sir Christopher Wren, the famous physic garden and the Chelsea Porcelain Works, now sadly moved to Derby.

In 1952, local tradesmen persuaded London transport to change the name of the tube station from Walham Green to Fulham Broadway. Up until then, Walham Green with its village connotations was a poor area, most notorious for its "green gang", a bunch of thugs, mostly teenaged, who specialised in mugging, burglary and antisocial behaviour.

Harsh Music of a Distant Drum

Dawn is breaking over one of Sir Christopher Wren's most exquisite masterpieces. Its colonnaded facade, lit by early sunlight, seems to glow, looking much younger than the centuries it has stood there. Beyond its majestic profile, the Thames, out of sight but still close, flows serenely and silently as it is too early for the chug and splash of river traffic to disturb its calm.

Inside the great building, there is gentle movement. Men go slowly about their morning business, unhurried and tranquil. Although it is scarcely 6.30 a.m., there are a few red-coated men walking softly around the cloisters. One or two are sitting on benches smoking pipes. All of them sport coloured ribbons on their chests, symbols of extraordinary deeds performed long ago.

Inside, rows of mahogany cabins all recently restored are the living quarters of the residents. A few paces along the corridor is the great hall where already a few old men sit reading and talking. Ancient flags hang from the walls, some so faded as to defy recognition. At one end of the hall is a polished table, on which the Duke of Wellington lay in state in 1852. In a glass case is the sabre belonging to Sergeant Ewart of the Royal Scots Greys and above it hangs the Imperial French Eagle of the 45th Regiment which Ewart captured during the Battle of Waterloo in 1815.

Beyond the hall the chapel is almost unchanged since Wren completed it two centuries ago. Old flags hang limply near the roof and there are glass cases holding golden candlesticks, ewers and gold plate.

There is a strong smell of beeswax in the air, but it could be some other polish, some twenty-first-century cleaning fluid alien to many of the old men in the chapel who associate cleaning duties with that wonderful mixture known as "soldier's breath" and "elbow grease".

Sergeant Major Tommy Wild walks slowly from the chapel towards his cabin. He has been up since five o'clock and is now looking forward to his breakfast. Matron has told him many times that he has no need to rise so early these days. He is, after all, she reminds him, 99 years old. But Tommy Wild is made of sterner stuff. Lean, hard, unflinching, unsentimental, even abrasive. He has fought in two wars, been wounded seven times, lost three fingers and an eye, but can still walk unaided and shave and dress himself. He has no living relatives. The British Army is his family; has been since he started out as a boy soldier aged 16 in 1916. There is no room for sloppy sentiment in Tommy Wild's life. You just got on with it.

On his way to breakfast hall, he passes another red-coated, white-haired resident. The man has the two stripes of a corporal on his sleeve. Tommy has the coat of arms of a warrant officer class one, regimental sergeant major.

'Happy birthday, Tommy,' says the corporal as he draws level with Tommy.

Tommy scowls. He is used to being addressed as Mr Wild. 'It's not my birthday till noon today,' he says gruffly. 'Till then, I'm still ninety-nine.'

The corporal smiles. Tommy Wild never changes, always the stickler for discipline, detail and truth. Other colleagues have arranged for Tommy to have a cake this afternoon, but it is being kept secret. After all, hitting a century is no mean feat. They know, however, that Tommy will show no emotion whatsoever over the celebrations. He won't laugh, he certainly won't cry, God forbid, and he will only offer his thanks in the most formal manner possible. But that's Tommy. Mr Granite Chips, ice for blood and pace stick for a spine.

He breakfasts on eggs, bacon, toast and tea and goes out into the cloisters to smoke a pipe, even though Matron and others disapprove. He used to be a fifty-cigarettes-a-day man until some callow doctor at the hospital told him it might shorten his life. So at eighty-two he switched to a pipe. He remembers, ruefully, how the arrival of cigarettes for lads in the trenches in 1917 was greeted with as much enthusiasm as letters from home.

He finds a bench and sits down, filling his pipe with tobacco from an old leather pouch. Other old men shuffle past, acknowledging him. He strikes a match and lights his pipe, savouring the nutty flavour of the smoke. Matron and one of the Royal Hospital medical staff are walking through the cloisters and stop to say good morning to Tommy. He rises instantly to respond formally to their greeting. The young medical officer hands Tommy a newspaper, which he accepts. Then Matron and her medical officer continue their rounds of the cloisters, eventually disappearing into the interior of the hospital.

Tommy folds his newspaper twice and tucks it in his tunic pocket. He'll read it later. Maybe. It'll be full of news about grotesque pop stars, useless politicians and pages of incomprehensible guff about health and keeping fit and diet and other modern nonsense. Even the cartoons are total rubbish. Drawn no doubt by long-haired layabouts who've never done a proper day's work in their lives.

Half an hour later, after finishing his pipe, Tommy wanders through the cloisters back to his cabin, where his strict routine dictates that he will take forty winks. He has done this every morning for the last thirty years; ever since he came to the Royal Hospital, in fact. Regular naps, light exercise and a good pipe represent Tommy's formula for a long life. He has never married, never even got close to it and he has no regrets about that.

The day unfolds at its usual leisurely pace and Tommy finds a few tasks to fill the time, helping in the small library, tidying his cabin. After a very light luncheon, Tommy naps for the second time that day and then unfolds the newspaper the medical staff gave him. He spreads it out on the small table in his cabin and changes his day glasses for a tiny pair of reading spectacles. On the front page is a black-and-white photograph of a British soldier who has been killed in Afghanistan by an improvised explosive device, an IED. He is no more than a boy, 19 years old, his face fresh and open with bright, shining eyes. He is wearing his dress uniform with its high collar and shining buttons.

Tommy studies the photograph closely, holding the newspaper up to his face. "Lance Corporal Lester", the caption reads, "killed on his nineteenth birthday". 'Lester was a fine soldier,' his colonel is quoted as saying. 'He died doing what he loved best, namely soldiering with his comrades.'

Tommy glances up from the paper at the clock on the cabin mantelpiece. It shows 2.00 p.m. Tommy has been 100 years old for just two hours. He looks back at the face of the boy soldier and it seems to be smiling back at him. Tommy can't look away. He can't even blink and Tommy, who has never cried, never wept, finds his eyes filling with moisture; hot tears spilling copiously down over his creased cheeks and dropping onto the newspaper which is spread out on the cabin table.

Through the vale of tears and beyond the smiling image of Lance Corporal Lester, Tommy sees dark shadows moving. He hears the crack of gunfire and smells the stench of cordite. The boy's smile fades and the picture becomes a scene of chaos. Tommy feels his boots squelching in mud and wind smacks against his cape. The hot tears, now turned to icy rain, sting his cheeks. Next to him in the trench, knee-deep in slime, his mate Dave Brent, a Chelsea lad and 16 years old like Tommy. A shell screams overhead and lands a few yards beyond their trench with a sickening explosion that makes the mud walls of the trench tremble. Dave pulls himself up to the edge of the trench and peers over into no-man's-land.

Tommy reaches out to restrain him, but before his hand touches Dave's shoulder, Dave's head is ripped from his shoulders and his torso falls back into Tommy's arms, the arterial blood from his neck spurting like a fountain over Tommy's arm and face.

Tommy draws in a breath and the image fades, dissolves and the boy soldier is smiling up at him from the newspaper again. But the photograph is wet with tears, which tumble down Tommy's cheeks in a relentless steam. His shoulders move, slowly at first, with silent sobs and he holds the crumpled paper close to his chest.

At four o'clock, Matron glances at her fob watch and turns to one of the old soldiers seated around her in one of the hospital reception rooms.

'Did you tell him four o'clock?' she asks.

Private Johnny Belcher nods. 'Oh yes,' he says, 'we told him a week ago.'

'And again this morning,' says another veteran.

'Well it's only just four o'clock,' says Matron, 'perhaps we should wait a few minutes before lighting the candles.'

On a large, round table in front of them sits an enormous iced cake decorated with an array of tiny candles – 100 in all, the chef has assured them. Around the waist of the cake is a ribbon in the colour of Tommy's old regiment. Matron smiles and looks at her watch again. Old soldiers are still filing into the room and taking their places in chairs arranged in a semicircle around the table. There is a buzz of conversation, punctuated by the usual geriatric coughs and the occasional volcanic sneeze.

Matron sits down and consults her watch again. She does this three times more, by which time all the colleagues who are coming to Tommy's birthday celebration have settled in their seats and an air of expectancy hangs over the room. It is now twenty minutes past four.

At four thirty-five a doctor, the Matron and two soldiers arrive at the door of Tommy's cabin. The door is ajar and swings open. Tommy is sitting upright on his wing-back chair, but his head is bent low onto his chest. He holds a newspaper in his hands and he is quite motionless.

The doctor goes to Tommy and feels for a pulse in his neck. There is none. He unbuttons Tommy's red tunic and places his hand over Tommy's chest. Then he turns to the others and shakes his head.

One of Tommy's friends, an 80-year-old, comes across and picks up the newspaper which had fallen from Tommy's hands. It is saturated with tears, but the boy soldier in the photograph is still smiling.

A Handful of People Might Know This ...

As early as the twelfth century, there is evidence of "restaurants" or public areas of cookery by the Thames in Chelsea. Flesh and fish could be obtained, fried, roasted, boiled or raw, accompanied, too, by ales or wines, but it is doubtful if they provided little more in the form of comfort, i.e. chairs and tables, cutlery, etc.

By the late seventeenth century, "eating" houses as they were now called had spread from the City to the then "country" suburbs like Chelsea and Fulham. Chop houses and taverns which offered more formal eating experiences were springing up, too. By the eighteenth century it was, however, the coffee houses that became the fashionable places to take refreshment. Here the "respectable" classes could take a dish of coffee or chocolate, then called chacolate, and glance at the newspapers or "penny dreadfuls" as they relaxed in their wigs and buckled shoes enjoying perhaps a pipe of fashionable tobacco.

Today, in the twenty-first century, Chelsea is still honeycombed with coffee bars, bistros, high-priced restaurants, snack bars and other eating houses, many of them of exotic ethnic origins.

And Chelsea swells can still be observed enjoying their leisure even in these straitened times with apparently no visible means of support. Today, however, they are not called swells but either toffs or Hooray Henrys. What fun.

In Fulham, in 1780 when houses on the east side of the high street were demolished, one was known as the home of the "Old Coffin Woman". A tiny, wizened crone and fearful of a pauper's burial, she kept a miniature coffin in her room. Sometimes she had it relined and oiled to give it an "oaken" look.

When she was forced to leave her house owing to impending demolition, she begged the authorities to allow her to take her coffin with her. They refused, placing her in the workhouse, but very generously storing her coffin until it was needed, which was when she died in 1852.

The Bad Seed

He liked to think of himself as a voluptuary and an exquisite, a truly gilded youth with an impeccable sense of entitlement. He lit a Balkan Sobranie cigarette and inhaled luxuriously. The brand was virtually unobtainable now, but like most rare things, could be conjured out of thin air by the simple process of writing large cheques to a certain tobacconist in St James' who knew a thing or two.

He stretched his 6-foot frame with the suppleness of a cat and expelled twin jets of perfumed smoke from his finely arched nostrils. It was 9.00 a.m. on a Monday and already spring sunshine was casting a gold shaft through the half-drawn curtains of his large, elaborately over-furnished bedroom. The bed itself, a four-poster of Edwardian provenance, was draped in swirls of pale blue silk; the four columns supporting the canopy of carved oak in a deep earthy brown, a thousand polishings having caused its patina to shine like glass.

He slid out from under the black satin sheets, Sobranie drooping from his lips, and stretched again. Before padding barefoot to the bathroom, a palace of ablution in black-and-pink marble, he glanced around the vast room with a proprietorial air. Fine rugs from Afghanistan, a Picasso print, an overstuffed chair covered in tweed, a dressing table with a half-dozen bone-handled brushes and a single rose in a fluted Lalique crystal vase.

Yes, this room did justice to the address, Redcliffe Road, one of Chelsea's finer streets. He loved the house with a passion. It was the perfect stage on which, and from which, he could conduct his glittering life, the large remainder of which still lay ahead of him like a vast, welcoming red carpet.

He was, after all, only just 22 years old. Born Mark Rillington on New Year's Day 1967 at Rostrevor Road, a somewhat down-at-heel thoroughfare directly off the Fulham Road, in, and here's the rub, Fulham. Much of his early life he had managed to erase, even at the age of 18 changing his Christian name from Mark to the infinitely more acceptable Marcus. He had also at that age inherited a fortune just shy of £2 million left to him by his father, who had died aged 60 in the little house in Rostrevor Road, leaving a widow, Marcus' mother, who within three months followed her husband to the grave. Orphaned during his last term at a very minor public school, Marcus had resolved there and then to reinvent himself and blot out those awful early childhood years.

Public school had passed in a blur, his academic achievements nugatory, but his sponge-like capacity to absorb the nuances and speech patterns of those his parents called "his betters", enabled him to pass himself off quickly as a faintly effete minor aristocrat.

Of course he lied extravagantly to his fellow pupils about the source of his father's wealth and he became a magnet for other socially ambitious lads when his father's largesse was showered on him in his last term at the ivy-clad, mullion-windowed former priory that only recently had become a fee-paying public school.

'Father was in steel futures,' he explained in serious tones. 'He anticipated the steel needs of various major industries, shipping, automobiles, white goods and so forth. He was always abroad with Mother, so I was brought up more or less entirely by my nanny, a dear woman; Irish, don't you know. And I was away at prep school as a boarder, too. No home life to speak of.' All lies.

The truth, alas, was more prosaic. Marcus' father, a rough-hewn proletarian, born out of wedlock in the Samuel Lewis Trust Buildings in Fulham's Walham Green, had left school at fourteen and sought employment in a scrapyard close to the New King's Road. Almost illiterate but with a sharp intelligence and an extraordinary head for mental arithmetic, he soon became manager of the yard. Then at twenty a junior partner with the owner, a fat, alcoholic Greek who conveniently died and Marcus' father was left running the yard. Within two further years, he was trading like a veteran with the help of an admiring and amazed bank manager. A natural entrepreneur with a harsh negotiating technique and ruthless application, he soon became known as the "Cockney King of Scrap".

He met Eve, a mild skivvy whom he rescued from service in a mansion in Belgrave Square when he purchased the Gothic iron railings they wanted replaced, and shortly afterwards they married and moved to a tiny terraced house in Rostrevor Road, which to both of them was like landing in the Fields of Elysium.

As his fortune from scrap-dealing grew, a second-hand Rolls-Royce was purchased and parked inappropriately outside the house in Rostrevor Road, dwarfing the few Morris Minors and Austin Sevens that now lined the street.

Marcus' childhood was excruciatingly conventional. A withdrawn, self-contained boy, he found co-pupils at his preparatory school coarse and aggressive. His father brusquely urged him to 'get a bloody grip', but his mother, nursing a lifetime of social bruises, rejections and humiliations, wept for her only child.

At length, with the subtle cunning common in women of her generation, she persuaded her bombastic husband to fund Marcus' education at a public school. 'Make a gentleman of him,' was her mantra and her husband grudgingly consented.

Stricken with a debilitating disease shortly after Marcus travelled to the Berkshire countryside to join his public school, Marcus' father grew weak and sentimental and revealed, in a rare moment of introspection, that he 'really loved the lad' and hoped he would make something of his life. This intelligence was a wonderful stimulus to his wife, who now felt her life's work was complete and her boy, Mark, would no doubt soar to heights hitherto unimagined.

She, too, passed away just fourteen weeks after her husband died. She was a gentle soul, who deserved better. Marcus took a day off to attend her funeral. His last term at school was beginning to cause him worry. His academic achievements were, as described earlier, quite dreadful. 'An idle dreamer,' his housemaster had opined in something of a frustrated fury. 'What, precisely,' the man had demanded of Marcus, 'do you propose to do with your life?'

'Live it to the full,' Marcus had drawled in the patrician accent he had recently acquired, and lit a cigarette, forbidden in his rooms, blowing a wreath of smoke towards the humiliated academic. The chameleon quality Marcus had taken on was his shield against reality and the stupendous news of his vast inheritance only served to reinforce it, making it virtually impenetrable. It was as if he was being compelled by an unseen hand to adopt the life of an eighteenth-century gentleman of leisure. He was contemptuous of the place from which he had sprung.

In order to achieve this curious role, it was vital for him to reinvent his parents, his life and his history. His reading at school had been thinly spread and he had no time for the classics. He had read and reread many times three books by American authors, devouring the prose, the social attitudes, the fierce sense of separateness they had seemed to celebrate. One was *The Catcher in the Rye* by J. D. Salinger, a tale of teenage angst and sexual awakening, the other two *The Great Gatsby* and *The Beautiful and Damned* by F. Scott Fitzgerald. Odd, indeed, that an English boy with such pretensions should have chosen two Americans as his literary lodestone. But there it was.

As far as sexual awakening was concerned, there had been precious little as far as Marcus was concerned. A fumbled and totally unsatisfactory coupling with a junior at public school confirmed that homosexuality, even of the milder sort, was not for him. But he was not repelled by it. The male body, his at least, was quite something. Thus, the roots of his incipient narcissism had been sunk deep, never to be wrenched free.

Shortly after the male-on-male action, or inaction as it might better have been described, he picked up a tart – recommended by a senior – in the small Berkshire town, the outskirts of which housed his public school. Although penetration and an exchange of bodily fluids had been achieved it was, to say the least, much ado about nothing.

After leaving school without so much as a backward glance, he moved into a suite of rooms at The Ritz on Piccadilly, from where he arranged for the house in Rostrevor Road to be placed on the market. It was snapped up almost immediately at a price many multiples more than that which his father had paid twenty years earlier.

During his first few months as the inheritor of a substantial fortune, he set about planning his immediate future. The bulk of his money was tied up in a wide range of dull, conservative shares his father had squirrelled away, but the couple of hundred thousand pounds that represented the residue of the disposal of Rostrevor Road gave him a cash bulwark for the short term. He rented two rooms in Cheyne Walk in Chelsea by the Thames – fabulous address, but one that swallowed great swathes of money from his current account – until he lit upon the house in Redcliffe Road.

The estate agent who showed him round was amazed at the ruthless sophistication of this 19 year old who, after standing briefly in the elegant panelled drawing room, turned to him and drawled, 'Yes, I'll take it. Make all the necessary arrangements.'

"All the necessary arrangements" it transpired, meant not just recommending a solicitor to handle the conveyancing, but also arranging for some immediate redecorations to be executed in advance of Marcus taking possession.

He wrote a cheque for £100,000 on the spot, post-dated as deposit, and pressed it into the startled estate agent's hand. Later, he telephoned his dead father's broker and issued a brief instruction to dispose of sufficient shares to cover the purchase of the house.

A couple of months later, he had taken possession of the house, furnished it, care of Harrods and Harvey Nichols, and sat in the window of the high-ceilinged drawing room gazing with languid anticipation at his future. Should he work? If so, at what? The few acquaintances he had picked up since leaving school were either doing "something" in the City or studying to be accountants, lawyers or doctors.

He decided that no decision needed to be made in the short term and he would spend his first two years of freedom just living. He had no great interest in theatre, art or music. He did, however, enjoy spoiling himself, eating at fine restaurants, having exquisite suits created for himself in Savile Row, taking long weekends in the Hotel de Paris in Monte Carlo, but not gambling. Even in his state of youthful euphoria, he knew that the odds against winning were stupendous. Gambling was for fools and rogues, but not for Marcus.

He wanted sex and in 1989 Chelsea was full of pretty, liberated young women. He met them at various parties thrown by near-neighbours, anxious to ingratiate themselves with this extraordinary young dandy who lived alone at Redcliffe Road. The first two girls he dated were disappointing sexually. Willing enough to copulate with him after the very first dinner at La Terrazza, they were not ready for his burgeoning and high-octane voluptuousness and furthermore, their post-coital conversation was shrill and mind-numbingly boring.

Girls, he decided, were like butterflies: gorgeous, frail and doomed to lose their colour in very short order. Girls were, in the end, just pretty diversions, so the very prospect of marriage, or even a long-term relationship, filled him with horror. He'd seen what marriage had done to girls he had met a year earlier, baby-making machines with their thickening hips and careless inattention to personal detail.

It wasn't a lot better for the boys who had become husbands, either. They were now breadwinners. The heavy anvil of the work ethic had dropped onto their young shoulders with a silent thud, squeezing from them any spark of individuality or zip or passion.

So work, any sort of work, was added to Marcus' list of things with which he was quite determined not to be associated.

In any shape or form.

Where, then, did he pick up his ideas, his tastes and his sharp perceptions of life? He was an inveterate "skimmer" of glossy magazines, a "dipper-in" of books on fashion or food or elaborate motor cars. None, however, were ever read right through. Far too boring; apart, of course, from *The Catcher in the Rye* and F. Scott Fitzgerald's *Great Gatsby* and *The Beautiful and the Damned*, the latter by far the most read and reread.

One paragraph had seared itself into his brain and in its elegantly harsh prose, written in 1922, it summed up Marcus' almost clinical terror of work or conventional marriage. The exquisite style of F. Scott Fitzgerald's was in a curious way more English than American; although later in the twentieth century, novelists like Norman Mailer or Truman Capote found a true expression of their "Americanness".

Scott Fitzgerald was writing about a cheap cafe in New York that was trying to emulate the more sophisticated watering holes in a better part of the city. Here, as Fitzgerald puts it, "consumers and the lower orders gather for their dull, but ritual enjoyment". The paragraph that so transfixed Marcus ran as follows:

> There on Saturday nights gather the credulous sentimental, underpaid, overworked people with hyphenated occupations, bookkeepers, ticket-sellers, office-managers, salesmen and most of all, clerks, clerks of the express, of the mail, of the grocery, of the brokerage, of the bank. With them are their giggling, over gestured, pathetically pretentious women, who grow fat with them, bear them too many babies and float helpless and uncontent in a colourless sea of drudgery and broken hopes.

And thus the carapace of contempt, cynicism and fear that covered Marcus like an invisible second skin, thickened, grew glass-hard and possessed him. How he hated "other people"; even his handful of acquaintances were treated with cautious disdain, but were drawn to him like moths to a flame.

He was something of an exotic oddity; 22 years old, rich, solitary and peacock elegant. But with no obvious history, no past, or none that anyone was ever permitted to probe or penetrate. He dressed in a faintly old-fashioned style and favoured high-collared shirts from Jermyn Street and boots in fine soft leather from Lobbs of St James. On certain mornings, as he contemplated another day of well-upholstered indolence, he would take a taxi to Curzon Street in Mayfair and have himself shaved in Trumpers – the hairdressers and perfumers that boasted a royal warrant in its window and had over the last century trimmed the locks of the British aristocracy and many of the ex-monarchs of Europe.

Just occasionally in his slow-motion arabesque of living, the breakfasts at The Connaught, the lunches, the teas at Fortnum's, the visits to his tailor in Savile Row, the fierce copulation with a Sloane Square girl whose pictures had appeared in *Tatler*, he would allow himself a moment or so of introspection.

He remembered his father, a burly, distant figure, brusque in manner and with a face prematurely creased with deep lines. He was seldom at home in the little house in Rostrevor Road; building a scrap-metal empire apparently required long, antisocial hours.

His mother, a gentle, nervous woman in thrall of her husband, colourless, cautious, always busy at some extravagantly trivial domestic chore, cooking meals of stupendous dullness, great heaps of mashed potato with slabs of bloody meat and soggy Brussels sprouts. When his parents engaged in conversation, it was brief and often monosyllabic.

In his early teens, before his father bankrolled his public-school education, Marcus used to strip naked in his little bedroom and examine himself in a full-length mirror. He was a slim lad, but already 6 feet tall at the age of sixteen. His face narrow with an aquiline nose and nostrils that seemed permanently on the cusp of a disdainful sneer. He was blonde, or rather straw-coloured, and until public school, his hair had been kept short, cropped in military-style by a local Sweeney Todd of brutal efficiency. His eyes were blue and of a coldness that even his doting mother found mildly unsettling. His body was smooth and lithe, with legs that would have been the envy of a dancer.

On these moments of self-appraisal, he would wonder just how different he was from his parents. His father was short, thickset, coarse-featured and his mother squat, grey, with all the prettiness expunged from her face by the business of living. Even her husband's growing affluence made no visible change in her. She was of that class that knew better than to ape her superiors. She lived, in fact, vicariously through her son, Mark. It was for him and him alone she nursed fantasies and ambitions. She fussed over him, worried about him, forgave him his youthful selfishness, his indifference, his sense of apartness. In flashes of extraordinary harshness, Marcus would mentally question whether or not he was the true fruit of his parents' loins. How could a grossly spoken, lumpen brute like his father and a trembling, self-effacing, overprotective, dumpy woman like his mother have produced this young Greek God in the making? These narcissistic reflections were regular features of his early teen years.

When he considered, much later, the prospect of career – or work, as his father would have put it – he only had to glance at his own hands with their soft palms and long pale fingers to know that any sort of physical labour was out of the question. His father's hands, spade-like and scarred, were so unlike his. Where Marcus' nails were buffed and delicate, his father's had been blunt and yellowing with dirt embedded deeply down to the quick.

And the scrap-metal business itself; it was an acute embarrassment for Marcus even to think about it. So once his fortune was secure, he blotted it out of existence. It had never existed. His mighty inheritance had … well, just materialised – a just and deserving cascade of riches that was surely his destiny.

And so, on that fine spring morning in Chelsea, in his opulent mansion as he finished his cigarette before showering and dressing, he had determined that he would at last, and finally, kill all the faintest traces of his past, the merest hints of the source of his wealth, so that nobody would ever know just how it had been sweated, accumulated and protected.

He was due to meet a very special person in the City of London that very morning. A man whose reputation had become legendary. A financial magician whose speciality was turning already substantial fortunes into mega-riches, a sort of Midas-by-proxy.

One of his acquaintances had drawn Marcus' attention to this fiscal paragon during a leisurely lunch at The Mirabelle.

'It was in *The Financial Times*,' the young man had explained to Marcus; a paper, like all the others, he never read. 'Yes, apparently a number of Hollywood films have placed their fortunes in this fellow's hands and by God, Marcus, he has quadrupled their wealth in less than four years!'

At this intelligence, Marcus pricked up his ears. 'Quadrupled, you say?' he had murmured.

The young acquaintance had nodded. 'Absolutely. He's apparently worth a billion himself.'

'Name?' Marcus had said, sipping his brandy.

'Oh, Zacharius or some such thing. Greek or Levantine, I don't know. It's all in the paper.'

'Get me a copy,' was Marcus' last request before they left the restaurant.

Now Marcus, in addition to being a social psychopath, was a young man of immense, towering greed. He knew little about the intricacies of money or financial products. But what he did know, with a certain stab of irritation, was that although he was rich, he wasn't mega-rich. He was not in the yacht-owning, private-jet-flying, Cap Ferrat villa-dwelling kind of wealthy class.

Perversely, he cursed his late father for not having invested more aggressively. If only the man had raised his sights a little more and not been satisfied with a shabby house in Fulham, a second-hand Rolls and a couple of million quid in safe, low-performing shares; shares that were not only of low performance, but also invested in dull, unglamorous enterprises. Heavy industrial concerns, often in the Midlands, a part of England that Marcus considered to be just this side of purgatory.

A meeting was arranged with a Mr Zacharius Lutreche after Marcus obtained his whereabouts from a three-day-old copy of *The Financial Times*. Although Zurich-based, he had a London office in Bow Lane in the City, a mere stone's throw from St Paul's Cathedral.

At eleven o'clock that morning, Marcus was escorted by an exquisitely dressed secretary, into a vast carpeted space furnished only with a desk the size of an aircraft carrier and a high-backed chair in which sat the said Mr Zacharius Lutreche. The immediate impression he exuded was one of power and confidence; saturnine of feature with glossy, neatly barbered hair as black as a raven's wing. His eyes were feline and slightly slanted, staring directly at Marcus from a high-cheek-boned, lightly tanned face. He wore a blue pinstripe suit of impeccable cut and on his left small finger, a diamond ring of great ostentation. Marcus put his age at about 40. On the desk in front of him lay a buff legal folder encircled by a pink ribbon.

He rose as Marcus approached and reached out his hand. As Marcus took it, he realised that Lutreche must have been 6 feet 8 inches at least, towering over him like a sleek predatory beast.

'Mr Rillington, do take a seat.' The voice was deep and resonantly transatlantic.

Marcus sat and crossed his legs and for the first time in his life, was feeling vaguely intimidated.

'Cigarette?' Lutreche pushed an onyx cigarette box towards Marcus.

Marcus took one and Lutreche reached across and snapped up a flame from a silver lighter.

'Mr Rillington,' Lutreche said, 'I am sure we both have many calls on our time. Therefore, I propose we cut to the chase and see whether an association between us is possible, desirable and of course profitable. I gather you are here as a result of an article in the London *Financial Times* and the recommendation of a friend. However, I think it appropriate that I should give you a more comprehensive explanation of what my organisation actually does. I know a little about you already, Mr Rillington.' He tapped the buff folder with his knuckle. 'I know that you are a financially independent young man and that you inherited a modest fortune from your late father. A gentleman who traded in metal and pig iron of all kinds. However, Mr Rillington, you are ambitious, ambitious to increase your fortune substantially. What you have is clearly nowhere near enough to carry you through life in the sumptuous style you have charted for yourself. Am I right so far?'

Marcus nodded. He was speechless, transfixed by Lutreche's directness.

'Very well, then,' continued Lutreche, 'this establishes a certain tentative bond between us at the outset. My job, Mr Rillington, is simple. I exist to make rich people richer and *very* rich. People richer than even they could ever contemplate. My service is unique and as a consequence, I charge very substantial fees to act on behalf of my clients. You realise, of course, that this first consultation between us is in the nature of a probing operation. For subsequent meetings, if there are any, I shall charge you at the rate of £5,000 an hour, non-refundable. Shall we proceed?'

Marcus took a long pull on his cigarette and found his voice; it sounded like a plea. 'Yes, let's proceed.'

'My life is about money,' said Lutreche in a soft, almost caressing voice. 'Its magnificence, its great lubrication of events, large and small, the myriad financial products that spring from it, the complexity of its manifestation in a hundred different currencies. I love the feel of banknotes, the crackle of a newly minted 1,000-dollar bill, the heft of a gold ingot. Money, Mr Rillington, is not just the best thing in the world, it is the *only* thing.

'Before I stray into dull technical detail about my operation, let me first tell you about just a few of my clients – all people of substantial fortunes when they came to me and all of whom are now worth fortunes that would make Croesus blush.' Lutreche then proceeded, in his slow, hypnotic baritone, to name a dozen eminently high-profile Hollywood movie stars, all of whom apparently were happy to confirm that Lutreche had quadrupled, sometimes sextupled, their already monstrous fortunes. Then he mentioned a few senior-ranking politicians, whose fortunes he was entrusted to nurse while they were in government service. The sums of money were quite simply mind-boggling, as were the fees Lutreche charged.

Before he took on a single client and asked them to transfer their entire fortune into his organisation's care, he required them to pay him £50,000 sterling, non-refundable. This was in addition to the hourly charge of £5,000, should further meetings be needed after the first one. It came as no surprise to Marcus to learn that few clients needed more than one meeting to reach a decision.

'Impressive,' said Marcus when Lutreche paused and drew on his cigarette.

'Of course,' said Lutreche. He then sketched in some very complex and technical details about what he described as his "vehicles of investment".

Up until this moment, Marcus had thought of money as cash in the bank, shares or things that money could buy such as houses, jewellery and motor cars. Lutreche took him through a journey of esoteric "financial products", hedge funds, put options, trusts, bonds, sub-prime mortgages, debt-purchase, default-hammocks and others which sounded as if they had been invented by a crazed Byzantine Grand Vizier in some corrupt mid-Eastern court.

By the time Marcus left the offices of Zacharius Lutreche in something of a daze, he had agreed to place almost two thirds of his wealth into the care of the man who had so eloquently explained his brilliant financial procedures. The retention of a few thousand in his current account was advised by Lutreche as "living expenses", while the bulk of his fortune would be turned from boring shares into some of the mysterious financial "instruments" Lutreche had explained earlier. The deal was for Marcus to tie up his money for a four-year period. There could be no early release from this commitment. Half-yearly he would receive a detailed statement of his worth, in pounds sterling; although no dividends or interest of any kind would be paid until the forty-eight months had expired. At the expiry date, he would receive just one cheque, which would include his original investment plus profits and other dividends.

'It will be,' said Lutreche with an air of finality, 'a cheque of such stupendous worth as to cause the walls of the Bank of England to tremble.'

For the next few months, Marcus' routine hardly varied. Rising late in Chelsea, he would brunch at The Connaught or meet so-called acquaintances for lunch at The Ritz, La Terrazza, The Mirabelle or Claridges. There were the odd trips to Paris or Rome, usually with one of his latest girlfriends; none of whom ever remained with him for more than just a few weeks.

He had recently discovered the joys of theatre and opera and was a frequent visitor to Covent Garden, where he paid excessively over the odds for a box. He bought a Ferrari, but destroyed it in a collision with a brick wall in Fulham after only two weeks. A slightly older acquaintance, a banker, suggested that Marcus might like to take up work in the City. Marcus greeted this suggestion with ill-concealed contempt. 'Work, old chap,' he drawled, 'is for peasants.' Far from being insulted, the banker found this approach "rather amusing, even bohemian". He even invited Marcus to spend a week on his yacht in the South of France. Marcus leapt at the opportunity. This would give him a chance to sample the real lifestyle he planned to enjoy when his Lutreche fortune was matured in four years' time.

He took to Cannes like a duck to water. The great harbour full of bobbing yachts, the sleek women draped across their decks and the air of effortless success, power and, above all, a total indifference to the rest of the world and its petty problems.

This was Marcus' kind of world. One he would inhabit, soon.

After a week in Cannes, he flew in his banker friend's private plane to Rio Janeiro and here he saw wealth of monumental ostentation, cheek by jowl with abject poverty. He rather liked the contrast. It underlined and illuminated just how rich the truly rich were and how useless the efforts of the poor, tax-paying, mortgage-burdened masses were when they tried to emulate them. He realised with a thrilling jolt that the rich needed the poor to exist. A world without poor people would have in some way reduced the status of the rich to being just comfortably off. And this, Marcus concluded, would simply not do at all.

A kaleidoscope of months followed, tumbling off the calendar like the withered leaves of a glorious autumn. His spending grew prodigious, his sexual appetite coarser. One girlfriend, the daughter of a famous actor, fell for his superficial charms, but baulked eventually at his gross demands. He cared not a jot for her rejection. He was a lithe blonde God who could pick and choose from countless hordes of foolish "liberated women". These poor bitches who didn't grasp the awful truth that the march to equality and freedom served the interests of the predatory male far more than their own, in spite of Germaine Greer's seminal book, *The Female Eunuch*.

He bought a Rolls-Royce Corniche and had it upholstered in unborn llama calf at vast, tooth-loosening expense. He paid for two dozen to lunch in La Famiglia in Chelsea, spurred on to this extravagance by some of his banker friends, who thought nothing of consuming two bottles of Dom Perignon at lunch or magnums of vintage claret at over £1,000 a bottle.

The mad whirl continued: weekends in Florence, same-day trips to Paris in private jets to lunch at Maxims.

One burning day in Monte Carlo, eighteen months after he had struck his deal with Zacharius Lutreche, he saw a yacht in the harbour – a vessel, although not large by Monaco standards, that was, to paraphrase Oscar Wilde, "the absolute personification of complete perfection". He wanted it, he needed it, he would have cut off an arm and a leg just to obtain it. Alas, it was not for sale and, as he realised with a jolt, he didn't have enough in his account to buy it in any case.

His spending had reached galactic levels. All the bills for his Chelsea house were taken care of by standing orders and although they were not inconsiderable, he had enough left to pursue his madcap life of indulgence. However, the real money, his real money, was still over forty months away, so on a whim he sought a meeting with his local bank manager in the Chelsea end of Fulham Road.

'Tell me,' said Marcus, inhaling from a rare Turkish cigarette available only through a pornographer/tobacconist in Soho, 'if I continue spending at much the same rate on a monthly basis, how long before, well, you know, how long before –'

The bank manager, a grey foot soldier in the great bank's crushed and exploited army of nonentities, smiled a thin, professional smile. 'Well, sir, you have been emptying your deposit account at a fairly brisk pace. I would say that in six months, you will need to reappraise your financial planning.'

'Six months!' said Marcus, who never even opened his bank statements. 'You must be joking.'

'No, sir. Your current outgoings have recently topped £20,000 a month. But of course, sir, you don't have the usual commitments, like a mortgage and so forth. However, as you know, I am aware that you disposed of your share holdings and the bulk of your earlier deposit account with us for, ahem, another investment.'

Marcus left the bank somewhat irritated, but nonetheless determined to continue his life at its present accelerated pace – forty months was not that far away, after all.

That autumn, scarcely three years before his Lutreche fund came to fruition, he encountered another jolt. His spending was now out of control. His wine and cigar bill alone was £5,000 a month. One evening after an elegant dinner at Annabel's and a brief bout of savage fornication with a phoney Arab princess in Earls Court, he returned to the Chelsea house and took a few snorts of cocaine – a recent, rather racy habit, he thought. Eventually, after tossing and turning on his silken bed, he fell into a deep sleep.

Not normally a dreamer, or at least one who could ever recall the following morning whether he had dreamed or not, on this occasion his dreams were vivid, Technicolor and real. His mother's face kept swimming into vision with her soft grey eyes, her half smile, and she would hold out her hands as if to embrace him. Then she would fade and her vision was replaced by his father's scowling visage. He was mutely mouthing some incomprehensible words of rebuke directed at Marcus. He awoke with a jolt, lightly perspiring. A cigarette and a gulp of brandy were enough, as usual, to calm him down and enable him to return this time to a completely dreamless sleep.

But later, the dreams returned, some so vivid as to leave him hollowed out on waking. He would sometimes stir in the early hours in a state that is halfway between consciousness and oblivion. He would experience night sweats that became increasingly copious, drenching his sheets with a clinging musk. Frequently, he would dream of his mother and as she loomed into his unconscious, he would suffer a pang of loneliness that smote him like a gong.

These dreams were highly ritualised, with his mother whey-faced and tragic, leaning over him to perform some trivial but caring duty, tucking him into his bed, her small hands bruised with age, or brushing his hair with a wooden-backed brush.

The most debilitating dream of all was one that had him suckling at his mother's breast. A suffocating, almost choking sensation would overwhelm him and he would wake in terror, his room suffused with the smell of his mother's milk. He knew this was no more than the manifestation of his nocturnally deranged imagination, but until full consciousness returned to him, it was real enough.

Yet in his waking hours, the business of living in the fast lane became pressing. Each week that passed was crammed with activities of essential triviality, lunching, jetting to Europe, entertaining groups of people – most of whom he despised and who regarded him as a meal ticket and a mildly entertaining eccentric.

There then occurred two events which tilted his life compass in a direction that could never be reversed. The first involved him mortgaging the Chelsea house. A banker friend arranged for him to raise £900,000 on the Redcliffe Road property against its current value of £1 million. He needed the money, he decided, not as an additional cash pool for current expenditure or to tide him over until the bulk of his enhanced fortune with Lutreche materialised, but to purchase a magnificent villa on Spain's Costa del Sol.

Another friend, a wealthy lawyer, had introduced Marcus to the prospect of getting on the Spanish property bandwagon, where profits of mouth-watering hugeness were there for the taking. The Costa del

Sol, stretching from Gibraltar to Marbella, was experiencing a frenzy of building, with not just British buyers seeking apartments and modest holiday villas, but hugely rich Arabs mopping up coastal acres to erect marble castles of eye-swivelling hideousness. All along the coast, earth-moving equipment, giant cranes and cement mixers gathered to gouge out new plots for building and erect, sometimes at breakneck speed, a variety of superficially dazzling homes. Mountainsides were being dynamite-blasted to flatten sites for skyscraper apartments and the small fishing harbours enlarged and modernised to accommodate the influx of elaborate floating gin palaces.

Marcus flew to Malaga with his new lawyer friend, a suave and persuasive Oxford-educated Indian, and was introduced to a glamorous estate agent with a clutch of stupendous properties on his books. Almost immediately Marcus fell in love with an immense villa on the coastline that had just been completed. In whitewashed Andalusian style with a red tiled roof, it had six bedrooms, a vast pool, garaging for five cars and was situated on a flat 2-acre plot.

In his usual impatient style, Marcus wrote a cheque on the spot for the asking price, £1.1 million. He knew that in addition to the proceeds of his mortgaged Redcliffe Road house, he would need to draw the remainder of his deposit account in London to complete the transaction.

The agent had seemed at first surprised and then delighted, explaining that certain procedures had to be gone through before he could close the deal.

But the deal was indeed closed in very short order and within a month, Marcus was the owner of a prime piece of Spanish real estate, or so he assumed, leaving the mundane details to his new friend, the Indian lawyer. But time was passing like sand in an hour glass. Nearly a year after the Spanish "adventure", he experienced the second life-changing event that was to tilt him off course in a direction that was irreversible.

He met a girl who flatly refused to sleep with him and promptly fell in love with her. This was an entirely new, rather frightening emotion for Marcus and for all his superficial sophistication, he hadn't the faintest idea how to cope with it. She was called Belinda, small, blonde and, in the language of the tabloid newspapers, "built like a pocket Venus". Just twenty-one, she met Marcus at Samantha's Disco just off Regent Street while she was celebrating her birthday with a bunch of noisy girlfriends and a couple of upper-class Sandhurst officer cadets on leave.

Exercising his man-about-town polish, Marcus had injected himself into their group, persuaded her to dance with him and then, as the scowling officer cadets watched agape, he took her phone number and promised he would contact her within twenty-four hours, make a date and take her to dinner. Her smile was utterly devastating and she ran a small hand through the tumbling blonde curls.

'Absolutely super,' she said, 'I'd be delighted.'

It was only after Marcus got back to his house in Chelsea that he realised something rather unusual had happened to him. Promptly next morning, he phoned her at a Hampstead number; a flat that he later learned she shared with two other girls. A date was fixed, a week hence, and Marcus prepared himself with particular care, selecting one of London's finest restaurants for the dinner and pre-ordering a magnum of vintage Krug.

What followed was a classic case of an overconfident and predatory young male, awash with testosterone, totally misjudging the nature and character of his intended "prey". Belinda was quite the most exquisitely beautiful girl he had ever clapped eyes on, but wise well beyond her years. She was training as a ceramics expert at the British Museum, her degree in art history having been earned at Oxford only a few months previously.

Conversation at their first date flowed seamlessly. She was witty, amusing and ambitious. She was also, she explained to Marcus, learning French and Italian at night school.

Marcus' flowering tumescence was enhanced by a cerebral lust. He just had to know more about this girl, see more of her, listen to her exquisite voice, possess her, devour her.

On the taxi ride back to her flat in Hampstead, Marcus attempted a clumsy lunge, but she deflected it with gentle skill. 'No, Marcus,' she said.

Baffled, Marcus was rendered briefly speechless but then, unusually contrite, asked in a soft voice if he could see her again.

'But of course,' smiled Belinda, 'love to.'

Marcus nearly melted into the scat.

A couple of months and eight dinners later, he had achieved a hello kiss and a goodnight kiss at the end of each evening, but no more. By the seventh date, her goodnight kisses became more passionate, more lingering, but even when Marcus was invited into the flat, her two flat mates were always there, watching TV or lounging around in pyjamas.

And so the friendship continued week after week, Marcus becoming increasingly besotted and frustrated. He sought relief with an ex-flame, but to his horror suffered an erectile dysfunction, making it clear that he couldn't touch another woman. In the spring, he managed to persuade Belinda to go to Paris with him, for the day, and after a wonderful six hours visiting all the famous sights, lunch at Grand Véfour and afternoon tea at the Georges V, Marcus was preparing to arrange for a taxi to transport them back to Charles de Gaulle Airport, when Belinda leant across and kissed him on the mouth.

'Why don't we take a room here for the night?' she said simply. 'I'd like you to make love to me.'

Marcus was at first stunned. He licked his lips, tasting the delicious flavour of Belinda's lipstick and then, with every nerve end jangling, went to the reception desk and booked a suite. Tomorrow, he mused, would be soon enough to arrange another flight home.

A week later, after the Paris consummation, Marcus was an emotional wreck. The sex with Belinda had been scalp-raising in is intensity, its beauty and, curiously enough, its innocence.

On arriving back in England, Belinda explained that she had to visit her parents in Yorkshire where they farmed 1,000 acres and therefore couldn't see Marcus again for a fortnight. She wouldn't give him her parents' phone number. 'Bit too soon to be phoning me at my parents' place,' she had explained.

For the next week, Marcus passed his time in a kind of glorious fugue, the memory of her kisses and her sweet body lingering even when he lay awake in his bed.

The second week saw him meeting with his bank manager.

'I'm afraid your deposit account is now empty, Mr Rillington, and your current account has just … er … £22,000 left in it. Now under normal circumstances, this would be adequate for –'

Marcus scowled at him. 'Twenty-two grand,' he said, 'that's more than you earn in a year. What's the problem?'

The manager, stung by this unpleasant jibe, managed to control his hurt and his displeasure. 'Just thought you ought to know, sir, that's all.'

Marcus rose imperiously and left, fuming. 'Bloody jobsworth,' he muttered to himself.

However, it was now only a year before his Lutreche fortune was due to materialise. Then, of course, he would be unassailably rich. Rich enough to marry Belinda and to hell with the rest of the world and its tawdry problems and pinch-assed bank managers.

Marcus remembered the precise time he made the phone call to Belinda's Hampstead flat. It was eight o'clock in the morning, exactly two weeks after she had travelled north to stay with her parents. One of her flatmates answered the phone.

'Belinda back yet?' he had asked.

After a brief silence, the girl, Felicity, had spoken. 'Belinda? Of course not. She doesn't live here any more.'

'What?'

'No. She's in Yorkshire. I'm sorry, who is this?'

'Marcus. Marcus, you know I –'

'Well, Marcus, I'm sorry. She's not coming back. Surely you knew?'

'Knew what?'

'Well, she got married last week to Roger. He's in the Blues and Royals, posted to Germany. That's where she's going next week. Sorry. Look, I've got to go; I'll be late for work.'

The vortex of despair into which Marcus was plunged was salted with manic fury. How could she? What kind of a gorgon had she turned out to be?

After Felicity had replaced her receiver at the Hampstead end, Marcus had spent a full minute with the phone in his hand, gazing at his reflection in a wall mirror. What was he to do? The knowledge he had just received inflicted pain that could not have been greater if he had been struck a blow in the solar plexus.

He finally dashed the phone back into its cradle with a hoarse, wordless cry. Above all he felt a sense of betrayal, of failure, of boiling self-hatred. This was not the way things were supposed to happen to him, to Marcus Rillington, playboy millionaire, man about town.

The prospect of intervening, flying up to Yorkshire or storming the flat in Hampstead, even in his cataleptic state, seemed futile.

He ran upstairs to his bedroom, stinging with these surging emotions, and flung himself across the silk covers of his four-poster bed. There he sobbed, pounding the mattress with both white-knuckled fists. Then, like a wounded animal, he curled himself into a foetal position and fell into a deep sleep.

He awoke an hour later, cheeks hot with tears but calm. The nightmare which was reality had passed. So Belinda had married another man. Let the worthless bitch rot in hell. This day, this very damn day, he would find another girl. His phone book was crammed with numbers of available females – he'd find one and fuck her till her teeth rattled in her skull. Lousy bitches – that was all they were fit for.

But two hours later, he had drunk three quarters of a bottle of Chivas Regal and snorted two lines of high-octane cocaine. Nostrils flared and stinging, his senses veering between clarity and intoxication, he decided to stay home. He didn't need food and he didn't need anybody. He smoked a couple of joints, took a hot shower, snorted another line, vomited, opened a bottle of champagne, drank half of it, vomited again copiously and finally fell unconscious on the black-and-white tiled kitchen floor, this time curled up, naked. He slept like a child without stirring for a straight seven hours.

It was a week later that a freshly barbered, elegantly suited Marcus emerged from Trumpers Hairdressing Salon in Mayfair and walked across the road to The Mirabelle restaurant opposite. He was to meet his Indian solicitor friend who had introduced him to the world of property speculation in southern Spain. The man had phoned only that morning requesting a meeting.

The Spanish deal, whereby Marcus had purchased for cash a huge villa in Marbella was, Marcus thought, remarkably neat. He had so far only visited the villa twice in two years, marvelling at its opulence and Moroccan drapes and furnishings. The place was let, rent-free, to an Indian couple, man and wife, recommended by his Indian solicitor, so that they could keep the place in good order for enough time for Marcus to sell it, as others had done with countless properties along the coast, at a vast and satisfying profit.

When he arrived downstairs in The Mirabelle with its fabulous courtyard and elegant white-draped tables, his Indian friend Tariq was already seated, sipping a dry Martini. The two men shook hands and Marcus sat down.

'Champagne cocktail,' said Marcus to the hovering waiter.

'Marcus,' said Tariq slowly, 'I have some bad, actually some dreadful news for you.'

Marcus stiffened. What kind of shit was Tariq going to shovel at him today? 'What the hell are you talking about?'

Tariq drained his glass and leant forwards over the table. 'I'm afraid there's a problem with the villa.'

'What fucking problem, for Christ's sake?'

'Please listen, Marcus. Look, I have to tell you that the villa was illegally built. The planning permission was phoney. The developer bunged the local planning officer and he issued a fake certificate.'

'What? What the fuck –?'

'Please, Marcus, let me finish. The crooked council employee is going to jail. The developer has fled, we think, to South America and the local authority is going to bulldoze your villa without compensation.'

'What bollocks!' cried Marcus. 'You can't be serious; they can't do that.'

Tariq nodded. 'I am deadly serious. They can and they will. We can appeal, of course, but that will cost money and take months.'

'What the hell, then, am I supposed to do?'

'Marcus, I'm sorry, but there is precious little else you can do.'

It was less than a month after his meeting with Tariq that Marcus received another blow which even his close friends, who were few, later described as a *coup de grâce*. Legal proceedings in the form of an appeal had been launched in Spain with Marcus being required to pay a Marbella lawyer £10,000 up front to secure his services. This he had done with bad grace.

The English newspapers were now full of details of this growing and widespread property scam directed, it seemed, at expats and other foreigners. As *The Times* laconically remarked, many wealthy and not-so-wealthy Brits seemed to leave their brains on the aeroplane when they alighted blinking into the Andalusian sunshine and reached for their wallets to join the Spanish property merry-go-round.

Mired as he was in this awful quagmire, and sensing that his luck was going through an even worse spell, Marcus was nonetheless ill prepared for the final blow. It was made even more painful by the fact that he learnt about it once again from the media. A secret investigation by Interpol had uncovered a monumental fraud perpetuated by Zacharius Lutreche. The same Zacharius Lutreche in whose care Marcus had entrusted his fortune.

A series of frantic phone calls to Lutreche's London office drew a blank; the number was discontinued. Further calls to his lawyer unpeeled the awful truth – Lutreche had been operating a classic pyramid investment scheme involving millions and he had been operating it for years. Hundreds of rich investors had been duped and drawn into Lutreche's spider web of financial planning with its promise of staggering riches.

For the first few years it had worked like a charm, with new investors' deposits paying the end profit of some of the luckier earlier ones. The bulk of their money Lutreche had been siphoning off to various accounts in South America, China and the Far East. An ex-employee of Lutreche's, working in a lowly capacity in the accounts department, had discovered the fraud and blown the whistle. An astute investigative journalist on *The Financial Times* had picked up the story and run with it.

Now somewhere in the East, Lutreche was being pursued by the police of several countries. But they were at pains to point out that even if they finally tracked him down, recovering even a fraction of the cash he had embezzled was a forlorn hope. *Private Eye* magazine published a brilliant cartoon showing Zacharius Lutreche seated at an opulent dining table in a hacienda in South America sipping from a goblet of blood. His other guests appeared to be Adolf Hitler, Ronnie Biggs and Elvis Presley.

A couple of months later, Marcus sat in the living room of his house on Redcliffe Road, still in his pyjamas, smoking a Balkan Sobranie and sipping a stiff Chivas Regal. It was eleven thirty in the morning. He hadn't washed or shaved for four days and the ashtray on his side table was overflowing with cigarette butts. A week earlier, he had wrenched the phone from its socket and unplugged the television set. He was, to all intents and purposes, a man in a catatonic trance. His bank statement lay open on the table next to the stinking ashtray. It showed he had £11,000 and a few pence left in his current account. The last conversation he had conducted had been nearly a fortnight earlier, with his lawyer. The man's words echoed around his brain like a glass marble in a bucket.

'Bluntly, Marcus, you are comprehensively fucked.'

Comprehensively. Such a compelling word with an air of irretrievable finality about it. He had missed his last three mortgage payments on Redcliffe Road, the debt still standing at £900,000. The Spanish property was no longer his and the pursuit of the recalcitrant developer had so far drawn a blank. The local Spanish authority had adopted a zero-tolerance policy towards illegal developments and already the bulldozers had moved in to raze Marcus' dream villa to the ground, reducing the pink marble facade and the 6-foot whitewashed walls to a heap of dusty rubble.

Marcus crushed his half-smoked Sobranie into the crowded ashtray and swallowed the whisky in a single gulp. He sat there for another hour, rocking slowly to and fro, but his facial expression was benign, almost tranquil. Then he began to laugh, softly at first, but rising to a howling crescendo that made his shoulders and hands shake uncontrollably.

When Barry Robinson, a clerk working at the local Gas Board in Walham Green, returned to his flat in Rostrevor Road just off the Fulham Road, it was about six o'clock. The day had been fine and sunny and the air was still warm. Robinson took his latchkey from his waistcoat pocket, but his hand froze mid movement. The door was 2 inches ajar and had been forced, splinters of wood hanging from the frame. Cautiously, he pushed it open and stepped inside. The tiny hallway was empty; nothing appeared to have been disturbed. Robinson, a bachelor, lived alone in the upstairs flat, the ground floor being let to an elderly retired couple he knew were on holiday.

Robinson, who had served in the Royal Navy, was no coward and clenching his fists, he proceeded to test all the doors in the ground-floor flat with his foot. They were all still locked as the old couple had left them. No attempt had been made to force them. He then proceeded to the bottom of the staircase that led to his flat and stood there for a moment. He detected no sound from the upper floor, but on the first step he saw that the stair rod had been loosened as if somebody had stumbled on ascent.

On the left in the hallway was an umbrella stand and Robinson drew a walking stick from it, holding it across his chest like a weapon. Then he mounted the stairs quickly and silently, pausing on the narrow landing at the top. He pushed open the kitchen door with his left hand, the walking stick now at the high-port position.

Empty.

Then the second door that opened onto his living room. Nothing disturbed. Sofa with scatter cushions, TV set, side table with lamp, small bookshelf full of paperbacks, an old rug purchased in Port Said during his navy days, wall-mounted electric fire. The bathroom, little more than a cupboard, was empty, too. On impulse, he checked the contents of his tooth mug, which usually held his cut-throat razor. It still did.

He backed out of the bathroom and turned to his bedroom door. It was open a crack, light spilling out in a thin shaft onto the landing linoleum. He nudged the door with his foot and it creaked open. The small square room looked untouched with its dressing table, single wicker chair and single bed with the dark blue candlewick cover. But on the little wooden stool next to the bed were a pile of clothes, neatly folded, and under the stool was a pair of brogues, highly polished and with little chains over the insteps. Then he saw that there was somebody in the bed, under the covers, breathing.

Robinson moved slowly towards it, the walking stick raised high, and reached out with his left hand to pull back the covers. A naked man lay curled there on his side, his thumb in his mouth. The man's eyes opened as Robinson exposed him and he gave a sleepy grin.

'Mum?' he murmured. 'Mum, is that you? Is Dad home yet?'

Robinson froze, staring down at the figure in his bed. The man looked young and slender and pale-skinned. Robinson put his age at about twenty. Then he let the covers fall back on the man's body and took a pace backwards. On the bedside table was a glass of water and what at first looked like a pile of rags, but on closer inspection was revealed to be a moth-eaten teddy bear of old-fashioned design with one glass eye missing.

Robinson moved cautiously out of the room and leant the walking stick against the wall. He picked up the telephone on the small hall table and very slowly began to dial the three digits: nine, nine, nine.

Outside the house, a few yards from the beginning of Rostrevor Road, a number 14 bus chuntered past, weaving its way along the Fulham Road towards Chelsea.

Only a Few People Know This ...

In the early 1950s at the Chelsea end of the Fulham Road towards South Kensington, there was a tiny shop, no bigger than a hole in the wall, that specialised exclusively in the sale of bread-and-dripping sandwiches. Slices of white bread were slathered with beef fat and the blood gravy from joints of meat, sold for one penny a slice, then salted. Most of the customers, if not all of them, were schoolboys from Sloane Grammar School, which was located in Hortensia Road.

The owner of the bread-and-dripping shop was a tiny Polish gentleman, who claimed to get through forty-five loaves of new bread every day. His source of dripping and gravy was, he said, a trade secret.

Schoolboys knew him simply as Polish Pete and the author of this book was one of his most prolific customers.

And Over the Border ...

In the eighties, the cult of "rave" clubs began to proliferate all over London. Here, avant-garde musicians and performers would gather to entertain young people of like mind and shock the "respectable" majority. Venues were sometimes raided by the police and moved elsewhere, often overnight.

One of the most notorious was Wetworld, which met regularly at the Fulham Swimming Pool on Lillie Road. Those in the know were invited to attended the rave and bring a swimsuit.

Fulham Borough Council claimed they knew nothing about these events and a council spokesman muttered, 'If they did take place, and we doubt it, the participants must have obtained illegal entry to the pool.'

A Policeman's Lot is Not a Happy One

As he pulled open the door of the black Humber Hawk, the policeman flinched involuntarily at the grossness of the sight that greeted him. The body of a man was propped upright on the back seat; his head was missing. Arterial blood still oozed from the neck stem and much of it was congealing on the white shirt front of the corpse, making it look like a scarlet bib.

The rear window of the car was splattered with what resembled a spaghetti pomodoro but was in fact the brain, bone and blood fragments of the man's head, blown clean off his shoulders by a shotgun blast. The window itself was still intact, the pellets from the double-barrels having embedded themselves in the back-seat upholstery.

The police constable pulled back from the grisly tableau and took a deep breath. Then with shaking hands, he took his whistle which was attached to a lanyard and blew a series of sharp blasts on it.

Some hours later after he had completed his report and the corpse had been removed, the car winched onto a breakdown truck and the crime scene taped off, the police constable walked to the rear of the police station where the canteen was located and collected a cup of tea and a small wedge of treacle tart. These he carried on a Bakelite tray to a small table at the far end of the canteen, where he sat gazing at the steaming brown liquid and the sticky triangle of loaded pastry. It was some moments before he could bring himself to take a sip of tea and it was harsh against his tongue.

The treacle tart lay inert and untouched on its plate until a fly landed on it and the policeman brushed it away with his hand. But the fly, crazed with lust for the sugary treat, swept back onto the surface of the tart and this time the policeman was obliged to kill it with a single blow from his teaspoon. Now the squashed insect lay spreadeagled on the treacle, its wings fluttering in the last post-mortem arabesque.

The policeman pushed the plate to one side, took another tentative sip of tea and then produced a pack of twenty Player's Navy Cut cigarettes from his pocket, removed one, lit it and inhaled so deeply that a casual observer might have concluded that the smoke had disappeared into his body, never to reappear.

A policeman at the next table, a balding fellow of about forty-five, glanced at his young colleague. 'You OK, Jack?' he asked.

Jack shrugged. 'Yeah, well, I suppose, yeah.'

A couple more constables came into the canteen, acknowledging Jack as they passed. A buzz of conversation sprang up, punctuated by the scrape of cutlery and the chink, chink of thick utilitarian cups. Wreaths of smoke drifted across the room and at a nearby table, a rubicund officer of enormous girth, with a face like a polished apple, belched with the resonance of a trombone. He was the oldest police constable in the station, a street copper who had pounded the Fulham pavements in his size eleven boots for twenty years. He was due to retire within a year on a pension so pitiful that his wife would have to continue working part time in a local florists to help pay the rent of their two-bedroom flat in Munster Road. But he'd saved a few bob, given his wife a handful of silver every Thursday on pay day for all of those twenty years and she, like most coppers' wives, had squirrelled it away in the post office. When he finally hung up his size elevens, there would be enough for a damn good holiday, maybe two, but not abroad. Frinton, probably, or Bournemouth if they avoided those fancy birthday-cake palaces along the seafront.

He belched a second time and patted his enormous belly. 'Bloody corned beef sandwiches,' he said and his accent was broad Lancastrian. 'Hey, Jack,' he said, turning in his chair, 'that dead'n you found, Sergeant tells me he was Freddie Gates.'

At this intelligence, there followed a rustle of interest from the other table. 'Who?' said Jack. 'Who's he?'

'Who was he, you mean,' said the big constable with a throaty chuckle.

'OK,' said Jack wearily, 'who was he?'

'Only the Featherweight Champion of England, that's who.'

At this, the room burst into gasps and exclamations of surprise, disbelief and incredulity.

'Yeah,' said the big constable, grateful to gain the attention of his fellow officers. 'Probably a gang hit. Freddie Gates mixed in bad company. Played the horses, got himself in debt, rough justice.' The big constable paused and took another huge bite out of his corned beef sandwich. 'And you know something; Freddie Gates never got knocked out, not even in 200 fights. Lost a few on points, of course, but he was never decked.'

'Why did he gamble, then?' asked a ginger-haired policeman sitting opposite the big constable. 'I mean, he must have made a bundle during his fighting years.'

The big constable chewed his mouthful thoughtfully. 'Spent it all. Nightclubs. Women. They all do it, these boxers. Thick as shit, and managers who rob 'em blind. Bloody tragedy.'

Jack gazed into the bottom of his empty tea cup and tried to blot out the rising buzz of conversation all around him. The big constable was expanding on his knowledge of the noble art and others were chipping in with other, more esoteric boxing anecdotes.

It was curious, Jack thought, that here in this London police station, in Fulham's Walham Green, very few of the accents were cockney or even southern English. There were Lancastrians, Yorkshiremen, Scotsmen, Welshmen, lots of Cornishmen and a couple of Devonians. The station sergeant, however, was a Londoner. A wiry whippet of a man, tall but narrow and with an accent of such proletarian harshness as to be almost theatrical.

Jack pushed his cup and saucer across the table, stood up and with a final glance at the treacle tart with its spreadeagled fly, walked out of the canteen. His bicycle, a red Norman Invader, stood in a rack provided by the station in the small courtyard area and he went over and unfastened the large leather saddlebag on the rear of the bike. From this, he removed a fawn raincoat and slipped it over his uniform tunic. Then he placed his helmet in the saddlebag and wheeled the bike outside onto the Fulham Road. He was off duty now and his journey home, if he pedalled fast, would be less than fifteen minutes. His big policeman's boots made the act of pedalling a little awkward and he had to splay his feet to avoid catching them in the chain.

The road was clear save for a blue Austin Seven that was following in the wake of a shiny red number fourteen bus, both heading south towards Putney. He turned right at Munster Road opposite Harold Laski House, the drab headquarters of the Fulham Labour Party. A big picture of Clem Attlee, the Prime Minister, adorned its front wall, but the grainy enlargement made him look like a bad portrait of Lenin. After entering Munster Road, he turned second left into Ringmer Avenue, a long street of terraced houses built during a frenzied construction boom at the turn of the century. Halfway along Ringmer he stopped, dismounted and pushed his bike over the pavement and into the tiny space in front of a house with a dark brown front door and an art deco starburst in stained glass above it.

He leant his bike against the wall and opened the front door with his latchkey. As he stepped over the threshold, his nostrils were assailed with the familiar smell of his wife's cooking. Something hot and meaty was being prepared and after hanging his raincoat on the hook behind the front door, he pushed open the door that led to the kitchen. His wife, arms white with flour, looked up and smiled. She was a small, plump woman of about thirty, blonde-haired, pale-skinned and with an air of bustle and of business about her. She wore a pale blue apron with her name, Barbara, stencilled on the front.

Jack kissed her lightly on the cheek and she responded by touching him briefly on the arm with a floury hand. A few words were exchanged, words of timeless ritual, not unkind words but empty of any real meaning.

Jack moved from the kitchen through another door into their small sitting room. A pair of check cloth slippers was placed in front of his armchair, a too-big piece of furniture they had purchased at Gamages in Holborn in a sale. It had a fat, square orange cushion and a cream-coloured antimacassar hanging over its back. This hideous item had been gifted to them by her late grandmother and any attempt Jack had made to have it consigned to the dustbin or the open fire, had been sternly resisted. 'It's an heirloom,' Barbara had protested.

Jack sat in the chair, unlaced his huge boots and transferred his grey-socked feet into the slippers. On the table next to his chair was an enormous walnut radio with a fancy mesh front and several knobby dials. The only other pieces of furniture in the room were a sofa in fake tartan, a round wooden table, four slim dining-room chairs, a tiny sideboard and an even tinier Moroccan pouffe, which was losing its stuffing from a split in its side. There were no pictures hanging on the walls as three of the four walls were covered with bookcases. Some of the books were hardbacks with coloured covers, but most were paperbacks with the famous Penguin logo on their spines. Barbara was always complaining about the books. 'Why do you need so many? They attract dust. If you've read them, why not get rid of them? What's the Fulham Library for?'

But Jack resisted. Books were his lifeline. His umbilical cord to real life. The escape route from despair. The prisoner's secret tunnel to a world of infinite excitement, drama and adventure. He had joined a book club when they had first married six years ago and received a new title every month. Novels mostly, some of them old classics by H. Ryder Haggard or Kipling, or modern novelists like Warwick Deeping and Dennis Wheatley.

'I like books,' he had explained patiently.

Barbara had tutted in her affectionate, wifely way, acknowledging that every man should have a hobby, but accepting that at least he wasn't a golf fanatic.

Jack leant back in the armchair and closed his eyes for a moment. He felt bone-weary, drained and faintly nauseous. Images danced before his eyes. Glimpses of dead flesh, headless corpses and thick, glutinous brain matter sliding down the surface of clear glass. Today had been his first sight of a dead body – six years in the force and this was his first stiff. He was surprised how much the thing had unsettled him. Colleagues had warned him, 'You won't find it a barrel of laughs, Jack!' But he hadn't fainted, though he had been unsettled. Not horrified, or even sickened, although now, a few hours later, he was experiencing a mild nauseousness.

He reached out and picked up a pack of cigarettes, lit one and sucked in a lungful of smoke. The nicotine hit was exquisite and he let it caress him from head to toe. What was he up to now? Forty a day? Fifty? No matter. He'd cut down soon. Maybe switch to cork tips. Craven "A", perhaps. But he liked the Player's Navy Cut. Craved the naked tobacco on his lips. Loved his seduction by the lady nicotine.

He glanced up through the open door that led to the kitchen, where Barbara was pounding a piece of dough as if it were a personal enemy. A strand of hair had fallen over her forehead and she brushed it away with her hand, leaving a smear of flour on her eyebrow. She was still a pretty woman, thought Jack; 32 years old, though. That was knocking on a bit; a couple of years older than him. They'd met shortly after he had come out of the Royal Air Force in 1942. That brief spell in uniform had been something of a dead-end, a non-event. Posted to Leicester, ground staff, clerical, aircraftman. Undistinguished. And the war still had three years to run. Now he was unemployed, living with his parents. Barbara had been working at a factory in Ealing, engaged in vital war work, packing fuses into cardboard boxes. They'd met at a Saturday-night dance in Fulham Town Hall. Great music, swing, jazz, even be-bop. A couple of waltzes and a foxtrot and that was it. Barbara decided he was the one and after the first meeting, on the way home to her parents' house in Doneraile Road near Bishop's Park, she'd let him kiss her twice and when he said goodnight on her parents' doorstep, she didn't stop him feeling her left breast through her pink overcoat.

For Jack, a reluctant virgin, this was the most erotic experience in his life so far and he, too, realised that such devilish passion could only be enhanced by marrying the girl. So six months later, they were wed at the All Saints Church in Fulham and they honeymooned in Folkestone. It rained.

His father, a retired clerk who had spent thirty-five years in the office of the Fulham Fire Brigade at Walham Green, had, together with his mother, an ex-nurse, urged Jack to contemplate a career. Apart from the obvious responsibility – he now had to support a wife – his parents felt that it was undesirable for a grown man to remain in their small house idling his time away. Barbara's, too, a cosy pair of extravagantly churchgoing vegetarians, felt their daughter's chosen life partner should set about, at once, becoming the breadwinner.

The matter became crucial when Jack and Barbara moved into his parents' spare bedroom – indeed, the only other bedroom – after the nuptial celebrations.

Jack, himself easy-going to the point of somnolence, had not the smallest notion of what he might do to earn a living. His education had been limited, a few years at Munster Road Secondary Modern had produced no visible results and then the RAF had claimed him for a period of utterly useless pen-pushing, idling, dreaming and cigarettes.

The dreaming, however, had been an important part of his growing up to adulthood. He was an avid reader, devouring almost anything he could get his hands on. Pulp fiction, old classics, history, science fiction. It became clear that when he left the RAF, he would seek a career of high adventure, unspecified, and earn sums of money unimaginable to ordinary mortals.

But just what precisely would he do? For a while, big game hunting seemed an attractive option. Then diving for lost treasure in the Caribbean. Professional football? He had been a handy outside left at school, admittedly only in the second eleven. But each enthusiasm waned as quickly as it had waxed and, virtually penniless, he had been demobilised from the RAF and moved in with his parents.

Now a married man with the grave and weighty responsibility that this state entailed, he was at last face-to-face with stark reality. The advice from both sets of parents was almost identical. Jack must seek secure, safe, pensionable employment. No risks must be taken. No chances snatched at. This advice, dredged up from the very depths of his parents' and his parents-in-law's respective souls was unchallengeable. The world was a dangerous place and Britain, emerging from the trauma of war, was financially and spiritually bankrupt. He must play it safe.

His father suggested the civil service, but Jack blanched at the prospect. It involved taking an entrance examination and that entailed the awful risk of failure, of rejection. His parents nodded sagely, as did Barbara's. They were of the "never volunteer brigade". "The soft option set". Ambition, even of the mildest sort, was to be avoided like the Bubonic plague.

'Look at me,' his father had announced, lighting an enormous pipe filled with evil-smelling black tobacco. 'Thirty-five years as an accounts clerk at the fire brigade. Same job. Safe. Good pension. Never wanted promotion. Never looked for it. Saw men who did. Went pear-shaped. Got above themselves.'

And so the pressure, relentless and subtle, had Jack casting off all dreams of shooting lions in Africa or plunging into the Caribbean deep with a spear gun or discovering new rivers in Peru.

It was Barbara, his new bride, blushing with the audacity of her suggestion, who mentioned the Metropolitan Police. 'Get a job as a policeman,' she said. 'Keep your nose clean there and you never get laid off and you get a pension.'

'And a free uniform,' chimed her mother, fingering a small crucifix.

'Not only that,' his father added, 'but it's not factory work.'

'Or being a navvy,' said his mother, revealing the great fear that many barely educated people in low-grade white-collar jobs had of being labelled working class.

This pernicious snobbery was prevalent in London in the early post-war years. It seemed to Jack's father, for instance, that toiling at a boring and low-paid clerical job was somehow more socially acceptable and status enhancing than wielding a shovel or getting your hands dirty in a factory or repairing a motor car. Those sorts of occupations were "common", and being common was almost as great a sin as being pushy or ambitious with ideas above your station.

Such talk had a numbing affect on Jack as the two sets of parents and his wife droned on articulating their own interpretation of paradise on earth. His father, a lifelong member of the Labour Party, had once said, in a rare moment of philosophical reflection, that England would soon, in his lifetime, become a benign socialist republic where poverty, inequality and its attendant ills would vanish like snow on a stove. Even Jack, with his complete indifference to political discourse, found this philosophy hard to square with his parents' petty anxiety about status and their desire not to be seen as common.

But blunted, cajoled and bored by the relentless outpouring of advice about his work options, Jack was anxious to bring the whole debate to some sort of conclusion. He glanced at Barbara and managed a wry smile. 'OK, then, the police idea sounds good. I'll have a think about it. We'll talk about it tomorrow.'

This statement effectively secured his release from the fusillade of cautious, fearful and faintly ridiculous advice he had been subjected to for the last hour. With a collective sigh of relief, the two families, now crammed into Jack's parents' small sitting room, turned their attention to the tea and crustless sandwiches that had been so meticulously prepared earlier by Jack's mother with her own fair hand.

A couple of days later, Jack applied to join the Metropolitan Police Force, an entirely cynical move as he entertained not the slightest doubt that they would reject him out of hand. The act of applying, however, might postpone further cascades of advice from Barbara and both sets of parents and give him time to contemplate other more desirable options.

To his surprise, not to say shock, the burly police sergeant in charge of recruiting at a police station in Victoria thought Jack an 'ideal candidate'. He went on to explain the procedures for joining, the training, the wages and, ye Gods and little fishes, the pension that would be available after the longevity of service even as a police constable. Promotion to the dizzy heights of station sergeant and beyond was open to all those joining, the officer explained. Forms were produced with important letter headings, long questionnaires and pamphlets that detailed the historic role of the London bobby from the days of Sir Robert Peel and the Bow Street Runners up to the present time.

Gathering all this information, Jack left the station in a daze, promising to fill in the forms and wait for the next stage – a second, more formal interview at a time to be specified and this time with a more senior officer, probably a chief inspector. Of course, back at his parents' flat, the news of his preliminary interview was greeted as if he had either swum the Channel, split the atom or discovered a cure for irritable bowel syndrome. 'It's only stage one,' Jack had protested weakly.

And so it was. But within weeks, Jack had been issued with a uniform, two pairs of boots, a whistle and a copious training manual. He was, to the delight of all, now an officer of the law (trainee) in the world's most famous police force. He was a London bobby.

It was six years on that he sat in his overstuffed Gamages' high-backed chair with its orange cushion and cream-coloured antimacassar, knitted by some distant relative of Barbara's in the shape of a snowflake. He lit a cigarette. Beyond, in the kitchen, he could hear the scrape, rattle and swish of cooking implements being handled and the fizzing sound of gas rings being ignited. Food would be on the table in fifteen minutes. It always was. That would be six o'clock, the regular time for their evening meal; unless of course he was on nights or "early turn". His whole life was a routine, a preordained structure which only rarely fluctuated and then in a fairly modest way.

But in those early days as a police recruit, he had heard such tales from the old hands at the Fulham Station he'd been assigned to; breathtaking tales of derring-do, of spectacular arrests, of master criminals being apprehended, of riots being quelled, of dash and verve and steadiness under the most awful provocations.

The truth, alas, was more a tale of tooth-loosening boredom; of slow, ponderous walks along the grey Fulham streets; of helping old ladies across the road; of wagging a finger at gaggles of noisy youths at

Walham Green; of standing for two hours at the Fulham football ground while the home side thrashed Chelsea in a local Derby – but facing the crowd, not watching the match; of helping the local park keeper locate a lost dog; of donning white gauntlets and directing traffic at the dangerous intersection between North End Road, Dawes Road and all those other damned roads that seemed to clog up with Austin Sevens, motor cycles and trucks whenever the barrow boys opened up their market stalls in North End Road.

And of course increasingly, the filling in of forms in triplicate, the transcribing of notes taken on the beat and other brain-numbing bureaucratic procedures. He felt he was drowning in a sea of worthiness. But all the while as the days and weeks and months rolled by seamlessly, Jack dreamed of escape from dull routine. His reading became prolific to the mild annoyance of Barbara. But she was, above all, an indulgent spouse. He dreamed of new horizons, of challenges, of drama, glamour, excitement; he wanted to be tested in the great furnace of life. Real life. A life not constrained by the soporific Fulham streets, but a life that embraced mountains, gorges, exotic people, roaring oceans and open skies where the young and brave would survive and flourish.

Just what form his role would be in this exhilarating new world remained unclear until a week prior to him seeing his first corpse. In the local paper, he had spotted a recruitment advertisement by a smart Italian typewriter manufacturer who was seeking young men with fire in their bellies who would, after suitable training, introduce their new range of "magnificent typewriting machines" to the world of business, here in London, the nation's throbbing capital. There wasn't a great deal in the advertisement that suggested mountains, roaring oceans or even mildly rippling streams, let alone exotic people, gorges and the rest. What did catch Jack's eye, however, was the sentence: It is not uncommon for our salespeople to earn over £1,000 in their first year, and more.

A thousand a year. An amazing sum in 1949. Limited though his formal education had been, Jack knew that one of the keys to freedom was money. A thousand a year, and more.

Jack tore the advertisement out of the paper, folded it and put it in his pocket. He would sleep on it. Let the idea of selling typewriters brew in his subconscious for a while and then, after a suitable period of gestation, make the awesome decision to apply.

Or not.

Then came the headless-corpse incident. The lifeless, congealing meat of a once-admired pugilist in his blood-splattered Vauxhall Cresta saloon. This, Jack concluded, was the most excitement he was ever likely to experience in his job as a beat copper in South West Six; an excitement that was tinged with nausea and not a little fear.

Enough already. If he was to break free and seek a better life for himself and the patient Barbara, it would have to be soon. Now, as he smoked his Player's Navy Cut in the big fat Gamages' chair, he knew the moment of destiny had arrived.

He removed the folded newspaper cutting from his tunic pocket, picked up a pen and filled in the short application form. A bold first step. He felt excitement, a hint of danger as he signed his name and placed the advertisement in an envelope he had removed from a drawer in the side table. He knew there was a book of stamps in the kitchen and after consuming Barbara's dark brown stew with its potatoes and cabbage lurking in the gravy, he would lick the stamp, affix it to the envelope and then, with a metaphoric roll of drums, go out of the house to the red pillar box on the corner and post it.

Barbara, of course, would be impressed, maybe a little fearful too. But hey, here was her husband, no longer just a bobby on the beat but a man about to determine his own destiny and earn £1,000 a year. Or more.

Then Barbara appeared in the doorway from the kitchen unpinning her apron. 'Darling, put out that cigarette, dinner is on the table.'

They ate in silence, which was not unusual. Barbara thought it was common to talk with your mouth full. The stew was hot and flavourless, the potatoes bland and over-salted, the cabbage as soggy as a drenched paper bag, but the bread and butter that accompanied the meal quite delicious. Jack mopped up the last puddle of gravy with a crust of bread and smiled.

It was customary after each meal for him to thank his wife for her exertions in preparing, cooking and serving it. It was a little ritual that gave both of them a buzz of mild self-righteousness. It was a routine that they had enjoyed since the first days of their marriage. But tonight, this night of deep and life-changing significance, Jack was going further. After the ritual thanks, he would reveal his plan for a roller-coaster life of typewriter sales, of £1,000 a year, maybe £2,000. Furthermore, it would take place beyond the restricting confines of Fulham. It would be up west and in the city, in the heart and lungs and liver and guts of throbbing London Town.

He thanked Barbara with the usual words and then he placed his hands in his tunic pocket. 'Darling,' he said, 'I have something to –'

Barbara's hand was raised to silence him in mid sentence. 'No, me first,' she said. 'Darling, we're going to have a baby.'

The words didn't register at first and Jack sat there dabbing his lips with a paper napkin.

Barbara reached across the table and placed her hand over his. 'Darling, you're going to be a daddy.' She uttered these words with such unfettered joy that he felt his heart miss a beat.

'Pregnant,' he said flatly.

'Yes, yes, darling,' burbled Barbara. 'I'm going to tell Mummy tonight; we must tell your parents tomorrow. Isn't it *wonderful?*'

'Wonderful,' said Jack. But his mind was spinning into a dark place, a confined space, a soft, embracing cell of a place where the fetters that bound him were swathed in silk.

'Oh, Jack,' Barbara continued, 'I'm so glad you've got a steady job now we're going to be a family. With so many young people today out of work it must be a worry to those with children. Oh, Jack, I'm so happy.'

Jack tried to force a smile to his lips. Of course it was good news. He had to acknowledge that it was good news. But how now could he proceed with his daring plan to throw caution to the wind and subject his dear Barbara and the foetus growing inside her belly to the helter-skelter of typewriter sales, up west and in the City, on commission only, even with the prospect of £1,000 a year? It was quite unthinkable. Irresponsible.

'How pregnant are you?' he asked, the rictus fixed to his face.

'Only about six weeks,' she said, blushing sweetly.

So six weeks ago, in the privacy of their little bedroom with its candlewick bedspread and heart-shaped dressing table, fake fur rug and mahogany wardrobe which was for the exclusive use of his wife, a recalcitrant sperm had found its way in the cavalry charge of orgasm up through Barbara's soft tissues and settled with a satisfying plop onto one of her tiny eggs.

His wife was pregnant.

He was to become a father.

He was not to become a £1,000-a-year typewriter salesman.

Not now, not ever.

After a pause that seemed to last a thousand years, Jack spoke.

'Darling,' he said, 'any chance of more stew?'

Barbara nodded. She was in a state of bliss. 'Of course, darling,' she said, rising from the table.

As soon as her back was turned at the small gas stove, Jack reached into his tunic pocket, removed the advertisement cutting, crumpled it in his hand and tossed it lightly into the waste bin a yard to his left.

'More potatoes, darling?' called Barbara over her shoulder.

Jack's grimace softened and he managed a genuine smile. 'More potatoes? Not half, darling. And cabbage. Must build myself up if I'm going to be a dad.'

Almost Every Schoolboy Knows This ...

In the 1960s the Italian restaurant Alvaro's opened in the King's Road. It was part of the swinging London scene and it became excruciatingly fashionable, counting among its customers film stars, art dealers, millionaire hairdressers, gangsters and, occasionally, the author.

Up until the early 1800s, the Fulham Road was lined with inns, malthouses and many wood-framed buildings and low thatched cottages.

Earlier, in 1392, Bishop Nicholas Braybrooke created one of Fulham's finest formal gardens and named it Goodyears.

Heartbreak

Anticipating the arrival of Brumby's coal cart was an exquisite part of the pleasure. The clip-clop of the majestic hooves on the hard tarmac, the whiff of dung and leather, the creak and jingle of the harness, the hoarse cry of the carter's boy as he manhandled a mighty sack of coal off the rear of the wooden cart and slung it across his shoulders. Then bent like Aeneas as he carried Anchises from the flames of Troy, the boy would lurch over the pavement to the front door of number 66 Hestercombe Avenue. Here, he would pause to expectorate an oyster of phlegm into the privet hedge and then lower the sack until its neck was directly above the open coal hole. Then swiftly, but with practised ease, he would loosen the thick cords at its neck and allow the Niagara of coal to hurtle down the sloping chute, where it raised clouds of dust that hung like smoke until carried off by the mildest of zephyrs.

At the front door, framed in its aperture, would stand a tiny, wizened figure. A woman of great age with a face so fissured and scored with lines as to resemble a moonscape.

When the last of the coal had whooshed down the chute, the carter's boy would wipe his hands on his leather apron and nod acknowledgement at the old crone. She would extend a skinny hand and deposit a coin in the pocket of the boy's apron. This was an unchanging ritual, for the woman, bent with years, believed that every transaction should be completed on the spot, in cash. Indeed, even the idea of credit or the issuing of a cheque or the acceptance of a delivery note would have been anathema to her.

'Thank you, Miss Salt,' the boy would say and turn back towards the great wooden cart where his master, the coalman, sat, still holding the reins of the carthorse. Sometimes after this delivery, the coalman would dismount and hang a feed bag around the neck of the horse, when it would gorge itself on oats and swish its tail, discharging Himalayan pyramids of straw-flecked dung. The ritual complete, the boy would remount the cart while the coalman snatched a brief cigarette and Miss Salt watched silently from the doorstep. Finally, the horse and cart would clop-clop away with a creak of wheels and a piping cry from the carter's boy.

Miss Salt would wait until the cart had turned into Waldermar Avenue at the apex of Hestercombe and turn towards the still-open coal hole. Then she would slide the metal cover over the hole with a push from her old-fashioned, high-buttoned boot. Job done and indeed dusted.

Miss Salt was reputed to be 100, but could have been older. Even she couldn't remember. She had lived at number 66 for decades, certainly since the house had been built in 1900. A spinster, born in London, parents unknown, but Miss Salt was a cockney original. Illiterate, but possessing a razor-sharp intelligence, Miss Salt was something of an enigma to her neighbours. She dwelt in just two tiny rooms on the ground floor of number 66 Hestercombe Avenue and in the phrase popular at the time, "kept herself to herself", venturing out only once a week with a straw shopping bag to acquire a few items of food from Shepherd's grocery shop to tide her through the next seven days.

Occasionally she would appear on the doorstep if a neighbour was leaving their house and engage them in a surreal one-sided conversation. In spite of her miniature frame – she was less than 5 feet in height – her voice had the resonance of a tramp steamer's foghorn.

Her most immediate neighbour was the local park keeper, a benign gentleman who exuded quiet, municipal dignity in his navy blue uniform and peaked cap as he prepared to walk the 2 miles to Bishop's Park, where he would exercise his authority along the gravel pathways, beside the beds of marigolds and around the sandpit and paddling pool provided by the benevolent Fulham Borough Council.

'Off to work, then,' Miss Salt would cry as the keeper pushed open the little iron gate in front of his house.

'Ay,' he would reply and move on with a stately tread.

This exchange, which was the full context of their conversation, had remained unchanged by word or inflection since time immemorial.

Other neighbours fared no better and Miss Salt's hoarse conversational thrusts remained rhetorical or merely verbless snorts directed at nobody in particular. Thoughtful people were set to pondering just what sort of life the old lady had led alone in her two rooms. The family who lived in the upstairs flat to hers on the ground floor had scarcely exchanged as much as a word with her for the past twenty years and early attempts at social intercourse had been met with icy indifference or a menacing scowl.

Miss Salt would emerge from her flat only once a day, usually in the morning. Then she would open the front door and stand in the porch, a bent, half-smoked cigarette dangling from her lips. Years of consuming these dog-ends of tobacco had produced a faint stain of nicotine that ran from the corner of her mouth up to just below her right eye. The forefinger and second finger of her right hand were dark brown up to the first knuckle and the nails were curved and yellow like a parrot's beak. Poised here on the doorstep, she would stand motionless in a grey woollen coat and her high-buttoned boots, with a thin cloud of cigarette smoke hovering above her bony skull. Her eyes were bright, amazingly so. They swivelled in their sockets like a bird's as she took in whatever activity was taking place in the avenue.

Nobody knew how she supported herself and most presumed she had some sort of pauper's pension or help from Fulham Council. The rent for her tiny flat was just £1 a week.

It was spring of 1949 that things came to a head. The weather had been typically foul, with heavy showers and icy winds sweeping through the Fulham streets, when her next-door neighbour, the park keeper, noticed that she had not been on her doorstep to shout a greeting when he left for work for over a week now. This struck him as odd and being a man of benevolence and neighbourliness, he rang the doorbell of her flat. There was no response and after three long rings he tried the bell of the upstairs flat. Within half a minute, the door was opened by the lady who lived there. She was in her dressing gown and from her appearance, it was clear she had just woken from a deep sleep.

She yawned and scratched her ear. 'Allo, Tom,' she said, for this was indeed the park keeper's name.

'Look, luv,' explained the park keeper, 'is Miss Salt OK? I mean, we ain't seen her for a week or more.'

The woman shrugged. 'No idea,' she said. 'We ain't seen her, neither. Never do. She don't tolerate company.'

'Have you tried her door?' said Tom patiently.

'No point,' said the woman adjusting her dressing-gown cord. 'She don't answer, but when the landlord comes, she's always on the porch with her pound to pay. Regular as clockwork.'

'Mind if I try?' asked Tom gently.

The woman stepped back and waved an arm. ''elp yourself. It won't make no difference. She don't answer no knocks nor rings. Not ever.'

Tom moved into the small hallway, which smelled of stale smoke and linoleum polish, and went to the blue door that was the entrance to Miss Salt's two rooms. He pressed the bell and it gave a piercing jangle. Then he noticed that it wasn't fully closed and he pushed it open. Inside the tiny room was dark – a spare space with a linoleum floor covering and in the corner what looked like a camp bed. There was also a round table, a chair, a sink in the corner with two big, old-fashioned brass taps, what looked like a tin box and nothing else. No cupboard, no wardrobe, no other furniture. On the floor, halfway between this room and the next, which was no more than a box room, lay the inert corpse of Miss Salt. She was naked, arms crossed over her chest covering the withered breasts, and her ankles also crossed as if in some devotional pose of death.

Tom gazed down at the emaciated body and sighed. 'OK,' he said, 'I must go and make a phone call. Don't touch anything, OK?'

The woman shrugged. 'No. I won't,' she said. 'Sure she's dead?'

Tom nodded. 'Oh yes, she's dead alright. Look, I won't be long. There's a phone box on the corner of Waldermar in the Fulham Road. I'll get the doctor.'

'Not the police?' said the woman.

Tom shook his head. 'No. Best get the doc. You stay in your flat. No need to be in here with ... with her ...' He pointed at the sad bundle of bones that had once been Miss Salt.

The woman sighed. 'Sad really, ain't it? But looks like she died peaceful.'

Tom led the woman out of the flat and half closed the door. 'I won't be long,' he said, 'no need to worry.'

The doctor, who had been kneeling beside the body, stood up and turned to Tom.

'Looks like her heart,' he said. 'Not surprising at her age. Now I'm going to have to get the council involved. There's no way I can find out who she was, where she was born, what her first name was. I suspect the council may know and I further suspect that her full history may be contained in that old metal chest ...' He pointed to a large, studded black box, the lid of which was secured by a double padlock. It was the one Tom had almost stumbled over when he'd first entered the old lady's flat.

'Well let's open it,' said Tom.

The doctor shook his head. 'Can't do that without somebody from the council witnessing it. Anyway, there's no key; it'll have to be forced open. I haven't the tools and my stethoscope would be quite useless.'

Tom managed a wry smile at this weak joke. 'Well I'd like to be here when it is open,' he said. 'The old girl used to say good morning to me every day for the past twenty-six years.

'And you still don't know her first name?' the doctor said.

Tom shrugged. 'Just Miss Salt.'

'Very well,' said the doctor. 'Now I must open a window. It's perfectly vile in here; she must have smoked incessantly.'

It was some days later after the body had been removed that the old metal box revealed secrets of Miss Salt's extraordinary life. She had been born Jemima Salt, daughter of Ebenezer Salt and Elizabeth, his wife. The birth certificate, faded and creased, showed the date of her birth to be 16 November 1847 at a house in Burlington Road, Fulham. It was clear from the two crosses on the certificate that bore her name, that both parents were illiterate. The doctor and an official from the Fulham Council, together with Tom the park keeper and Miss Salt's landlord, a Mr Percy Pryke, were present. Mr Pryke explained that he had inherited the house at 66 Hestercombe from his father in 1922 and Miss Salt was already there as a tenant. It was his father's wish that the lady remain there for the rest of her life. So as a dutiful son, Percy Pryke complied with his father's wishes.

'She had no folks,' said Pryke to the sombre council official who was making notes in a tiny book.

'And no friends,' said Tom, 'just neighbours.'

The council man said she was receiving no help with rent or anything else and wondered how she supported herself. 'We shall have to make enquiries at Somerset House,' he said somewhat pompously; although it was not apparent to the other witnesses to the opening of Miss Salt's box just what relevance Somerset House had to the matter in hand.

It was not quite a Pandora's box but a trove of sorts. Among the clutter of worthless junk, cheap necklaces, brass rings, pressed flowers between sheets of brown paper and cotton handkerchiefs, two items emerged that proved to be of most significance.

It was, however, some weeks later after these items were handed over to a journalist on the local *Fulham Chronicle* that the final jigsaw puzzle of Miss Salt's life was complete, or very nearly complete.

Even in 1949, the resources of the local newspaper were impressive and inspired by the possibility of an "exclusive", the paper set about analysing the two items extracted from the trunk. One was a sepia photograph of a British soldier in uniform and on the reverse of the photograph was the name O'Reilly. The other item was in fact a bundle of letters, the writing faded and in some cases illegible, about a dozen in all. They were all addressed to Jemima but as the envelopes were missing, it was uncertain which address they had been sent to.

They were love letters, simply phrased but obviously heartfelt. They were all from a man called Rohan. They had all been written in the year 1865, when Jemima had been 18 years old.

The young journalist had taken the photograph to the Imperial War Museum and from the uniform and the name on the reverse, had determined that it was a picture of Private Rohan O'Reilly of the 57th Regiment of Foot, the West Middlesex, known as the Die Hards.

The letters had been sent over the vast stretches of the ocean from New Zealand. It was clear that Jemima's beau had met her before he sailed with his regiment and the letters were cries from the heart at their separation.

Private Rohan O'Reilly had died in the battle of Otapawa when assaulting a fortress held by rebellious Maoris. A spear had entered his heart. The date was 1866, a year after his letters home had ceased. The commanding officer at the time, Colonel Hamilton Browne, wrote how proud he was of his gallant Irish soldiers. It was an established fact that the Middlesex Regiment in the nineteenth century recruited mainly from Ireland.

Additional research by *The Chronicle* uncovered a few more sparse details about the life of Jemima Salt; details that were married to the good doctor's report on what he discovered when he examined the body. Jemima Salt was 102 when she died and was *virgo intacta.*

"A Lifetime of Celibacy and Lost Love" was the breathless headline when *The Chronicle* broke the story of Jemima Salt. Slowly, the pieces of the puzzle fell into place. Jemima had met Rohan just before he sailed to New Zealand with his regiment. Already orphaned at eighteen, Jemima had worked as a scullery maid in a house on the Chelsea border, just off the Fulham Road, and Rohan, the son of a plasterer, had fallen for the pretty, fresh-faced young Londoner. Having pledged lifelong love and fidelity, Rohan had sailed away never to return. On arrival in New Zealand several long weeks later, his letter-writing had commenced and then ceased within the year.

This conjured the heart-rending image of a young girl, too proud to admit to her lover that she was illiterate, receiving and keeping his letters like precious icons not only through her youth, but also beyond into her sad final years. *The Fulham Chronicle* journalist wrote:

> It is particularly poignant to surmise that Jemima Salt opened each letter, kissed it and then placed it unread in her metal box, to be treasured and revered forever. We can only hazard a guess at how many times over the last eighty-four years Jemima Salt took those letters out of their box and held them close to her breast as a comfort through the long reaches of the night.

The only tiny piece of the puzzle that was never solved was just where did Jemima Salt's money, sparse though it was, come from? On her death, just £5 was found in her purse.

As Everybody Knows ...

Henry VIII married Jane Seymour at the Chelsea Old Church in 1536 and Sir Hans Sloane was buried here in 1753.

The modern statue in front of the church is of Sir Thomas More, King Henry's Lord Chancellor who was beheaded in 1535 for refusing to bow to Henry's religious reforms.

In 1728 Lewis Vaslet, a French schoolmaster, opened the Fulham Academy at a house in Burlington Road – the back lane to Fulham High Street. One of the pupils at the academy was Lord Compton, the young son of the Earl of Northampton.

A later owner of the academy was Dr Robert Roy, who had previously run a successful school in old Burlington Street, Piccadilly. It was during this time that the Fulham school received the name Burlington House.

Muscles, Testosterone and Love

'Imagine, if you can, a man standing over 6 feet tall with shoulders the size of basketballs and biceps bigger than a sprinter's thighs.' The boy reading this breathless prose aloud paused for a moment and cleared his throat. 'And furthermore, he is British and tipped to be the next Mr Universe.'

His audience, another boy of about the same age, fifteen, nodded in appreciation. 'Great,' he said. 'Fantastic.'

The reader extended the magazine towards his companion, carefully, as if handling a sacred icon. 'There's a picture,' he said. 'Have a butcher's.'

The other lad took the glossy book and scrutinised the double-page spread. It consisted of a large photograph of a huge man in shiny blue briefs, his body oiled and gleaming, his muscles bulging beneath the skin. So massive were his biceps and pectorals that he appeared almost deformed.

'Cop a load of those measurements,' cried the boy, pointing to a panel of statistics in the corner of the photograph. 'Fantastic.'

'Yeah,' said the other boy, taking the magazine back. 'Chest 52 inches, biceps 18 and a half inches, waist 30 inches, thighs 26 and a half inches, calves 17 inches. Fantastic.'

'Reg Park,' said his companion in reverent tones. 'Born in Leeds. Dad a jeweller. Do you think he can beat Steve Reeves?'

'The Yank? Sure he can. Steve's great. But a bit smooth, know what I mean. But Reg, well, he's got bulk and killer definition.'

Both boys hesitated to take in this assessment. The boy who had been reading nodded sagely. 'And did you see that picture of Reg's lat spread in last month's *Muscle Power*?'

The other lad shrugged. 'Can't afford it. I only see it when you nick it from the club.'

At that moment, the door to the small room in which the two bodybuilding aficionados were sitting swung open and a woman in a pinafore stood there. She was small, greying and looked tired around the eyes.

'Tea's ready,' she said, 'Doug better go home now.'

'Can't he stay?'

The woman shook her head. 'No, he can't; it's nearly six o'clock. His mother will be worrying.'

Reluctantly the two boys, who had been seated on the bed, stood up. Doug, the visitor, threw a final admiring glance at the open magazine with its spread of the gigantic Reg Park, his bronzed thighs braced like young oak trees, and then picked up his blazer and followed the woman out of the bedroom and down the narrow stairs to the hallway. At the front door, he turned to bid farewell to his friend.

'Bye, Bill, see you at the club Friday?'

Bill looked sideways at his mother and tried to make a non-committal noise that would convey a negative to her and a positive to Doug. This was accompanied by a rather overdone Gallic shrug.

'Is that a yes or a no?' said Doug plaintively.

'That's a yes,' interjected Mother, wiping her hands unnecessarily on her flowered pinafore, 'but only if he finishes his homework first.'

'Great,' said Doug, 'see you then. Bye, Mrs Reed. Bye, Bill.'

The dining room at 7A Clonmel Road was no more than a box room measuring 10 feet by 12 and when the house had been first built in 1908, it had been described by the selling agent as a "back parlour". It gave out to a tiny scrap of garden of about the same size which sported a bird bath, a stunted pear tree and a shed of doll's house dimensions.

Bill's mother, as resourceful as any other lower-middle-class woman aspiring to convey gentility, had managed to squeeze a round table and four chairs into the dining room, plus a Lilliputian sideboard with barley-sugar legs that contained the family's "best" china.

Around this table sat Bill, his mother, his sister, Ruth, and his father, the redoubtable Archie Reed. The evening meal was being consumed, corned beef hash, potatoes, cabbage and carrots all lying silent in a pool of thick brown gravy. The pudding that would follow was a large lump of suet that had been cooked in the oven inside a white cloth and on being released would be drizzled with golden syrup direct from the tin.

First course complete, with plates scraped clean using slices of white bread, Mother placed the log of suet in the centre of the table and prepared to carve it with a knife like a loaf.

'None for me, Mum,' said Bill as the knife hovered above the suet.

'What?' said Mother. 'You can't be full. Come on, just a little.'

'No, Mum, I don't want any.'

At the second refusal, Archie Reed pushed his own plate forward. 'Well I'll have his. What's the matter with him, anyway?'

Mother sank the knife into the suet and a wisp of steam escaped. 'Oh, there's nothing wrong with him. It's just a fad.'

Archie scowled and dabbed his lips with his napkin. 'A fad, what sort of fad?'

'He says he mustn't overdo the carbohydrates.'

'Overdo the carbo ... Who's been stuffing his head with that nonsense?'

'Oh, he read it somewhere.'

'Where?'

'In that magazine of his. You know; the keep-fit thing.'

'It's called *Muscle Power*,' said Bill urgently. 'It's really good on diet and protein and stuff.'

'*Muscle Power*?' said Archie. 'Is that the book I saw lying around in his room?'

Bill winced inwardly. He thought he'd hidden the magazine under his bed. How careless he had been in leaving it open on his eiderdown. 'Yes,' said Bill. 'It's really good. American.'

'American?' said Archie. 'Have you seen it, Mother?'

Mother nodded. 'Of course.'

'Bit homo, isn't it?' said Archie.

'Archie!' admonished Mother. 'Really.'

'It's about weightlifting,' said Ruth, keen not to be left out of what promised to be an interesting discussion.

'Weightlifting!' cried Archie. 'Lots of greasy men poncing around in little girls' pants.'

'It's a *bodybuilding* magazine,' said Bill desperately. 'Weightlifting is just part of it.'

'He gets it from the club in Putney,' said Ruth, her 13-year-old spirit rising to the role of mixer.

'What club in Putney?' demanded Archie.

'The Saint George's Bodybuilding and Weightlifting Club. It's above the pub on the embankment.'

Archie turned to Ruth. 'How do you know all this?'

Ruth shrugged. 'I just do, that's all.'

'And it's not for homos,' said Bill.

'I doubt if Ruth knows what homo means,' said Mother. 'She's only thirteen. I think we should change the subject. Really, this conversation is very rude.'

'Now hold on just a minute,' said Archie. 'I want to know a bit more about this Saint George's Club. How long have you been going there?'

Bill tried to look nonchalant. 'About three months.'

'What for?'

'For training. With weights. Full body workout.'

'Why?'

'Because I want to improve my physique.'

'What's wrong with your physique?'

'I'm too skinny.'

'Too skinny! Well eat your flippin' suet pudding. That'll put some weight on you.'

'Archie, please,' begged Mother. 'Look, he goes to the club with Douglas, from Wandsworth Bridge Road. It's a proper club with facilities and proper supervision. Sort of athletic club. It's better than playing in the street with rough types from Walham Green.'

Archie sighed, unable to comprehend his wife or his son's logic.

I don't like that book,' he mumbled. 'Grotesque. I only saw a couple of pages. Bloke there all covered in grease, straining like he had constipation, all his veins sticking out and big lumps under his arms. Big lumps, like bloody wings!'

'Language, Archie,' said Mother desperately.

'He was spreading his lats,' said Ruth triumphantly and Bill threw her a poisonous look.

'His lats?' said Ruth.

'Latissimus dorsi,' Bill explained. 'The big wing-like muscles on your back. We've all got them.'

'He knows all the names of the muscles, don't you, Bill?' said Ruth mischievously.

'Yes,' said Mother, 'all in Latin names, too.'

'Are you all mad?' said Archie, baffled. 'Who wants to know stuff like that?'

'Well it's like anatomy. Like what doctors learn,' said Bill. 'It's very interesting.'

'Alright, then,' said Archie, adopting a cunning tone, 'let's hear some of 'em.'

'Some of what?' said Bill.

'Some of these Latin muscles.'

'Go on,' said Mother, almost proudly, 'He does know them, Archie. Go on, dear, tell your father.'

'Well,' said Bill, suddenly pleased that the attention was now on him. 'These muscles across the top of your shoulders are called the trapezius. The actual shoulder muscles are called deltoids, chest muscles are pectorals or pecs. Upper-arm front is biceps, back of upper arm are your triceps. A three-headed muscle. Thigh muscles, quadriceps, vastus internus, inside the knee, vastus externus outside the knee. Oh! and the big back muscles like wings, latissimus dorsi.' Bill paused and smiled. 'There are the smaller muscle groups like –'

'Enough already,' said Archie, but he was clearly impressed. 'Yes, well, you certainly know your stuff. But why do they have to be in bloomin' Italian? Can't we have English names for our flippin' muscles?'

'Don't know,' said Bill.

'Alright now, that's enough,' said Mother. 'Archie, your suet pudding's getting cold. Would you like some syrup on it?'

Archie nodded. Maybe his son was secretly training to be a doctor. Nothing would surprise him now he was at that fancy grammar school in Chelsea. Yes, a doctor. It was a warming thought, provided of course he didn't become a shirtlifter into the bargain. He'd have to keep an eye on the boy and see how things developed. Mother seemed content, though.

Archie reached for the tin of golden syrup and prised off the lid. On its side was a label showing a picture of a lion couchant and in black lettering the words: Out of the strong came forth sweetness. Archie tilted the tin and a stream of pure golden syrup drizzled down onto the great slab of suet that lay half collapsed now on his plate.

*　　*　　*

Later in his small bedroom, Bill stood in front of the cracked mirror that revealed the full length of his body down to the knees. He was wearing just underpants and socks and he sucked in a lungful of breath and tensed his pectoral muscles. After three months of bench presses, they already showed a minuscule increase in definition. Then he flexed his right arm, bringing his fist up to his head as if saluting. His bicep, however, was still no bigger than a gull's egg. He pressed his arm against his side to make it look larger, but it was a complete failure. He sighed and moved closer to the mirror, placing the palms of his hands on his thighs and expelling all the air from his lungs. *Muscle Power Magazine* had told him in last month's issue that the manoeuvre would allow the rippled definition of his abdominals to become "enhanced". Mostly, though, it made his ribs stick out from under his skin like a xylophone.

But his belly was flat. Not an ounce of subcutaneous fat to be seen. That was something to be proud of. His thighs, however, were nothing to write home about. Many weeks of squats with 120 lb barbell on his shoulders had produced pitiful results. A slight improvement in the way his quadriceps were defined perhaps, but no perceptible increase in bulk. Nothing remotely like the balloon-like oiled upper legs of Reg Park or Steve Reeves or John Grimek, whose limbs were featured regularly in muscle magazines; but it was only three months, after all, he reminded himself with a rueful shrug. He must be patient. And just get on with the training. Maybe increase the leg repetitions, four sets of fifteen squats instead of three.

And then there were his calves. His hopeless, skinny, useless calves. He had done heel raises with his toes on the edge of a wooden block while carrying two 10 lb dumb-bells until his calves had screamed with pain. He had stood on tiptoe in his bedroom for five minutes every night before going to bed and woken up each morning with cramp. The circumference of his lower limbs, after this ruthless pounding, still remained a derisory 13 inches. In shorts his legs looked like a couple of white broomsticks vanishing into wrinkled grey socks.

Full-frontal body examination now over, he turned side on to the mirror to catch a glimpse of his back. Both shoulder blades still stuck out, reminding him that his posture was in need of serious attention. The skin across his shoulders, under which lay the pocked trapezius muscle, was whiter than milk and scored with acne spots. Some were just the dead scars of past eruptions, but many were newly flared, angry and ripening.

He felt himself lucky, however, that his face was completely clear of spots. Other teenage friends were plagued with this adolescent curse that disfigured their cheeks and foreheads and left them scarred for life.

He turned away from the mirror and picked up his shirt. It was time to go downstairs and do his homework, maths, which he hated with a passion bordering on insanity.

This task completed, very badly as usual, he would then be free to walk down to Bishop's Park to see if Rosie was down there. The exquisite, pouting, slender, auburn-haired, dark-eyed Rosie with whom he was hopelessly in love.

When Bill had first been introduced to the Saint George's Bodybuilding and Weightlifting Club, he had been just a shade apprehensive. It was, after all, just a big attic room above a pub situated on the Putney side of the River Thames. To reach the club floor, you were required to push through the usually crowded public bar to a back staircase that led up to the top of the building. When Bill and his friend Doug had made their first visit, they realised it was simply a place where young, mostly working-class males went to build up their physiques and develop muscles that would impress their girlfriends. The club consisted of a large square room with reinforced floorboards that contained several sets of dumb-bells, barbells, chest-expanding springs like hinged stirrups, leather benches and chinning bars.

All the devotees who visited the place up to three times a week for a "workout" followed carefully planned programmes of exercises using the equipment that at first glance looked like redundant items from a medieval torture chamber. The joining fee was £1 and subsequent visits half a crown, with no time limit on how long you stayed; provided, of course, you left before the pub closed at 10.30 p.m. Bill and Doug were among the youngest members of the club, where the average age was about 20.

Some of those who had been training regularly for years possessed extraordinary physiques, rare in London in the early fifties. One club star called George was a 6-foot-3-inch lorry driver with a shock of curly white hair; although he was not yet 25 years of age. He had built up a massive physique with a barrel-like chest and shoulders as wide as a door.

Another lad of eighteen had managed to develop his pectoral muscles – his "pecs" – to such a degree that his mates nicknamed him Jane Russell after the mammary-abundant American film actress who had recently starred in a movie called *The Outlaw* wearing a skintight, off-the-shoulder blouse.

Another fellow, a swarthy, squat man with an eagle tattooed over his chest, although only 5 feet 3 inches tall, had developed thigh muscles that measured 29 inches, exactly the same size as his waist. His day job was as a packer in a gin-bottling factory.

To an outsider, many of the members of St George's Club would have been considered a bit "freaky", self-obsessed young men with limited intellects who perhaps preferred "training" to boozing downstairs with beer-sozzled mates in the pub.

To Bill and Doug, however, the club stalwarts were role models, men with physiques to aspire to. Goals to be attained. 'After all,' big George had said, shrugging his mighty shoulders, 'having a good body don't half pull in the crumpet. No bird likes a weed. Know what I mean?'

This was the clincher for Bill. A glorious physique that could draw admiring females in their droves, or at least one in particular – the magnificent Rosie. Trouble was, his training partner and closest chum Doug was also in love with the magnificent Rosie. So with romance and testosterone bubbling up inside their respective 15-year-old bodies, both Bill and Doug had decided that only by developing physiques of Michelangelo proportions would they stand even a ghost of a chance of being notices by the said magnificent Rosie.

But here, as Shakespeare might have said, was the rub. Neither boy had admitted to the other of this heartfelt longing; neither of them had ever admitted that it was the magnificent Rosie who haunted their dreams and fuelled their burgeoning sexual fantasies. Both masked the manifestations of their lust by pretending the object of the bodybuilding regime was simple self-improvement, with of course the prospect of an added bonus that they might be generally, but unspecifically, more attractive to the opposite sex. A further curious ingredient was added to this bubbling adolescent stew of mutual secrecy and shared heartache.

So far, neither Bill nor Doug had actually met the magnificent Rosie. They had seen her, gazed upon her, marvelled at her, but that was "it", and a profoundly unsatisfactory "it" to be sure. It had all begun one evening in early spring when the two boys had strolled along the long road that led to Fulham's Bishop's Park. This route, sloping down from trolleybus-choked Fulham Palace Road, took them past the municipal tennis courts, a tree-encircled haven that was situated opposite the decidedly upmarket Park Mansions. Doug, as usual, had travelled up from distant Wandsworth Bridge Road, a good twenty minutes' brisk walk to Bill's home in Clonmel Road.

As the two boys drew level with the clubhouse, a game of mixed doubles had just started on the main court and four young people, two lads and two girls, were prancing about over the surface of the tennis court in shimmering white shirts and shorts.

Bill and Doug stopped, mesmerised by this display of athleticism and sartorial elegance. "Thwack", went the ball as the quartet warmed up and "thwack" again as it was returned. One of the girl's returns hit the net and she stooped to retrieve the ball. As she bent, her hair tumbled over her face. She picked up the ball and turned back to the baseline, brushing the blonde mane back over her ears with an impatient gesture.

It was Rosie. The incomparable Rosie; her lightly tanned skin already blooming prettily from her exertions, her long, slim legs emerging from a pair of tiny, tight-fitting shorts.

Doug and Bill were rooted to the spot, neither boy uttering a sound, but both of them holding their respective breaths as if hypnotised by the sheer magnificence of what they saw. After a few seconds, Bill nudged his companion and said, in a casual, offhand manner, which was entirely unconvincing, 'That's Rosie.'

Doug swallowed hard, his juvenile Adam's apple rippling. 'Yeah, I know,' he said.

Further conversation was impossible; indeed, would have been sacrilegious.

The four tennis players finished practice and the game began in earnest.

In truth, none of the players was very good, but there was a great deal of leaping about and cries of anguish as second serves crashed into the netting. Doug and Bill's eyes never left Rosie. She jumped and scampered, she served with a slow overarm movement, she leapt up to return a high ball, her blonde hair fluttering as she ran.

After the first set, Bill and Doug managed to tear their gaze from this vision to ascertain just what kind of male person had been so privileged, indeed blessed, to be chosen as Rosie's tennis partner. He was about seventeen, maybe eighteen, deeply tanned and, both lads noted, possessed of a very fine physique. Strong-muscled thighs and calves, broad shoulders and a flat, hard stomach. Not exactly the build of a weightlifter, but certainly no gangling, skinny weed.

A sense of urgency swept over the two boys as they watched Rosie start serving in the second set. Of course her partner would be a mini Adonis. There was no way a girl as perfect as Rosie would have anything to do with a less-than-splendid male specimen.

Later in Bishop's Park, as they enjoyed ice-cream cornets, Doug and Bill discussed the merits of Rosie, the tennis goddess, but in a deliberately casual, almost offhand way, neither boy wishing to reveal the surging, gut-wrenching, hormone-raging, heart-racing, groin-stiffening urges they both felt.

A week later, more or less recovered from the emotional watershed they had experienced at the tennis courts, both boys stepped up their training at St George's Weightlifting and Bodybuilding Club. Bench presses, overarm curls, triceps curls, squats, sit-ups, dumb-bell presses from the incline bench, bent-over rowing, heel raises.

At home, both their mothers, and to a lesser extent their fathers, were baffled by the obsession with the high-protein diet they now seemed addicted to. In Bill's case, his father was pleased, if mildly surprised, that Bill now gobbled down Mother's suet pudding and golden syrup as if his life depended on it.

With his pocket money, Bill had purchased an enormous gallon-sized tin of high-protein supplement in powder form. It had been advertised in *Muscle Power* magazine and was apparently "guaranteed to pack on the bulk if added to a healthy diet".

The sudden switch to an obsession with weight gain had come after both boys had read an article by a famous world heavyweight weightlifter called John Davis who said, 'Young athletes must go for bulk. Once "size" has been achieved, only then should they strive for muscle delineation.'

It was a eureka moment. For months and months, both Bill and Doug had been following the wrong course of action, watching their diet, driving their mothers crazy with their fads and sweating their weights down to dangerous levels with their routines at the St George's Club. Now, both boys were going broke for bulk.

Both lads had gained weight eight weeks after this switch in emphasis, Bill from 9 stone to an impressive 10 and a half, and Doug from 8 and a half to 10. And it showed. As they pressed the barbells and curled the dumb-bells and squatted and sweated, they displayed a new confidence. Bare-chested and glowing, they posed at the end of each session in front of the big mirror in the club dressing room, which was in fact no more than a corridor.

Once a week, usually on a Friday evening, they would saunter past the municipal tennis courts at Bishop's Park where, more often than not, the golden Rosie was playing. Not, however, always with the same male partner and both lads silently but simultaneously made mental notes that this mild promiscuity was a clear signal that Rosie was not "spoken for" or, as their cruder friends from the Walham Green area had put it – Rosie wasn't being knocked off by some regular stud. She was, after all, only sixteen and in 1949, even in Fulham, 16-year-old girls were usually still virgins.

It was twelve weeks after the start of their intensified weight training that Bill and Doug encountered something of a breakthrough in their sterile infatuation with the glorious Rosie. They had both puffed and sweated their way through a particularly strenuous routine at the St George's Club and now, bodies glowing, muscles pumped, white T-shirts clinging to their pectorals, they sat on a wooden bench to enjoy the spectacle of Rosie playing singles with another girl.

It was clear – although neither Doug nor Bill uttered a word – that both of them were planning with icy discretion and debonair elan to actually approach Rosie and in the words of the science fiction writers, establish first contact. Before this daring and momentous action could take place, however, they suffered an unscheduled interruption. A gangling, acne-pitted youth with a squint in his left eye lurched into view from behind the half-timbered clubhouse. He wore a faded leather jacket, baggy trousers and carried a large broom. His eyes, or at least one of them, alighted on the muscular duo as they sat on the wooden bench, slack-jawed at Rosie's perambulations.

'Allo!' he cried in a hoarse, penetrating falsetto.

'Oh God,' muttered Bill, 'it's Lenny,' as indeed it was.

Lenny, the part-time cleaner-cum-groundsman at the municipal tennis courts. A benevolent council, recognising Lenny's medical problems, namely that he was a an orphan, harmless and insane, had given him the role, three evenings a week, of sweeping up the area around the clubhouse and polishing the brass taps in the Gents washroom. Notwithstanding these defects, Lenny was an astute observer of human nature.

He waddled across towards Bill and Doug and gave them a death's-head leer. 'Fancy 'er, do ya?' he cried.

Doug and Bill cringed but remained silent.

Lenny tapped the side of his nose with a gnarled forefinger already stained dark mahogany with nicotine. 'She goes up the Lady Margaret Church Hall of a Saturday for the dance. Regular.'

'How do you know that?' blurted Doug, instantly regretting it.

'Aha,' said Lenny, wiping a thread of saliva from his lower lip. 'You do fancy 'er, then?'

'Shut up, Lenny,' said Bill, prickly with embarrassment.

''ow do I know?' said Lenny, leaning on his broom in a conspiratorial manner. 'Cos I cleans out the shithouse at the Lady Margaret Hall of a Saturday night. It's me uvvah job. She's always there. Pretty as picture. Lovely frocks. All the lads want to dance with 'er, know what I mean?'

'Bugger off, Lenny,' said Doug.

Lenny shrugged; he'd fielded worse insults in his brief twenty years.

'Bugger yourself,' said Lenny and he limped away with his broom at the half port.

Later on the way home, Doug turned to Bill and said, 'Lady Margaret Hall? D'you know where that is?'

Bill nodded. 'Yeah. It's a church hall just off Putney High Street. Dance there every Saturday night. My sister sometimes goes, with a friend. Bit posh, really, Lady Margaret's; lots of people from Wimbledon.'

'Wimbledon?' said Doug, whistling. 'Blimey.'

'Yeah,' said Bill, then after a long pause, 'we could go. One Saturday. If you like.'

Doug considered this for a moment. 'What, to dance?'

Bill nodded. 'Yeah, well, it's not far. We could walk over Putney Bridge. Only half a crown to get in.'

'I bet there's lots of smashing girls there, from Wimbledon and that.'

'Oh, lots. Plenty. All looking for it.'

'You reckon?'

'Yeah.'

'Prettier than Rosie?'

'What?'

'The girls at Lady Margaret's of a Saturday. Are they prettier than Rosie?'

'Well, yeah, bound to be. I mean bloody Wimbledon; it's in Surrey, you know.'

'Yeah. Blimey. Just imagine. Lots of girls prettier than Rosie.'

'Wanna go?'

'OK. When?'

'Next Saturday!'

'Yeah. Why not? Let's go. We can wear our new T-shirts.'

During the following seven days, Bill ate prodigiously at home to the delight and amazement of his parents. His mother had observed his weight gain with genuine pride, for it was a compliment to her culinary skills, and his father, when he deigned to appear from behind his copy of the *Daily Express*, expressed mild approval, too.

He was a trifle put out by Bill's insistence on sprinkling his high-energy protein powder on every meal, including the suet pudding, but he was nonetheless satisfied that his son was no longer in danger of becoming a wiry, slim-hipped, prancing poof who would bring shame and ignominy on the family.

'Where do you get that stuff?' he asked, pointing at Bill's 1-gallon tin of high-energy protein he kept under the sideboard – with Mother's approval.

'It comes from a health laboratory in Cornwall,' said Bill, who had already had a second helping of mashed potato, sprinkled liberally with the light brown protein powder. For some reason, this triggered off a curious reaction from his father.

'Ah! Cornwall,' he said, lowering his *Daily Express*, 'that's where I intend to retire with your mother, in due season, of course. Cornwall, England's most southerly county.'

Bill noticed his mother avert her eyes and emit a shallow sigh.

'Yes, Cornwall,' continued his father, 'a place of mystery and history, thatched village and stuff.'

'We've never been,' said his mother as she began to clear the plates from the table.

But Bill's father was on a roll; Bill had never seen him so animated. 'The place names for a start,' he said, standing up and brushing the crumbs from his waistcoat. 'Names to conjure with. Names soaked in history. Villages like Cripplesease, Washaway, Grumbia, Mellangoose, Praze-an-Beeble, Fiddler's Green, Bugle, Frogpool, Goonbell, Gweek and Mabe Burnthouse ....' He paused with a faraway look in his eyes. 'But I'm stuck here in bloody Fulham.'

'Language,' said Bill's mother, but without conviction.

Bill, however, found his father's recitation of Cornish place names had triggered off a reverie of his own. He found himself mentally listing the muscle groups he still had to work on for maximum development: deltoids, triceps, latissimus dorsi, biceps.

His mother, who had witnessed all this verbal and mental nonsense before, broke the spell by dropping a saucepan in the kitchen with a clang. Bill left the table and went to his room and his father retreated behind the *Daily Express*.

Saturday night and Bill and Doug were dressed to the nines. Both wore skintight white T-shirts with the words NABBA printed on the front. This stood for the National Amateur Bodybuilding Association; their burgeoning pectorals and a hint of deltoids were enhanced by the garment. Both also wore elephant-grey gaberdine slacks and black plimsolls.

The walk over Putney Bridge was brisk. A cool wind was blowing off the Thames. Their destination: the Lady Margaret Church Hall in Putney; a daring excursion for two 15 year olds. Although it had not been discussed, both boys knew that tonight, this very night, one of them would dance with the magnificent Rosie; provided, of course, she actually showed up. But the ubiquitous Lenny had been clear on this point. 'Always there,' he had said, '... lovely frocks.'

Bill's master plan was to identify Rosie early in the evening and make a beeline for her before his friend and, let it be said, his rival Doug had gathered his wits. Fortune, he believed, favoured the bold.

Doug on his part was determined on an identical course of action.

The Lady Margaret Church Hall was a rundown sort of place nestling between rows of early Victorian terrace houses. It was no rival to the more exotic Palais-de-Danse at Wimbledon or indeed the equally flash Hammersmith Palais, but such temples of glitz and glamour were well above Bill and Doug's pay grade.

The hall was quite large with a raised stage at one end, on which sat a group of musicians consisting of a pianist, a drummer, a saxophone player and a guitarist. All were amateurs and stalwarts of the Church. It was considered daring that such devout followers of Christ should allow themselves to crank out funky dance music each Saturday which would, older members of the community felt, only encourage lascivious thoughts among the impressionable and probably goad them into physical contact with the opposite sex.

As Bill and Doug entered the high-ceilinged hall, having paid their respective half-crowns over the trestle table at the entrance, they observed the traditional layout of the place and the disposition of the 100 or so young people already gathered there. Below the stage was a table covered with a paper cloth from which lemonade, Tizer and Coke was dispensed, all at sixpence a glass. No alcohol was permitted in Lady Margaret's Church Hall. A church warden, a wizened fellow with industrial-strength dandruff, was always on hand to see that temperance was not only maintained, but was also seen to be maintained.

At the stage end, a knot of girls had gathered, all in frocks, some pretty, some plain, but all in a state of excited anticipation. At the other end, a smaller group of boys stood around like badly herded sheep.

This was standard procedure in 1949. Only after the first dance would the sexes mingle.

Bill and Doug positioned themselves at the boys' end of the hall among the Brylcreemed throng, many of whom were sporting the latest fashion craze: the thick-rubber-soled shoe known in sophisticated circles as the brothel creeper.

Almost immediately the churchwarden, who had ascended the wooden steps to the stage, announced: 'Just to get things going, the first dance will be a quickstep.'

At this signal, like greyhounds unleashed, a clutch of lads made a direct assault on the group of girls at the far end of the hall. Bill, sensing he was perhaps a bit slow on the uptake, moved swiftly after them, with Doug a pace or two behind. Then over the heads of the lads leading the charge, Bill saw the unmistakable profile of the magnificent Rosie and his heart fell like a stone. The testosterone-charged mob ahead of him were at least six deep and most of them surrounding the magnificent Rosie. He saw a tall lad with a faux-suede jacket and greasy hair addressing her and Rosie responding with a shake of the head. Ye Gods!

she was refusing him. Then another, a short lad with spiky ginger hair, he, too, received the shaking-head treatment.

Now Bill was only two behind. The others in their too-long drape jackets were crowding in, but then one of the lads turned away muttering the words, 'She don't do quickstep.'

The remaining boys broke away like a parting wave and began trudging back to their end of the hall. Bill, with the sense of timing and initiative he had honed while at his grammar school in Chelsea, remained where he stood, with Doug at his shoulder. Then with an elegance and confidence that belied his 15 years, he stepped up to within a pace of the magnificent Rosie and said in a clear, ringing voice, 'May I have the next waltz, please?'

Rosie, who was masticating a piece of gum with ferocious intensity, paused in mid munch and her jaw dropped an inch. 'What?' she said.

'The next waltz,' repeated Bill, and he was conscious of Doug's hot breath fanning the lobe of his right ear, but Bill was in control of the situation now and he smiled at Rosie, a big, lovely smile. 'The next waltz, may I have it?'

Rosie seemed transfixed, her eyes wide, her golden curls shimmering, then she smiled back an equally lovely smile. 'Yeah,' she said, glancing at her companions, two lumpy girls who continued chewing their gum, unmoved by this momentous initiative.

'Oh, thanks,' said Bill and observing the strict etiquette that prevailed in such situations, he turned to move back to the boys' end of the hall. In doing so, he nearly collided with a crestfallen Doug, whose face displayed the bitter self-loathing of one of life's losers.

But they had scarcely taken two steps, when they were halted by magnificent Rosie's cry of, 'Oi, wait a minute.'

Both boys turned at this peremptory command. Rosie had recommenced chewing her gum but paused again and shifted it with her tongue to the corner of her mouth.

'You two twins?' she said, pointing an exquisite finger at them.

Bill and Doug exchanged glances. 'Twins?' said both of them simultaneously.

'Yeah,' said Rosie, 'same clothes, you know, like Siamese twins.'

At this, her two lumpy handmaidens cackled their appreciation of this witty rejoinder.

'Well, actually,' began Bill, but Rosie gave a shriek of laughter.

'What's your names?' she said.

'Our names?' said Bill, baffled.

'Our names?' repeated Doug, stunned.

'Yeah, what are your names?'

'I'm Bill,' said Bill.

'And I'm Doug,' said Doug.

'Well now,' said the magnificent Rosie, crossing her dainty ankles, 'why don't your brother, Doug, ask my sister to dance?'

'Your sister?' said Doug.

'Yeah,' said Rosie, 'she's just there ...' Rosie pointed to a slim girl with her back to them. 'Josie,' she called, 'come here a minute.'

The girl thus addressed turned and faced them. Bill felt his heart stop dead in his chest and Doug nearly fell over. Josie was a mirror image of Rosie, same blonde curls, slim body, peachy skin, full pink lips.

'Well go on,' urged Rosie, 'ask her for the next waltz. She's my twin sister.'

At this moment, as Bill and Doug's lives changed forever, a ragged figure emerged from a door beside the stage. It was Lenny, carrying a bucket and a mop. He observed the frozen tableau before him – Doug and Bill motionless, transfixed by the double vision of loveliness of Rosie and Josie – and gave them a vigorous thumbs-up sign. Then he looked up at the churchwarden, who was still up on the stage, while the musicians ground out the remains of the quickstep, and cupping his mouth with his free hand shouted above the din, 'Ere, Mr Truscott, the men's bog's backed up again.'

Sporting Heroics

The gymnastics master at Sloane School, Chelsea during the 1940s was a Mr Galloway. He worked part time at the school and his proper job was a professional footballer for Chelsea FC. The author can proudly confirm that he learnt not only how to vault a training horse in the gym with Mr Galloway, but also how to legally shoulder-charge an opponent off the ball during a soccer match without killing him.

In the late 1940s, during a soccer match at Craven Cottage between Fulham FC and Blackpool, the author ran onto the pitch at the conclusion of the game and obtained an autograph from the fabulous England and Blackpool star – Stanley Matthews.

Larceny, Laughter and Diamonds

There could be no more blissful state than to be young, unattached, strikingly handsome and already possessed of a respectable fortune in London in the middle of the 1960s.

Johnny Ransome fitted the bill to perfection. Just twenty-eight, clad in the finest cloth that could be cut in Blades at the top of Savile Row, shod by Lobbs, the King's bootmaker, hair tonsured by Vidal himself, shirts, ruffled, extravagant and rainbow-hued by Turnbull & Asser, skin-clinging jeans from Granny Takes a Trip in the King's Road, handmade cigarettes jetted in from Egypt – oval-shaped, exotically perfumed and delivered in boxes of 1,000 every fortnight.

Luncheon? Daily. Of course at Alvaro's in the King's Road, Terrazza in Soho and Schmidt's in Charlotte Street. No Angus Steakhouse or chain of dreary pubs ever enjoyed his custom. And most nights, except Mondays, it was dinner at The Mirabelle or Tramp or just occasionally Annabel's. He found the horsy-guffawing of the upper classes and their bovine women a distinct pain in the arse.

Thus, life in London passed in a blur of pleasure for Johnny Ransome. His flat, oh so daringly modern, was in a converted thirties house on the Fulham–Chelsea border in Fernshaw Road which, owing to the explosion of youth culture, pop music, drugs, rock and roll, sex and hallucinatory substances, was now considered to be "trendy". Less than five years earlier, Johnny and his cohorts would have described it quaintly as a festering shithole. No estate agent could explain this phenomenon, but there it was. The dividing line between upmarket Chelsea and ropy old Fulham was now virtually invisible.

But how did Johnny Ransome differ from another London hedonist born twenty years later, the ubiquitous and ultimately tragic Mark Rillington, whose perambulations and conceit are chronicled in the early chapter of this collection of cautionary tales? Well, to begin with, Mark Rillington was a snob and a poseur, doomed to live with the fact that his fortune had not been earned but inherited. His rejection of his past and of his own parents' love made him an object of ridicule and contempt by those very people he sought to emulate. His descent into madness and untimely death are a matter of pity, his short life, like a flawed meteorite, doomed to flare briefly and then be extinguished.

Johnny Ransome, however, was a peacock, bright figure basking in the social explosion that was the sixties, and he was his own creation. An orphan at six, raised in a council home just off the Fulham Road in Walham Green, Johnny's lifestyle was a result of personal effort. Not a penny had come his way from blood relatives. His education nugatory but his streetwise wisdom awesome.

It was perhaps inevitable that he would become a successful burglar at the age of 15. Now although it is the accepted wisdom that all burglars are successful until they are caught, in the case of Johnny Ransome many other factors came into play. To begin with, his career was chosen, not blundered into. He perceived, even as a young teenager, that in the Swinging Sixties, appearing to be successful was just as important as being successful. He read the glossies and the excitable tabloids and he bought the records of the new, hot British pop groups.

He also understood that acquiring stuff, all kinds of stuff, was the key to entrenching the image of success and upward mobility. He saved enough from his first legal job as a packer in a gin-bottling factory to buy a very smart suit, shirt and shoes in London's Carnaby Street, where it was hysterically claimed by almost all the gossip and social columnists that this was the epicentre of swinging London, the Mecca of fashion and style.

It was later, however, after his first year of housebreaking, nobbling, nicking, fencing and other mild forms of larceny, that he realised that Carnaby Street and its imitators were not in fact citadels of high fashion, but temples of schlock, tat and gross bad taste.

This realisation struck him like a gong while burgling a fine Chelsea house on Cheyne Walk. Having gained entry by squeezing his slim 9 stone down a chimney, he found himself, after popping the family jewels into a small sack, riffling through the master of the house's wardrobe. A row of Savile Row suits of impeccable cut and a dozen pairs of exquisite shoes riveted his attention. There was also a drawer of folded silk and satin which he ran his hands over.

'This,' he murmured to himself, 'is the real fucking gear.'

And of course it was.

By now he had established a number of reliable contacts both in Fulham and Soho, and overseas, where his acquired merchandise could be fenced at a fraction of their true cost of course, but nonetheless providing Johnny with 100 per cent profit every time. The suits in Cheyne Row and other items of clothing and footwear were by stupendous coincidence all close to his size. So he nicked the lot: shoes, suits, shirts, ties, socks, pants, the whole shooting match.

From that day onwards, he only burgled houses while wearing suits, silk shirts and crocodile loafers. He loved his work, which was mostly conducted in daylight. Nobody queried a handsome, well-groomed young dandy, impeccably shod and clothed, wandering casually through Eaton Square, Mayfair and South Kensington. Often he would lunch in The Grenadier Pub behind Wilton Place, Belgravia and listen to young, chinless gallants talking incontinently about their affairs and of their homes and cars and parents' vast estates in the Home Counties. Storing this intelligence was no trouble for Johnny Ransome; he was blessed with a photographic memory. These slender leads often led him to his next major hit.

One of his most spectacular successes was after hiring a Land Rover acquired with a fake driving licence. He drove into Hampshire and plundered a Queen Anne mansion of a set of six fine Sheraton chairs, a rare porcelain jug from China and a diamond necklace of such splendour that two of his fence contacts tried to outbid each other to obtain it.

This netted Johnny £6,000 in cash. A hell of a lot of money in 1962.

Now at the ripe young age of 28, with over thirteen years of burglary experience on his CV, he began to educate himself. He read improving books, *Teach Yourself Economics* and *How to Win Friends and Influence People* by Dale Carnegie, even *The Wealth of Nations* by Adam Smith. This erudite list was supplemented by the novels of Somerset Maugham, Kingsley Amis and Evelyn Waugh. Plus of course the occasional pinch of trash by American blockbuster authors and some extraordinary pornographic tomes by various madwomen from North London who scribbled under assumed names to protect their identities and left-wing credentials.

He also enjoyed the company of a half-dozen girlfriends but so far, none had captured his heart. His loins certainly, but his heart remained resolutely un-captured. To these pretty butterfly creatures, he was just a living manifestation of swinging London, young, effortlessly well-off and rather exciting. 'What did he do for a living?' they would ask at some point of the relationship. His reply was later to prove to be too clever by half. 'I'm an economics graduate,' he would say. 'I acquire merchandise, enhance its value and dispose of it profitably.' This pretty lie would be delivered with a sardonic smile and a flashing eye. Jack the Lad made flesh.

And how the girls loved it. The word entrepreneur wasn't much in evidence in the early sixties but had it been, Johnny Ransome would have been its true model.

As he approached his twenty-ninth birthday, his housebreaking became increasingly dangerous. He targeted some of London's finest houses and apartments in Eaton Square, Knightsbridge, Chelsea and Mayfair. Spice was added to his adventures by the occasional country house raid. His skill was extraordinary and self-taught. There was no safe combination he couldn't crack, no security system he couldn't circumnavigate. His method of operation, usually in broad daylight, was his hallmark.

The small but influential network of fellow crooks and fences in London were amazed at his enterprise and how he managed in all these years to evade not only detection and capture, but even to avoid being interviewed by the police. He simply didn't fit the bill as a burglar. Nosey investigators from Her Majesty's Inland Revenue when politely enquiring how he maintained his lavish lifestyle were comfortably neutralised when, as a cover, he had invested a little money in a trendy clothing store in the King's Road and its annual turnover, through infusions of laundered cash, appeared to be very profitable. His partner, a trusty Jamaican and failed rock drummer, was delighted to have Johnny bolster his business.

By paying tax promptly on even a fraction of his ill-gotten gains, Johnny had deflected HM Inland Revenue to look elsewhere for their prey. He also, during this fake excursion into the rag trade, learnt a great deal about bookkeeping and accountancy. It was simple. The shop, cutely named Johnny and Jo-Jo's, appeared to buy a vast amount of second-hand clothing in various markets like Petticoat Lane and Camden Town, for cash. Then it would be sold. At a fair profit. Again just for cash. But mostly these were ghost purchases. Tax would be promptly paid on the profit and the books of Johnny and Jo-Jo's shop kept in immaculate condition. Thus in a good month, Johnny might have netted £2,500 in fenced merchandise, but only £1,000 would go through the little clothing shop. Of course a few shirts and flared jeans would be traded just to keep up appearances, but mostly it was a ruse to keep the Revenue at arm's length.

Jo-Jo loved the arrangement. Out of this mostly ghostly merchandise – i.e. that didn't exist – Johnny paid him a proper weekly wage with all the appropriate deductions. It was, in the language of the street, "A neat little stitch-up".

As he grew bolder, and richer, he grew a shade more careless, even cavalier in his housebreaking. It even gave him a vicarious thrill when some wretched lowlife ex-con was arrested and charged with crimes that he himself had executed. This caused a little unease among the thieving community in Soho and the East End. It was OK for them to admire Johnny's daring success, but quite another thing for one of their own kind to be stuck with the consequences of his brilliant work.

Shrewdly, Johnny was aware that resentment among thieves was as strong as honour and he arranged, through an intermediary, for any old lag who was doing time for a crime Johnny had committed to have the old lag's family compensated with a fat packet of cash to tide them over while the unfortunate fellow did his bird.

All the while new challenges confronted Johnny in his work. New high-tech security systems, armed guards, Dobermann pinschers as big as donkeys, tripwires, delicate sensors that when disturbed sent out howls of electronic din at such an intensity of decibels as to shatter the eardrums of an elephant within half a mile's distance from the spot where it had been activated.

All these devices and more besides were overcome by Johnny's almost supernatural ability to neutralise, disconnect or simply circumnavigate all of them and emerge, in broad daylight, suited and booted like Beau Brummell, clutching a large Gucci bag or suitcase crammed with choice merchandise.

For his occasional forays into stately homes or country house hotels, he used either a 1936 Rolls-Royce or a large white van, often painted with a spurious logo of a fake removal or repair company.

One fresh spring morning, Johnny was enjoying a coffee and a slim cigar at a coffee house in the King's Road. He had glanced through the pages of *The Times* and the *Daily Express* and in the showbiz section of the latter, he learned that a very famous film star and his equally famous actress wife were due to arrive in London to make a major movie. As an avid movie buff since his teen years, Johnny knew that this particular Hollywood couple had a thing about expensive jewellery. Very expensive jewellery. Maybe not the Koh-i-Noor, but pretty close nonetheless. He further understood that they were to be ensconced in a private house rather than a hotel during the filming and their off-duty hours would almost certainly be spent shopping conspicuously in Bond Street and Hatton Garden for rings, bracelets, necklaces, earrings and other trinkets; provided, of course, that the said items were both vulgar in the extreme and buttock-clenchingly expensive.

The film, the publicity blurbs suggested, was to be a crime-caper movie shot entirely in London locations. The budget, for 1962, was immense.

Johnny mentally filed this information and finished his coffee.

When the megastars Liz and Richard arrived, he would keep a close check on their movements, both public and private.

A month later, to the usual blitz of publicity, the recently married megastars jetted into Heathrow from Los Angeles on a private plane. Interviews were given, limousines drawn up on the tarmac and countless photographs of the grinning duo plastered over all the newspapers. Filming was due to start in a week, giving Liz and Richard time to recover from jet lag, appear on both BBC and ITV and indulge in a little light retail therapy.

By their third day in London, they had visited Cartier in Bond Street, a shop in Burlington Arcade that specialised in Fabergé eggs and other old Russian artefacts, and made a further two visits to some small jewellery shops in Hatton Garden. When asked by reporters what they had purchased, their spokesman, a lugubrious American with steel-rimmed glasses and a crew cut, explained that this was a private matter. The jewellers, too, maintained a "lips sealed" policy but by the Friday, the dam had burst.

Richard appeared outside the house they had rented on Cheyne Walk in Chelsea with a fur-draped Liz at his side. She was wearing a diamond necklace thicker than a baby's arm and drop earrings which could have doubled as chandeliers for a family of rich dwarves. 'Just a token of my love,' said Richard as Liz smiled, revealing more teeth and more cleavage than seemed entirely necessary.

Cameras clicked and a particularly raffish reporter from a tabloid newspaper called out, 'How much did you pay, Richard?'

'You cannot put a price on perfection,' said Richard as Liz squeezed his arm.

The pendant on the end of her necklace, which nestled between the monumental globes of her world famous breasts, glinted with an ethereal red light and Liz fingered it delicately.

'This ruby,' said Liz, in a breathy whisper, 'is over 200 years old.'

A well-dressed reporter from *The Times* nudged his companion. 'It's the Maharajah of Wahimor's,' he said. 'He took the British side during the 1857 mutiny and we rewarded him with a vast pension, so it is said. He was already one of the richest men in the world. He was murdered in 1890 and his vast collection of jewellery passed to his son, Emir, who, as often happens in these dynastic sagas, frittered away his fortune on horses, expensive European courtesans and at the tables of the casino in Monte Carlo. It was bought by an oil tycoon's widow in the twenties, who kept it locked in a safe until she died in 1950. She must have sold it to a London jeweller, because nothing has been heard of it since.'

The tabloid journalist who had listened to his erudite colleague on *The Times* waved his hat at Liz to catch her attention. 'Where did you buy it?' he cried.

'I didn't buy it,' said Liz sweetly. 'Richard did.'

The crowd loved this and cheered.

'OK,' said the reporter, undaunted, 'I'll ask Richard. Hey, Richard, where did you buy it, Cartier's?'

Richard shook his head, took out a gold cigarette case and made a great performance of extracting a black-tipped Balkan Sobranie, lighting it with an enamelled lighter and blowing a perfect smoke ring. 'We bought it in a jeweller's shop. Here in London. And we paid cash. That's all I'm prepared to say, except ...' Here Richard paused theatrically and took another pull on his cigarette. 'Except that paying cash meant carrying the money in a specially designed wheelbarrow handcrafted by blindfolded nuns in Outer Mongolia. Any other daft questions?'

A publicity man stepped in front of the pair and raised his hands. 'That's all, chaps. No more questions. Thank you.'

Then Liz and Richard stepped over the threshold of their rented Cheyne Walk mansion and the big, studded black door closed with an expensive clunk behind them.

Johnny Ransome knew Cheyne Walk quite well – three years earlier, he had burgled a house two doors away, collecting a brace of fine Rolex watches and a tray of antique rings, which he fenced for £3,000 in cash. Now, standing at the back of the crowd watching Liz and Richard disappear into their fine eighteenth-century town house, he smiled a slow smile and allowed his gaze to drift to the upper floor of the building. This was where the bedrooms were, six of them, each with their own bathroom. He was presuming the layout of this house was similar, if not the same, as its neighbours' on either side. Classical examples of the very finest in eighteenth-century architecture.

The middle floor with its slightly proud window sill would be the high-ceilinged drawing room, of that he was certain. He was also certain that the wall safe would be there, too. He dropped the cigarette he had been smoking onto the pavement and crushed it with his heel. As he turned and walked away towards the Embankment, he was already planning his mode of entry. After his success three years ago, it was likely that security along the whole terrace of houses had been improved. No matter, Johnny Ransome would find a way. He was a mirror image of the great Houdini. Whereas Houdini could escape from almost anything by a combination of physical dexterity and mental discipline, he, Johnny Ransome, could gain entry to anything, by the same methods.

He was strolling along Cheyne Walk two days later in his velvet-collared coat, a curly bowler hat completing the impression of a wealthy young city gent taking an early morning constitutional.

Liz and Richard had left the house at dawn, being chauffeured by Rolls-Royce out to Shepperton Studios to begin filming. The camera crews, who had gathered to witness their departure, had now dispersed and Cheyne Walk was silent, save for the elegant figure of Johnny Ransome, who sauntered past with an unhurried gait, casing his target with forensic concentration.

At eleven fifteen precisely, still wearing his bowler, Johnny Ransome gained entry to the house on Cheyne Walk. (The law firm of Zobadiah, Cripps and Spengler have advised my publisher that revealing Johnny's method of entry would not be in the interest of public security. Suffice to say, it required a combination of gymnastic skill and mental discipline unknown outside the ancient yoga masters of Jaipur in India.)

Once inside, Johnny's sensitive fingers soon discovered the subtle tumblers and the number sequence of the huge wall safe that was positioned behind a fine oil painting of a Highland stag by Landseer. Less than five minutes later, he was strolling along the Embankment by the Thames, the Maharajah of Wahimor's necklace wrapped in tissue paper snug inside his jacket pocket.

Back in his Fernshaw Road flat, Johnny took off his hat and coat, placed the necklace on the coffee table, lit a cigar, poured himself a stiff whisky, sat down and made a telephone call.

After three rings, the number Johnny had dialled was answered with a guttural, 'Yes?'

'It is remarkably good weather for this time of year,' said Johnny.

'Remarkably?' the guttural voice replied.

'Beyond remarkably,' said Johnny.

'Well, will ze weather break soon?' came the rasping response.

'Very soon,' said Johnny. 'Can you get here before the usual expected storm?'

'There is a flight from Amsterdam at six. I could catch that.'

Johnny looked at his watch. 'You'd better get your skates on. It's midday here.'

'So tonight?' said the other voice. 'Usual place?'

'Yes,' said Johnny. 'I'll be there from ten o'clock. I'll wait.'

'If I can get a seat on the six o'clock,' said the other.

'You will. You always do,' said Johnny. 'Goodbye.'

Hans van Droog was 70 years old but looked much older. His face was creased like an old cavalry saddle and his pointed, Vandyke beard snowy-white. He was close to clinically obese, with great slabs of meat encircling his waist, arms and thighs and his hairless skull scored with wrinkles and other skin imperfections. His eyes, jet black and shining, were those of a predator, a jaguar perhaps, or even a wolf. He was Europe's most successful jewel fence. His fifty-five years in the diamond trade had given him knowledge of fine jewels and their heritage second to none.

Above all, he had the precise worldwide contracts necessary for the execution of his trade. He knew people in Rio de Janeiro, Cairo, Moscow, Monte Carlo and Marbella who would *always* buy the stolen merchandise he acquired. As a middleman, he was simply the best. His speciality was speed. A hot item could usually be on its way out of Holland to its ultimate owner within twenty-four hours of him receiving it. And he always made a profit on his transactions. Payment was never made in Amsterdam, but to his numbered Swiss account in Zurich.

He sat in the window of his magnificent house overlooking the Herengracht Canal and stroked the neck of his fat, overfed Persian cat.

'Beyond remarkably,' Johnny Ransome had said. That was Code Red. The highest. "Beyond remarkably" simply meant that his young friend in London had lifted something of spectacular, almost legendary value. Hence the need for him to fly to London tonight, strike the usual deal with Johnny and bring the item or items back to Amsterdam prior to him unloading it to one of his vastly wealthy contacts somewhere in the world.

He'd need a lot of cash, if Johnny could be believed, and Johnny usually could. He went to a mahogany drinks cabinet and opened the door. There were no drinks inside, but it was lined with narrow drawers. Each one contained bundles of currency in big denominations: dollars, sterling, pesetas, Swiss francs, German marks. He took out several bundles of 100-pound notes and a few 500-dollar notes and slid them into a briefcase, snapped it shut and locked it.

He pondered for a while on what hot item Johnny Ransome had recently lifted. He'd seen more than just a few in his lifetime as a super fence and his knowledge of rare gems was legendary. He knew that the skill in cutting diamonds was vital if their value was to be enhanced, as was keeping the backs of diamonds open so they remained transparent and glowed with great intensity. He had handled some extraordinary pieces in recent years: Lovite, blue chalcedony, amethyst-and-diamond earrings, blue topaz and green tourmaline necklaces encased in 18-carat yellow gold, emerald-and-diamond drop earrings once owned by the late Duchess of Windsor and countless other pieces that had passed legally through Tiffany in New York, Fred in Monte Carlo and Cartier in Paris and London.

Finally, he closed the cabinet door, picked up the phone and booked himself a first-class seat on the six o'clock flight from Amsterdam to London.

Smithfield Market in London is a legendary trading place for the meat trade. High-ceilinged halls and vast refrigerated cabinets display the carcasses of beef, lamb and pig all dangling from huge metal hooks. Men in white coats and small skullcaps manhandle great slabs of meat from the back of lorries and hang them on these hooks prior to their journey to various butchers' shops, supermarkets and restaurants through the whole of England. Even late at night there is always activity in Smithfield Market.

Just off the market in a side street, Johnny Ransome sat at a plastic-topped table in a small cafe sipping a mug of hot, strong tea. He glanced at his watch – it showed ten thirty precisely. Only one other table was occupied, by a couple of meat porters in white coats. They were large, fresh-faced men built like wrestlers with broad shoulders and big spatulate hands. They were both tucking into plates of egg, chips, bacon and tomatoes over which generous portions of brown sauce had been shaken.

Johnny took out his cigarette case, extracted a cigarette and lit it. One of the meat porters called for more tea and the cafe owner, Spanish Toni, came from behind the counter with a vast brown teapot. At that moment, the glass door that led to the street swung open and Hans van Droog came lumbering into the cafe. He was wearing an ankle-length leather overcoat that exaggerated his bulk and a black cloth cap. He carried a small suitcase and had a 9-inch cigar stuck in his mouth.

'My dear Johnny,' he said and the two men shook hands.

Johnny looked across at the two meat porters and then at Spanish Toni. The cafe owner rubbed his nose and made a small movement of his head. So for the next few moments, Johnny and van Droog made loud, inconsequential conversation about football, the price of animal feed and the exorbitant cost of air travel.

At length, when the two meat porters had scraped their plates clean and drained their pint-sized mugs of tea, they stood up, stretched, belched and each put a few coins on the table, which Spanish Toni swept up with a winning smile and bade them goodnight.

Once they had gone, Spanish Toni went to the door of the cafe and turned round the Closed sign. Then he turned off the outside lights and pulled down the window blinds.

'Anything to eat, gentlemen?' he said to Johnny and van Droog.

'Tea,' said van Droog.

'Same again,' said Johnny.

Spanish Toni poured two large mugs of tea and replaced Johnny's first drink with a new one.

'No sugar,' said Johnny and Spanish Toni melted behind the bead curtain into the back parlour.

Van Droog took the cigar out of his mouth and laid it on the edge of the plastic table, already scarred with countless cigarette burns. 'So vot have you got, Johnny?' he said.

Johnny Ransome took a package from his inside pocket and unwrapped it. The Maharajah of Wahimor's necklace lay incongruously on the plastic tabletop, glinting brightly under the cafe's strip lighting.

Van Droog ran a gnarled forefinger over the necklace in a light caress. 'Wahimor,' he murmured. 'Ah! yes.'

Then he picked it up and kissed it. He seemed to be testing its coolness. Johnny had seen him do this before. It struck him as a faintly obscene gesture. Then van Droog turned the necklace over in his hands a few times before he laid it flat on the table. He took what looked like a small eyeglass from his pocket, an item he had had made in South Africa at vast expense, and screwed it into his right eye. Then he lowered his head until his face was inches from the necklace and scanned it, millimetre by millimetre, back and forth a dozen times. He turned it over and did the same again. Then he took a tiny ruler from his pocket and measured the necklace's length, followed by the width of the ruby pendant. He sat gazing at it for a full minute before removing the eyeglass, which he polished with a silk handkerchief and placed back in his pocket.

'Well, how much?' said Johnny, used to van Droog's performance as a prelude to bargaining over price.

Van Droog sucked his teeth and then sighed. 'How much, Johnny?' he said. 'Well, my dear friend, this piece is priceless.'

Johnny Ransome shook his head. 'Oh, come on, Carl,' he said, 'let's not get all theatrical. Give me a price.'

'I said priceless,' repeated van Droog softly. 'What I mean is that I cannot give it a price.'

'What the hell is that supposed to mean?' said Johnny.

'Because it is a fake,' said van Droog.

Johnny stiffened. 'You've got to be joking, Carl. This piece was bought by big Richard –'

Carl raised a paw. 'Calm yourself, my friend,' he said. 'It is a fake. Believe me, an astoundingly good one, too. And you know I can't deal in phoney merchandise. However, I can tell you that this fake is one of the best I've ever seen. But the dimensions are just off, the cut is not quite right and so on. But, my dear Johnny, I know who made it. Only one man could execute such a sensational copy. One man. Here in London. In Hatton Garden. Almost certainly. The guy is a genius. He doesn't need to fake because he is hugely rich and successful already. But he likes the thrill, the game, the challenge. He is the master.'

'How much do you think he charged Richard?' asked Johnny.

'No less than a million,' said van Droog.

'Wow!' said Johnny.

'He would have had a fake certificate of authenticity and all the relevant documents. Knuckleheads like this Richard wouldn't know a fake if it crawled up their arse and bit them.'

'So that's it,' said Johnny. 'Couldn't you shift it for a few grand to one of your punters?'

Van Droog shook his head. 'No way, Johnny, my friend. I won't touch it. If tried to palm that off on one of my special clients, I'd be in the bottom of Herengracht Canal with my throat cut before you could say … what is it, Johnny? Bill Robinson?'

'Jack Robinson,' said Johnny glumly.

'So I'm off, my friend,' said van Droog. 'Better luck next time. No hard feelings, OK?'

Johnny nodded. 'No hard feelings. That's business.'

Van Droog smiled, showing uneven yellow teeth.

'Yes, that's business, Johnny. However, let me give you this.' He took a small square of paper from his pocket and wrote on it, then handed it to Johnny. 'This is the name and address of the man who made this superb replica. He is almost certainly the man who sold it to your arrogant film star. What you do with this information is up to you. Now I must go. Goodbye. See you next time.'

*　　*　　*

The shop in Hatton Garden was tiny, less than 5 feet square, and was dominated by an old desk with a scarred leather top. The walls were lined with glass cases of watches, earrings, necklaces and rings. Behind the desk sat a tiny man with a domed bald head, pince-nez spectacles and a velvet jacket.

The shop door opened and Johnny Ransome walked in. 'Mr Rubins?' he said politely.

The little man nodded and smiled. 'How can I help you?' he asked, adjusting his spectacles.

'To coin a phrase,' said Johnny, sitting in the small chair in front of the desk, 'let's cut to the fucking chase.' He tossed the necklace onto the desk and pointed at it. 'I congratulate you on a wonderful piece of work, Mr Rubins, but you are a very naughty boy. However, naughty though you are, I think we can do business.'

Rubins' face had paled and he glanced around nervously.

'No, I'm not a policeman. Your secret is safe with me, for the moment.'

'Where did you get this and when?' blurted Rubins and his spectacles fell off.

'Oh, hasn't it hit the papers yet? My daring raid? It will sure as eggs are eggs. Then the shit will really hit the fan. Now here's the deal, Mr Rubins. And to coin another cliché, it's an offer you can't afford to refuse. We're in the same business, you and I, Mr Rubins. Honour among thieves and all that crap.'

'What deal?' said Rubins in a whisper.

'OK. Quite simply,' said Johnny, 'I know you sold this piece, I know who to and I know you made it yourself here on these crappy premises. Why for God's sake? You're worth a few bob yourself. However, that's by the by. Now here's your choice. Either you can tell me to get lost, politely of course, in which case I shall take the necklace to the authorities claiming I found it. I shall reveal that it is a fake. Oh yes, I have people cleverer than you who can confirm that it is a fake. If I do that, you will face jail time. OK? Alternatively, Mr Rubins, I can go along with your brilliant little scam, let the two film stars screw the insurance company for a substantial sum and chuck the necklace in the Thames; after, of course, you have given me, in cash, precisely two thirds of the million quid you sold the necklace for to those two dumb actors. Why two thirds? Well, because I'm a sport and you deserve a little reward for your efforts. I will settle, therefore, for £750 grand in cash and not a penny less. Deal?'

Rubins looked at first as if he was going to faint. 'Cash?' he murmured. 'You can't be serious!'

'Oh, I am,' said Johnny, 'deadly. And I bet you've got it here in your safe. After all, it's only seventy-two hours since you pulled off this stroke, you crafty little man, so I'll just smoke a cigarette while you totter off to the back of the shop and get the money. Oh, and any currency will do, dollars, francs, I'm not fussy. And just thank your lucky stars you're dealing with a gentleman thief, Mr Rubins. I have acquaintances in the trade who would have first broken your legs before taking the money and then they might even have torn your lungs out of your chest before leaving with the full million quid.'

Rubins stood up and smoothed down the front of his cardigan. 'I don't need to go into the back of the shop,' he said. 'I keep the money here, in this filing cabinet. Burglars always go for the safe, in which I leave a little. Works every time.'

'Thanks for the tip,' said Johnny. 'Now go and lock the front door, come back and open that bloody filing cabinet and give me the money. Slowly, Mr Rubins, one note at a time. We might as well enjoy the process and after all, we're both professionals at the top of our game.'

When the story of the theft of the famous Maharajah of Wahimor's necklace hit the press, there was a frenzy of excitement. The BBC sent a TV crew and two top reporters to interview Richard and Liz, who seemed to bask in the glow of their misfortune.

Johnny, strolling along the Embankment opposite Cheyne Walk, glanced at the date panel on his wristwatch. It was now less than 100 hours since he had gained entry to the house across the road and just less since the meeting with van Droog and Rubins had taken place. The three quarters of a million, in four different currencies, was in his sock drawer at Fernshaw Road. Old Rubins' tip had been a good one. Safes were just a magnet for thieves.

Johnny leant against the parapet and gazed across the Thames. He'd bought a copy of *The Evening Standard* earlier, the afternoon edition, and it contained blazing headlines about the theft of the Wahimor necklace. A subheading caught his eye: Insurance company offer reward of £100,000 for the return of the Maharajah of Wahimor's stolen necklace.

Johnny put his hand in his breast pocket and his fingers closed round the hard coldness of the necklace. His plan had been to dump it in the Thames. It had served its purpose and both he and old Rubins had profited from it. But a reward of another £100 grand! Wouldn't that be something? Liz and Richard would get their fake bauble back, the insurance company would be saved a fortune and everybody would be happy.

He folded the newspaper carefully and continued strolling along the Embankment. Just where, he pondered, should he "discover" the lost necklace and return it to the authorities to claim his £100 grand?

Then he stopped and leant against the parapet again. Could be risky. So far, the caper had gone pretty smoothly and three quarters of a mil couldn't be sneezed at.

He took the necklace out of his pocket, dropped it over the parapet and walked away. Let it sink to the bottom of the Thames and be lost forever, he thought, smiling. But he hadn't realised that it was low tide and the necklace had fallen into the mud of the Embankment where it lay, uncurled and glinting, waiting, silently, beautifully, for some other lucky punter to pick it up and start another chapter in the life of this fine priceless gem.

True or False? Who Cares?

The new Saatchi Gallery in the King's Road is now rated as one of the best modern-art galleries in the world. In 2009, a naked cyclist tried to ride his bike into the gallery, but was subjected to a citizen's arrest by an 80-year-old woman. No charges were preferred and the cyclist apologised and put on a raincoat provided by a sympathetic passer-by.

In April 1902, the municipal swimming baths were opened at Waltham Green. The opening ceremony was conducted by the mayor, who then dived into the water to cheers from the other dignitaries who were in attendance. There is no record – and I've checked – whether or not the mayor actually wore a bathing costume or jumped into the water in his three-piece suit, mayoral chain of office and spats.

I'd like to think he did the deed fully dressed!

Rags to Riches

Freddie wasn't certain whether describing himself as a street trader was marginally less damaging to his image than being called simply a barrow boy. It was not a calling he had chosen independently, but one into which he had drifted almost casually after, it has to be admitted, some urging from his father, Jack.

Father, a leather-lunged, red-faced slab of a man had worked a barrow in the North End Road Market in Fulham since before the crucifixion of our Lord, or so it seemed. The stout construction of his barrow with its steel-encircled wooden wheels resembled a military supply wagon of the sort that served the gallant British Tommies in the Crimea, India and other exotic locations.

Freddie's father, who had left school entirely illiterate, had nonetheless at age 15 gained employment as an assistant to an old-time market trader whose speciality was fruit and vegetables. Over the years that followed, he had learnt the harsh lessons of capitalist enterprise and surprisingly, the basic essentials of economic theory and practice. By the age of 30, steeped in the arts of salesmanship, barter, exaggeration and thrift, he had his own elaborate barrow in the North End Road, which now displayed a variety of merchandise – much of which could also be seen in tiny chemists or grocers or even department stores, but not at the reduced prices that Freddie's dad was able to afford. Just how he managed to sustain such tempting discounts was a conundrum that would have baffled the most erudite minds in the City of London, but sustain them he did.

Vaseline, Vick inhalers, aspirin, cough linctus in green bottles, crepe bandages, shaving foam, razor blades, unguents with quasi-medical names that served no purpose other than to cause those who applied the substance to their bare skin to reek like a tart's boudoir, sugared fruit in fancy shapes, tins of nuts, jars of golden syrup, sweet biscuits, chocolate biscuits, crackers, plastic flowers of hideous design, leather gloves in the "one size fits all" shapeless category, silk stockings and woolly jumpers. Variety, then, was the spice that raised Freddie's father's merchandise above those of his fellow traders.

Freddie was the only son of his parents, Jack and Millie Granger, and from the moment he was born it was decreed, assumed, expected and anticipated that on achieving maturity, Freddie would join his father in the North End Road and there enhance the flow of merchandise from barrow to eager consumer, to the profit and satisfaction of all concerned.

Freddie, like his father, was of a straightforward and uncomplicated nature. The family lived in a small, rented, two-bedroom flat in Kilmaine Road, which even in the 1960s was considered to be a shade less than salubrious. Kilmaine Road lay off Munster Road and consisted of terraced houses built between 1890 and the start of the twentieth century. Slightly better than the average two-up two-down designed for the urban poor, they all had a patch of stamped earth at the rear, pitifully described as a garden by the landlords who at best could only extract about £1 a week rent for each of the two flats in every house.

Jack and Millie paid their rent promptly, in cash, to the landlord who came to collect each Friday on his bicycle. His name was Ahmed and he was as brown as a chestnut and always wore a general service medal ribbon on his jacket lapel to show that he had served as a loyal soldier to the King in the British Army during the 1939–45 conflict. Born in Fulham of Indian parents, Ahmed was one of the first of his race in the metropolis to become a successful entrepreneur. Some twenty years would pass before virtually every tobacconist and newsagent shop in London would be owned and run by these splendid chaps and their families.

Jack and Millie entertained no prejudices and rather admired Ahmed, even though Jack insisted on calling him Sabu. Ahmed had a ripe cockney accent and an addiction to Player's Navy Cut cigarettes. 'I'm a fifty-a-day bloke,' he would boast and just occasionally when takings were low from Jack's barrow, the rent would be paid in cigarettes; obtained, of course, mysteriously, by Jack from one of his suppliers at stupendous discounts. Thus, on such occasions, Jack made a profit on the deal and Ahmed, a shrewd operator himself, actually admired Jack for what he was doing.

'This is how things were, Jack,' said Ahmed, puffing on a freshly lit Player's Navy Cut, 'before the invention of money. It was called barter and the practice was very popular in the old country. So my dad told me!'

Jack didn't actually give a toss about Ahmed's commercial family history, but he always humoured his landlord. 'So long as both sides are happy,' he would say, 'then the deal is good!'

Ahmed would then fasten his cycle clips, place the cellophane-bound cigarette boxes into his saddlebag and pedal off along Kilmaine Road whistling a jaunty, military air.

Millie Granger, Freddie's mother, was a prototype of the working-class homemaker. Although their flat was tiny, it was buffed, scrubbed and polished to a fine sheen and the faded tartan sofa cushions seldom left unplumped. The scullery, for no such thing as a kitchen existed in Kilmaine Road, was stone-floored with a big sink, a wooden draining board, a gas oven and a cupboard. In this tiny space, Millie Granger produced hot meals of stupendous variety three times a day.

Freddie had failed the eleven-plus and therefore was not scheduled to attend one of the many fine grammar schools in London at that time. He failed, not because of any lack of intelligence, but purely because he was an idle daydreamer. His ill-read but street-smart father expressed no displeasure at his son's poor academic performance. To him, "schooling" was a waste of time and the sooner Freddie got through his statutory few years at Munster Road Secondary Modern, the better for all concerned. 'I mean to say,' mused his father, 'what bleeding qualifications do you need to run a bloody barrow?'

And so it came to pass that Freddie, at fifteen, left Munster Road Secondary Modern and immediately started work in the North End Road dispensing merchandise with his father to the head-scarfed and cloth-capped Fulham denizens who flocked to the Grangers' barrow like moths to a flame, six days a week.

However, unlike his father, Freddie could read; indeed, it could be said that from the age of 5, he read copiously. He read *The Beano* and *The Dandy* comics, and he read fat American comics smuggled into school by his mates. In other words, he was an avid consumer of stuff with little or no literary merit. Even this trivial junk failed to spark off any interest in things academic. Most maths was boring and yet he could add up very quickly and was fast at mental arithmetic. But algebra and all the other subjects left him stone cold.

So his school days passed in a blur, with him earning only the mildest praise from his teachers for his prowess on the football field. When he left Munster Road and entered adulthood, he took to the business of selling like the proverbial duck to water. Within his first few weeks, he made his father inordinately proud. His style was less confrontational than his parent and whereas Jack was inclined to be a bellower, Freddie preferred gentle persuasion. In his clear South London accent, which was not quite the raw cockney brogue that surrounded him in the North End Road, he developed "a line" that mesmerised the largely female shoppers as they shuffled along the road with their wicker baskets and pushchairs crammed with infants.

Occasionally, when Freddie and Jack had a consignment of male-orientated merchandise to shift, they would address a crowd of cloth-capped local artisans. The landlord of The Swan Pub at Walham Green would have given them a tip-off that fine goods were on offer at the Grangers' barrow and so they would gather to hear of the stunning discounts and mind-bending quality of the items to be sold.

It is hard to recreate the excitement Freddie's sales pitch could create here in cold print. But it was, in a word, magic. The goods being dispensed at "miraculously" low prices – Freddie's words – vanished like snow on a stove and the sturdy artisans would return to the pub, or go home, loaded with industrial-sized tubs of Brylcreem, razor blades, woolly hats, hobnailed boots, giant tins of baked beans, leather belts and very occasionally and dangerously, packets of condoms; which in the sixties were called contraceptives in polite society and regrettably spunk bladders by the lower orders.

The tip-off, which came from the landlord of The Swan, was in fact Freddie's unconscious and entirely instinctive foray into merchandising and promotion. He bunged the landlord, sometimes in cash, sometimes in cigarettes – his father's speciality – and in return the landlord would spread the word among his customers that Jack and Freddie's barrow was something of an Aladdin's cave and what was on offer on any particular day was too fabulous to ignore.

As year passed on year, Freddie's role on the North End Road barrow became the main reason for its continued success. Father Jack, who had developed mild laryngitis owing no doubt to all his bellowing, played less and less prominently in the front line, devoting most of his energy to purchasing or what today would be called archly, "sourcing".

1964

By his late teens, Freddie's sales method had become exquisitely theatrical. He seemed able to hold large crowds of shoppers spellbound while he extolled, in stunning detail, the virtues and benefits of each item on offer. Although a confident young man, Freddie was never arrogant. He was forceful and persuasive in a non-threatening sort of way, whereas Father Jack rather exuded menace, even chivvying hesitant purchasers to, 'Come on, darlin'; make your bleeding mind up!'

The turning point in young Freddie's life, one hesitates to call it thus far a career, unfolded as follows.

On a brisk October morning, when a weak sun had just broken through a thin film of cloud over the smoking rooftops of the North End Road, Freddie was addressing an early crowd of women on the virtues of stocking their larders with quart-sized bottles of pickled onions, tins of goose fat and industrial vats of imitation Marmite. As his dazzling peroration reached its climax – the women were already rummaging in their purses for recalcitrant half-crowns – a tall man in an astrakhan-collared coat appeared at the rear of the crowd. He looked out of place in the North End Road with his collar and tie and grey homburg, but he was watching Freddie with intense concentration.

When the pitch ended and the actual process of buying and paying began, the stranger remained stationary, at least until a gap appeared between two stout ladies, both bent on acquiring tins of sardines, pickled onions and as much imitation Marmite as could be crammed inside a shopping bag. He approached Freddie with a dazzling Clark Gable smile.

'My dear sir,' he boomed, 'may I congratulate you on a performance that would have done justice to the great David Garrick himself!'

Freddie, who was wrapping a bottle of pickled onions in brown paper, looked up at the stranger and smiled. 'Very nice of you to say so, guv'nor. Love your hat. And your coat. Very classy and no mistake. Now, sir, if I may be so bold, what you need to complete the ensemble is a nice woolly scarf and I have just the thing.' With this, Freddie produced

119

a long bright red scarf with a flourish, then continued. 'Hand woven by blindfolded nuns in Tibet. It's yours for ten bob, squire, or two for fifteen shillings.'

The stranger gave a yelp of ecstasy and produced a crisp white five pound note from the folds of his coat. 'Yes, yes,' he cried, 'and my dear sir, a bottle of your pickled onions, nay two, if you please, and keep the change!'

Momentarily stunned, Freddie gazed at the stranger then handed over the merchandise with a broad grin, took the proffered fiver and rang a little handbell he kept on the side of his barrow. The stranger doffed his homburg, took the two scarves, wound them both around his neck, picked up the bottles of pickled onions, bowed low and melted away into the crowds.

A week later, when Freddie had almost forgotten about the incident, the fellow reappeared similarly robed and hatted, but this time he was accompanied by six young men in smart suits, white shirts and stripy ties. They all wore neat bowler hats and carried rolled umbrellas.

Freddie nudged his father who was helping that day unpacking crates of tinned condensed milk. 'He's here again,' he said.

'Who?' croaked Jack.

'The geezer who bought two scarves and two bottles of pickled onions.'

'Blimey,' said Jack, nudging his son. 'Looks like he's brought a bunch of undertakers with 'im this time!'

Now Jack's voice, though croaky, still travelled and his pert observation about the stranger's companions was heard by the stranger and he emitted a hearty laugh.

'A student of human nature, I see,' he boomed. 'But not entirely accurate, if I may be permitted to contradict your verdict.'

Jack glanced at Freddie and Freddie glanced back at his father. Their unspoken conclusion was that the homburged gent before them was some sort of harmless lunatic.

'Permission granted, cock,' said Freddie.

'Aha!' cried the stranger. 'Well now, my dear sirs, these compadres, these youthful companions are trainee sales representatives for a well-known provisions conglomerate that operates worldwide against fierce competition. And if I may say so, their job is, or will be when they are trained, to introduce a variety of canned foodstuffs to the retail grocery business. And what a variety it is, too. But forgive me, kind sirs, I must not overstay my welcome. Suffice to say, I bring them here today to witness a classic demonstration of sales techniques, a master class if you will, of just how to attract, engage, persuade and ultimately satisfy a customer following the ancient principles first noted in ancient Greek markets and later Rome. Also hinted at in the seminal work of self-improvement, *How to Win Friends and Influence People* by Dale Carnegie, himself a shining example of the American dream made flesh!'

Here, the stranger paused and wiped a fleck of foam from the corner of his mouth. 'And you, dear sirs,' he continued, 'are no doubt asking yourselves who is this man? Who is this importunate wretch who invaded my sacred selling space accompanied by a gaggle of ambitious novices? Yes, indeed, it is a question both pressing and legitimate.'

'Alright, cock,' said Jack, scratching his ear, 'who are you?'

'Aha!' exclaimed the stranger. 'Direct and to the point. I, as it transpires, am Sebastian Runcorn, Professor of Communications and Marketing and my consultancy, Runcorn Direct, has been engaged by a number of blue-chip corporations to help train their dynamic sales teams of the future. Sales training is big in America, kind sirs, and I, Sebastian Runcorn, am one of the first pioneers of sales training in this kingdom.

'Today, as you may have discerned, is practical training day; live action, so to speak. And now, before I leave, I shall ask my class,' he waved a hand towards the six acolytes who stood rather sheepishly in line alongside him, 'I shall ask them now to purchase at least one item from the cornucopia on offer from your wheeled appliance as a token of their appreciation of the lesson in basic sales techniques you have been so good as to provide.'

With that, the six bowler hats moved forward and began buying mops, tins of mushroom soup, socks, brooms, nasal sprays, yellow dusters, bottles of preserves and next year's calendars featuring the lovely Marilyn Monroe showing thighs that gleamed with an incandescent sheen. In all, Freddie took twenty-eight pounds, fifteen shillings in less than five minutes.

'Job done,' cried the stranger. 'Farewell, gentlemen. If I am spared, I shall return with more students. Lavish sales are a certainty. Goodbye!'

*   *   *

Later, over supper at Kilmaine Road, Freddie and Jack tucked into large platefuls of mashed potato, pork sausages and beans, which was Millie Granger's speciality. This substantial treat was accompanied by two bottles of brown ale, the very finest that Watneys could brew; although Millie made do with a glass of Tizer.

First plates wiped clean, Millie then served great steaming slices of spotted dick left over from Sunday lunch and drenched each helping in thick yellow custard. All three of them ate this in silence until, finally satiated, Jack pushed back his chair, produced a Player's Navy Cut, lit it, inhaled deeply and said to Millie, 'That nutcase ponced up to the barrow again today; brought six others with him. I reckon he was slumming, taking the piss out of us.'

Freddie shook his head. 'No, Dad, you're wrong. I mean to say, he bought gear and so did his mates or whatever they were; took nearly thirty quid.'

'Well what was it all about, then?' said Jack. 'He said he was training them or summat. Complete bollocks if you ask me. Still, I'm grateful for the sales; can't look a gift horse in the arse.'

'Jack, really,' admonished Millie. 'If you're going to talk dirty, I'm going to make tea.'

Freddie laughed and touched his mother's arm. 'Two sugars for me, Mum,' he said as she bustled out of the tiny space into the ever tinier scullery. Then he turned to his father, took a proffered cigarette, accepted a light, puffed and then sat back as if in deep contemplation. 'You know, Dad,' he said at length, 'something big happened today; something I can't quite get a handle on, but something really big. Huge, in fact.

Jack Granger frowned. 'I dunno what you're talking about, son,' he said.

'Well I'm not sure myself,' said Freddie, examining the glowing tip of his cigarette. 'I know it sounds daft, but I think that maybe my life is about to change forever, about to catch alight in some way. Know what I mean?'

Jack pulled a face. 'What, because of that geezer who swallowed a dictionary and his little mates? Is that what you mean?'

Freddie shrugged. 'Just a feeling, Dad. Just a feeling. We'll have to wait and see.'

At this point, Millie bustled in with a pot of tea and three mugs decorated with Fulham club colours and the two men's introspective dialogue dribbled to a close.

1967

The following weeks unfolded with what appeared to Freddie unusual speed. Each Thursday Professor Runcorn showed up in the North End Road with half a dozen of his trainees, some from insurance companies keen to teach their "apprentices" the art of salesmanship, others from vast organisations like ICI and Shell. The routine was always the same. Runcorn and his companions watched Freddie go about his business for at least twenty minutes and then led by Runcorn, they all came forward and made multiple purchases.

In the fourth week, Freddie took nearly £150 in ten minutes.

Then Runcorn turned up with just one companion eleven weeks on. He was a bearded fellow in a corduroy jacket carrying a thick folder under his arm.

They watched Freddie go about his usual business, and it was a particularly busy Thursday, until a brief lull in activity occurred.

Runcorn raised his homburg and smiled at Freddie and his father. 'Gentlemen,' he boomed, 'may I introduce you to Mr Raymond le Maitre. He is a TV producer with one of our most dynamic independent television companies. They hold the franchise for the London area. I am, as it happens, a major shareholder in the company and it is at my request that Mr le Maitre is here today.'

Freddie glanced at Jack and they both shrugged.

Le Maitre stepped forwards and shook Freddie and Jack's hands over the displays of fake Marmite, bottled pickles, woollen mittens and lavatory brushes. 'Well, I'll cut to the chase,' he said. 'I'm making a documentary about London's street markets and I'd like to film you as you work.'

Freddie nudged his father and smiled. 'Oh you would, would you?' he said.

'Definitely,' cried Runcorn, 'and we'll pay you.'

'How much?' said Jack and Freddie simultaneously.

'Two hundred and fifty quid,' said le Maitre.

'We could make you a star!' yelled Runcorn

Freddie turned to his father and patted his arm. 'Told you something big was going to happen!'

Jack gave a throaty laugh. 'And so you did,' he said. 'Psychic or what?'

*   *   *

Events followed at what could only be described as breakneck speed. Le Maitre and a team of men with cameras, lights, vans, girls with short skirts and clipboards and a fierce-looking director wearing cowboy boots and a tasselled suede jacket arrived a month later and began filming.

It passed in a blur as Freddie and his father went about their business in the usual way. But Freddie knew, with an iron certainty, that this was the definite turning point in his young life.

1971

The documentary *London's Street Markets* was transmitted twelve months later, achieving the highest ratings of any documentary since the TV company began transmissions in 1955. Freddie became an instant star. Although happy with the £250 and the publicity it gave him and Jack for their barrow in the North End Road, Freddie had not the smallest idea of just how things would now unfold. Runcorn's visits with his "apprentices" tailed off; apparently he had sold his "consultancy" to an American marketing firm and Jack at least thought that was that. It was fun while it lasted and he now presumed that they would just carry on their business in the usual way.

1972

Exactly a year later, Jack turned to his son as they sat with Millie in the Cafe Royal restaurant enjoying a fine lunch of oysters, champagne and beef Wellington.

'Well I was wrong, wasn't I?' he said. 'I couldn't have been more wrong if I'd forecast that Winston Churchill would swim the Channel.'

Freddie, exquisitely attired in a pinstripe suit from Savile Row, took a sip of champagne and smiled at his parents. 'It was just a feeling I had, that's all.'

'I knew you could do it,' said Millie proudly. 'I always did.'

Freddie's book *The Gentle Art of Salesmanship*, dictated to a very pretty girl from one of Europe's top business publishing houses, had sold a million copies in paperback. Shortly after it had hit the bookstalls, the TV company who had made the documentary approached Freddie and offered him the role of presenter of a chirpy light-entertainment show entitled *London's Living Legends*. The thirteen episodes were a runaway success and Freddie, taking to that success like a duck to water, was celebrating his twenty-third birthday with his proud but astonished parents in the Cafe Royal, the same Cafe Royal in which Oscar Wilde and other great figures of the past had celebrated their successes.

'Well,' said Freddie, patting his increased girth, 'fabulous grub, Mum; nearly as good as your bangers and mash. Now finish your champagne, we've got a plane to catch. The Jag will be here in fifteen minutes.'

'Hollywood,' said Millie dreamily. 'I still can't believe it. My boy a movie star.'

'Fancy old Runcorn turning up in America like that,' said Jack. 'It really takes the biscuit. And taking a job at Universal Studios. He was a shrewd one that Runcorn geezer,' continued Jack, fingering the knot of his Hermes silk tie, the first he had ever worn in his life.

Freddie nodded. This level of profundity was rare, coming from his father. 'I think he's probably one of the canniest salesmen in the world. I mean to say, he sold *me*, first to London ITV and then the biggest publisher in Europe and now, without me ever having seen a script, he's sold me to Universal as a leading man in some blockbusting epic that doesn't yet have a bloomin' title.'

'I'll drink to that,' said Jack, draining his glass.

At this point, a waiter approached their table carrying a newspaper. 'Mr Granger, your car is here. And I thought you might like to see the headline in *The Evening Standard*.

Freddie took the paper and unfolded it. The headline blazed across the front page read:

Super Sales Star Freddie to take Mum and Dad to Hollywood.

1999

The house in Esher was a faux classical Georgian job with tall windows and a treble garage. Sir Frederick Granger sat in the exquisitely panelled library smoking a thin cheroot and sipping from a cut-glass tumbler of Famous Grouse whisky. It was a sad day. His father, Jack, had died earlier aged 88 in a Bournemouth nursing home five years after his wife, Millie, who had passed away in her sleep while cruising the Mediterranean.

Now Freddie, still unmarried at fifty-four, was quite alone. In spite of the loss of his last parent, Freddie wasn't completely downcast. It had been a roller-coaster life so far and hopefully there was more to come. Professor Runcorn had emailed him a week earlier from California, where he now farmed 2,000 acres and marketed llama sperm as a miracle face cream. He was ninety-eight and a half and still busy. In two months, he told Freddie, he was to marry for the fifth time to a pneumatic blonde from Arkansas, who had worked as his in-house nurse for the past year. She was nineteen. His email also suggested that Freddie might like to take time off from his busy schedule in Europe and become a visiting fellow at UCLA, lecturing on marketing and salesmanship to young Americans who were pursuing their own American dreams. Freddie had printed out the email and now reread it. "Visiting fellow" sounded grand. Almost as grand as his knighthood.

From barrow boy to TV presenter, best-selling author, star of Hollywood movies, Chairman of six blue-chip companies, unpaid commercial ambassador for the British government working alongside members of the royal family. Would becoming a "fellow" at an American university be the cherry on the top of his cake?

Or a step too far?

He put down his glass and walked over to the desk where his computer was situated, booted it up and tapped out a reply to Professor Runcorn:

My dear Sebastian,

Your kind suggestion that I become a kind of quasi-academic is flattering, but I must respectfully decline. I am, after all, what I am described as in my passport – quite simply: a salesman.

Your old chum,

Freddie

P.S. I'd have liked some of your llama sperm on my barrow in the North End Road forty years ago. I reckon I could have shifted a bundle. Good luck with your impending nuptials and take your weight on your elbows, like a gentleman.

Gentrification Gone Mad?

In the early 1980s, the company P. & O. and Globe bought 20 acres of deteriorating industrial sheds, wharves and other detritus in Fulham and with astonishing speed turned the riverside site into Chelsea Harbour – a luxurious complex of houses, flats, restaurants and more flats. The actor Michael Caine and the film and theatre critic, the late Sheridan Morley, bought two of the early purchases of penthouses.

Fulham's historical connection with transport was maintained in the early 1900s by the works of Rover and Rolls-Royce in Farm Lane!

God Only Knows

The alarm clock emitted its piercing ring at precisely 7.00 a.m. Hestercombe reached out a hand and fumbled for the stop button, missed it and sent the brass clock crashing to the floor, still ringing. 'Oh shit,' he muttered, sitting up in bed. A weak, dawn sunlight was filtering through the net curtains and he could hear the central heating kicking in, which was something of a comfort.

He leant out of bed, grabbed the alarm clock and after silencing it, hurled it with a neat overarm lob across the room where it landed, face up, on a small chair. Hestercombe smiled a slow smile of satisfaction. He was still in form as a lethal spin bowler six months before the cricket season started.

He rose, stripped, showered, shaved and sat on the toilet for ten minutes contemplating the day ahead. Or at least the morning ahead. All Saints Church, the ten o'clock service. That was about all on the itinerary for Sunday. Newspapers would be flipped through after lunch, and lunch wouldn't be much to write home about. He hated cooking for himself, but as a bachelor his options were limited. Maybe he'd just heat up that bit of beef left over from last week with a few spuds. Just boiled. Roasting the buggers was too much of a hassle.

Finally dressed, he took the meat out of the freezer and put it on a saucer in the kitchen to let it thaw before lunchtime. It felt as hard as rock and had turned a funny sort of grey colour. He plugged in the kettle, let it boil and made a quick cuppa. Nice and strong. Couldn't stand all this herbal crap people kept going on about. He liked it almost black. And hot. No sugar and only a touch of milk. Except this morning, the dribble left in the jug overnight had turned rancid so he poured it down the sink. Domestic trivia, he thought, is a pain in the arse.

He drank his tea, rinsed the cup under the cold tap and came downstairs to the hall. His fawn raincoat was hanging on the banister and because he hadn't put it neatly on a hanger, as his late mother had insisted, a lump had sprung up in the back of the raincoat where the cheap gaberdine material had been stretched by the banister knob. When he slipped on the coat, it made him look like the Hunchback of Notre Dame.

'Notre Dame.' Now that was a church he wouldn't mind going to. He loved Paris, but of course that was just idle dreaming. He was an Anglican, after all.

As usual as he left the house, he began asking himself the usual questions. This churchgoing habit, what was that all about? Was he truly a believer? Or did he go to church now he was fifty-five as a sort of insurance policy, just in case there really was a God? Well was there? His late mother had never questioned her faith. Just accepted it. But it was natural, wasn't it, to question your faith? Certainly in this day and age.

Oh alright then, he *did* believe in God, really did. But lots of the stuff that went with it, like the ritual of religion, well that just clouded the issue. I mean to say, Virgin Birth, give me a break. Who really swallows that kind of guff?

Well lots of people, actually.

Were they gullible fools? Or just people showing real brass-bound, unshakeable faith?

And all this stuff about Jesus coming to save us all. Save us from what? Tell that to the widow of a soldier blown apart in the war or a child born blind.

> Sing to the listening earth
> Carry on every breeze
> Hope of a world's new birth:
> In Christ shall all be made anew?
> His word is sure, his promise true.

And this business of the Crucifixion. A faith that is supposed to be "love"-based has as a symbol of a half-naked bloke nailed up on a bit of wood with blood spurting out of his side. And what was Communion if not simulated cannibalism? Very nice. Big deal. And yes, Jesus did suffer, being crucified isn't exactly ballroom dancing, but lots of people suffered much worse things, like the Jews at Auschwitz – and they didn't drone on for 2,000 years about saving the rest of us. Oh no. During the last two wars, again Germany, both sides had priests or clergymen at the battle front praying for victory. Both praying to the same God, presumably. I mean, the Nazi God wasn't some fellow called "Fritz" and our chap "Reg".

He was the *same*, the *only* God. How did he choose who won the war? Maybe he didn't. 'Let the silly sods sort it out themselves,' he probably said.

Bit of a cop out though, isn't it?

Good things happen. Thank you, God.

Bad things happen. 'Not me, squire,' says God. 'You've got free will,' adding, 'even though I am all-powerful! Alright, already!'

> The God whom you have longed to know
> In Christ draws near, and calls you now.
> In Jesus all shall find their rest,
> In him the sons of earth be blest.

And what about miracles? Pick up thy bed and walk. Healing the sick. The feeding of the five thousand. Bread and fishes or stuff and nonsense? Did Lazarus leave a diary?

Now life after death, that's a really tricky one. Mother passed away five years ago and was that it? Just a pile of bones and flesh that has rotted away to dust? Or did her spirit, her essence, her personality, her capacity for love, did they really exist? And do they exist now in some other sphere they call Heaven? Well do they? Actually, I think, I believe they do.

Blimey, that's one doubt whacked on the head. So I believe there is life after death, more or less. Let's just put that to one side, on the credit side if you like.

There's one hell of a lot on the debit side too, though.

Never mind.

Press on.

Hestercombe paused at Fulham Palace Road and waited for the lorry to pass before crossing. Then he cut through Bishop's Park en route for All Saints Church and lit a cigarette.

Almighty God,
Purify our hearts and minds,
That when your Son Jesus Christ
Comes again as judge and saviour,
We may be ready to receive him
Who is our Lord and our God.

As he passed the municipal tennis courts, Hestercombe passed a young woman jogging along in shorts. She had long, tanned legs, with a neat, firm bottom and breasts that wobbled prettily beneath her white T-shirt. Hestercombe felt a stirring of ancient lusts. He *enjoyed* these feelings. Sex, other than for the procreation of children inside marriage, was sinful, wasn't it? Oh come on, God – it's 1985, for God's sake. Hold on, that statement was ridiculous, 'Come on, God – it's 1985, for God's sake!'

Hilarious.

Just a figure of speech, though.

But it raised a serious point: if there is a God. And the evidence, Hestercombe was beginning to realise, was pointing towards the affirmative, weakly, but nonetheless in favour of His existence. Blimey, another doubt kicked into touch. He dropped his cigarette and trod on it.

But back to the point of sexual desire. God must have put it into man. Placed it there deliberately and hopefully into women. Except probably not that Molly Jenkins of Ringmer Avenue, who had rejected Hestercombe twenty years ago and married a postman who, it was rumoured, was impotent. Hestercombe had remained a bachelor since he had been thwarted in love. Too late now to cry over spilt milk.

He pressed on through the bandstand area of the park and alongside the path that ran parallel to the River Thames. A swan floated serenely by and when he reached the big meadow, he saw bluebells under the shade of the giant plane trees that lined the meadow. A thin cloud above had melted away and a sudden shaft of golden sunlight shone through the treetops. Hestercombe gazed upwards to the great blue canopy of the sky. 'Space,' the scientists had said, 'goes on forever.'

Now that is a bit difficult to swallow. The agnostics and the atheists can't explain that in scientific terms, can they? Yet they reject the existence of God on the grounds that he cannot be proved in scientific terms. Talk about having your cake and eating it.

Well bully for you, chaps; you can't explain space going on forever either, can you?

Well can you?

Course you can't, you pillocks.

Sorry, mustn't get too judgemental.

Only 200 yards now from All Saints Church and a woman passed Hestercombe pushing a small child in a pram. He sees the tiny, cherubic face with its innocent blue eyes and experiences a stab of mixed emotions. Sadness that he is childless and joy at the miracle of life.

The *miracle* of life.

> Father in Heaven
> Who sent your Son to redeem the world and will send him
> again to be our judge:
> Give us grace to imitate him in the humility and purity of his first
> coming,
> That when he comes again, we may be ready to greet him
> with joyful love and firm faith,
> Through Jesus Christ, our Lord.

Hestercombe is in the church courtyard now, passing old lichen-covered gravestones. Spring flowers have added a splash of colour to the grey of the stone. A sparrow perches on one, cheekily, and watches Hestercombe walk by. Sunshine is striking the kaleidoscope of colours on the stained-glass window above the door and Hestercombe pauses to admire it.

All this life. All these wonderful things all around him. Pretty girls, flowers, babies, birds, trees, nature in all its glory. Of *course* God existed. All this didn't just happen by accident. It was God's work – stands to reason. And as for the scriptures and the Bible, was it the Word of God? I mean God actually talking? Did he dictate it, in Hebrew, Greek or English? Who knows? But does it matter if it is in fact the *Word of Man* or, to be more precise, the words of *many men*? Many good men who lay down a set of fine principles by which their fellow men and women should live. Principles which are best reflected in the Ten Commandments or as Hestercombe preferred to call them, the "ten jolly sensible suggestions".

As he approached the church door, it opened and the verger stepped out. He was a small, rotund fellow with a bald head and pink cheeks. Hestercombe always thought he looked like Friar Tuck. His gown was neat and his white bib spotless.

'Morning, Jack,' said Hestercombe.

'Good morning, Rector,' said the verger, 'beautiful day.'

Reverend Hestercombe nodded and walked into the tranquillity of the church, the perfume of the polished wood and the big scented altar candles enveloping him in a warm embrace.

> Fling wide the gates, unbar the ancient doors;
> Salute your King in his triumphant cause.
> He comes to save all those who trust his name
> And will declare them free from guilt and shame.

Sort of.

Fancy That ...

At the annual Chelsea arts ball in the late fifties, young bohemians turned up for the event in deliberately provocative costumes.

Long before the punk rock craze began and before Johnny Rotten was born, there were people at the ball dressed as Nazis, in black bin liners, see-through plastic macs, bondage trousers and crotchless knickers. Hair was spiked, faces painted and some girls exposed the pubic area, neatly shaved into heart shapes.

Happy days.

At least ten bishops are buried in the grounds of Fulham Palace. There are also monuments to William Rumbold, who carried Charles I's Royal Standard at Nottingham when the civil war broke out, and to Thomas Carlos, whose father, Colonel William Carlos, hid in the oak tree at Boscobel with the future King Charles II after the Royalists were routed at Worcester in 1651.

The Creative Historian

It was tough for Timothy after his father fell ill. At only 15 years old, he found himself now more or less head of the household, which he shared with his mother and two younger sisters.

Mother, who was in her late forties, was not in the best of health. The sixty-a-day cigarette habit and her propensity for fried Mars bars and chips had been less than helpful in maintaining her work ethic. For nearly twenty years she had "toiled", her word, at the home of a minor aristocrat in Cadogan Square as a daily help. Sir Joshua Hunter's main residence was a castle in Cumbria, but he used the Cadogan Square flat as his London pied-à-terre. Mother had therefore spent two decades on her knees, metaphorically speaking, polishing, dusting, scraping, buffing and moaning around the six big rooms which, she maintained, were "stuffed with more bleedin' furniture than a Gamages warehouse".

As the years passed, she grew more careless in her duties and the resident housekeeper, a martinet of formidable demeanour who exalted under the name of Mrs Bessie Rucktrimmer, was more than once required to rebuke Timothy's mother for her shoddy, alcohol-induced, work practices. But although she survived for many years, the last straw proved to be her being discovered asleep and dead drunk, in Sir Joshua's four-poster bed on the fourth floor.

Her dismissal from her job coincided with the onset of her husband Ned's ill health. He had been a council employee for some thirty years, engaged in what in the twenty-first century would be described as "waste collection and disposal". In 1966 he was called a dustman. However, the physical demands of his job put paid to both his hamstrings and his sacroiliac and he quit work with the council, spending the bulk of his time, namely all of it, sipping warm beer or placing money he could ill afford on horses and dogs. Miraculously it seemed, Ned occasionally made a good bet and he was able then to make a contribution to the family fortunes.

This was all very well until his wife lost her job and with it the modest income that kept the five of them just about above the breadline. Timothy's sisters, Annie and Trish, were 11-year-old twins and as such unable to make any sort of meaningful difference to the state of the family's fiscal situation. As the stark nature of their predicament became clear to them, it was decided by Timothy's mother that "steps would have to be taken".

The first of these was for them to dispose of unwanted knick-knacks that lay around the house in a kind of untidy profusion. For reasons beyond analysis, Timothy's parents had accumulated a cornucopia of the weirdest schlock. Alongside the Coronation mugs and plaster bust of Clem Attlee and the signed black-and-white photographs of George Formby, the toothy, northern, banjo-playing comedian, were various other items. Hideous vases; Victorian lace-up boots; beer mats; paper bags of chipped marbles; felt berets; straw hats; kettles without handles; unopened books of Latin grammar; seven hammers; a hideously constructed ship in a bottle; a small but useless device designed to pluck rogue hairs from the nostrils of gentlemen; some giant brass tongs; a broken fender; an old leather waistcoat minus pockets and buttons; a rusty flat iron and fourteen unopened tins of Cross & Blackwell's baked beans in rich tomato sauce, plus lots of other stuff of much less interest and indeed less notional value.

It was to fall upon 15-year-old Timothy to turn this Aladdin's cave of tat into hard cash. He was, after all, at the local Sloane Grammar School situated in Hortensia Road, Chelsea, a mere two streets away from where the family resided on the very cusp of the Fulham–Chelsea border. With his grammar school education and exposure to a sprinkling of middle-class boys whose parents' finances didn't run to public school fees, he was well placed, it was thought, to offer the collection of family junk to one or more of the second-hand shops and antique emporiums that proliferated in the Fulham and the King's Roads.

Protest was futile. Mother's decision was not only final, but it was unchallengeable.

'Look,' she explained, taking a deep swig from a bottle of Gordon's Gin, 'we gotta wheelbarrow in the cellar. In perfect nick. Wheels and everything. Now, Tim, my lad, you just load as much as you can into the barrow and trundle off down the Fulham Road and see what you can shift. Won't be much, I grant you, but blimey, what other options have we got? And you've developed such a nice way of talking. Go on, son. And if we can scrape up enough for the next few weeks' rent ... I'll be finding another paid position before you know it.'

At this her husband, Ned, released a throaty laugh. 'You'll be lucky, luv; you'll need references to cop another job in service.'

'Never you mind, darlin',' said his wife, tapping the side of her nose. 'I can write me own bleeding references.'

During this exchange, Timothy and his sisters listened silently, each in a mood of familiar resignation. The girls, being young, thought this was just another crisis that would pass without too much pain. But Timothy, wise beyond his years and one whose eyes had been opened by the eccentric teaching methods that were a feature of Sloane Grammar School, felt this heteroplasmy in family affairs was no less than an opportunity he, despite his youthfulness, could richly exploit.

The following day, being a Saturday, Timothy retrieved the wheelbarrow from the cellar of their tiny house and began to load it with the various items to be disposed of. Ann and Trish gave a helping hand. He tried to be selective, choosing only those pieces he thought might possibly have at least some value to a keen-eyed purchaser or that could be used as bric-a-brac. A couple of old flat irons, the brass fender, a rusting and blunt carving knife with a remarkably preserved bone handle, an unopened tin of chocolate with a picture of Prince Albert on the lid, a pair of enormous grey socks, a single boxing glove of ancient design suitable for the left hand, an elaborate birdcage with a pair of tiny swing doors. Painstakingly, Timothy sifted through heap after heap of junk, placing in the wheelbarrow less than one in ten items he found. His mother had obviously been hoarding stuff for decades.

The wheelbarrow was creaking under the weight of objects Timothy had stacked there and the last item to be included was a brace of hoops, each about the size of a man's hatband but covered in black-and-white beads. Timothy turned them over in his hands to see if they contained any clue as to what they were, but they yielded no information. He placed them top of the pile and declared the job complete.

'This afternoon,' he said to his sisters, 'I'm off down the Fulham Road.'

His mother, who had been dozing in an armchair after a liquid lunch, opened an eye approvingly. 'You're a good lad and no mistake,' she murmured.

'Mum,' said Timothy. 'What are these two ring things, the ones covered in beads?'

His mother shrugged. 'What, those? Well, I don't know exactly; pretty things though, aren't they?'

'Where did you get them?' asked Timothy.

Mother shrugged again and Timothy couldn't help but note that the shrug was accompanied by a brief flush of the cheek. From the corner of the parlour Ned, who had just roused himself from a deep torpor, released a cackling laugh. 'She nicked them from Sir Joshua's house, didn't you, Amy?'

Mother reacted like a speared animal. 'Damn you,' she shrieked. 'I didn't nick them. They was a going-away present when I quit work at Cadogan Square. They're antique.'

'Going-away present!' cried Ned. 'Pull the other one!'

'You watch your mouth, Ned,' Mother cried. 'After twenty years cleaning his bloomin' house, I was entitled. It was my redundancy money, sort of.'

'OK, OK,' said Timothy, anxious not to get embroiled in a morality drama. 'So they're antique, but antique what?'

'Well,' said his mother slowly, 'they're from Africa. I think.'

'Thanks, Mum,' said Timothy, who had now learnt that pressing his mother for further information would be fruitless and likely to detonate a pointless family argument.

At this point, Trish offered to make everybody a cup of tea and the moment of tension passed.

Timothy presented a wonderfully eccentric sight as he wheeled his barrow with precariously balanced bits and pieces along the Fulham Road. The pavement stones being a trifle uneven in this neck of the woods, he found it easier to manipulate the barrow in the road itself. After crossing the bridge that marked the boundary between Fulham and Chelsea, he passed Hortensia Road in which stood the daunting brick edifice of the Sloane Grammar School. On the left just past Fernshaw Road and Edith Grove, he halted outside a small shop with mock bay windows of concave glass. From the crowded shelves of old china ornaments in the window and the two-piece suite on the pavement outside, it was clearly the premises of a dealer in items of second-hand nature.

Timothy manipulated his barrow up over the pavement and pushing the glass front door open with his buttocks, he backed into the shop dragging the barrow behind him. A bell jangled as he crossed the threshold. When he turned round, he saw a stout man wearing a leather apron sitting behind a small desk. Obviously the proprietor. An encouraging cardboard sign hung on the front of the desk. It read: Whole house clearances a speciality.

There was only one other person in the shop – a white-haired fellow of distinguished appearance wearing a fawn raincoat who was examining the spines of some leather books that lined a shelf next to the desk. The rest of the space was taken up with a jumble of furniture, pots, pans, second-hand frocks and leather lampshades of revolting design.

'Can I help you?' said the man seated behind the desk.

'Well, yes,' said Timothy. 'I wonder if I could interest you in any of this …' He waved a hand over the barrow.

'I doubt it,' said the man gruffly. 'What you got?'

'Well, various things,' said Timothy anxiously.

'I can see that, son,' said the man, 'and it's mostly crap. Tell you what, though; I'll give you ten bob for the barrow.'

'What?' said Timothy, baffled.

'Ten bob,' said the man. 'You can take the rest of the junk elsewhere. I suggest the dump. It's useless.'

'What about £10 for all of it,' said Timothy, 'including the barrow?'

'Don't be impertinent,' said the man. 'It's ten bob for the barrow and you can sod off. Take it or leave it. I'm running a business here, not a bleeding charity.'

Timothy stood his ground. 'The barrow's worth more than ten bob,' he said.

The white-haired fellow in the raincoat put back the book he was scrutinising and turned to face the proprietor. 'I think the boy is right. The barrow is worth more than ten shillings. It's a sturdy piece of work, mature wood with two handy rubber grips. Why don't you give him two pounds?'

The proprietor sucked his teeth for a moment and then nodded. 'OK. Two quid and that's it.'

The white-haired man smiled at Timothy. 'And give him a sack to carry all the contents of the barrow,' he said.

The proprietor opened a drawer in his desk and took out two pound notes then he grabbed a large hessian sack and stood up. 'Empty the barrow,' he said, throwing the sack towards Timothy.

Timothy took the handles and tipped the barrow sideways. All the bits and pieces spilled out and scattered on the floor. Then he began to pick them up and stuff them into the sack while the two men watched him. When he had finished the task, the proprietor gave him the two pound notes and took possession of the empty barrow. Timothy lugged the sack outside and then turned and grinned at the white-haired man who had returned to studying the book spines. 'Thank you,' he called, but the man made no response.

Timothy hoisted the sack over his shoulder and began to walk along the road. The load was very heavy and he had to stop and rest after 100 yards. He changed the sack to his other shoulder and started again, but it was no good. He'd never get far with this uncomfortable weight. He leant against a lamp post and dabbed his sweating face with a handkerchief. If he could find a dump or a place to leave the sack, that would be it. Mother would have to be content with two pounds. Not quite a week's rent, but what else could he do?

He knew there were at least three more second-hand and antique shops along the Fulham Road as far up as South Kensington, but getting there was out of the question. Then, as if appearing out of thin air, the white-haired gent in the fawn raincoat drew level with him and smiled.

'You'll need a hand with that,' he said.

Timothy wasn't too sure how to respond to the man's offer. 'No, well, thanks, but no thanks. I'm just dumping it.'

'I don't think that's a very good idea,' said the man. 'Look, my shop is just around the next corner. I'll help you carry the sack there.'

'Your shop?' said Timothy.

'Yes, my shop. As I am sure you know, there is more than one second-hand dealer in this stretch of London. I buy as well as sell and today I was interested in some of Steve's old books. See, I've bought one.' He held up a tiny leather-spined volume. '*Life of Nelson,* an exquisite miniature published by James Cundee of Ivy Lane, Paternoster Row, London in 1806. Author Joshua White Esq. Now 1806 is significant. It was one year *after* the Battle of Trafalgar. Old Steve had no idea, but I still paid him fifty pounds for it.'

'Wow!' said Timothy. 'What will you sell it for?'

The old gentleman laughed. 'Sell it? I don't think so. Not yet a while. But who knows?'

'Why did that man, Steve, give me two pounds when you told him to?' said Timothy.

The old man took a grip on Timothy's sack and helped him lift it. 'Come on,' he said, 'it's not far to my shop.'

They walked on slowly carrying the sack between them, Timothy in his grey pullover and slacks and the white-haired gentleman in the fawn raincoat.

'Here we are,' said the man as they reached the corner of Hollywood Road. 'My place.'

It was a small shop with a double window and a shiny red front door. A sign in the window said: Objets D'Art and Curios. Above the red front door on the lintel were printed the words: Septimus Crabtree.

The old man opened the door with his key and they carried Timothy's sack inside. 'Now then,' said the man, 'I am Mr Crabtree. Who are you, young man?'

'Timothy.'

'Good. Now sit you down on that chair and let's have a look at what you've got. There's something in particular I want to examine.'

Timothy emptied the sack and the contents scattered across the wooden floor. Crabtree crouched over the pile and pulled out the two hoops covered in beads.

'Two questions, Timothy,' said Crabtree. 'First, why are you selling, or at least trying to sell all this stuff and secondly, where did you get these?' He turned the hoops over in his hands carefully.

'OK,' said Timothy, 'my mum's lost her job, my dad can't work and, well, we need the money.'

'I see,' said Crabtree, 'a sort of fire sale.'

'What?' said Timothy.

'Never mind. I suppose your father and mother can claim the dole, can't they?'

'I've no idea,' said Timothy.

'Well, two pounds isn't going to help much, is it?' said Crabtree.

Timothy shook his head.

'And where did you get these?' said Crabtree, holding up the hoops.

'My mum. From her work, I think. They're African. But I don't know what they actually are.'

'Very well, Timothy. I'll tell you what these are. They are Zulu head rings made of black gum and decorated with black-and-white beads. Probably quite old, but it would be difficult to establish precisely how old.'

'Are they valuable?' asked Timothy.

Crabtree turned the rings round in his hand and sighed. 'Not really. They are fairly commonplace; however, they could be invested with some serious values.'

Timothy looked blank. 'I don't understand.'

Crabtree walked over to a small table in the shop and took off his raincoat. 'I'm sorry, Timothy, I'm rambling a bit. Suffice to say that I'm afraid most of your stuff is not worth a penny piece – as it is.'

'As it is?' said Timothy.

'Look, let me try to explain. The book I bought from Steve half an hour ago, to Steve it was just an old book, one of a job lot he bought recently. But if he had bothered to look, really look at that book, he would see that it is in fact a rare piece of publishing history, an object of desire and fascination. Not just a book.'

Timothy looked puzzled. 'I still don't understand.'

Crabtree waved him silent. 'Timothy, I believe you are a pupil at Sloane Grammar School, are you not?'

Timothy nodded.

'I know that from your tie. You see, it's not just a tie – it's a tie which has had personality invested in it. It is a Sloane tie.'

Timothy glanced down at his tie and fingered it nervously.

'And furthermore,' Crabtree continued, 'I recognised it because I taught history at Sloane for twelve years. I retired six years ago. Now a teacher's pension isn't much to live on, Timothy, so I decided to invest my savings in this little shop, where I am proud to boast I can put my knowledge, indeed my love of history into good use. For the first year or so, running this shop alone, I realised I couldn't compete with the grand antique emporiums in Chelsea and Kensington or indeed the cheap junk shops along the New King's Road. I was caught in the middle. But then, like a starburst in my head, I saw what I had to do. I had to make sure that every item I sold in my shop had to have a *history*, or as my young friends in the advertising industry tell me, a USP!'

'A USP?' said Timothy, who was beginning to lose the will to live.

Crabtree was clearly some kind of nut, a sort of mad professor. He stood up and reached for the empty sack.

'No, wait,' said Crabtree, 'it will profit you to hear me out. A USP means a unique selling proposition. You, Timothy, have in your possession a pair of run-of-the-mill Zulu headbands. Just suppose, Timothy, just suppose you asked me to sell them for you. I would do it willingly and split the proceeds with you. And the proceeds would be a great deal more than two pounds or even fifty!'

Timothy put down the sack and looked hard at Crabtree. He didn't *look* crazy. Excited, yes, but kind of normal. Like most teachers. Even retired teachers. 'So what would you do?' he asked.

'Well, I am giving away the secrets of my trade, but as we are both products of Sloane School, so to speak, I will do so willingly. I would stain each of these headbands with a little blood, from a beef joint I keep in my refrigerator, a leftover from yesterday's solitary lunch. I would let it dry then I would sit down at my little typewriter over there and type out a short history of the headbands. It would go something like this, Timothy.

'A fine Zulu headband, circa 1879, worn at the Battle of Rorke's Drift by Prince Dabulamanzi KaMpande, younger brother of King Cetshwayo. The prince survived being shot at by one of the defenders of Rorke's Drift, one Private Hook, but the bullet glanced off the headband and caused it to fall from the prince's head whereupon Hook retrieved it. The prince suffered only a scratch and Hook retained the ring as a souvenir. Hook later received the Victoria Cross for valour. I obtained it many years ago from one of Hook's last remaining relatives now long deceased. Price of the ring £150.'

'Blimey!' said Timothy. 'But, Mr Crabtree, all that stuff, how do you know about it, I mean how can you tell?'

'I can't. Every word I would type would be … no *not* a lie, definitely not a lie, Timothy, but an invented history. A charming fantasy. Indeed, I may have stumbled over the exact truth about the ring. Who could prove or disprove my little story?'

'But there are two rings,' said Timothy.

'Yes, Timothy, and when I had disposed of ring number one, I would do exactly the same with ring number two.'

'Same story?' said Timothy.

'Oh yes. If it works once, it'll work twice.'

'Sounds a bit dodgy to me,' said Timothy.

'Dodgy is such a proletarian word, Timothy,' said Crabtree, 'and I thought grammar school was supposed to expunge all traits of working-class speech from your vocabulary and afford you entry into the minor bourgeoisie. But that is of little consequence at the present time. Now, Timothy, let me make you a proposition. You were dispatched by your impoverished parents with a wheelbarrow full of assorted junk in the hope that by disposing of it for cash, you might temporarily ease the family's straitened circumstances. So far your efforts have been scandalously ill rewarded. Am I right so far?'

Timothy nodded.

'Well, now I have told you how I operate utilising my knowledge and my, albeit modest, powers of persuasion, I can offer you the following golden opportunity. Leave all your junk with me overnight and come back to my shop tomorrow, Sunday, I am open on Sundays, and I will have selected a number of items from that pile of tat now spread over my floor and given them all a history, a personality and, of course –'

'A USP?' said Timothy.

'Precisely,' said Crabtree. 'And you, young Timothy, will share the proceeds of any sale on a fifty-fifty basis. Finally, as I like the cut of your jib, and also as a token of my confidence in both you and my own dazzling gifts of scholarship, invention and hyperbole, here is ten pounds in cash, which you may take as an advance on any future sales.'

Timothy's mouth was hanging open.

'Here, take it,' said Crabtree, who had removed two five-pound notes from his tweed jacket. 'Today's haul, therefore, with the two pounds from your sale of the wheelbarrow, will be a princely –'

'Twelve pounds,' blurted Timothy.

'Oh! a mind as sharp as a box of chisels,' said Crabtree, laughing. 'Now off you go. You will be the bearer of good tidings when you get home and who knows, Mother may bake you a pie. Be sure to tell her about Sunday, it's all square and above board. Be here at eight o'clock. We have work to do before I open my doors to the bargain-hungry multitudes, who I can assure you will flock to Hollywood Road with money burning holes in their pockets.'

Timothy's return home, while not on a par with Hannibal's successful negotiation of the Alps, was a triumph of sorts.

'Twelve quid,' said Mother. 'That's over two weeks' rent.'

Timothy nodded modestly. 'Yes, and more to come if I go back on Sunday.'

'This bloke,' said Ned, who had roused himself from a tobacco-induced stupor, 'is he, you know, all right?'

'All right?' said Timothy. 'What do you mean?'

'Well, you know, I mean he's not, he's not married, you say, so I was just wondering ...'

'He used to teach history at Sloane. He's a very clever chap,' said Timothy.

'Sounds a right character,' said Mother. 'Maybe if he's a bachelor, he might need somebody to do for him at home.'

'I don't think so, Mum,' said Timothy quickly and his mother shrugged.

'Just a thought,' she said. 'That would be neat, wouldn't it? You helping him to sell off our old tat and me dusting his fender!'

Ned gave a coarse laugh and lit another Craven "A".

Timothy was up and gone by seven thirty on Sunday morning and rang the doorbell outside Crabtree's shop at seven fifty-five precisely.

'Come in, come in,' said Crabtree. 'Door's open.'

Timothy walked into the shop and saw Crabtree kneeling on the floor with an army of assorted items spread out before him. There was a flat iron, the left-handed boxing glove, a birdcage, a small brass fender, what looked like a grubby dog's bone and a rusting 6-inch blade.

'I was up most of the night, Timothy,' said Crabtree, 'pecking away with my two fingers at my ancient Remington giving the items you see before me what, precisely?'

'A USP,' said Timothy.

'Absolutely. My dear Timothy, I have invested in these commonplace objects a new life, a history, a new identity, even!' Yes, I have now a story, a narrative which refers to each object and will, if I am not mistaken, enhance their value if not beyond the dreams of avarice, then certainly more than they would command if left unbaptised, so to speak.'

'Where are the Zulu rings?' asked Timothy.

'Oh, in the back room,' said Crabtree. 'They were the first to be dealt with. Just as I told you yesterday. We shall of course offer them one at a time. Now, let me show you what I have written about all this other stuff.' He seized the bone and hefted it in his hand. 'You probably didn't even realise you had this in your barrow. It *is*, of course, an animal bone. Part of the thigh of a horse or, to put it more precisely, it was the thigh of a horse. Now, Timothy, now, my dear boy, it is a fragment of the femur of Copenhagen, the Duke of Wellington's horse which carried him throughout the Peninsular War and the Battle of Waterloo in 1815. The animal is buried at Stratfield Saye, Wellington's country home. Unusual though it was for a horse to have its own personal burial plot *and* headstone, it is even more unusual for the gardener employed by the great Duke at the time, to retain a fragment of bone as a souvenir before the dead animal was interred. Lost for several years, it came into my possession through a distant relative of the selfsame gardener. A fact, dear Timothy, that cannot be proved, or challenged, or indeed denied.'

'Will anyone believe it?' asked Timothy, staring at the unlovely object.

'Oh, they will if they can be persuaded to pay £75 for it! Belief, unshakeable, will follow this item as any vendor of historical artefacts will confirm!

'Now, Timothy, gaze upon the rusty blade, a mere 6 inches, without a handle, a discarded carving knife, perhaps. Not so, now that I have given it a backstory, a new and dreadful history. This is the blade that, on 30 December 1916, Prince Felix Yussupov plunged into the body of Rasputin! He was aided in the assassination of the czarina's confidant by the Grand Duke Dmitri, who first poisoned him with food and drink, then shot him and before throwing his bullet-riddled body, still alive, through an ice hole of a neighbouring canal, thrust this blade that I hold in my hand now, deep into Rasputin's black heart. Death, when it finally came, was by drowning. But the blade? I obtained it, years ago, on my travels to Russia. Do you like that one, Timothy? Neat, eh?'

Timothy shrugged. It was beginning to sound like gibberish to him, but Crabtree's enthusiasm was infectious. Crabtree seized the boxing glove and pulled it over his left hand. 'The very same glove,' he cried, 'that Joe Louis, heavyweight champion of the world, was wearing when he thrashed Max Schmeling, Hitler's sporting hero, in 1938, although I may be a little hazy about the date. I think £100 for this item would not be considered extortionate!'

He threw the glove aside with a flourish. 'And this neat little birdcage, a fine fretwork of wire and palm wood, is of course the same cage in which the Princess Po-Hua, daughter of the Chinese Emperor Yuan-Shun, kept her tiny songbird, which was a secret gift from her favourite eunuch Pa-La. And the date? Oh! I think AD 1353 should be close enough, but the item is fragile. Should fetch a least £135.'

'What's a eunuch?' said Timothy.

'Never you mind,' said Crabtree, whose face was now flushed with excitement. 'Look at this, dear boy. Gaze upon *this*.' He picked up the rusty flat iron. 'Base metal it may be,' he cried, 'but this instrument, if I may so describe it, was used by Beau Brummell's valet to keep his pantaloons in spick order.'

At this moment, the telephone on a small table started ringing and Crabtree leapt up to answer it. 'Yes, yes,' he said, 'about twenty minutes. Yes. Thank you.' Then he clapped his hands in an authoritative fashion. 'Chop-chop now, Timothy, our first customers are on their way.'

'What?' said Timothy.

'Oh yes, I'd better explain. I have an arrangement with a tour operator in the West End who specialises in organising culture visits for overseas visitors. Their itinerary, in addition to visiting London's historic sights, always includes a foray into either Portobello Road, Camden Market or here along the Fulham Road. Naturally, Timothy, for a little … er … consideration, my friend makes sure his little group always visit my shop. Its reputation as a purveyor of the exceedingly rare and exotic is, if I may say so, with all due modesty, now quite international. Today's group are bric-a-brac and curio collectors from the fine city of Tokyo in Japan. Make haste, Timothy. Place the little typed cards against each of these items here displayed and prepare to receive our guests.'

'Well I'll be jiggered,' said Ned, putting his half-smoked Craven "A" into an ashtray. In front of him on the kitchen table was a neat pile of banknotes, fivers, tenners and singles.

'How much did you say our stuff made?' said Timothy's mother who was sitting opposite Ned.

Timothy shrugged modestly. 'Oh, £222.'

Ann and Trish, standing alongside their brother, shrieked with joy and hugged him.

'And that was just our share!' said Mother.

Timothy nodded. 'Yes, all our stuff ... well, virtually all of it. Went for a total of £444!'

'I'd like to give this Mr Crabtree a big wet kiss,' said Mother gleefully.

Ned winced and took a drag on his Craven "A". 'So you'll be going back with more stuff?' he said.

Timothy nodded. He felt 10 feet tall. A victorious warrior home from some bizarre conflict in which he had triumphed single-handedly. 'Oh yes, but not for a while. Mr Crabtree is going on holiday for a couple of weeks – to Bruges.'

'That should give us time to clear out anything else we've got in the attic,' said Mother.

'I suppose so,' said Timothy.

'Well now,' said Mother, rising, 'I'm going round the cake shop to buy cream doughnuts. We need to celebrate!'

'Whoopee!' cried Ann and Trish.

Timothy just smiled a slow smile and Ned took too deep a draw on his Craven "A" and started to cough like a horse.

Timothy's history teacher at Sloane School was a Mr Middleditch, a stern academic with a dry way of teaching. History was a serious subject and no injections of levity were permitted during his lessons. He was intrigued when Timothy told him of his experiences with Septimus Crabtree and even more intrigued when he learnt that Crabtree had once been a history master at Sloane.

'I've only been here five years,' said Middleditch, 'so I would have missed him, but his name is familiar and his reputation colourful if not notorious!'

'Notorious?' cried Timothy. 'How do you mean?'

'I think, Timothy, you must convey the intelligence you have just imparted to me to the headmaster. He will no doubt explain. He has been head of Sloane for over twelve years.'

Five minutes later, Timothy was sitting in the headmaster's study with Mr Middleditch. The head, Mr Guy Roab, had listened to Timothy's tale with keen attention then lit one of his famous Turkish cigarettes.

'Timothy,' he drawled in an accent that hinted of an officers' mess in British India at the turn of the century, 'Crabtree didn't retire from Sloane, he was required to leave; conduct unbecoming and so forth. Poor show all round. Nothing *criminal,* you understand, but a poor show nonetheless.'

'What did he do, sir?' said Timothy.

'He played fast and loose with the history he was supposed to teach. Made things up. Told whoppers, in fact. Great big whoppers. When a school inspector challenged him after a complaint from a parent whose son had been told some cock-and-bull story about Queen Elizabeth I having invented roller skates, I had to speak to him. You know what his excuse was? Said it made history *more* interesting. More *accessible,* if you please. This from a man who was telling 12-year-old boys that the Charge of The Light Brigade in 1854 in the Crimea was conducted on zebras requisitioned by the army quartermaster as all of Lord Cardigan's cavalry horses were sick with flu. I mean to say, it was quite outrageous. Why are you laughing, Timothy?'

'Sorry, sir,' said Timothy, who had noticed that the usually taciturn Middleditch was himself smiling behind his hand.

'Anyway,' said the headmaster, 'Crabtree left the school and soon became involved in a series of, well, I don't know how to describe them. Maybe "scams" is the right word. He set up an antique shop and began selling utterly worthless junk at exorbitant prices to gullible foreign visitors by creating completely phoney histories for them. As near criminal as you can get.'

'Yes,' said Timothy wistfully, 'he's very inventive.'

The headmaster wagged a finger at Timothy. 'My advice to you, young man, is to avoid any further contact with the man. I hope you will reveal to your parents the true nature of Crabtree's fraudulent personality. You may have profited from his sleight of hand, but such gains are tainted, Timothy, do you hear? Tainted.'

'Yes, sir,' said Timothy.

'Very well,' said the headmaster, 'may you learn from this unfortunate experience. Now you'd best get back to class.'

When Timothy returned home after school, his parents received the news about Crabtree's true nature with a degree of insouciance.

His mother shrugged. 'Oh well,' she said, 'no harm done. We still made that two hundred quid and you've done nothing wrong.'

'Pity, though,' said Ned, 'could have been a nice little earner.'

In spite of the headmaster's warning, two weeks later Timothy went back to Crabtree's shop on the Hollywood Road after school. He hadn't told his parents. To his surprise, the windows were boarded up and the name Septimus Crabtree had been removed from the lintel. A notice hung on the door: Gone Away. Timothy stood at it for a few moments and then walked away along the Fulham Road. The events of two weeks ago now seemed like a rather curious dream. Had it really happened? The money was real enough, though, and somehow Timothy couldn't regard it as in any way tainted.

Timothy's mother found employment six months later as a part-time housekeeper for a wealthy Arab family with a flat in Eaton Square.

Father Ned had enjoyed a string of luck with the horses and turned a £20 stake into £300.

Both Alice and Trish had passed their eleven-plus and entered the local girls' grammar school.

Timothy continued to work hard at Sloane, paying particular attention to history.

It was two years before Timothy heard another word about Septimus Crabtree. A small news item in the local *Fulham Chronicle* revealed that retired schoolteacher Septimus Crabtree had been found guilty of some misdemeanour under the Trade Descriptions Act and fined £200. He was also being sued by the landlord of a small shop in Pimlico for arrears of rent. Unfortunately for the landlord, Crabtree had disappeared again and was thought to be somewhere on the Continent.

'Probably Bruges,' mused Timothy.

A further year passed and Timothy's studies in the sixth form at Sloane were bearing fruit. He had applied for and been successful in obtaining a place at Cambridge University, where he was to read history. The day before he bade farewell to his proud parents to catch the train to Cambridge, a postcard arrived at the flat. On one side was a picture of a canal in Bruges and on the reverse, a Belgian postage stamp and a short message written in a neat hand:

Timothy,

Congratulations. Study hard. Enjoy and learn. But don't be ashamed to add a little garnish to the hard facts they give you at Cambridge. It will make history so much more fun.

Septimus Crabtree

Believe It or Not ...

Before she became Prime Minister, Mrs Margaret Thatcher lived in Flood Street, Chelsea and was once photographed with a shopping basket over her arm in the Fulham Road. Dennis was seen to slip into the Queen's Elm pub for a swift noggin.

The North End Road Market, just off the Fulham Road, originated as a family concern, many of the stalls passing down from generation to generation. Some of the named are still familiar today, the Johnsons, Hurrens, Coleshills, Seabys, Frosts, Lees and Kerrins. The author's mother and wife both shopped there in the 1950s.

And the Year is 1946

Fulham

Conjure up in your mind's eye a morning in early autumn, in a small flat in Fulham's Hestercombe Avenue. Imagine a tiny stone-floored kitchen with a sink, a draining board and a four-ring gas oven. A few battered pots and pans hang from nails hammered into the plaster walls and over the sink stands a small woman, a bantam hen, white-haired but slim with a patterned apron around her waist. She is washing up two plates and some cutlery from the breakfast she and her husband have just enjoyed of eggs, bacon, toast and marmalade. It is still only six o'clock, but the husband has left the flat, mounted his bicycle and begun the several mile cycle ride to the police station in Pimlico where he works as a station sergeant.

As the washing-up is completed, the woman removes her apron and pours herself a cup of tea. There will be an hour's respite before she rouses her two children from bed, feeds them and sees them both off to school. During this lull in her domestic activity she enjoys a moment or so of introspection, reviewing her life and, to a lesser extent, her future.

Chelsea

Imagine a day in early autumn in a fine three-storeyed house in Chelsea's Sloane Avenue. Conjure the vision of a sumptuous bedroom with high ceilings, exquisitely corniced, and a four-poster bed draped with silk. In it, propped on swansdown pillows, a woman in a lacy bedjacket is sipping from a porcelain cup of Earl Grey tea.

At her side, a maid in a black-and-white uniform stands with a tray on which is a silver teapot and milk jug. The woman in bed nods acknowledgement as the maid refills her cup.

'I'll run your bath, ma'am,' she says, putting the tray on a beautiful lacquered side table, 'and lay out your navy blue suit?'

The woman smiles. 'Yes, the blue today. Charity luncheon at The Ritz. Oh, and Miriam, tell Chef I don't want kippers again today, just a boiled egg. And some fruit. Has my husband left yet?'

The maid picks up the tray, curtsies and moves to the door. 'Yes, ma'am,' she says, 'the Rolls picked him up half an hour ago.'

The woman looks up at the elaborate ormolu clock on the marble mantelpiece. It is nine thirty.

When the maid has withdrawn, she sinks back onto the pillows and enjoys a moment or so of contemplation. In the bathroom next door, she hears the sound of running water.

Fulham

Although scarcely fifty, the woman's hair has been snow-white since she was thirty-five. It's a hereditary trait but in no way detracts from the fact that her face is still pretty and unlined. She has bright greyish eyes and a small rosebud mouth. There is not a trace of make-up on her face, although later she may apply a little powder. Each night, she slathers her face with Pond's Cold Cream and it is this ritual, she swears, that keeps her looking young.

She came to London from Wiltshire fifteen years ago, having followed her husband, also from Wiltshire, who sought a job with the Metropolitan Police. Her accent still betrays her country origins, but not his. Leaving school at thirteen to help raise six brothers with her elder sister, she has had a hard life so far, but not an unhappy one. In spite of the lack of formal education, she possesses a keen, sprightly intelligence. She reads avidly the *Daily Express*, popular fiction, some classics her husband obtains from his book club. She is an ardent listener to the BBC's Home Service. The world outside her own is a vast, challenging place. She wishes she could see more of it.

But she has never set foot outside England or travelled on an aeroplane. Some of her old relatives in Wiltshire have never left Salisbury. She knows there is so much more to life than just raising children and growing old in a London flat. But it is her lot and she is by no means unhappy. She is free of the curse of ambition, for herself, but not for her children, in whom she invests all her dreams and hopes and affection.

Chelsea

After bathing, the woman sits in front of a large dressing table and allows the maid to arrange her silky auburn hair into a chignon. At fifty, her neck is still as smooth as alabaster and her bosom firm. She is a remarkably beautiful and glamorous creature whose life so far has been one of uninterrupted pleasure.

After early schooling in Hampshire and later at a finishing academy in Switzerland, she possesses all the effortless confidence of those blessed with both looks and money. As a debutante, she has met the king. Her season is still talked about. She has been married to her husband, a staggeringly wealthy baronet, since she was twenty-two. They have six children, two boys and four girls. All are away at private boarding schools. At home here in Chelsea, she and her husband, who works for the Bank of England, enjoy the domestic services of a maid, a butler, a chef, a housekeeper and a chauffeur. The butler and the maid travel with them at weekends to their country estate outside Salisbury where they retain another live-in cook.

She is not too worried about her two sons, even though they both flunked university, being idle and drawn to a life of parties, drinking and gambling. They will both have a secure private income and will anyway be found "places" in the city firm with whom their father has connections.

The four girls are more of a worry. The only objective she has for them is a good marriage like hers. If that means eschewing romance or falling in love, and other wet bourgeois concepts, they should do very well and keep the whole dynasty machine ticking over very nicely. She just prays that Caroline, her youngest who is a bit of a romantic, doesn't fall for some middle-class spiv, a young subaltern in an unfashionable regiment perhaps or, God forbid, a salesman. However, it will be OK if she loses her virginity to somebody unsuitable. Provided she is careful. It is no bad thing for a well-brought-up girl to bring a little sexual expertise to the marital bed as chances are her husband will be a virgin, too.

Fulham

After seeing both children off to school, the woman sets about the intense ritual of keeping the flat up to a state of cleanliness that the matron of a hospital would appreciate.

There is only one appliance in the flat which can assist with the chores; a hand-operated Ewbank carpet cleaner. Everything else needs elbow grease and lots of it. The grate must be cleared of last night's fire. Ashes removed. The grate's tiled surround polished.

The beds made, sheets washed by hand in a tin bath, hung out to dry in the yard. The tiny kitchen must be cleaned. The food supply checked. Are there enough vegetables for tonight's supper? The small jar on the lounge mantelpiece which contains the rent money must also be checked as the landlord calls today, on his bike, to collect. Another jar, slightly smaller, contains a few coins set aside in case of medical emergencies, the dentist, the doctor. She must also check in her handbag for shilling pieces as the electricity is on a pay-as-you-go meter. Budgeting is a task which on their small income needs care and attention. All bills are paid promptly, weekly and in cash.

Thursday is pay day, when her husband hands over his pay packet unopened. She will give him his cigarette money and deploy the remainder in housekeeping and children's pocket money. This is her life. There is no leisure, no cinema visits, no pubs and one short holiday a year in England in a cheap boarding house by the sea. Only years later, when her daughter goes on the stage as a chorus girl in a London musical to the immense delight of the family, do she and her husband visit the theatre. Only later, when her son goes in the army and after serving abroad, starts a career in the commercial world, does she feel that her life's work is complete. The future promises, in the far distance, the prospect of grandchildren and that warms her heart as she settles into the routine of just living.

Chelsea

The woman slips her arms into a fine fur coat and checks her appearance in a tall mirror in the hall. The maid opens the front door and she crosses the threshold onto the pavement outside. Her husband's Rolls, having deposited him at the bank, is now ready to sweep her off to her first appointment in what will be a typically busy day. She is to meet an old friend at The Ritz for a fund-raising lunch. After this, she has a hair appointment in Mayfair with one of London's most fashionable hairdressers, then at four o'clock, a fitting at her dressmakers. It is vital she has the right clothes for the approaching season. Chiropodist at four forty-five promptly then to Claridges for a light tea. Home at six just in time for cocktails with another friend who has popped in. While sipping her Martinis, the butler comes into the room with the cook's menu for dinner. They are entertaining twelve people that night. The pressure is dreadful. Decisions. Decisions. Decisions.

'Tell the cook not to plan smoked salmon as a starter,' she says. 'It's so middle class. And I think after the pheasant, a little iced water to clear the palate before the last course. My God, why do I employ a cook, anyway, I seem to do *all* the work … well, the planning, anyhow.'

The butler conceals a smile. 'She is only temporary, ma'am. The new cook starts in a fortnight.'

'Thank God for that,' she says. 'I'm quite drained after having to plan all these dinners and on top of my charity work, too.'

'Yes, ma'am,' says the butler, turning away to conceal a grimace.

This he knows is her life. And what is more, she actually believes it is one of pressure and decision-making and selfless attendance at charity lunches and all the rest. It is likely to go on like this until she reaches old age when, God willing, she can quit London and spend her declining years in the country surrounded by dogs, cats and hopefully, exquisitely mannered grandchildren.

Living? It's a tough old business, but somebody has to endure it.

Very Few People Know This, But ...

In fashionable Cheyne Row, there is a memorial plaque to Margaret Damer Dawson, who was the founder of the first women's police force. She died in 1920 aged only 45 years.

Further on along Cheyne Row is the home of Thomas Carlyle, one of the nineteenth century's true intellectual giants. The house is now a National Trust Museum.

The Manor of Fulham was granted to Waldhere, the fifth Bishop of London, in about AD 800. His estate consisted of 120 acres and according to The Domesday Book, was sufficient to support 1,000 hogs on the acorns and beech trees in his wood.

In those days, the estate extended its boundaries as far as Acton and Brentford.

Star-struck

The sculptor was a lean fellow sallow of complexion, but his 6-foot frame offered a commanding presence. His moustache was luxuriously white and curled upwards to meet his equally dense eyebrows. He glanced up at the brass clock on his studio wall. It showed seven fifteen. Early morning sun was already streaming into the big, high-ceilinged room and motes of dust danced furiously in its golden shafts. The sculptor was a frenzy of activity, pushing a leather chair into a corner under the room's large picture window, realigning the butcher's block table into the centre of the room. It was on this he would work the soft clay that would eventually be the template for the final bronze bust he had been commissioned to execute.

His housekeeper, the dedicated Mrs Tregunner, a Cornishwoman of impeccable loyalty and great age, tottered into the studio from the small kitchen that adjoined it.

'I heard a car drawing up outside,' she said, her West Country accent still balm to his ears even after she had spent half a century in London in his service.

'Then, Mrs Tregunner,' he said kindly, 'if he is true to his reputation, it will indeed be him. I see it is seven fifteen precisely. Would you be so good as to let him in?'

Mrs Tregunner nodded. 'I will indeed. It will be a pleasure.'

The sculptor rearranged a few of his implements on the table. To the untrained eye they more than a little resembled the cutting and slicing devices employed by surgeons in the preparation of some major life-saving operation. On shelves displayed around the studio were head-and-shoulder busts in gleaming bronze of the sculptor's previous commissions. He was a celebrated artist, much fawned over by the art critics and those journalists who regarded themselves as both champions and defenders of traditional art forms in music, stage, cinema, dance and of course sculpture.

The tabloid newspapers however, who cared little for things aesthetic, found him irresistible prey not for his art, which even they acknowledged was stupendous, but for his private life. Unmarried, but the seducer of several beautiful society women, the sculptor was the personification of the noble savage. Leaving his Truro school at fifteen with a dire educational record, he drifted from job to job until moving to London just before the war in 1930 to work as a bootblack at The Ritz Hotel. Just how he moved, untrained from skivvy to sculptor with a studio in Chelsea was now a polished legend. Some say he learnt his craft by a brief spell as a bricklayer, others that he picked up his amazing style while on the production line in a plasticine factory. But whatever the truth, which he would never reveal, he was now, at the dawn of the fifties, the most famous and celebrated artist of the age. Today, coincidentally, was his fifty-fifth birthday and his only concession to this brief stroke on the cosmic clock was to arrange for a bottle of iced Dom Perignon to be placed in a silver bucket alongside his sculptor table, together with two glasses.

Mrs Tregunner, who had reappeared, smiled and drew a deep breath. 'Your sitter has arrived,' she said.

A pace behind her was a man of medium height, stout of build and with a bald head. He was wearing a business suit of black coat and striped trousers and was carrying a silver-topped walking stick. The sculptor stepped forward and shook his hand. The visitor's grip was firm. 'Welcome,' he said, 'and on time.'

The visitor made a self-deprecating shrug. 'Busy time for both of us. I hear you like an early start, too.'

The sculptor nodded as Mrs Tregunner took the visitor's topcoat and cane. 'Actually it isn't really early,' he said.

The visitor grunted and looked around the room. 'So this is your workplace?' he said.

The sculptor nodded. 'My factory, yes. Handmade goods a speciality.'

'I take it you want me to sit in this chair?' said the visitor and without waiting for a reply, he placed his broad bottom on the leather seat and stretched his legs. 'I sit down too much,' he said. 'I'm developing an arse like a Turkish pasha. Can't abide exercise, though. Smell of sweat makes me sick. Do you mind if I smoke?'

The sculptor, who had picked up a sheet of paper and charcoal crayon, shook his head. 'Please yourself,' he said, 'I intend to; helps me concentrate.' The sculptor made a brief sketch of his visitor's face – a childish, crude scrawl that simply recorded the dimensions of the man's head. Then he picked up a tape measure and walked over to the sitter. 'Need to measure the distance between nose and chin. And between the eyes. Plus your head circumference.'

'As long as it's not my inside leg,' said the visitor with a gruff laugh.

The sculptor ignored this and proceeded to take and then jot down the sitter's various measurements. Satisfied at last, he went to a small cupboard at the side of the studio, opened its doors, lifted out a large lump of brown clay, still moist, and carried it over to his work table. 'Now you don't have to sit stock-still,' he said, 'but try to look a half-head to your right and keep your mouth shut. I'm sorry; I mean keep you lips closed.'

'You are not the first person to tell me to keep my mouth shut,' said the visitor. 'It is my wife's daily incantation!'

'OK,' said the sculptor, 'this first couple of hours are important. Would you like some music? Mozart? Vera Lynn? Fats Domino?'

'Eclectic tastes, I see,' said the visitor. 'No thank you, silence would be a treat.'

The sculptor nodded and patted the great lump of clay as if it were a pet animal. Then he looked hard at the visitor, letting his eyes travel slowly from the man's head, down his fleshy face, past the jutting chin to the thick, bull-like neck which sat on narrow, sloping shoulders. The eyes, pouched with age, were nonetheless bright and shining. Those eyes that had witnessed beauty and hideousness, eyes that had closed in sleep exhausted after conflicts as a soldier in foreign lands, eyes that had outstared mortal danger, eyes that had wept in sadness and rage, many, many times. And the man's hands, short fingers like sausages, the hands of an artisan. But the nails were buffed and neat. The nails of an aristocrat. His body was unimpressive. Pear-shaped, wide-hipped. A great spread of buttocks that in their youth had sat astride a prancing stallion or two. But the great head was the prize. The object of the sculptor's full attention.

Each line, each wrinkle earned over a lifetime of triumph and tragedy and love and hate. That face, not handsome but fiercely striking, a little too puffy now, pinkish in the cheek but still smooth.

A curl of smoke rose from the cigar the visitor was smoking and he smiled at the sculptor. 'You won't try to flatter me,' he said. 'I want a true likeness.'

The sculptor smiled and picked up a small spatulate knife. 'Certainly not, Prime Minister,' he said, 'I wouldn't dare. Would you care for a glass of champagne?'

Most People Have Forgotten That ...

Chelsea is famous for having a bun named after it and is the word before "Pensioner's" who live in the famous Chelsea Hospital. It has also more recently become associated with big four-wheel-drive vehicles called Chelsea tractors.

The elastic-sided boot, fashionable in the seventies, was called – you guessed it – the Chelsea boot.

And a certain type of delicate porcelain was dubbed "Chelsea", too.

Last but by no means least in this galaxy of associations, Britain's first ever televised church service was broadcast from the Royal Hospital Chapel in 1949.

In 1789, London suffered one of its coldest winters ever. It was so cold that the Thames froze over and a frost fair was held near Putney Bridge on the Fulham side of the river. Booths were erected with puppet shows, roundabouts and refreshment tents. Crowds of people wandered across the thick ice enjoying themselves. Among the revellers were the Bishop of London, Beilby Porteus, and his wife.

Double Dutch

'I know a woman,' said Ravenscroft, 'who speaks entirely in clichés.'

His companion and drinking buddy, an emaciated wreck of a man, nodded faithfully. It was clear that Ravenscroft, a burly red-faced builder and local sage, was about to impart on a rhetorical journey of sharp insights, social observation and philosophical penetration. Thus warned, rail-thin Fernshaw, a retired dental technician, took a cool sip of his half pint of Guinness and made the only reply possible before Ravenscroft's deluge of *merde de cheval* overwhelmed him.

'Tell me about her,' he said.

They were standing in the saloon bar of The Red Lion, which was situated on the curve of the Fulham Road that led past Walham Green, the notorious yobbo-infested corner of the borough, and on towards the Chelsea Football Ground and eventually the Shangri-La of South Kensington.

'Tell you about her?' echoed Ravenscroft, wiping Guinness foam from the corner of his mouth. 'How long have you got?'

Fernshaw shrugged. It was going to be a long night.

Ravenscroft placed his Guinness, a pint glass in his case, on the bar counter, produced an untipped Piccadilly cigarette, the brand that claimed to have won countless Palmes d'Or in ciggy competitions worldwide – although Fernshaw thought this was all bull shine and advertising puffery – and inhaled like a deep-sea diver who had just been rescued from the briny Pacific.

'Her name is Esmeralda Duncannon and she lives in a flat in Burnfoot Avenue. I have met the woman on countless occasions and I can tell you … indeed, Fernshaw, I can positively guarantee that if you perchance made her acquaintance, you would be with me in claiming she is the cliché queen of the twentieth century.'

'How so?' said Fernshaw, in what he hoped was an uncontroversial tone of voice.

'How bloody so?' cried Ravenscroft. 'I'll tell you bloody how so.'

'Thank you,' said Fernshaw, shrinking onto his bar stool.

'For example,' yelled Ravenscroft, 'you meet her on her doorstep, while passing her house you understand, you meet her and it's perhaps raining. Raining.' He repeated the word so that Fernshaw was fully aware of the weather situation surrounding this anecdote. 'I say, "Good morning, Miss Duncannon," and she says, "Good weather for ducks," or, more annoyingly, "It never rains but it pours!" I spotted her in a queue at Frost's Market the other day and I asked her how she was, you know, a polite inquiry. She said, "Mustn't grumble." Infuriating. Then as we parted company, she called out, "Bye-bye. If you can't be good, be careful." Bloody hell, then only a month ago, I overheard her talking to a neighbour in the Ritz Cafe at Walham Green. The waitress – that slag from Lewis Trust Buildings – served her a cup of tea and put a saucer of sugar on the table. Know what she said? Do you bloody know what she said?'

Fernshaw made a sort of whimpering noise signifying his urgent desire to know just what Esmeralda Duncannon had said in that poignant cafe situation.

'She said, "No sugar, I'm sweet enough!" Can you believe it? And when her friend, some nondescript scrubber from Ealing, asked her if she was going on holiday this year, do you know what the annoying cow said?'

'No,' said Fernshaw, taking a gulp of Guinness purely for medicinal purposes.

'She said,' yelled Ravenscroft, '"Chance would be a fine thing!" Then at that meeting in the Armourers' Hall off Wandsworth Bridge when Sir Oswald Mosley was giving a speech, good bloke Mosley, wrongly accused by lefty poofs of course, but I digress, while Mosley was speaking about crime and punishment, she turned to her neighbour, that fat tart from Hammersmith, and said, can you credit it? She said, "Hanging's too good for them." And, "The lash is the only thing they understand."'

'Really?' said Fernshaw.

Ravenscroft's eyes bulged and he threw his arms wide. 'What goes up, must come down; look before you leap; pride before a fall; nobody's perfect; Bob's your uncle; a stitch in time butters no parsnips; people who live in glass houses shouldn't undress with the light on.' His voice rose to a thin shriek and then, like a felled tree, he crashed over backwards onto the floor of the pub, cracking his skull on its polished surface.

At his funeral, Fernshaw threw a handful of dried flowers into his grave. The local vicar who had conducted the service smiled at Fernshaw and said, 'It's what he would have wanted.'

Fernshaw pulled up the collar of his coat and turned away. 'Don't you bloody start,' he said.

Are You Aware That ...

All that is left of Sir Thomas More's old house that once stood in Bishopsgate in The City is fifteenth-century Crosby Hall. It was dismantled and rebuilt on the riverside in Chelsea in 1908. In the last ten years, it has been given a facelift and is now a neo-Tudor mansion of great magnificence, but privately owned.

The first record of a market in the North End Road was 1713, the same year that the famous pub The Cock opened in the terrace known as Melmouth Place at the south end of the road. Its publican, Ted Pimm, was notorious for his half-dozen bull terriers, which would chase those customers who had become aggressive with drink out onto the street.

The Learning Curve

It is some years now since I taught history at one of Chelsea's most famous grammar schools. It is, alas, no longer designated a grammar school and resides now under the unlovely appellation of "comprehensive".

In my day, some decades past, it drew boys of all classes to its bosom, provided they had passed the now richly maligned eleven-plus examination. Working-class children, sometimes from excruciatingly poor backgrounds, mingled with the offspring of newly impoverished middle-class parents, whose dwindling fortunes made it no longer possible for them to afford the fees at Marlborough, Eton, Winchester or even Eastbourne. The social cocktail worked pretty well, I recall, enabling exceptionally bright boys to progress beyond the sixth form to Oxford or Cambridge University. The compulsory wearing of school uniform was an important element in creating a sense of unity at the school. All boys in the same blazers, white shirts, caps and ties ensured that no lad from a humble background would feel upstaged by richer pupils who might look superior to their less affluent friends.

Today, with uniforms abandoned in most schools, children, like their often unlovely parents, dress with that sumptuary abandon that incites rage and disgust among those who believe self-respect starts with a disciplined approach to personal appearance.

However, I like to think that during my time as a teacher of history, I made a potentially dull subject become alive and exciting without ignoring the "set" books recommended by the educational establishment. I taught history as a narrative, something both thrilling and mysterious, something that reached beyond mere dates and lists of events. Once a year we managed to take a small group of pupils abroad, mostly to Europe, where they could stand on famous sites of history and see for themselves the architecture and lifestyle of people whom they had previously only read about.

I was accompanied on these short tours by the geography master, a fine academic who shared my view that history and geography are closely linked subjects. In those far-off days, it was always surprising how different pupils responded to these trips. Obviously the financial cost to parents had to be kept to a minimum, so things like accommodation and food was of necessity a touch spartan. What I found fascinating was how some pupils, when urged to take up the opportunity of a trip abroad, seemed lumpen and resistant, anticipating no doubt that the visit would consist of tours to crumbling buildings and museums and lots of boring, foot-weary trudging around cathedrals and boggy battleground sites. As a matter of fact, stripped of the adjectival epithets, that was pretty much what they were. Other pupils remained wide-eyed and receptive, like juvenile sponges soaking up the experience with obvious joy.

We, the geography master and I, took groups to Paris, Brussels, Rome and once to faraway Istanbul, which my pupils found "splendid" that it once had been called Constantinople. For me, the most memorable trip was to the greatest city on earth – Venice. I should perhaps qualify that statement. It is my personal opinion that Venice deserves such an accolade. Many others disagree, but there we have it, an example of the myriad opinions held by seekers after the Holy Grail of historical, geographical and even architectural truth.

The visit had been in the late 1940s before the Great Festival of Britain had been launched in 1951. We were a small group, two masters and only six pupils, all of whom were just shy of 15 years of age. There were two boys who remain vivid in my memory, both very bright but from hugely different social backgrounds. There was Crispin who, as the name implies, was from an upper-middle-class family who could be best described as enjoying a life of reduced circumstances. "Reduced circumstances" in their case simply meant that the Humber Hawk was second-hand, the wines at home decidedly non-vintage and there was no way Crispin's father, an only modestly successful solicitor, could afford public school fees for his son or two daughters. Crispin was tall for his age, something of an athlete and with long, flowing Byronic locks. His accent, honed at his prep school in Chelsea, an establishment his father could afford, was delightfully patrician; although his vocabulary was, it seemed, limited.

Then there was Jack, a roughly spoken lad whose father had died when Jack was just three and whose mother scrubbed other people's floors for a living. Jack was on the short side, stocky in build and with that slight coarseness of feature that is unfortunately a common proletarian inheritance. Jack, however, was a talker, his vocabulary extraordinary for a 14 year old. While his grammar was occasionally awkward and his speech peppered with the slang of the Fulham streets, he could chatter nineteen to the dozen for what seemed hours.

So our little party began its walking tour of Venice; a gondola trip was promised on the last day of the visit. On day one, we stood in St Mark's Square, "the biggest open-air living room in Europe", and I gave our group a brief introduction. Venice, I told them, is planted on its timber piles midway between the east and the west, or as Goethe once described it, "The marketplace of the Morning and the Evening Lands". I told them how these spongy, muddy islands of the lagoon became over the centuries a magnificent, glittering Republic, a great trading state and vast naval colossus, poised as Jan Morris said, between Rome and Byzantium, Christianity and Islam.'

Of how Venice came to call herself Serenissima and decked herself in cloth of gold and how over the years, great palaces of extravagant beauty sprang up creating a vivid Venetian style that is still copied to this day, nearly 1,000 years on. How their doges rode in fabulous golden barges along the Grand Canal, how trade and gossip was conducted by the great Rialto Bridge. I reminded them of how in Shakespeare's *Merchant of Venice*, Antonio greeted Shylock with the words, 'How now, Shylock, what news on the Rialto?'

I told them how they were once invaded by Napoleon and now were invaded by tourists. I told them of the sights we would see on our trip, the stunning mosaics of St Marks, the glass-blowers of Murano, the carnival masks, the staggering works of art by Titian, Canaletto, Bellini, Tintoretto, Tiepolo. The awesome sculptures, the dark prison in which Casanova languished, the Bridge of Sighs, the sleek, unique and beautiful black gondolas, the smells of the Fabriche Nuova Fish Market, the limpid canals that honeycomb the city.

This city, I told them, this paradise of stone and silk and glass and minarets and marble, this awesome place that was Vivaldi's birthplace, that still rings with his music is, in a word, unique. Then we started where all tours of Venice start, in the great Basilica of St Mark's. Before we crossed the threshold, I asked the group to raise their eyes to the rooftops and to observe one of the greatest equestrian statue groups on earth. The four horses of St Mark's cast not in bronze, but mostly in copper, and looted by the Venetians from Constantinople and placed on the Basilica's rooftops. Later, of course, in the seventies, the originals were moved inside to protect them from Venice's supposed pollution, even though they had survived outdoors for 1,600 years exposed to salt, sea and air. Then inside the Basilica itself to marvel at the Byzantine extravagance of its decoration and to survey the amazing fourteenth-century mosaics in the baptistery.

It was here that I noticed how Jack had become transfixed. Not, I hasten to add, by my oratory, which I must confess was a trifle gaudy, but by the artefacts on display. His young eyes seem to drink in the penetrating beauty of the tapestry, the mosaics, the mighty Byzantine lamps, the silken cords, the whole magnificent atmosphere. He was a boy transformed.

Crispin, however, seemed bored to the point of unconsciousness. He yawned and he gazed when he gazed at all. Not at the magnificence of that which surrounded him in such exotic profusion, but at the sun-bronzed legs of a young female American tourist, whose attempt to show respect by covering her head with a lace handkerchief was somewhat negated by the fact that the tightness of her cotton skirt, stretched like a drum skin over her peachy buttocks, revealed the line of her skimpy panties.

We moved on from St Mark's to the Doge's Palace with its quatrefoil tracery, completed by genius craftsmen in 1440, and then to Jacopo Sansovino's arcades for the library of St Mark. These described once by the great Palladio as the "richest building since classical antiquity".

We crossed the lagoon in a motor launch to visit the Campanile of San Maggiore and take in the panoramic view of the Giudecca Canal and Santa Maria della Salute, Longhena's great seventeenth-century votive church.

My heart lifted as I saw Jack draw breath in amazement at this panorama, but my spirits dampened a touch when I observed Crispin, hanging at the back of our group, thumbing through a magazine. I later discovered it turned out to be a publication called *Razzle*, which consisted of colour photographs of women in various stages of undress and some, my geography colleague assured me, of young girls displaying their naked breasts and glimpses of their genitalia. It was pointless to rebuke the boy, so I didn't. I just pressed on. Jack's interest more than compensated for Crispin's lewd indifference.

The day rolled on and we visited galleries, small museums, one extraordinary one given over to the history of the Stradivarius violin, great churches with monstrously large organs, merchants' palaces built on the very water's edge, shops that specialised in writing paper, pens and ancient mixtures of ink.

In all these places, Jack was an enthusiastic observer. Crispin, alas, only became animated when confronted with Giovanni Bellini's painting of *A Young Woman at Her Toilet* circa 1515. He was heard to mutter, 'They didn't have very big tits in those days, did they?' I must confess, I blushed with embarrassment.

After a lunch of indifferent pasta, we took the group to Murano for an exhibition of glass-blowing, then finished the day with the promised gondola ride. Jack trailed his hand in the lagoon water looking blissful and Crispin fell asleep.

After the allotted four days, we returned to London, Jack clutching no less than five coloured guide books to Venice and a small Venetian vase for his mother. Crispin bought some cheap cigars, "for his father" and a rather vile plaster statuette of the last Doge Lodovico Manin, because he claimed the image looked like Frankie Laine, an American singer of popular songs. My geography colleague was of the opinion that Crispin would tell his parents the whole trip was a waste of time, whereas young Jack would pore over his handbooks and look forward with concealed enthusiasm to his next visit.

Thirty years on, as I write these words, I know that Jack does in fact work as a guide in Italy for a well-known tour company having learnt Italian, not at my school but by correspondence course.

Crispin, drifting in and out of the advertising business, finally married an exotic dancer who bore him eight children, but divorced him after eleven years of marriage when he was caught in flagrante delicto with the Chinese au pair.

Such, as they say, is the rich tapestry of life.

175

Few People Realise That ...

Close to the site of the old pottery at the junction of New King's Road and Fulham Park Road was the house Elysium Row, circa 1738. It was used as a sanctuary for orphaned girls during the 1866 cholera epidemic.

The home was run by the wife of the Bishop of London, a Mrs Tait. She has been compared to Florence Nightingale, who famously cared for British soldiers in the Crimea, many of whom were suffering from cholera.

The Fulham Road was once called the London Road, a very apt title. Earliest records are dated 1442, but by the eighteenth century, this narrow, muddy lane was flanked on both sides by market gardens and was becoming popular as a residential area for wealthy families tired of crowded and unsanitary Central London. Here were built the venerable estates of the Holcroft and the Cleybrooke families, both of the Tudor period.

All disappeared, of course, by the nineteenth century.

The Art of Exaggeration

People are seldom, in reality, what they seem. For years, young Sebastian Henshaw took his neighbours at face value, or at least he accepted without demur the description of them provided by his father, who at age 65 believed he had been invested with penetrating insight by God. 'I can see right through people,' his father was fond of saying. 'I can sum them up in a trice.' And so it seemed to young Sebastian through all his teenage years.

One who was subjected to his father's deep analysis was Captain Smallbone, who lived across the street in Hestercombe Avenue and was frequently seen in his officer's uniform complete with Sam Browne belt and peaked cap. Across his chest he sported a few bright medal ribbons. 'Seen a lot of conflict that man,' Father pronounced. 'Shot and shell. Wounds everywhere. Bayoneted by the Japs. Blown up by the Jerries. Secret missions. Very hush-hush and the fellow survives with a metal plate in his head.'

At the time, young Sebastian found it mysterious if not baffling that war-ravaged and heroic Captain Smallbone seemed to spend a lot of time in the house across the road with his wife, a large woman with a fur coat too big for her. He would disappear for perhaps a week at a time and then return to Hestercombe Avenue for six weeks or more. He would leave the house in the morning and catch a bus up west, often in uniform, and return at six in the evening. It was therefore assumed by Sebastian that in those brief excursions away from Hestercombe Avenue, he was engaged in warfare most bloody. It was still difficult to appreciate how Captain Smallbone could face down the might of the

177

Hun in Europe one week and then after six weeks in London, fly off to the Far East to engage with the Japanese Knights of Bushido.

When he once politely enquired of his father how such a rigorous itinerary could be sustained, including the various wounds the gallant Captain was supposed to have suffered, his father tapped the side of his nose with a nicotine-stained forefinger and said, 'Secret missions. Look at the man's medals pinned on personally by the King, I've no doubt. He'll be promoted general soon.'

It was only after young Sebastian completed his own national service in the army some years later that the true history of madcap Captain Smallbone emerged. The Captain was not in any combat unit but doing valuable work in the Royal Army Pay Corps. He had never been abroad or heard a shot fired in anger. His medal – singular – was the General Service Medal. His daily trips were to Whitehall, where he exercised his skills as a trained accountant and his occasional absences were to army finance conferences in Salisbury where he lectured.

When young Sebastian raised these awkward facts with his father, his parent had shaken his head more in sorrow than in anger. 'That my own son should be such a cynic. Captain Smallbone has done his bit for his country. I know the truth but I have no intentions of dignifying your unwarranted slurs with any kind of rebuttal. I'm too old and too tired.'

Shortly after this, Sebastian's father died in his sleep and his mother remarried the postman. After national service, Sebastian had returned to Hestercombe Avenue, but he only stayed briefly after his father died so that he might find a flat of his own in Chelsea and seek work to support himself. Before he quit the family home in Hestercombe Avenue, he took the trouble to uncover the true history of other neighbours in the road, all of whose backgrounds had been chronicled, verbally at least, by his late father.

There was the aristocratic gentleman next door, Mr Ripley, always neat as a pin in his suit with a waistcoat and a silver watch chain stretched across it. He had been wearing spats. 'Top financier,' father had said. The tiny flat next door was merely his London pied-à-terre and his main home was an Edwardian pile set in 1,000 acres in Putney.

Putney?

This was the clue that revealed the truth. Mr Ripley was a hairdresser in residence at Whites Club in London. It was from snipping the locks of the gentry that Ripley had adopted his airs and graces and polished shoes, watch chains and spats. He owned no house in the country and was always behind with his rent. His wife took in ironing to supplement their income.

Then there was old Mrs Trestle from number fifty-two.

'Showgirl,' his father had said, 'once danced in the Folies Bergères in Rome. Refused an offer of marriage from Anthony Eden, one of England's top politicians.'

Apart from knowing that the location of the Folies Bergères wasn't Rome, young Sebastian also discovered that the ubiquitous Mrs Trestle was a retired prostitute from Hounslow with a harelip and shingles. Her husband, long deceased, had been a plumber. Anthony Eden, Sebastian was sure, had never even met poor old Mrs Trestle.

Then there was the case of the priapic milkman. This fellow, his father had stoutly maintained, was a sex-fiend of predatory inclinations who had ravished most, if not all, of the females in the SW6 district. The milkman – a balding Welshman called Owain Jones – delivered supplies of the cows' bounty in glass bottles door to door from his horse-drawn cart. Countless housewives had lain spreadeagled in anticipation of Owain Jones' tireless, thrusting loins, according to Sebastian's father. 'A glance at his groin,' he had whispered, covering his mouth with his hand, 'would be enough to confirm his proclivities!'

Sebastian had noticed, it is true to say, the sinister sausage-like bulge in Owain Jones' pants, but this was later to be revealed as his money-purse, which he kept under his outer clothing for safety reasons. He was also wholly innocent of the lecherous liaisons credited to him and lived a life of blameless innocence with his sister, an undernourished spinster with flat feet and a pronounced lisp.

Thus it was, as the years passed, more and more of Sebastian's father's wild inventions and false histories were exposed to the blinding light of truth.

Now married and living in some comfort in Chelsea, Sebastian sat one evening in his study enjoying a postprandial cigar and pondered that eternal question: Why had his father been such a fantasist? Apart from the wretched Owain Jones, all the people whose lives had been imagined by his father had been recreated as heroes or giants of art and commerce. He clearly subscribed to the notion that you should, wherever possible, never speak ill of anyone. It was only several years later that Sebastian learnt that he wasn't his father's legitimate son.

Certainly he was the fruit of his late mother's loins, but the seed had been sown by the postman, whom of course she later married.

Sebastian accepted this intelligence with stoic calm. Perhaps if he and his wife eventually had children, he would invent an entirely different history of his own background and that of his non-father, too. What would he let him become? Big game hunter, philanthropic schoolmaster, champion boxer, sabre-fencing champion of Bulgaria where he had secretly been born?

Whatever it was, Sebastian was determined that his children would only know his version of the truth.

People Have Probably Forgotten ...

The celebrated painter J. M. W. Turner, sadly no relation,[1] lived at 119 Cheyne Walk. It is a small, unpretentious house and at the height of his fame as an artist, this humble son of a barber, uncouth and rough in manner, decided to disappear. But in fact, all he had done was to change his name to "Puggy" Booth and shack up with an enormous, flabby Scotswoman called Sophia Caroline. He died at 119 Cheyne Walk a dishevelled figure, although his work had made him a very rich man.

One of the grandest houses in Fulham was Brandenburgh House, built for Sir Nicholas Crispe in the late seventeenth century. Sir Nicholas was a slave trader who was granted the right to trade with the West Indies and Guinea in 1632. He became very angry in 1637 when he perceived rival traders were muscling in on his patch. 'Interlopers,' he stormed, 'were infringing my monopoly by transporting "nyggers" to the West Indies.' Not only a nasty piece of work then, Crispe couldn't spell, either!

---

1. Although I can't be certain, my daughter, Jane, is a brilliant artist, so maybe we are related ...

Rising Star

It had been something of a day for Laurence Binfield; perhaps one of the most significant days of his life so far. At ten o'clock that morning, he had been called into his boss' office and informed that he was being promoted to head of his department with a substantially increased salary.

The advertising agency where he worked was a young, dynamic organisation which handled a clutch of hot media accounts and Laurence, originally hired as a trainee client contact executive, had shown an early aptitude for smooching the agency's advertising customers and bridging that vital gap between the slightly anarchic but brilliant creative people who wrote and produced the actual advertisements, and the pinstriped businessmen who were the account executives. It was a glamorous job even working on accounts that were designed to promote products that removed "under-stains" or jars of glutinous sludge that "eliminated wrinkles".

Work was frenetic and exciting. The agency offices were in Covent Garden. The "lunch culture" was in full swing and the recruitment of brilliant young graduates who were stunningly beautiful, mini-skirted young women, a major feature of the company's ethos.

At 30 years of age, Laurence was on the fast track and no doubt about it. As he waited outside the agency's excruciatingly modern glass-fronted black building in Long Acre, he glanced down at his recently purchased Gucci loafers, a symbol of vaunting ambition and accelerating success, and fingered the lapels of his two-piece suit from Huntsman of Savile Row.

A taxi cruised up to the kerb and Laurence climbed in. 'Tite Street, Chelsea,' he said, savouring the words.

Tite Street – one of London's most iconic addresses, very close to the fabled Cheyne Walk. And that's where Laurence lived, albeit in a rented flat that he could, until recently, hardly afford. But now, with these extra thousands coming in, well, almost anything was possible. Save a bit, perhaps. Certainly sell the Anglia now that his new job included a shiny new Jaguar. And he'd have enough for a deposit on a place, maybe in Tite Street, and of course, a gargantuan mortgage to seal the deal.

As the cab rattled along Shaftesbury Avenue past the London Pavilion and the statue of Eros in Piccadilly Circus, Laurence allowed himself a moment or so of self-congratulatory introspection. He had married young, to Zenda, and began a roller-coaster ride to success and affluence. Zenda, herself a bright geography graduate, had obtained work at an international oil company, where she had been a management trainee. She was now a full-time mother and housewife, although for some reason Laurence couldn't fathom, she didn't enjoy being described as such.

Zenda was such a pretty, sexy girl, he mused, although she had put on just a little weight lately and truth to tell, her legs weren't quite up to the smooth, coltish standard of those mini-skirted dolly birds at the office. And the children, lively and splendid, full of energy and mischief.

How pleased they would be when Laurence told them of his promotion, and how proud. Of course the new job might involve a bit of overseas travel, Switzerland probably once a month to the HQ of a major client and certainly New York and the south of France for marketing and sales conferences. All very exciting. Glamorous hotels, fine dining, rented yachts, club-class travel and all paid for the by agency. He'd bring presents back for the family, naturally; some nice jewellery for Zenda and some smart board games or toys for Timmy and Kathy.

The cab trundled past Harrods in Knightsbridge and made a left at Beauchamp Place. Then it cruised past Ristorante San Lorenzo, London's very hottest "must-be-seen" eatery. Princess Diana, Dustin Hoffman, Joan Collins and David Frost were regulars. As was Lawrence. On expenses, of course. In the immortal words of Frank Sinatra, 'Life was a gas!'

He hoped that his new company car, the latest Jaguar, would be in British racing green, but that was not a point he would push. Mustn't be too greedy. Still, it would be no hardship to get rid of the 7-year-old Anglia, which had 120,000 on the clock, dodgy tyres and a paint job that needed stripping down and redoing. He might get three hundred quid for it. If he was lucky. Then a dark thought entered his brain. Zenda used the Anglia most days, taking the children to school in Putney. It was littered with discarded sweet papers. Laurence didn't fancy his new Jag being cluttered up to look like a kid's bedroom. And in any case, he didn't think it would be appropriate for Zenda to have the car except at the weekends. He had a parking spot at work, so he could drive to the office every day.

But Zenda?

Bit of a tough one, that. If he sold the Anglia, what would Zenda use? He sighed and pushed that question to the back of his mind to deal with later, much later. Nothing, but nothing, would sully the mood of excitement and power he was now enjoying.

The cab pulled up outside a neat nineteenth-century house in Tite Street with a shiny black front door and a bay tree in a wooden box on the doorstep. Laurence winced as he glanced at the taxi meter and carefully counted out banknotes to pay the driver. He only had just enough, including a mingy tip. The cabbie took it with a grimace and accelerated away with a spurt of loose tarmac like Stirling Moss at the Monte Carlo Rally.

Laurence took the latch key from his waistcoat pocket and unlocked the front door. It led into a spacious hall tiled in black-and-white marble. Straight ahead was a fine staircase that went up to the second and third floors. Laurence and Zenda's flat was on the ground floor: two bedrooms, a living room, kitchen and bathroom. Laurence walked along the hall and turned left. Another door, with scuff marks at its base, was open a crack and Laurence went inside. The inner hall was small but carpeted in beige. A child's plastic wheelbarrow leant against the wall and there was a suspiciously orange stain on the carpet. Beyond the double doors ahead of him, Laurence could hear the voices of his children.

'That's my chair,' Kathy was saying and Laurence recognised tears in her voice.

'No, stop it!' This time a sharp yell from Timmy.

'Timmy, get off.' Kathy again.

Then a blood-curdling scream and the sound of some object being dropped.

'Now see what you have done!' Zenda's voice, raised and angry.

Laurence pushed open the door and stepped inside. Kathy and Timmy were struggling to gain possession of a tiny child's chair. The floor was covered in soft toys, books and one sandal. Zenda was on her knees picking up what looked like a broken vase. Timmy was picking his nose as if seeking the Holy Grail up his left nostril and Kathy was weeping loudly and unconvincingly, but in possession of the prized plastic chair.

Nobody looked up at Laurence, who stood there and placed his crocodile-skin briefcase carefully on the floor. 'What's all the fuss about?' he said.

Kathy stifled a sob. 'Timmy tried to take my chair.'

'She pinched me!' countered Timmy, removing his finger from his nose and examining the result of his excavation.

Zenda looked up. 'Did you get the loaf?'

Laurence shook his head in a guilty fashion. 'Sorry, no.'

'Oh! Laurence,' said Zenda, standing up with the shattered pieces of vase in both hands. 'I phoned and told Betty to remind you.'

'I know, I'm sorry,' he said. 'Why couldn't you go out and –'

'Because the damn car won't start and I didn't fancy walking up to the King's Road. Anyhow, you've got a bakery next door to your fancy office.'

'I know, I'm sorry.'

'You know Kathy and Timmy like toast before they go to bed. They've been driving me mad all day.'

At this, both children broke into howls of despair and Timmy reinserted his finger into his nose.

'Don't do that,' yelled Zenda. 'Both of you go to your room, now.'

The two children shuffled off towards the door, brushing past Laurence on the way.

'Don't I get a "hello Daddy" kiss, then?' he said.

Kathy made a feeble attempt at kissing his hand, missed and hit his coat sleeve, leaving a smear of saliva. Timmy went past howling and slammed a door behind him.

Zenda dropped the shattered vase fragments into a wicker wastepaper bin and wiped her hands on the front of the apron she was wearing. Her blonde hair hung across her face and she brushed it back with a swift movement of her hand. She looked tired and there was a smudge of lipstick in the corner of her mouth.

186

'Did you come home in a taxi?' she asked.

Laurence nodded smugly. 'Yes, I did, and I'll tell you the reason why. Do you know –?'

'Oh! Laurence,' Zenda interrupted, 'for God's sake! We're behind with the rent as it is and next term's school fees are due. If it wasn't for my father paying them occasionally, we'd have to take them out.'

'How often does your father pay?' demanded Laurence. 'I thought you did.'

Zenda sighed. 'Honestly, Laurence, do you really think I can afford the school fees every quarter out of my housekeeping allowance? Get real.'

'OK, OK,' said Laurence, 'I'll give you more. For Christ's sake, Zenda, you might have mentioned it earlier.'

'Well I'm mentioning it now. And we've got the telephone bill in today.'

'Alright, Zenda. Please. I can claim some of that back from the company.'

Zenda sank into an armchair and folded her hands over her lap. 'That's what you always say. Look, I need a drink.'

'I'll get you one,' said Laurence. 'Gin and tonic?'

'Yes,' said Zenda, 'except there's no tonic.'

'Oh! for Christ's sake, Zenda,' mumbled Laurence, going over to the small drinks cabinet.

He poured two glasses of gin, sloshed in a few spurts of soda and handed a glass to Zenda.

As she sat there slumped in her chair, she looked older than her thirty years, Laurence thought. She had closed her eyes and for a moment, Laurence assumed she was asleep. He decided to tell her his exciting news after dinner when the children were in bed. From the small bedroom on his right, he could hear the muffled screams and yelps that always seemed to accompany their playtime.

Zenda looked a bit of a mess, actually. She was holding the gin and soda against her chest, but her eyes were still shut. Her left stocking was wrinkled at the ankle and she had what looked like a chocolate stain on her pale blue silk blouse. Just what did she do all day while he was at work earning their living? OK, she had to get the children off to school in the morning, but after that, she had the rest of the day to herself – a day of leisure, in fact! Probably gossiped on the phone with some of her friends – all mothers with plenty of time to laze around – reading her copy of *The Guardian*, a paper Laurence couldn't abide. He was a *Telegraph* man. Did she realise that it was down to him, the warrior-provider, the hunter-gatherer, to struggle in the commercial jungle of Covent Garden to provide the lifestyle they both believed was theirs by right? While he was exercising his finely honed judgement in the challenging media world, taking risks, making snap decisions, often involving many thousands of pounds, she was probably in Peter Jones looking at bloody curtains they couldn't afford, yet. And why did she let Timmy and Kathy leave their debris all over the flat? You couldn't take a step without treading on a plastic toy or woolly rabbit. And lately, their sex life had gone a bit, well, downhill. All the zest and passion of the early years had melted like snow on a stove.

OK, he had fallen asleep on the job recently, but he'd been to a business cocktail party, for Christ's sake. Business, not bloody pleasure. And yes, he had taken a half-dozen large G and Ts. But even so, wasn't it a wife's duty to excite her husband, make him welcome in the marital bed? Not just lie there thinking of England or worse, smiling at his inability to raise an erection. For Christ's sake, that really was humiliating.

He stormed out of the room and into the kitchen, where two plates of salad covered in cling film were on the counter. So there would be no hot dinner tonight. Typical. He'd worked his balls off all day, won a promotion and all he got is a plate of sodding rabbit food.

And there was no tonic, either.

He looked up at the calendar pinned to the side of the refrigerator. It showed a stunningly pretty blonde in a tight blouse and jodhpurs, her full lips moist, red and pouting. Laurence knew her. She was a model; had done a lot of work for the agency. I could get it up with her *any* time, he mused, even if I'd drunk 2 gallons of gin and jogged naked over heated coals in the Sahara Desert! My God! he was in his sexual prime and it was being wasted, squandered. No, that was unfair. They would probably "do it" tonight and everything would be OK. Yes, he mustn't be too hard on Zenda. Anyway, when he told her of his promotion and the extra money, especially the extra money, she'd be as randy as a butcher's dog! No, that was crude and unjustified, a shameful thing even to think. He took a slug of gin and soda. Christ! it tasted like shit.

'Darling,' it was a cry from the living room, from Zenda. 'I've just remembered; there's some tonic in the medicine cupboard in the bathroom. God knows why I put it there.'

Laurence went into the small bathroom, stumbling over a child's wooden train, opened the doors of the medicine cabinet and a cascade of toothbrushes, aspirin bottles and eyebrow pencils scattered into the washbasin. He saw the bottle of tonic in the back of the cabinet, removed it, unscrewed the cap and went back into the living room.

Each of them finished their gin and sodas and Laurence recharged their glasses with tonic and a lot more gin and slumped down in the armchair.

'I'm knackered,' he said, taking a long draught from his glass.

Zenda looked at her husband from behind her drink. He had kicked off his Gucci loafers and now sat in his socks. His big toe was poking out of a hole in one of them. Why he had to spray money about on silk socks she simply didn't know. They just laddered like women's stockings and you couldn't mend them. He couldn't begin to understand or appreciate how difficult it was to manage their very expensive lifestyle on his income from the agency. He still didn't know how to observe the niceties of living together, even after eleven years. He still left his dirty underpants on the floor of the bathroom for her to pick up. He still pissed on the bathroom floor, occasionally. And even after stuffing his face at lunch in San Lorenzo's or Scalini's or Langan's, he would expect a three-course cooked meal in the evening, and more often than not, he couldn't eat it.

He was useless about the house, too. Couldn't change a light bulb and wouldn't ever read instructions on how to assemble a flat-pack kitchen cabinet, usually ending up by slinging it, accompanied by a torrent of filthy language, into the little yard at the back of the house. And as for the children's school fees at that splendid school in Putney, well, her father had warned her, 'He's a lovely chap,' he had said, 'but he must learn to walk before he can run. Ambition is all very well but, Zenda, my dear, pride often comes before a fall.'

Her mother loved him, though. Thought he was the bee's knees. And he had been a dashing young man when she first met him. But he was, she supposed, like most modern men, an unreformed but amiable savage who needed a woman more than he would ever admit. It was easier for men. They were cosseted by their mothers until they reached maturity and then, more often than not, handed over to a wife, whom they expected to carry on the same level of coddling, plus sex and childbearing. My God, life was unfair. And if there was a God, and as a *Guardian* reader she doubted it, he was certainly a bloke and a Tory. On the other hand, she'd never met a socialist she actually liked. Po-faced, sanctimonious, chippy and boring. Just like *Guardian* readers.

Maybe God was neutral, after all, but still a bloke.

The ham salad was quite tasty and Laurence opened a bottle of Sancerre. Zenda had sliced the leftover potatoes from yesterday and mixed them with some plum tomatoes and olive oil. Before they had sat down to eat, off Villeroy & Boch plates, Laurence had given Timmy and Kathy their baths and put them to bed while Zenda took a shower and washed her hair.

Once tucked up in their beds, side by side in their small bedroom, the two children had fallen instantly asleep. Laurence thought they looked like little angels as he kissed them lightly on their foreheads before putting out the light and leaving the room.

After supper, Zenda and Laurence watched the nine o'clock news and he finally told her about his promotion. She kissed him and gave his hand a squeeze.

'My clever husband,' she said.

Laurence kissed her back and slid his hand over her thigh. 'And I'll get the Anglia fixed up, resprayed and all that, now I'm getting a Jag.'

'Thank you, darling,' said Zenda.

A little later, naked in bed, Laurence pressed his face against Zenda's perky breasts and she hugged him close. He adjusted his weight and repositioned himself, poised to commence the age-old act of marital consummation.

From outside their bedroom door, a heart-rending cry ripped the air. It was Kathy's voice, rising to a thin wail.

'Mummy,' she cried, 'I got a tummy ache.'

Laurence rolled off the spreadeagled form of his wife, swung his legs off the bed, slipped on a pair of boxer shorts and tottered to the door.

Zenda gazed at his retreating figure and smiled. He wasn't such a bad father and husband, after all, but his bum was beginning to lose its firmness.

No, Really? Not a Lot of People Know This …

It is a myth that cockneys are defined as Londoners who live within the sound of Bow Bells. A book on the *Poor of Chelsea* published by Merridew of London in 1699 claims that the origin of the word means "Milksop" or "Mummy's Boy", a form of insult. So a cockney was a lad who had been so pampered in his upbringing that he was a pretty useless member of the working classes. Today, in the twenty-first century, he'd be called a "Big girl's blouse".

So now you know.

Fulham Football Club was founded in 1879 by lads who attended the Sunday school at St Andrews in Greyhound Road. They played on various grounds until they managed to acquire the broken-down Craven Cottage and its surrounds, which had been almost destroyed by fire. The first stand at the ground was erected in 1906. Parish records show that one of the lads who founded the club was a Mr M. Caine. Not a lot of people know that, either!

A Woman of Vast Importance

Mrs Woods was, by all accounts, a woman of formidable reputation. In 1953, she was well into middle age, but the legend persisted that she had been a heart-stopping, mouth-watering beauty in her youth. She towered above her diminutive husband, Bennett, and the whisper among her curtain-twitching neighbours in Munster Road was that she exercised control over little Bennett by means of genital manipulation.

Dermot Hillier, who ran a small greengrocery in Munster Road and was something of an amateur historian and student of human frailty, claimed that the relationship between Bennett and his Amazonian spouse was not unlike that which existed between Mrs Simpson and King Edward VIII during the abdication crisis of the 1930s. The wretched Bennett, it was further claimed by Dermot Hillier, was actually Mrs Wood's sex slave and willing victim of her humiliation techniques.

The wretched Bennett himself knew of these unkind stories that swirled around the neat terraced houses strung along Munster Road, but a lifetime of obscurity and a stoic disposition made him immune to such jibes. He continued working quietly for Fulham Borough Council as a clerk in the department responsible for organising street cleaning and was rarely seen out with Mrs Woods, who seemed to spend an inordinate amount of time indoors at their modest but immaculate house on Munster Road but a stone's throw from Dermot Hillier's vegetable emporium.

Like most married couples, they had fallen into a settled routine of daily life that was, after thirty years, now so entrenched that it would be impossible for either of them to deviate from it. The rigidity of the routine had been determined by Bennett's one minor misdemeanour early on in their relationship. After only six months' marriage, the act of consummation had not taken place. Both parties had been willing to give it a try, but to put the matter bluntly, the great difference in their physical bulk and height had made the process of mounting, and sadly penetration, quite impossible.

After a number of bruising attempts, where Mrs Woods kept all her clothes on including a hat, they decided that the intercourse business was not all it was cracked up to be. The very last courageous throw of the dice, so to speak, was when, in a frenzy of tumescence, young Bennett had removed his socks and his vest, for the first time, and tried a soupçon of foreplay by placing his left palm over Mrs Woods' vast snow-white marshmallow of a breast.

She had shrunk away from his touch with a thin, piercing cry, 'Don't be filthy.' When he transferred his sweaty hand to her lower abdomen to seek an alternative erogenous zone, she had uttered the ultimate erection-shrinking epithet, 'Never, ever touch me *there*,' and that was that. They fell apart in silence and from that day henceforth, slept in separate bedrooms.

But both were persons who believed quite firmly in the sanctity of marriage, thus divorce or separation were not things even to be considered.

After a year, however, of this sexless union, Bennett, who was a rising star in the Fulham Municipal Firmament, was promoted to assistant to the deputy chief clerk in the drains and street cleansing department. His ground-breaking suggestion for the design of a new flange cover for some of the old Victorian drains was a clear sign he was a man to watch. The increased remuneration which was attached to his new job went a little to his head. On a whim one evening, he invited Miss Rutherford, a typist, to join him in a glass of sherry at The Red Lion in Walham Green. Miss Rutherford, a mousey 25 year old, readily accepted, her current boyfriend being abroad with the Royal Electrical and Mechanical Engineers, where he held the rank of lance corporal.

After only the second Harveys Bristol Cream, Bennett, in a frenzy of animal lust, leaned across and kissed Miss Rutherford on the cheek. She blushed but did not resist. Emboldened, Bennett kissed her again on the lips, but at this, she gave a kittenish scream, slapped his face and fled.

A sense of shame and self-loathing overwhelmed Bennett and he ran from the pub and caught a number 14 bus straight home. His confession to Mrs Woods was a fine example of humility and he hoped it would prompt a sympathetic response from the craggy Amazonian, who listened to his words with folded arms and a thunderous scowl.

'You disgust me!' she hissed. 'You are little more than an animal. Don't ever think you can try that with me, *ever*. And don't think I will divorce you; I wouldn't give you that satisfaction.'

From that moment, Bennett's life was set in a pattern. He would go to work and bring home his wages and Mrs Woods would keep house and of course keep up appearances.

Now Mrs Woods was an avid but untidy reader of eclectic tastes who, in spite of a limited formal education, was keen to improve herself. However, her enthusiasm for literature was blighted by the fact that she could only remember snatches of what she had read and even then, was confused as to their origin. As a result of this mental aberration, she was inclined not only to misquote the works of Shaw, Shakespeare, Coward and Hemingway, but also to mix them up in a kaleidoscope of verbal confusion.

On the day of Bennett's confession, after condemning his lewd behaviour in The Red Lion, she had turned on her heel and thrown the following majestic, aural thunderbolt in his direction. 'As Julius Caesar said in George Bernard Shaw's *Merchant of Venice*, man is a faithless wretch, God wot.'

Every weekday from then onward followed the same pattern. Bennett would rise from his single bed in the tiny spare room, shave and perform his ablutions in silence and after dressing, he would go to the kitchen and prepare breakfast. When the table was laid and the kettle coming nicely to the boil, he would call Mrs Woods down to join him. She would descend the stairs with a stately tread and then, in a voluminous orange dressing gown, pink fluffy slippers and with her hair in curlers, survey the repast Bennett had prepared.

'Eggs too runny. Toast burnt. Butter tastes funny. Can't you get anything right? Your pathetic culinary expertise reminds me of the immortal words of Queen Lucretia of the Netherlands in Noel Coward's epic poem, *The Rape of the Lock*. Don't cry for me Argentina, too many cooks spoil the broth, but one husband utterly destroys it!'

Bennett, anxious beyond sanity to secure her forgiveness for his heinous behaviour, tried desperately to please her, to win back her respect and what he hoped might even be her love.

After a month of her complaining about the paucity of Bennett's breakfasts, he rose an hour earlier than usual and prepared a range of several breakfasts. White toast with runny eggs, brown toast with bacon (crispy), scrambled eggs with cold ham, porridge, cornflakes, fried tomatoes and poached eggs, tea, coffee, various juices, iced water. Their tiny kitchen was a whirlpool of activity each morning and finally when Mrs Woods approached like a galleon in full sail, he prayed that at least one item on offer would please her. She would pause in front of the groaning sideboard while Bennett stood a respectful distance away, wiping his hands nervously on his apron, the plastic one decorated with a facsimile of the last three popes.

After poking her finger in the plate of scrambled eggs and sniffing at the cold ham or even licking a crust of toast, Mrs Woods would make her decision. It varied, but even after consuming the breakfast of her choice, her verdict was always damning

'Tasted funny. Did you wash your hands before preparing the food? Your nails look filthy to me. God preserve us if you poison me. And why do you leave the kitchen in such a mess? Were you born clumsy?'

Then, when the painful ritual was finally completed and Mrs Woods belched with the resonance of a trombone, she swept out of the kitchen and upstairs to the bathroom, where the thunderous ceremony known in high medical circles as "the evacuation of the bowels" took place.

Bennett tried to mask the ear-splitting sounds of Mrs Woods at stool by switching on the radio, but she would scream from above to turn it off. It was rare for her to reappear downstairs before Bennett left for work and when she did, his mode of transport, choice of raincoat, hat and gloves were subjected to a withering stream of biting criticism.

'You are a disgrace,' she would hurl at him. 'That raincoat makes you look ridiculous. I am reminded of the soul-rending speech made by Mr Pickwick in Ernest Hemingway's heart-stopping musical, *Two Gentlemen of Verona: on Ice*. Get thee behind me, Satan, and I shall rend my raiment, so says the Lord, in my Easter bonnet.'

Only once did Bennett dare to correct her misquotations, but received an acidic put-down for his pains.

'How dare you correct me,' she cried, 'you read nothing but the *Daily Express* and *Stamp Collector's Gazette*. I, however, as you well know, am *well read*.' She waved towards the crammed bookshelves with a triumphant gesture.

And so the painful morning ritual continued month after month, season after season. Evenings were no better, Bennett returning home exhausted from a day of flange-designing or drain inspections in the Wandsworth Bridge Road, when Mrs Woods would regale him with details of her quite dreadful day. Appliances often broke. Migraines were frequent. She felt giddy. The next-door neighbours were "common" and she refused any sort of social contact with them. Why didn't Bennett buy some new furniture? The old sofa was a death-trap; a loose spring had almost speared her through the upper thigh. After the tirade subsided, Bennett set about preparing the evening meal, an event that invariably drew a firestorm of criticism from Mrs Woods.

But he pressed on, looking each day for a chink in her attitude that might hint of the small beginnings of forgiveness. When she complained of his snoring, even though he slept in the next room, he moved his bed downstairs into the hall.

'Perchance to dream!' she had bellowed. 'And by this sleep we end the Ides of March on a merry note. Oh, who will rid me of this turbulent priest?'

He tried to win a least a soupçon of gratitude from her by once producing a small bunch of violets, purchased from a street vendor on the way home from work, but she shrieked in dismay, 'You know I'm allergic to violets! I'll be sneezing all night, throw them away.'

'But, dearest,' Bennett had said, 'I didn't know. I'll bring gladioli tomorrow, I promise.'

At this, Mrs Woods had narrowed her eyes. 'What have you been up to? Not your filthy, lecherous tricks, I hope. You can't just buy me off with a bunch of flowers. Who have you interfered with? You slavering beast, tell me, confess, confess, I demand it.'

Bennett tried vainly to calm her down, even patting her hand in what he hoped was a non-threatening, almost affectionate way.

She drew back her hand as if it had been scalded. 'F. Scott Fitzgerald summed it up,' she screamed, 'in his ground-breaking novel, *The Old Man of the Sea*, when the heroine Ann of Cleves declares – I cannot blame thee now to weep, for such an injury would vex a saint much, more a shrew of thy impatient humour.'

Bennett shrugged and withdrew to the kitchen. He would, however, keep trying.

After Mrs Woods had retired to her room, her cheeks wet with tears, her mind filled with gross images of her husband's shameless infidelity, he put on his apron and began to prepare a tasty dish of shepherd's pie. Cooking calmed Bennett down and he found the ritual of preparation gave him time to think and to reflect on just how his life had come to such a pass.

When he had first met her, a shy but statuesque girl of twenty, he had fallen in love with her at once. She was handsome rather than pretty, with jet-black hair piled high on her head in the fashion of the time. At 5 foot 11 inches, she towered over most of her contemporaries, male and female, and Bennett at a paltry 5 foot 5 inches felt positively dwarfed. But he didn't entertain any delusions about becoming a candidate for her affections. To start with, he was already balding at age 20 and his physique could best be described as puny, but he did enjoy walks in Bishop's Park and along the Thames towpath at Putney; in fact, it was on such a mud-stained excursion one autumn Sunday that they had first met.

For the first six months, their relationship consisted of just that, muddy strolls along the Thames Embankment. While she was also a regular visitor to the Fulham Library, 'I'm quite the bibliophile,' she explained, Bennett's hobby was confined to stamp collecting and occasional Airfix model making.

Their first kiss sealed the deal, so to speak. It happened by accident when, during one of their Sunday perambulations, she stumbled in the soggy ground and Bennett, reaching out instinctively to prevent her falling, brushed her cheek with his lips. She had smiled coyly and suggested that perhaps they should get married. A stunned but overjoyed Bennett agreed instantly and experienced his first real pang of surging lust. They married and, both being orphans, chose a registry office in Walham Green to conduct the ceremony.

After a brief sex-free honeymoon in one of Frinton's most luxurious hostelries – Mrs Woods suffering from her ladies' time of the month – they returned to Fulham, place of their birth, and began the curious, awkwardly clumsy relationship as a married couple.

In its way, it worked quite well – even though Mrs Woods subjected the wretched Bennett to a Niagara of misquotations every evening when he returned from his work on drain clearance and his career-enhancing speciality in the design of flanges. Mrs Woods' quotations were grotesque but littered with Churchillian conviction. They were on the whole benign until, that is, the incident in The Red Lion, when Bennett's craving for forbidden flesh led him to lunge at the unfortunate Miss Rutherford, fiancée of an absent lance corporal who, while serving his King and country abroad, had been shamefully cuckolded.

Bennett realised, too late, that confessing his loathsome behaviour to Mrs Woods had been a mistake. What he should have done is buttoned his lip, begged God for forgiveness and carried on as normal. Alas, hindsight is not a comforting thing and Bennett now realised that he would have to suffer the consequences of his honesty until the grave or even beyond. He unravelled the scenario in his mind as he peeled the potatoes and sliced the onions in preparation for the planned shepherd's pie, but as he performed these rituals, he was struck by a great hammer of truth. He realised that in spite of the humiliations, the insults, the rejections and the revulsion she felt for him, he was still in love with her.

He laid down the potato peeler and said the words out loud, 'I love you, Enid.' Tears followed, but could have been encouraged as much by the onions as by his emotions. If he could prove his love, he mused, just demonstrate in a truly convincing way that he, Bennett Woods, rising star in the Fulham Council's Drains and Flanges Division, really did love her, perhaps a line could be drawn in the sand and, more importantly, perhaps she would be persuaded that she loved him, too. But what would be needed to achieve such a result? He cooked for her, he slept downstairs to ensure she had an undisturbed night's rest, he only bought himself clothes that she had approved, he had never seen her naked, even on honeymoon. He did all that he could in order to please her and it was to no avail. What was needed was a gesture of monumental significance, something majestic, Carthaginian, something perhaps even of Olympian grandeur.

But what?

Then he was struck again by the hammer of truth. Yes. At last. The solution. He would give her the ultimate proof of his love. But the plan, such as it was, would need meticulous planning and involves some risks. But ye Gods and little fishes! it would work. It had to. There was no denying it. Alleluia!

Later that evening when Mrs Woods descended to take dinner, Bennett had taken great care to prepare an alternative to the shepherd's pie – a roast chicken with broccoli – just in case she rejected his first offering with her usual snarl. He smiled graciously at her and held out a chair.

'Would you care for a little wine, perhaps, with the pie?'

She eyed him with suspicion, but sat in the offered chair. 'Not if it's like the usual muck you try to force down my throat. It calls to mind one of Richard Brinsley Sheridan's most famous lines from his unforgettable drama *Charley's Aunt*. If music be the food of love, let vultures gripe my guts. Take away these chalices. Go brew me a pottle of sack!'

Bennett shrugged and poured a glass of lemonade, a bottle of which he always kept in reserve.

Miraculously this evening, she consumed his shepherd's pie without a murmur. But after rejecting his shop-made apple pie and insisting on a large hunk of Cheddar, she cast a critical eye over his appearance.

'I don't like that tie,' she said.

Bennett immediately removed it and tossed it into a nearby waste-paper basket.

At this, Mrs Woods' gaze was loaded with scepticism. 'Why did you do that? Didn't I choose that tie for you?'

Bennett nodded. 'Yes, dearest. You did. But as you now disapprove of it, I cast it aside without regret.'

'Well,' she said in a puzzled tone of voice, 'you didn't have to throw it away. You could have just hung it up.'

Bennett felt a surge of triumph. Ye Gods, she was weakening. 'Whatever you say, dearest,' he said and retrieved the tie from the waste-paper basket.

Mrs Woods eyed him suspiciously. 'What's going on?' she said, brushing a crumb of Cheddar from her lower lip.

Bennett drew a deep breath and pulled himself up to his full height. 'I love you,' he said.

At this, Mrs Woods flinched as if struck by an axe or pricked with a sharp instrument. 'Love me!' she hissed. 'You don't know the meaning of the word. Vile adulterer!'

'But I do love you,' insisted Bennett, 'and I intend to prove it, beyond all doubt.'

'This I will have to see,' said Mrs Woods with a cruel laugh. 'This could be a shattering moment. A confessed lecher and reprobate who openly assaults innocent girls in public places in defiance of his marriage vows, claiming he loves his wife! Pah! Stuff and nonsense or, as the great German poet Guy de Maupassant put it in his musical cavalcade, *The Importance of being Ernest*, 'When daisies pied and violets blue and lady-smocks all silver white, and cuckoo buds of yellow hue do paint the meadows with delight, the cuckoo then, on every tree, mocks married men; for thus sings he: Cuckoo! Cuckoo! Cuckoo! O word of fear, unpleasing to a married ear!'

Bennett shrugged and folded the tie carefully in his hand. 'You may well say that,' he cried, 'but I do love you and you shall have proof!'

'I won't hold my breath,' said Mrs Woods, belching discreetly. 'And the potatoes were overcooked.'

The acquisition of a small handgun was a good deal easier than Bennett had previously anticipated. A colleague in the Drains, Sewers and Flanges Subdivision of the Fulham Borough Council had offered invaluable but unintentional advice.

'Picking up a shooter down the Lewis Trust Buildings is a doddle, apparently. Some ex-con who also served in the British Army in Korea now flogs old .38 service revolvers to the borough's villains, so my brother, who's a policeman, tells me! Makes you wonder what the world's coming to, eh, Bennett?'

Bennett had affected mild disinterest in this intelligence, but warehoused it carefully.

Now, three months on and possessed of an envelope stuffed with £200 worth of five pound notes, Bennett was lounging at the corner of one of the tall, grim structures that was part of the Lewis Trust Buildings. Erected by a charitable trust in the early part of the twentieth century, it was now a low-rent home for the urban poor. With the collar of his Gamages waterproof coat turned up and a Player's Weight cigarette dangling from his lip, Bennett looked like a refugee from a cheap detective novel. But he was a man possessed by demons, his mission crystal clear. He was to furnish proof, beyond any scintilla of doubt, that he truly loved Enid, his wife, and was thus deserving of her forgiveness and the rekindling of her affections for him.

He dropped the cigarette on the asphalt pavement and crushed it under his heel. To his right was a dark blue front door to a ground-floor flat. The number corresponded to the information his colleague at the council had unwittingly supplied. Drawing in a deep breath, and with his hands shaking slightly, he pressed the doorbell.

The shop in Fulham Road was double-fronted, but its bow windows had latticed metal shutters fixed into the frames. Mannequin dummies beyond the window were draped with a selection of fine ladies' fur coats. The exquisite skins displayed included the pelts of leopard, ocelot, mink and other endangered species, all of whom had been cruelly slaughtered to satisfy the lust for profit of the fur traders and the simpering egos of countless silly women.

Bennett pushed open the glass door that led into the shop and drew a shiny blue-black .38 service revolver from his mac pocket. The rotund fellow behind the counter glanced up from the ledger he was scrutinising, his eyes wide. Behind him, a wall clock struck 9.00 a.m. precisely and Bennett, levelling his weapon at the man's chest, waited until the discreet chimes had faded before speaking.

'The mink stole, I think,' he said, removing the safety catch with a metallic click.

'Are you mad?' cried the man and he reached down below the counter.

Now Bennett, who had never handled a revolver in his life before, made the lightning assumption that the fellow was reaching for a weapon of his own and panicked.

The sound of the shot was deafening and the velocity of the bullet, as it struck the man's chest, threw him against the wall and he slid down it, glassy-eyed.

A great roaring sound filled Bennett's head and he stood for a moment, still as a statue, the revolver smoking in his hand. Outside in the Fulham Road, a number 14 bus chuntered past the window as Bennett, with slow deliberation, undraped an exquisite stole from its mannequin, removed its 3,000-guinea price gag and stuffed it into his canvas holdall.

At four minutes past nine on that very same morning, Mrs Woods entered the greengrocery emporium of Mr Dermot Hillier. A few other women stood around examining the cornucopia of swedes, parsnips, King

Edward potatoes, carrots, lettuces, cabbages, tomatoes, radishes, onions and leeks on display. Mr Dermot Hillier, who was occupied placing some tomatoes in his brass scales, looked up in surprise as Mrs Woods entered this shop. She was wearing a purple top coat and a hat with a feather in it, leather gloves and an expression of vague, almost dreamy introspection. That morning, she had awakened as usual, performed her ablutions and descended to the kitchen. The table creaked with a display of breakfast delights and jugs of fruit juices that would have done justice to a grand hotel. There was also a note from Bennett:

Dearest,

Had to leave early upon my mission. Hope you find something to your liking on the table. I shall return.

Bennett.

PS My mission is to prove I love you.

PPS I do.

This plaintive written cry from the heart had somehow found a chink in Mrs Woods' emotional armour and plunged her into an uncharacteristic mood of reflection tinged with a soupçon of guilt. Yes, guilt – an emotion she thought had been expunged from her range of feelings forever. Had she been too high-handed in her assessment? Perhaps! But he was a man and as her late mother had warned her, they were weak vessels, slaves to their unsavoury lusts and prone to faithlessness. Their marriage now had spanned a decade and a half; he was a fair provider, but was all his cringing and glutinous provision, the separate sleeping arrangements and so on a mask to conceal a hideous secret life?

Or was this grossly unfair? And was she judging him too harshly? But wait. What of his first act of disloyalty and sexual incontinence? Was it no more than a stolen kiss as he had confessed, or a hideous lie to deflect her from discovering the truth? Had he in fact torn the unfortunate girl's underclothing from her trembling loins and taken her roughly from behind in broad daylight, in full view of a pub crammed with beer-slurping perverts, leering voyeurs and hairy degenerates?

These conflicting scenarios swirled inside her head, causing her to wobble slightly, and to steady herself, she placed a hand on a wooden tray containing a pyramid display of Brussels sprouts. The carefully arranged vegetables, balanced precariously, were immediately disturbed and tumbled from the tray, bouncing onto the wooden floor.

Mr Dermot Hillier reacted with the snap of authority he was noted for and flinging his arms up, he sent the brass scales and half a pound of tomatoes flying across the shop. 'What the heck!' he cried as Mrs Woods, doubly shocked by the twin cascades of fruit and veg, fell sideways against another tray of carrots and sent them hurling in orange confusion to join the Brussels sprouts.

Another customer, an elderly lady with a walking frame, screamed and a small terrier that had sauntered into the shop from the street outside began to bark hysterically.

Mrs Woods, taking a step back, placed her foot on a sprout, which caused her to lose her balance and she fell, none too gracefully, onto the floor. In so doing, she struck her head against the corner of a wooden cabinet containing some particularly splendid beetroots and was rendered unconscious. Dermot Hillier sprang from behind his counter with the agility of an arthritic panther, his intention being to come to the assistance of an infrequent but valued customer. But the scattering of loose vegetables impeded his progress across the floor of the shop and with a strange keening cry, he fell directly onto Mrs Woods' inert body.

At the same time, the invalid lady released her walking frame from nerveless fingers and she, too, slid to the floor in a faint. The terrier, maddened by these scenes of chaos, made a rush for the glass door that led out of the shop, but as it was closed he struck it with such considerable force that he bounced and fell foaming at the mouth across Dermot Hillier's neck, who now covered Mrs Woods' Amazonian framealmost completely.

Mrs Woods, who recovered consciousness as Dermot Hillier's paunch pressed against her hips, nevertheless kept her eyes tightly closed.

'Bennett,' she murmured, 'Bennett.'

Her arms encircled the unfortunate greengrocer's waist and she joined the fingers of her hands in a vice-like grip in the small of his back. This had the effect of driving all the breath out of his lungs and he emitted a choking sob. Mrs Woods arched her back in a thrusting movement, her eyes still closed, and began hyperventilating. Then, releasing one hand, she started pounding her clenched fist on the wooden floor.

'Bennett!' she yelled. 'Yes, yes, *yes*, yes! *Yes!*'

Her whole frame seemed to swell and rise up, carrying the trapped greengrocer with it, and then she collapsed like a punctured balloon and Hillier rolled off, moaning softly.

The stunned terrier, lurching across the shop, foam bubbling at the corner of its mouth, raised a leg and urinated on the walking-frame lady's handbag, which she had dropped as she fainted.

Another customer, an American plumber, struck at the dog with his rolled-up copy of the *Daily Mirror*, but the animal avoided the blow and nipped him sharply on the ankle.

At this stage, for no reason that could later be established, all the lights in the shop fused and a tray of Cox's Orange Pippin decanted themselves onto the already fruit-and-veg-strewn floorboards.

The feelings of shame and guilt that overwhelmed Mrs Woods when she staggered to her feet to survey the scene of carnage all around were profound. The wretched Hillier was crouched in a corner of the shop, his nose bleeding, while the invalid walking-frame lady was being offered a boiled sweet by the American plumber, who had bravely ignored his own injury inflicted by the incontinent terrier. Her cheeks inflamed and her left stocking in a wrinkled pool over her shoe, Mrs Woods fled from the shop and scurried along the street.

Passers-by fell back as she gathered speed, for here was a rare sight in Fulham on an October Tuesday – a middle-aged madwoman, her clothing awry, her feathered hat half obscuring her face, moving like a racehorse along the Fulham Road, past The Red Lion, past the library, into Clonmel Road and all the while yelling in a clear, almost operatic voice, jumbled quotations and snatches of self-flagellating doggerel. Any passing medical man would have immediately diagnosed the first symptoms of Tourette's syndrome.

'May these same instruments which you profane, never sound mote! In acclamations hyperbolical! The boy stood on the burning deck, as queer as a week-old kipper; did he fill his arse with broken glass and circumcise the skipper? God Save the King. Oh come let slip the dogs of war, for I am weary of this petty world! Oh woe! She is as false as water. A diabolic whore. Is their no shame in the body's treachery? Cry Harry, God and Cleopatra for the glory of France!'

Still concussed and raving but in a quieter voice, Mrs Woods arrived home and flung herself onto the sofa. Her eyes swivelled in their sockets and she took off her hat. The ostrich feather was bent and she tore it off and flung it across the room. Where was Bennett? Where was the man she had so cruelly and wantonly betrayed, and with the greengrocer? 'Oh shame and humiliation. Where is thy fatal sting?'

At first, Mrs Woods didn't realise that Bennett had entered the room. She was sitting on the sofa facing the small fireplace, her head in her hands, her great boxer's shoulders heaving with sobs.

'Dearest,' Bennett said. 'My dearest.'

She turned and there he was, a small, rumpled figure, his face gleaming with perspiration and a magnificent mink stole looped over his right arm.

'But, Bennett,' she blurted, her eyes trying desperately to focus.

Bennett waved an admonitory finger. 'No, don't speak, Enid,' he said. 'I implore you, before you rebuke me for my sins, hear me out.'

'But, Bennett,' she cried, 'I, too, have sinned. I have betrayed you, surrendering to the festering, unchaste throbbing of my own vile body's appetite, and with the greengrocer. It's enough to make the pope fuck a goat.'

Bennett's jaw fell slack. 'Enid, dearest, what are you saying, the language. My God, are you drunk?'

'Yes,' she cried, 'drunk with shame.' Then she clutched a hand over her throat, 'Oh my God, did I say the "F" word?'

Bennett nodded. 'I fear so, dearest, and some gibberish about betraying me; was that a quotation from *Othello*? You really do have an encyclopedic knowledge of the Bard. But, dearest, I beg you to hear me out. Let your eyes feast on *this* ...' He held out the mink stole and gave it a gentle shake. 'Here, my beloved, is my proof. Proof of my love for you.' He offered the stole to Mrs Woods and she took it, her mouth open, her eyes as wide as saucers. 'Proof!' cried Bennett excitedly.

Mrs Woods slipped the mink stole over her shoulders and stroked it. 'Oh, Bennett,' she sighed, 'but where? How?'

Bennett gave a nonchalant devil-may-care laugh. 'To prove my love for you, dearest,' he said, 'I killed a man and took the fur. What further proof do you need of my devotion and faithfulness?'

'You killed a man?' cried Mrs Woods.

'Yes. Shot him dead. With *this* ...' He produced the revolver from his mac pocket and tried to twirl it cowboy-style, but it fell to the floor with a clatter.

'Oh my God!' said Mrs Woods, clutching the fur stole close to her body.

'Oh yes,' continued Bennett in a conversational tone. 'The animal who once proudly wore this skin was itself murdered, deliberately, its fur ripped from the carcass while it was still warm. Most important to remove the fur before putrefaction kicks in, so I am told.'

'You did this thing, this vile deed for *me?*' Mrs Woods cried.

Bennett nodded coyly. 'I did. And, dearest, the mink really suits you!'

Mrs Woods smoothed her hands over the silky fur. 'Do you think so?' she purred. 'Oh, Bennett, my heart is overflowing. I am reminded of Orson Welles' towering performance as Long John Silver in the unforgettable gangster epic, *Scarface*, where he declared his love to Lady Gay Spanker with the searing words:

A thousand kisses buys my heart from me
And pay them at thy leisure, one by one.
What is ten hundred touches unto thee?
Are they not quickly told and quickly gone?
Say, for non-payment that the debt should double,
Is twenty hundred kisses such a trouble?

'Oh, Enid,' sighed Bennett, 'you certainly know your Dickens!'

He took a step towards her, his arms outstretched, and Mrs Woods clutched him to her bosom. He raised his face towards her, puckering his lips for a kiss, but before their mouths could touch, there exploded a great commotion from the street outside. The squeal of tyres, the howling of sirens and a sharp slamming of car doors.

Bennett ran to the window and looked down into the street. There were two police cars parked in the road, the blue lights on their roofs still flashing, two uniformed policemen and a plain-clothed officer standing behind the vehicles. The latter held a large loudhailer and the other two carried high-velocity rifles.

The officer with the loudhailer, one Sergeant Liphook, raised it to his lips and cried in stentorian tones, 'Bennett Wood, this is the police. You are completely surrounded. Throw down your weapon and descend to the street in an orderly manner, with your arms raised.'

Mrs Woods, who was standing at Bennett's shoulder, pushed him aside and raised the sash window. 'He's not here,' she yelled, 'go away.'

Sergeant Liphook glanced at his colleagues. 'My God, he's got a woman up there, either a hostage or his moll. The man is dangerous. Constable Truscott, fix your sights on that window!'

Bennett retrieved his revolver from the floor and stood beside his wife at the window. 'You'll never take me alive, copper!' he screamed and Mrs. Woods shook her fist.

'No, never.'

'Good grief,' said PC Truscott, 'she's his accomplice. Look out, sarge, he's got a gun.'

Bennett levelled his revolver at the first police car and squeezed the trigger. All three policemen ducked as the bullet struck the windscreen, but there was no shattering of glass and the missile bounced off the car and rolled into the kerb. PC Truscott picked it up with a gasp of incredulity.

'Blimey, sarge,' he said, 'it's a rubber bullet.'

Sergeant Liphook took the bullet from Truscott's hand and squeezed it. 'Hard, but not lethal,' he said. 'Same sort of bullet used on the fur-coat merchant. Knocked him for six, bruised but otherwise unhurt.' He raised the loudhailer again. 'Now listen, Mr Woods, nobody will get hurt if you come down quietly, with the woman.'

Bennett was gazing at the revolver in his hand, his mouth gaping. 'Rubber bullets!' he said. 'That swine in the Lewis Trust Buildings sold me a dud! But they can still get me for attempted homicide!'

Mrs Woods tapped him on the shoulder. 'Never mind that now,' she whispered, 'I have a plan.'

Below in the street, Sergeant Liphook, flanked by his two constables, had decided on storming tactics and moved towards the house, all three of them adopting a curious, crouching run. PC Truscott kicked in the front door, which fell from its frame with a splintering crash, and they ran two at a time upstairs to the first-floor flat.

They dashed into the small sitting room, the window of which overlooked the street, but it was empty. As were the other three rooms, the bathroom and the kitchen.

Sergeant Liphook pushed his trilby onto the back of his head and turned to PC Truscott. 'Can you Adam and Eve it! They've bloody well vanished into thin air.'

The frenzied press speculation that followed these events focused on the actual fur robbery, the incompetence of the constabulary and the mysterious disappearance of Bennett and Mrs Woods.

The police, meanwhile, had alerted ferry terminals and airports, while detectives combed the Fulham streets for clues. The Woods' flat was stripped and several employee colleagues of his at the Fulham Borough Council were interviewed, all to no avail.

Curious though it is to relate, truth as usual being stranger than fiction, it was six months later that a young lad, a twentieth-century "Mudlark" no less, was trudging along the Thames towpath in his search for hidden artefacts dropped from passing barges, when he came across a curious sight. In the sluggish river tide close to the muddy bank where he stood, he saw a shabby, saturated fur stole floating in the scummy froth. It looked very much like something discarded by a party reveller from a passing pleasure steamer.

He reached out with the stick he was carrying and pulled the stole out of the water and onto the muddy bank. As he did so, a fragment of Lewis Carroll's *Through the Looking Glass* drifted into his consciousness, a narrative piece he had recently been studying at school:

> Ever drifting down the stream,
> Lingering in the golden gleam,
> Life, what is it but a dream?

Then, to his surprise, he recalled another brief verse, not by Lewis Carroll but a poet unknown:

> Why so swift to grasp the dream,
> Mad to learn the story's ending,
> Filth of all hues and odours foul
> Drowned to death and to hell descending.

Picking up the saturated fur carefully, he placed it in his plastic holdall. Later at home, he would dry it out then ascertain its value. As the ancient saying goes: The River Thames will in the end offer up all its hidden secrets to a wondering world.

The spot where the mink stole was recovered corresponded with the exact spot where Mrs Woods and Bennett first met nearly sixteen year ago.

Such is the random nature of circumstance, coincidence and the many exotic threads that make up the great quilt of life. Or so William Shakespeare didn't say.

You'll Never Believe This, But ...

In 1862, Silas Miller, an 18-year-old apprentice potter, was apprehended by the police on the Chelsea Embankment for behaving in a dangerous fashion. He was attempting to shoot ducks with a bow and arrow. The police, on realising the young man was very drunk, confiscated his arrows but allowed him to keep the bow.

A lady's maid who was passing by witnessed the incident and after the constable had moved off, she gave the boy a shilling so he could buy some more arrows.

At the end of the nineteenth century, on a triangular site at Walham Green, a variety theatre was built, the Granville, designed by prolific theatre architect Frank Matcham. In the early days, with its plush red seats and fancy dome over the entrance, it provided local residents with the very best variety entertainment.

By the 1950s, it had become run-down and TV had virtually killed off variety; although the author remembers with a guilty smile sneaking into the "Gods" in 1949 and paying half a crown to see *Nudes of all Nations* and other slightly shabby acts of acrobats and singers well past their sell-by date.

The Granville was demolished in 1971.

Ignorance is Bliss

'There's English,' said Rathbone, drawing on his Player's Navy Cut as if his life depended on it, 'and there's French, Italian, German, Spanish, Dutch and bleeding Greek, too. Yes, all European languages, they are. Continental, I think the word is. But, my friends, there is another language, a very special one, here in Fulham. And it is a bit like the language of a secret society only spoken by its members. No, don't laugh, my friends, listen. Yes, listen to your old Reggie Rathbone and maybe you might learn something. Some tiny shaft of knowledge could penetrate those thick skulls of yours for a change.'

Reggie Rathbone took another drag on his cigarette and its tip glowed red in the dingy half-light of the saloon bar in The Swan at Walham Green. The barman, a rotund fellow with a domed, hairless head and a tiny Hitler-esque moustache, slid another foaming pint of mild and bitter across the counter.

'OK, Reg,' he said, 'what is this other language? Esperanto, is it? I've read about that.'

Reg Rathbone gave a snorting laugh. 'No, mate. Not bleeding Esper-sodding-ranto. No way. That's some old bollocks dreamed up by a bunch of tosser politicians. No, I'm talking about a lingo that exists here in bloody Fulham. Yes, down the town hall if you must know.'

'Down the town hall?' said the barman, grinning.

'Down the Fulham Town Hall, yes,' said Reg, blowing smoke in fine jets from both nostrils. 'And it's called town-hall speak. Yes, that's what it's called.'

The small crowd who had gathered round Reg, the sage of Walham Green, emitted a kind of collective rustle and all seemed to clear their

213

throats at the same time. There were five of them, all men, mostly in their late twenties, all of them smoking like chimneys and sipping pint glasses of beer. There was Dick who was a postman, Les the builder, Tom the insurance salesman and the Ponting twins, Bill and Bernie, who ran a barbers in Munster Road. They could be described as members of the respectable working class.

Reg took a swig from his pint glass, wiped the foam off with the back of his hand and nodded, almost to himself. He knew he had a captive audience, did Reg. His acolytes hung on his every word, looked upon him as something of an oracle. This was because he had been to Sloane Grammar School in Chelsea and was therefore "educated". The others were all products of scrofulous secondary moderns, where the only subjects in which they obtained any knowledge whatsoever were masturbation, football and smoking. Reg was also forty-five, a man with a lifetime of experience and a job as a reporter on the local *Fulham Chronicle*. The fact that he had scarcely risen through the editorial ranks beyond reporting weddings, funerals and late-night punch-ups at the Lewis Trust Buildings was neither here nor there. He was out there in the real world, a word spinner, an observer of society, a man who wore three-piece suits from Cecil Gee, a raincoat with epaulettes and a hat with a greasy band around the rim, just like Frank Sinatra or Hollywood reporters in "B" gangster movies.

'I will give you a few examples of town-hall speak,' said Reg, belching discreetly. 'Yes, for example, if you or I cop a rise in our wages, that's what we call it, a rise in our bleeding wages, OK? In town-hall speak, however, they say their "emoluments have been enhanced". And if you or I have a crash in the old jalopy, they don't. They have a "vehicular altercation". If old Neddy the 80-year-old drunk from Dawes Road flashes his dick at a passing schoolgirl, you know what he is doing? He is "indulging in inappropriate behaviour" or is guilty of "indecent exposure". No bugger from the town hall ever "puts his money in the slot" when he's phoning from a red phone box. Oh no, he is "inserting the correct coinage necessary".

'I tell you, boys, it's another bleeding language, town-hall speak – there's no other name for it! Mind you, a bit of it has rubbed off on the Old Bill. Yes, two young people are found shagging in the bushes in Bishop's Park. Well, they are not shagging as far as our constabulary are concerned. Oh no! Do you know what the police say they are doing?'

The barman, who was polishing a glass, responded to his cue. 'No, Reg. What do the police say they were doing?'

Rathbone gulped a mouthful of mild and bitter. 'They were engaged in sexual congress.'

The barman frowned. 'Sexual congress. Don't you mean intercourse?'

Rathbone shook his head vigorously. 'No, I don't bloody mean intercourse. It's bloody congress. That's the word.'

'You can hardly call that town-hall speak,' piped up a raincoated youth with a shock of red hair. He was Dick the postman.

Rathbone glared at him. 'What? What? What are you saying?'

The youth gave a toothy grin. 'Town-hall speak. You can't say that sexual congress is town-hall speak, Reg. It's more like police speak.'

'Or copper jargon,' shouted Les the builder, who had just finished his third pint of the evening.

'What the hell are you talking about?' cried Rathbone, who was not used to his anecdotes and tall stories being interrupted, let along challenged.

'All I'm saying, Reg,' persisted Dick, 'is that if the police use their own funny phrases and that, well, it can't be called town-hall speak, that's what I'm trying to say. I mean town-hall speak is what is spoke by people at the –'

'I bloody *know* that,' yelled Rathbone. 'You are being pedantic.'

'What's that, then?' said Tom the insurance salesman.

'What's what?' roared Rathbone.

'Pedantic. What's it mean?' said Tom.

'Bloody hell!' cried Rathbone. 'Are you completely dumb, Tom? For Christ's sake! Pedantic, well, it means, it sort of means, it describes a person, well, who's a pedant.'

'I know what pedantic means,' exclaimed Bernie the barber and all eyes turned to him. 'It means nit-picking.'

Gales of laughter followed this remark and Rathbone looked as black as thunder.

'Well, yes, that is so,' he said pompously. 'Nit-picking. Quite.'

'Well if it means nit-picking,' said Bernie, stroking his elaborate side whiskers, 'why did you call it pedantic? That sounds like town-hall speak, if you ask me.'

'I wasn't asking you,' said Rathbone, crushing his cigarette out in a glass ashtray.

'Can't be called town-hall speak,' said Tom, giggling.

'Or police speak,' cried Les triumphantly.

'No,' said Bernie, 'I know what it is. It's Rathbone speak.'

'That's not funny!' thundered Rathbone, but his words were almost drowned by raucous peals of laughter. 'Sod the lot of you!' said Rathbone, taking out another cigarette and lighting it. 'Waste of time trying to improve *your* minds. I don't know why I bother.'

'Never mind, Reg,' said the barman kindly, 'have another drink. Mild and bitter?'

Reg nodded. 'Thanks, Jack,' he said.

Bernie came over and touched his elbow. 'Only having a giraffe, Reg. No offence intended.'

Rathbone shrugged. 'None taken.'

Les joined them at the bar and pushed his empty glass towards Jack, the barman. 'I would be grateful, landlord,' he said in a faux upper-class accent, 'if you would be so good as to recharge my glass receptacle with some alcoholic fluid. On receiving said intoxicating beverage, I will reimburse you with the appropriate coins of the realm.'

'You talk dirty like that in my pub and you'll have to stand the next round for all the lads,' said Jack, laughing

Rathbone turned and rested his elbows on the bar counter. 'I concur with those sentiments indubitably,' he said.

Bernie the barber turned to Les and nudged him. 'Know what *that* means, don't you, Les?'

Les shook his head. 'Not really, Bernie. Pray, enlighten me with your erudite explanation.'

Bernie raised his glass and saluted Rathbone. 'Roughly translated,' he said, 'what Reg actually said was "up yours"!'

The laughter that followed was profound and long-lasting and could be heard as far away as the old fire station in the Fulham Road.

Lots and Lots of People Know This, Maybe ...

The headmaster of the Sloane Grammar School in Chelsea was Guy Boas, a brilliant Shakespearean scholar and formerly librarian at the famous Garrick Club in Covent Garden. The author attended Sloane School in 1946 and fifty years later became a member of the Garrick Club.

In 1851, Fulham was still largely rural and its population heavily weighted with Irish labourers who worked on what was called "The Land of Cabbages" at Fulham fields.

It is interesting to note that the West Middlesex Regiment, formed in 1757 in the Fulham area almost 100 years earlier, drew many of its recruits from Ireland and continued to do so even up to the 1950s, when the author served with the Regiment in Austria.

Forbidden Lust on Council Property

'The sense of anticipation was palpable; it was in the air, like electricity.'

The man who spoke these words was in his sixties, his face creased with the ravages of age, his bald dome protruding like a speckled egg from a fringe of wispy white hair that covered his ears. Although he wore thick spectacles, his eyes were still bright, shining behind the lenses and darting from side to side as he surveyed his audience of four, who sat cross-legged in front of him.

'Today,' he said, waving a manicured hand, 'you are so sated with experience, so spoiled for choice, your appetites so dulled by excess, that you have lost your sense of wonder and the heady thrill of anticipation.'

His four listeners shifted their positions uncomfortably. The eldest of them was fifteen, the other three lads just fourteen.

The 15 year old yawned. 'Oh come on, give us a break, Uncle, change the record.'

The old man shrugged and stroked his chin. 'Another thing that has been lost,' he murmured, 'a sense of respect. It's all part of the same pattern. Even at your age, you are suffering from information overload, a kaleidoscope of sensations and experiences on offer, a surfeit of choice. It can only end in tears, if it hasn't done so already.'

One of the younger boys glanced at his watch, a twin-dialled diver's timepiece with a gold bracelet.

'And you have all the toys of the modern world at your fingertips; too soon, in my view, for you to appreciate them fully. That watch, Simon, that glittering badge of affluence that encircles your wrist cost more than I used to earn in a year sixty years ago.'

All four lads groaned in chorus. 'Gotta go, Uncle,' said the eldest and stood up.

The old man sighed; he enjoyed the company of his nephew and his friends. But after half an hour in his company, they were impatient to get on with their own lives.

He cursed himself silently for once again failing to rein in his tendency to lecture them and drone on about the "good old days" or sometimes, the "bad old days". He had intended to have a grown-up chat with the four of them, all down from their public school in Yorkshire. But he had failed to listen to his wife's warning.

'Timothy,' she had said, 'to those boys, you aren't just yesterday's man, you're the day before yesterday's man. Banging on about your life in the fifties would about as much appeal to them as watching paint dry.'

There followed brief handshakes between the boys and their host just as his wife, Polly, a pretty 60 year old, came into the room.

'Just off, then?' she said breezily. 'Won't you stay for tea?'

'Obviously not,' said her husband, 'they have a schedule to follow.'

'Now, Timothy,' she said, 'no need for that.' Then she turned to the boys. 'Shall I phone for a taxi?'

They giggled and Simon shook his head. 'No need, Aunty. Dad's car will take us back to Hampstead.'

'Oh,' said Polly, 'what time?'

'Well,' said Simon, 'it brought us here and it's still outside. So we can go anytime.'

Timothy, who had raised himself painfully from his armchair, went across to the window and looked down onto the street. A beige Bentley was drawn up at the kerb with a uniformed chauffeur behind the wheel. Timothy turned and faced them.

'No,' he said, 'I'm not going to give you the satisfaction of saying it.'

'Saying what, Uncle?' said Simon slyly. 'In your day, you'd have gone home on a bike?'

Timothy gave a mirthless laugh. 'Actually, no, Simon, I'd have caught a bus.'

Amid giggles and a hug from their aunt, the four lads piled out of the room and clattered downstairs with Aunty following.

Timothy went back to the window and watched the Bentley pull away with his wife waving goodbye. Then he limped to his armchair and took a fat Cohiba Cuban from his humidor, clipped the end with a gold cutter, lit it with a wooden match and inhaled the rich, aromatic smoke.

Polly reappeared and shook her head. 'Timothy, you do really set yourself up for it, you know.'

Timothy nodded glumly, 'I know,' he said, 'I'm sorry.'

Later, over dinner, he was more relaxed, comfortable in his wife's company and warmed by a fine bottle of Chateau Lafitte Rothschild. They had been married nearly thirty years but were childless and this made the frequent visits from Simon, their nephew, all the more important to them. His brother, the dazzlingly successful Thomas, a star journalist on *The Times* and a frequent presenter of upmarket arts programmes on ITV, had been married four times, each union ending in divorce, but Simon was the only child of the first marriage. Thomas' esoteric lifestyle meant he was away from London much of the year and even when Simon came down from school in Yorkshire, he was frequently alone in the family house in Hampstead with just servants for company.

Over the years, he had become used to visiting his uncle and aunty in their house in Chelsea and Timothy had assumed, discreetly, the role of surrogate father to young Simon, and his wife surrogate mother. Timothy's career in accountancy had been successful, too, and he was a partner in a city practice that included as clients several blue-chip companies, both national and international.

But in spite of this success and their fine Queen Anne house in Chelsea just off the King's Road, he was, compared to his brother, just another childless, middle-class professional whose lifestyle was predictable, comfortable and dull.

Both his and his brother's beginning had been modest, their father a labourer, mother a laundress, born in a tiny terraced house in slightly shabby Sherbrooke Road in Fulham. Both boys had scraped through the eleven-plus and gained entry to the Sloane Grammar School in Chelsea. Thomas, being two years older than Timothy had arrived there first. By the time Timothy turned up, Thomas was soaring, excelling both academically and on the sports field, whereas Timothy's progress was just ploddingly successful. He was the sort of man who would be described by future employers as a safe pair of hands.

Both boys were called up for national service and joined the army. Thomas gained a commission in a fashionable infantry regiment and then two years later, Timothy's spell in khaki saw him achieve the rank of corporal in the Royal Army Pay Corps.

On leaving the service Thomas, who had acquired the polish and social patina of an English officer, began a career in journalism and serial marriages. Each of his wives, including young Simon's mother, was rather flashy, money-driven and extraordinarily beautiful. His first marriage, however, didn't take place until he was forty-five. Each of his wives, in spite of their sexual attractiveness, played second fiddle to Thomas' exploding and self-obsessed career. Simon had been born when Thomas was over fifty.

Steady old Timothy met Polly, a quiet, decent dental technician and married her after just a year's mild courtship a couple of decades before his brother had hitched his first marital knot. Apart from the disappointment of being childless and both rejecting the solution of adoption, they had nonetheless enjoyed a steady, happy and satisfying union.

Now in the early evening of their lives, they seemed keener than ever to maintain contact with young Simon, their nephew, particularly as Thomas, his father, was away more than he was at home.

The latest on this front was that Thomas, now sixty-five, was cohabiting with a dusky Tunisian ballet dancer one-third of his age. The popular press had reported gloatingly on their liaison and published photographs of the couple, limbs entwined, at various nightspots in London, Paris and the south of France. Just what the effect of this gallivanting had on young Simon was hard to say, but it caused Timothy and Polly distress.

Dinner finished, Timothy selected another cigar from his humidor and sat in his armchair by the tall window overlooking the street.

Polly cleared the table then picked up a fine quilt she was finishing and joined her husband in a chair next to his.

'I heard you talking to Simon and his friends earlier,' she said. 'I heard you say something about a sense of anticipation, yours, I presume, being palpable and being as electricity in the air or atmosphere. Timothy, what was that all about?'

Timothy sighed and for a moment his face disappeared behind a cloud of cigar smoke. 'I was just thinking aloud, really,' he said softly, 'contrasting my life at fifteen. Way back then in Fulham, a time of innocence and enquiry, the slow discovery of new things, new experiences. Such a sense of wonder we had then – unlike today, when almost every experience can be enjoyed at the touch of a computer mouse.'

Polly put down her quilt and smiled at her husband. 'Oh, I see, one of your usual anti-computer diatribes. Honestly, Timothy, you're behaving like King Canute.'

'No, no,' said Timothy, 'not at all. Look, if you must know, I was going to try to convey to those boys the extraordinary thrill of my first, my first really sexual experience.'

Polly's eyes widened. 'Timothy! Really. What on earth –'

Timothy raised a hand, palm outward. 'No, let me finish, Polly. Look, I know you don't like talking about this stuff, but I just thought, what the hell, these modern kids think they invented sex. They don't see us as sexual beings at our age. Well, fair enough. I was sure my mum and dad never "did it" when I was twelve or even fifteen, or at least I blotted the idea out of my mind.'

'I thought you were a virgin when we married? We both were!' said Polly, frowning.

'Yes, yes, we were. I was alluding to my first sexual experience and that fell a lot short of actually, well, you know, "doing it".'

'I think you would have bored those boys to death,' said Polly, snatching up her quilt. 'I don't know what's come over you. Honestly, Timothy. And you would have embarrassed them, too.' She got up from her chair and went over to the door. 'And please don't tell me about your first sexual "experience". I can think of nothing more boring. Now, I'm going to make a cup of tea.' She slid wraithlike from the room, her usual tactic when a subject she disapproved of was about to be discussed.

Timothy sat for a moment in silence and then re-lit his cigar, which had burned unevenly and then gone out. The sense of anticipation was palpable – the phrase he had used earlier when talking to his nephew resonated inside his head, triggering a kaleidoscope of memories so vivid he could almost taste, smell and touch them.

It was in 1949 when he was barely fourteen and his good friend Smudger had promised him a cornucopia of such delights to be savoured on the following Saturday that he actually trembled with excitement. Now Smudger, whose proper name was Sidney, was also fourteen but wise beyond his years and lived with his parents in a tiny flat in the Lewis Trust Buildings at Walham Green. This great slab of what today would be called social housing was home to Fulham's urban poor, Smudger's parents among them.

Both Timothy and Smudger were pupils at the Sloane Grammar School in Chelsea, having passed the notorious eleven-plus entrance examination. While Timothy was an average pupil, with little interest in things academic, Smudger, the cockney bantam, was possessed of a fierce native intelligence and a mind so enquiring as to be almost obsessive. Scarcely an hour passed without Smudger asking questions, begging for information, challenging his teachers and generally demanding that he be told the secrets of life, love and the universe.

This fantastic zest for knowledge led quite naturally to Smudger frequenting Fulham Library every single day after school. Timothy, although reluctant to join him at first, soon succumbed to Smudger's persuasive powers and the pair of them became fixtures in the library, where literature of varied quality was consumed, to the benign amusement of the librarian – a lady with teeth like a horse but a kindly smile.

It was on the Wednesday before the fateful Saturday that Smudger revealed to Timothy his plan for both of them to lose their virginity in the Lewis Trust Buildings, together with two other boys and three girls. That the sexes didn't quite match in numbers did nothing to quell Timothy's sense of awe at his cockney chum's organisational skills and persuasive techniques. The two other lads, Dennis and Jack, were also fourteen but they, unlike Timothy and Smudger, were from a secondary modern school, where their academic achievements were nugatory.

The three girls, Pat, Rita and June, were, Smudger solemnly claimed, all sixteen. Ye Gods! the prospect of older women had set Timothy's pulses racing, not least because he had long lusted after the exquisite June, she of the flaxen hair, white ankle socks and navy blue gymslip.

'It's all fixed,' Smudger had explained as he and Timothy sat in Fulham Library. 'Mum and Dad are going to the pub. Usual time. They'll be there till ten. Always are. I gave them my paper-round money to spend cos it's Mum's birthday on Saturday. It was my present, you see, so they'll be in The Swan till closing time. And the girls, well, they can't wait to come to the party. I'm getting some brown ale in. Yeah. How about that, Timothy? And some orange juice for the girls. And fags, too. I got two packets of Player's Navy Cut under my bed. And not only that –'

At this point, Timothy had raised a hand to stop Smudger's flow. 'The girls, Smudger, I mean do they know, are they, you know, I mean, do they ...?'

Smudger grinned at his chum's embarrassment. 'Don't worry about that,' he said with emphasis. 'We shall seduce them.'

These words emanating from a 14 year old struck Timothy like a hammer blow. 'What?' he said feebly.

'Yes,' continued Smudger in a conversational tone, 'you know, just like Tarzan and Jane in *Tarzan of the Apes*.'

Now this book by Edgar Rice Burroughs, the first in the Tarzan series, had been read and reread in the Fulham library by both boys until the pages were imprinted with their thumb marks and certain pages folded down at the corner.

'Oh yes,' said Timothy. And one particular passage came back to him, the one where the Ape Man, after swinging through the trees and rescuing Jane Porter, turned to her and "did what any red-blooded male would do, by covering her upturned face with burning kisses". Well, there you have it. Simple, really.

'Course you know he was really a posh lord,' said Smudger. 'Seduction and stuff came natural to him.'

'Yes,' said Timothy, 'Lord Greystoke. Yeah, but it doesn't tell how ... how he, you know.'

'Look, Timothy,' said Smudger impatiently, 'you just follow your instinct, one thing after another.'

'But s'pose the girls don't want their upturned faces covered with burning kisses?'

'Don't be silly,' said Smudger, 'course they will. Stands to reason. Look, they're getting a choice of orange juice plus, and here's the thing, Timothy, I got some records, really great. Stan Kenton's *Peanut Vendor*, fantastic, and Frankie Laine's *Jezebel* and Johnny Ray's *Cry!*'

'Where did you get those?' said Timothy, impressed.

'Borrowed them. Bloke next door. He's got a fantastic collection. He lent me his gramophone, too. It's all going to be great. I mean, Stan Kenton, that trumpet, he plays it ... well, it's fantastic. And Johnny Ray, wow! The girls will go nuts.'

Timothy computed this information silently. Brown ale. Cigarettes. Orange juice. Jazz records. An amazing package to be sure, but it still didn't provide chapter and verse about the actual mechanics of seduction. After the burning-kisses routine on the upturned faces of the girls, assuming they allowed such a liberty in the first place, what was the next step? He wracked his brains and then, like a light going on in his head, he recalled a passage from a book by Hank Jansen. A book not to be found in the Fulham library but one obtained from a barrow boy in the North End Road who specialised in what Timothy's parents described as "mucky literature".

Hank Jansen's paperbacks were written in that wisecracking Raymond Chandler style, often set in Los Angeles, where blonde women always seemed to be pouting at tough policemen who kept their hats on in the house. It seemed that the successful seducer would, after overwhelming the object of his affections with the statutory burning kisses, slide his hand over a heaving bosom. Timothy found some difficulty in imagining a woman's bosom actually heaving, but you had to assume that Hank Jansen knew what he was talking about.

At this stage of the proceedings, it seemed, almost miraculously half an inch of the girl's thigh would appear above her stocking top and then, as the seducer's hand slid from heaving bosom to this new area, the girl would release a choking cry and "cling to her man like a limpet". What followed, even Hank Jansen skated over. But whatever it was, it left the girl "heavy-eyed and gasping". The seducer, it seemed, then lit a cigarette and exhaled twin jets of smoke from his nostrils.

So that was it. Just follow the formula. Easy …?

The front cover of most of Hank Jansen's paperbacks featured stage three of the proceedings just described. The girl, always a blonde, usually wearing a skintight shirt or blouse, was clearly in the actual process of "clinging to her man like a limpet" and her long-lashed eyes had been painted to convey a certain "heaviness". (These paperback covers were always painted.)

The man in the illustration was square-jawed, suited and often wearing a small, rather silly hat. He, too, was on the very cusp of oscillation, his grim lips inches away from the pouting scarlet mouth. While one of his arms was around the girl's waist, the other was reaching down towards, yes, you've guessed it, the 2 inches of exposed lady-flesh above the stocking top.

Having studied countless lurid book covers featuring an almost identical disposition of participants, Timothy nonetheless couldn't recall a single one that featured the sliding-of-the-hand-over-the-heaving-bosom manoeuvre. Still, he reckoned he had enough acquired knowledge to get him started, plus the fact that all his silky seductive moves would be accompanied by either Stan Kenton's piercing trumpet blast, Frankie Laine's bellowing rendition of *Jezebel* or Johnny Ray's high-pitched wailing of the hit number Cry. That was not all. There were also to be untipped cigarettes and, be still my beating heart, brown ale. In bottles. Watneys Best, to be sure. Oh yes, and orange juice just in case.

However, the memories and the heightened sense of anticipation came flooding back to Timothy now after so many years.

The fatal Saturday finally arrived and after buttered crumpets and a boiled egg for tea, Timothy casually informed his parents he was going round to Smudger's place at "The Buildings" to listen to some jazz records. His parents didn't really approve of their son going to the Lewis Trust Buildings; it was rather common in their view and full of rough types. The fact that Timothy's parents were only fractionally less rough than the denizens of The Buildings and their own tiny flat just one block away was an irony lost entirely on both – and Timothy.

In a freshly pressed white shirt, long grey trousers and black plimsolls, Timothy surveyed his reflection in the hall mirror before leaving home. His acne had faded a little and his dark hair was plastered over his skull with a little parting on the left side. He looked well cool – or just warm, perhaps.

As he walked the half mile to the Lewis Trust Buildings, he was conscious of a growing tension in his stomach. He hoped it would fade once he was in Smudger's flat – a glass of Watneys might well settle it.

The flat, venue for the planned illicit debauch, was up a flight of stone steps to the first floor of the buildings. The communal light bulbs that had been designed to illuminate the gloomy, windowless stairwells had long been vandalised and the ascent to Smudger's place was conducted in total darkness.

On reaching the green front door of number 2A, Timothy rapped on it with his knuckle. It opened and framed in the aperture was the ubiquitous Smudger, brown ale bottle in one hand. A small, slight boy but with bright, shining eyes and a riot of curls that were the envy of all the girls in the vicinity, little Smudger was something of a teenage heart-throb with all the swagger and cockney confidence that he and all the other street urchins seemed to acquire naturally.

Timothy was the last to arrive, the six other youngsters spread around the minuscule sitting room of the flat. There was Dennis, a gangling, oafish lad with the personality of a week-old kipper. His dad was a local dustman. He sat silently in the corner of the room. Then there was Jack, a dusky boy whose mother was Jamaican and his father Irish. He was a well-built muscular lad with a reputation as a good swimmer and ping-pong player.

The three girls sat together, crushed up against each other on the sagging sofa which dominated the room. June, Timothy's forlorn hope, was a tall, thin girl with flaxen pigtails and a slight cast in one eye, but she exuded confidence and a certain innocent sexuality.

Rita was the senior girl in attendance, nearly seventeen and already the proud possessor of a womanly bust and full, pouting lips; indeed lips that the artist who illustrated Hank Jansen's paperbacks would have been pleased to copy.

Finally Pat, a girl Timothy had never met before. She was petite and fresh-faced, with auburn curls and very white teeth with a cute gap in the front row.

All the girls were wearing frocks and sandals. Of white ankle socks there was no sign. Timothy took this as a very encouraging omen. Frocks were much prettier than gym slips and you could see the girls' knees. Rita and June were holding beakers of brown ale, but Pat nursed a glass of orange juice. Smudger, as master of ceremonies, got things going by placing a Stan Kenton record on the gramophone, ostentatiously lighting a cigarette.

'Fag, anyone?' he offered suavely.

The girls declined but Dennis, Jack and Timothy quickly accepted, lit up and proceeded to blow smoke in a clumsy attempt to appear sophisticated, even dangerous. Smudger sat on the arm of the sofa and patted Rita on the shoulder.

'Wanna dance?' he said.

Rita, impervious, just grimaced. 'Can't dance to this,' she said.

Indeed, Stan Kenton's frenetic rhythms didn't suggest any close-contact smooching.

Then, displaying the elan for which he was famous, Smudger took June by the hand and led her out of the sitting room and into his small bedroom that was situated by the kitchen.

Rita shrugged and crossed her bare legs with a flourish. This galvanised Jack into action and he sat himself down on the sofa, slipped his arm around Rita's meaty shoulders and began kissing her on the mouth with clumsy urgency. She offered neither resistance nor encouragement but sat there passively while Jack gave it his best shot. The speed at which this had happened seemed to unnerve Dennis, who leapt up and went to the bathroom, slamming the door behind him.

Timothy suddenly felt vulnerable. Smudger was probably already at stage two in the bedroom with the lovely June, Jack was eating fat Rita's face, Dennis was locked in the lavatory from which strange noises were emanating and little Pat, cute little Pat with the pretty frock and shiny pink legs, was sitting on the sofa in front of him. Timothy pushed the cigarette to the corner of his mouth with his tongue and made a hesitant step towards her. Her eyes met his and she smiled a smile that lit up the room. God she was pretty. Her face was small and triangular and her auburn curls reached to her shoulder.

Almost in a daze, Timothy realised that the surge of emotion that overwhelmed him was not sexual. There was no stirring in his adolescent loins but something else, something more profound. At that moment, he wanted to kiss those rosebud lips, to absorb them into his own, to taste and feel their softness. Stan Kenton's musical climax was at hand, the strings and brass of his band sugaring the atmosphere with a pounding, all-enveloping rhythm.

Pat, who was seated on the sofa, inched away from the lascivious Jack and his coolly indifferent partner, uncrossed her neat ankles and stood up as if to greet in an old-fashioned, rather formal way. Then she smiled a brilliant 100-watt smile and her teeth were so white and shiny.

'You can't kiss me with a fag in your mouth,' she said and her accent was pure Eliza Doolittle before the Professor Higgins makeover.

Timothy snatched the recalcitrant cigarette from his lips. Was he actually taking the lead in this momentous, unfolding drama?

Awkwardly, breathlessly, Timothy took a further pace towards her. But he found his arms hanging loosely at his sides, his cheeks burning with what could have been either embarrassment or excitement. My God, the sophistication of this 16 year old was turning him to jelly.

Now inches from her face, Timothy leaned even closer. He could smell the peppermint on her breath, see the glistening shine of her exquisite brown eyes. This was it, then. Stage one. The covering-of-her-upturned-face-with-burning-kisses routine, Tarzan-style. Their lips touched. Oh so softly. Feather light, gossamer to gossamer.

Then a door slammed in the corner of the room and Smudger appeared, shirt untucked, cigarette in one hand and a bottle of Watneys brown in the other.

'June's got a bit of a headache,' said Smudger. 'Gotta turn the music down and yeah, gotta turn the lights down, too. Hey, look at Jack, blimey.'

Jack removed his lips from Rita's mouth and turned towards Smudger. 'What's wrong?' he said.

'Nothing,' said Smudger defensively. 'I'll just turn out the lights. Gotta candle in the kitchen. I'll put it in a beer bottle.'

'Very romantic,' murmured Pat, who was still close to Timothy although the kiss had been aborted.

The magic of the moment, too, had evaporated and Jack, turning back to the inert bulk that was Rita, attempted to clasp his mouth over hers, but she turned her head. Far from accepting this as a rejection, Jack placed a hand over Rita's right breast and squeezed it like a motor horn. Rita yelped and pushed his hand away, so Jack slid it onto her bare pink thigh.

At this moment, Smudger reappeared from the kitchen with a lighted candle stuck in the neck of a beer bottle and he went over to the brass light switch by the sitting-room door. "Click" and the place was plunged into darkness, save for the feeble gleam of candlelight.

June's silhouette appeared behind Smudger in the doorway to the bedroom they had recently occupied and although her face was in shadow, her flaxen hair appeared to be in a state of disarray.

The door to the bathroom suddenly swung open and a shaft of light struck the room followed by Dennis, whose face appeared to be as white as chalk.

'I been sick,' he said, to nobody in particular, and seized a bottle of beer that stood on a table by the bathroom door.

The Stan Kenton record completed its climax with a swirl of brass and the gramophone needle continued to scrape the edge of the record with a sound like a tiny saw attacking a plank of wood. Smudger, ever vigilant as master of ceremonies, went across and by the guttering candlelight, changed the record to one by Frankie Laine, the barrel-chested songster from America whose top notes, it was claimed, could shatter fine porcelain. As the first notes of *Jezebel*, his number-one hit, filled the room, Timothy was conscious of Pat moving closer to him. Then he felt her lips touch his again and instinctively, he reached out and embraced her. They stood there for a long moment, Timothy dizzy with pleasure as he savoured the exquisite chaste kiss and Pat's fresh, clean smell.

In the darkness behind, he heard the sound of clothing being torn and Rita's piercing cry of, 'Oi! Steady!' Then he felt a tap on his shoulder and turned reluctantly away from little Pat to see Smudger standing there at his side.

'Ere,' said Smudger in a hoarse whisper, 'you'd better 'ave one of these.'

Timothy looked down at Smudger's outstretched hand, but in the gloom couldn't make out what he was holding.

'What is it?' said Timothy, also in a whisper.

'Durex,' said Smudger. 'I only got two. Jack'll 'ave to go without.'

Now Timothy, who had never seen a contraceptive in his life, was spiked with a surge of fear. 'What!' he said.

'Go on, take it,' hissed Smudger. 'And get Pat in the other bedroom. Don't take off the covers. Do it on top of the bed. Know wot I mean?'

Timothy didn't have a clue what he meant, but sweating with terror, he took the small packet from Smudger's paw and pocketed it.

Smudger then moved away towards the bedroom door where the dishevelled, smiling June was waiting.

'Ain't got no aspirin,' said Smudger, gently pushing June back into the bedroom.

As he closed the door behind them, Timothy heard June give a gurgling laugh. Her headache apparently had not compromised her sense of humour.

Dennis was upending a bottle of brown ale into his mouth and the shaft of light from the bathroom showed beer running down his chin.

Jack and Rita still grappled on the sofa, but Jack's seduction technique seemed to be paying off because the girl now lay prone with Jack on top of her, both still clothed; although what looked like a fragment of lacy cotton hung over the arm of the sofa.

Frankie Laine was in full voice:

If ever the devil was born
Without a pair of horns,
It was you-o-ou, Jezebel,
It was you-ooo!

Pat's hand slid into Timothy's as she led him across the room towards the other bedroom. Ye Gods! Smudger's parents' bedroom! A sense of unreality overwhelmed Timothy. Here was this exquisite creature leading him across the room towards the holy of holies, the parents' bedroom. Was he destined to lose his pathetic virginity in such a place, while its true occupants sat innocently in the public bar of The Swan quaffing Guinness and sweet sherry with impunity?

The parents' bedroom, a tiny square room, was illuminated by a single bedside lamp with a fringed pink shade. The light it cast was, on the whole, suggestively romantic.

Pat led Timothy to the double bed and then sat on it, her knees together and her hands in her lap.

'Have you ever done it?' she said suddenly. 'You know, properly?'

Timothy gulped. This was a serious test. He tried a debonair smile but it froze on his face. 'Well, you know –'

'You haven't, have you?' said Pat softly.

Timothy shook his head.

'Me neither,' said Pat. 'Nearly did once. With Smudger.'

This was more information than Timothy required right now and he felt his cheeks glow with embarrassment and irritation.

'Well shouldn't you undress me?' said Pat coquettishly.

Timothy stumbled towards her and plucked at her cardigan.

She pushed his hand away and tutted. 'It's got buttons, silly,' she said and proceeded to undo them.

Timothy knelt at her feet and tried to embrace and kiss her, but she held him off.

'Shouldn't you undress, too?' she said.

Now totally confused, Timothy stood up, unfastened his belt and stepped out of his trousers. Pat removed her cardigan, unbuttoned her blouse and revealed a small lace-trimmed bra in pink and white. Then she lay back on the bed, her hair spilling out against the pillow, her frock having ridden up to reveal her slender thighs.

Trouserless but still in his vest, shirt, socks and plimsolls, Timothy knelt on the bed in a sort of hovering position, his hands placed either side of her head. He kissed her again, this time fiercely, and then kissed her chest on the little section that was exposed between the cups of the bra. Emboldened, he slid down until his face was touching her knees and on impulse, he gave each kneecap a lick.

Pat giggled and pushed him away. 'That tickles,' she said.

Inside Timothy's fevered brain, he tried to recall the various stages of seduction he had discussed at length with Smudger and the other lads. What stage was he at? Was it two? No, the girl was still wearing clothes. He slid his hands along her thighs until his fingers touched the elastic of her knickers. Pat grew rigid, her thighs tightly shut. Then a great clunking truth hit him like a sledgehammer: he could not proceed any further until he himself was "ready".

He reached down and touched himself through his Y-fronts. His manhood lay there like a limp noodle. This was going to be a disaster. He removed his pants and dropped them to the floor. Then he remembered what Smudger had pressed into his hand and grabbed his discarded trousers. He rummaged in the pocket until he located the small square envelope which contained ... whatever it contained.

Kneeling up on the bed, he peeled the flap of the envelope and removed a sticky roundel of thin rubber. What the hell's name was he supposed to do with that? He manipulated it until it had stretched out to what seemed an excessive length. Then, with trembling fingers, he tried to actually put it on his flaccid penis.

Of course it was impossible.

He tried again, forcing the end of his member into the open end of the rubber. It hung in a loop not unlike one of those wind socks at Croydon Airport on a calm day.

Pat, who was watching this performance, turned away and put her face in the pillow. Her frock had risen now to reveal a lot more of her legs.

Timothy, kneeling there with the wrinkled rubber dangling, suddenly felt a stirring in his loins. My God, this was it. It was, however, a slow business and Timothy tried to encourage it with his hand. A few more minutes, surely, and they'd be at it like proverbial rabbits.

Just as Timothy thought things were looking up at last, the room was flooded with light and Smudger's voice rang out with bell-like clarity.

'It's bloody ten o'clock and Mum and Dad will be on their way home.'

There followed a *Keystone Kops* scramble as Timothy recovered his trousers and Pat sat up, blushing and pulling her skirt down.

'Look,' said Smudger, 'I gotta hide the beer bottles under my bed. And empty the ashtrays. Hurry up, Timothy, for Gawd's sake.'

Outside in the sitting room, Dennis, Jack and Rita were plumping the sad little cushions on the sofa and feverishly flapping their hands in an attempt to disperse the cigarette smoke.

'You'd better all go,' said Smudger, panic in his voice. 'My dad will take a strap to me if he knows wot we've been up to.'

So the six guests, Timothy, Dennis, Jack, Rita, June and the exquisite Pat gathered their bits and pieces, handbags, raincoats, scarves and with brief farewells, fled from Smudger's flat and out into the cold concrete stairway that led down to the street.

As they spilled out onto the open concourse around the Lewis Trust Buildings, they almost collided with a middle-aged couple walking unsteadily towards the entrance to the flats. The man was a little bantam of a chap with a cloth cap and heavy workman's boots. The woman, who was taller, wore a headscarf and an overcoat with a fake fur collar.

Timothy sat at the window, gazing down at the Chelsea street. It was so long ago, yet the memories, the smells, the sounds, the tactile sensations, were still fresh.

Polly came back into the room carrying a tray of tea with teapot, cups and a plate of chocolate biscuits.

'You've been crying!' she said, looking intensely at her husband.

'Not at all,' said Timothy brusquely. 'Just something in my eye, grit or something. It's OK, though. It's gone.'

Polly poured the tea and handed a cup to Timothy. 'You know something, darling,' she said kindly, 'there's no fool like an old fool.'

Timothy nodded silently but thought, yes there is a fool like an old fool and that's a very young one.

Some Facts are Just Bizarre ...

At the Royal Hospital, Chelsea, home of the famous Chelsea Pensioners of which today there are about 400, there is an unusual statue in the area known as Figure Court. It is of King Charles II in the dress of a Roman emperor. In a nearby private house in Tite Street, the owner, an artist, has a small replica of this statue, but dressed as Elvis Presley.

The very first church to be built in Fulham was 857 years ago, in AD 1154.

During excavations in 1880, some foundations were discovered, including a stone attached to the shafting of a window frame. In the same year, All Saints Church was built, its architect being Arthur Blomfield, the son of the Bishop of London.

Today, in 2012, it retains its ancient tower, Kentish stone facade and fine battlements. The author was christened at All Saints Church in 1935.

War and Peace

The Victorian terraces of Waldemar Avenue run down to the busy junction with Fulham Road. Built by Cubit's in the early part of the twentieth century, they are deceptively spacious, consisting of three storeys with small walled gardens at the rear.

In an upper bedroom in a middle house along this terrace, a 16-year-old boy stirs in his sleep. He is strong-limbed and tall for his age. A fuzz of early beard growth decorates his cheeks and on the door of his bedroom hangs a coloured photograph of a lady called Pamela Green. She is quite naked but discreetly posed, her arms crossed over her loins and her glossy thighs closed.

The boy, who we shall call Benny, sits up, yawns, scratches his tousled mop of hair and prepares to meet the challenges of another day.

Chaum-ni, South Korea, 1951

On this bleak pass, fringed with boulders and shale, and in freezing, bone-chilling frost, an 18-year-old boy sits propped up against a tree stump. He is wearing a windproof jacket and forage cap provided by the American Army, even though he is a soldier in the British Infantry Regiment 1st Battalion, the Middlesex (the Diehards). He has only dozed overnight and his rifle is still held across his lap, the magazine fully loaded. Since the communists in North Korea had invaded the South, a United Nations force had been dispatched to expel them.

His battalion, including many national servicemen like him, are about to face a massive assault by the massed ranks of Chinese infantrymen.

The boy, whom we shall call David, feels his bowels churn with fear as his platoon sergeant calls his men to prepare to defend their position on the ridge. Half a mile away, in a forward position, a Middlesex patrol have reported a large Chinese troop movement clearly bent on recapturing the ridge at Chaum-ni, now occupied by the British and the Americans who earlier had seized it from the enemy.

Fulham

Benny, having completed his brief ablutions, dresses in cord slacks and a sleeveless cotton shirt with two breast pockets. It is his best shirt, one of just three he owns.

Downstairs, he hears the sounds and smells the aroma of breakfast being prepared by his mother: bacon, eggs, tea and toast. In the small kitchen of the house, his mother is indeed standing over a frying pan at the gas stove.

'What time is Reggie picking you up?' she says.

'About eight,' says Benny, pulling up a chair and sitting down at the kitchen table.

'Looking forward to it?' his mother asks.

Benny nods, already spooning cornflakes into his mouth. 'Yeah. Festival of Britain. *Daily Express* says it's really fantastic. That big Skylon thing, blimey, it's like the Eiffel Tower.

'Not quite,' smiles Mother and she loads a plate with two eggs and a rasher of bacon, thus completing the week's ration. 'There's so much to see there,' she says. 'The Dome of Discovery, pavilions, water splashes and so on. But be careful, there are pickpockets about.'

'Oh, I'll be all right, Mum,' says Benny. '*Daily Express* says it's the most wonderful thing since the Great Exhibition of 1851, exactly 100 years since.'

'Oh yes,' says Mother, 'today will be a great adventure.'

Chaum-ni, South Korea

David is lying flat on a muddy ridge and gazing down his rifle sights at the sloping ground just ahead of him. Already there is a whizz and whine of small arms' fire coming from a line of straggly shrub about 200 yards away.

His platoon sergeant, who is thirty, still has an unlit cigar stump in his mouth, which he chews rhythmically. Along the line, past twenty other riflemen, is the platoon commander, a 19-year-old second lieutenant, also a national serviceman. This is his first action also and in spite of being "in command", he looks to his more experienced sergeant for the odd hint of advice.

'Here the bastards come,' says the sergeant, spitting out the cigar stump.

Through his sights, David sees the straggly shrub suddenly part as if struck by a wave and from it bursts a line of Chinese soldiers, hundreds of them, three-deep but spreading into a wide arc and all running up the slope with their automatic weapons held low. There is a deafening burst of machine fire and the crack of rifle shot. Smoke billows up, obscuring David's view, and he cannot tell whether the firing is from his own troops or from the approaching Chinese. A gust of wind clears the smoke for an instant and less than 50 yards away, a bunch of Chinese soldiers are running full tilt towards the British line, firing from the hip.

Lead is striking the turf only feet from where David is lying and suddenly the soldier next to him emits thin shriek and half kneels. The front of his light khaki jacket shows a spreading stain of crimson and he falls forward onto his face.

David scrambles to his feet just as two tiny Chinese, both about 5 feet tall, rush towards him screaming. David struggles to fix his bayonet, but the sergeant yells, 'Shoot them!'

Fulham

Benny and his friend Reggie are on the top deck of a number 14 bus chuntering along the Fulham Road. Their plan is to get off at Piccadilly Circus and walk down the Haymarket, along the Strand, over Waterloo Bridge and onto the South Bank, where the Festival of Britain site is located.

Reggie produces a five-pack of Woodbines and the two boys light up, giggling.

'Let's live dangerously,' says Reggie and Benny nods vigorously in agreement.

'Yeah, why not?' he says. 'It's boring not to.'

Chaum-ni, South Korea

David feels the 4 inches of his bayonet sink into the little Chinese soldier's stomach and with a gasping cry, he falls over, blood spouting from his mouth and nose. The Chinese soldier, who in the brief seconds his face is exposed under his too-big forage cap looks about 15 years old, squeezes the trigger of his weapon. But it fires wildly, spraying bullets several feet wide of David.

His sergeant shoots the Chinese soldier in the face with his rifle, firing from the hip, and the youngster collapses onto the corpse of his comrade.

Waterloo Bridge, London

Benny and Reggie are halfway across Waterloo Bridge by now and the sun has come out from behind a row of scudding clouds.

'Look!' says Benny, pointing, 'see the Skylon.'

Reggie shields his eyes and follows the direction in which Benny is indicating. The slim steel edifice stands proud against the pale sky.

'My mum says it's a symbol of peace, now the war's over.'

'Yeah,' says Reggie, Woodbine hanging from his lip. 'Six years since we kicked old Adolf's bum.'

'There won't be no more war,' said Benny firmly.

'Don't know what you're talking about,' says Reggie. 'Communists, it's in the *Daily Mirror.*'

'Communists,' says Benny, 'they were on our side in the war, weren't they?'

Reggie shrugs. 'Yeah, but this thing is in Korea.'

'Where's Korea?' says Benny, who mostly reads the sports pages of the *Daily Express*, which has in fact reported the Korean conflict quite extensively.

'Out east,' says Benny. 'Out east, Korea is, I think.'

Chaum-ni, South Korea

The enemy, repulsed in their attempt to reclaim the ridge at Chaum-ni, lost forty-eight dead, who lay sprawled on the slopes, victims to the deadly rifle fire of the British Infantry. Many prisoners have been taken, many of them scarcely in their teens. Wiry, scared-looking Chinese boys.

David, who is unhurt, offers one of them a cigarette, which is accepted with a quivering hand.

David's sergeant is barking orders through the drifting smoke. Seven Middlesex soldiers have been slain. But the ridge has been held.

David's young platoon commander, a second lieutenant, walks towards him, revolver in hand. The sergeant grins. He knows the young officer hasn't fired it, but he has shown great courage in leading the resistance to the waves of charging Chinese soldiers.

'Organise the burial party,' says the officer.

The sergeant salutes smartly. 'Yes, sir,' he says, 'will do.'

South Bank, London

Benny and Reggie walk into the area in which the great Festival of Britain is taking place. It is something of a magic fairy land to the two lads. There are lots of people milling around and pretty girls in summer frocks, eating choc-ices. Benny drops his cigarette and crushes it under the heel of his sandal.

'That red-haired one, she's very pretty.'

Reggie nods; he feels like a child let loose in a sweet shop.

'And the blonde one. Blimey. Spoilt for choice. Better do the Festival first, though. Do all the rides and the Dome of Discovery. OK?'

'Yeah,' says Reggie, 'we can chat them up later.'

Chaum-ni, South Korea

David is bone-tired, emotionally and physically spent, but he is carrying out the most important part of his post-battle drill, cleaning his rifle. First, he pours boiling water down the barrel, which is scored with carbon. Then he takes from his pouch a small oil bottle, a length of cord and a patch of cloth, "a four-by-two", and proceeds, with trembling hands, to conduct a "pull-through", just as he was taught in his basic training.

An American airplane roars overhead and dips its wings. From behind a cloud, a weak sun has emerged. But overhead, circling, are big winged birds that to David's untrained eye look remarkably like vultures. But does Korea have vultures? he muses.

Smoke is drifting over the ridge and all around is a frenzy of activity as David completes his rifle cleaning. Maybe tonight, if things quieten, he will finish writing the letter to his parents in Waldemar Avenue in Fulham, but only if his hands stop shaking.

Here's a Couple of Things you Might not Know ...

According to popular tradition, the idea of setting up the Royal Hospital, Chelsea for old soldiers came from Charles II's mistress, Nell Gwyn, who was so moved by a wounded soldier hobbling up to her and begging for alms that she prevailed upon the King to establish at Chelsea a permanent home for military invalids.

The more realistic explanation, however, is that King Charles was inspired by the Hôtel des Invalides in Paris, founded by Louis XIV in 1670.

According to Francis Grose's *Provincial Glossary* published in 1789, Putney and Fulham got their place names according to vulgar "game-playing" between two sisters. These two (unnamed) females both built churches on each side of the Thames, but only had but one hammer between them. They interchanged it by tossing it across the river on command of the words, 'Put it nigh,' on the Surrey side of the water.

On the other shore, the Fulham side, the cry was, 'Heave it full home,' thus the two churches and the two villages were named Putnigh and Fullhome, which of course over centuries became Putney and Fulham.

Quite frankly, dear reader, if you believe that you'll believe anything, but it's a cute little fable, is it not? Either that or Francis Grose was a couple of sandwiches short of a picnic.

The Majesty of the Law

The police constable was of substantial girth, but his 16 stone was distributed fairly evenly over his 6-foot frame. His cheeks were pink from the fresh wind that blew off the Thames in Fulham's Bishop's Park and his size-11 boots, gleaming with a sergeant-major shine, crunched over the gravel surrounding the children's sandpit by the artificial paddling pool.

A knot of six boys, all about 14 years of age, were engaged in ferocious and bloody combat. One of them, the smallest, was cowering in the sand, while the other five rained kicks and punches at his head and body. Blood flowed from his mouth and nose as he tried to shield his face from the assault.

The constable reached out one ham-sized fist and seized one of the attackers by the scruff of the neck, lifting him clear off the ground. Then he spun him round and delivered a sharp smack across the lad's cheek. The other four drew back but made no attempt to run.

One of them, a burly fellow in a ragged T-shirt, made a threatening gesture with a clenched fist, but the constable grabbed him by the arm, pulled him towards the other lad and with a turn of speed and great dexterity, banged both their heads together. They both yelped with pain and the constable adjusted the chinstrap on his helmet before turning to the other three.

'Anybody else got any bright ideas?' he snapped.

The three stood sullenly around their fallen victim, eyes downcast.

The injured lad stood up and wiped his nose on his sleeve, leaving a smear of blood.

'You all right?' said the constable.

The boy nodded. 'Yeah, I'm OK.'

The constable gave a long sigh as one almost bored with the proceedings and turned back to the sheepish five. 'All right, then, what was all this nonsense about?'

No answer. Just a shuffling of feet and some exaggerated sniffing.

'Come on,' said the constable, 'talk to me. You, you little toerag, what's going on?' He pointed to the lad he had slapped. 'Why were you hitting this boy?'

After another silence, the tall lad rubbed his head. ''e called Jacob a Jew boy.'

'What?' said the constable.

''e called Jacob a Jew boy.'

The lad who had been the brunt of the assault suddenly grinned. 'Well 'e is, ain't 'e?' He pointed to the fourth lad, a slight fellow with a shock of dark, lustrous curls.

'So,' said the constable, 'the five of you attacked this lad because he called *you* Jewish? Is that right?'

The five nodded, including the Jewish lad.

'Do you know something?' the constable said, 'I'm ashamed of all of you. Ashamed of you. Do you hear? First of all, *you*,' he said to the boy who had been pummelled by the rest, 'why did you decide to insult this lad? You meant to insult him, didn't you?'

The lad wiped some more blood from his nose and shrugged. 'My dad says the Jews take all our money.'

'Oh he does, does he?' said the constable. 'Right, I'd like your name and address.'

The lad gave it and the constable wrote it in his handbook. 'Now you lot,' he said, addressing the five, 'what this boy said was not only wrong, but wicked. Do you hear? We've just fought a war against a bunch of Fascists who went about murdering all sorts of people, including Jewish people. And it was a just war, and we won it. But that doesn't mean because a stupid boy shouts a vile insult at another you should kick the living daylights out of him. I mean to say, you there,' he pointed at the tallest of the five, 'you've got ginger hair. How would you like it if some gang of lads gave you a pasting because he called you a ginger nut? Course you wouldn't. Now listen to me, all of you. First of all, *you* who called out that deliberate insult, apologise. Go on, say you're sorry. And shake hands.'

'What?' cried the lad. 'But they attacked me!'

'Apologise. Do it now.'

'Sorry,' said the lad in a low voice.

Jacob shrugged. 'OK,' he said.

'Now shake Jacob's hand,' said the constable.

He did. Briefly.

'Now you lot, you're a bunch of bullies and that includes you, too, Jacob. You attack a lad, five to one, and you kick him when he's down. Disgusting behaviour. Now I could arrest the lot of you, but I'm not going to. However, if I see any of you again, in this park or anywhere else, either fighting or yelling vile insults, I will arrest you. And that would be unfortunate. Your mothers would be ashamed and, Jacob, yours would be especially. Joining in a mob attack. So now, you five apologise to this idiot and say you are sorry for attacking him. That means you do say sorry for the bullying. Go on; do it.'

The five shuffled towards the bloodstained lad and mumbled their apologies.

'Now bugger off,' said the constable, putting his notebook back in his pocket.

The six of them sloped off and to the constable's surprise, the lad who had been attacked walked alongside Jacob like they were old friends. The constable buttoned his pocket and sauntered off towards the exit from the park. The address he had been given was just five minutes away and the name was familiar. A family called Stanton lived there. Old man Stanton, the attacked boy's father, was a member of the British Union of Fascists, led by Oswald Mosley.

The constable reached the address in five minutes and rang the doorbell. No reply. Maybe Stanton was at work, at the Gas Board, as a fitter. He was about to turn away, when a window opened on the ground floor and Stanton, a shaven-headed 50 year old, looked out.

'Yeah,' he said belligerently.

The constable removed his helmet and rubbed his chin. 'This is not an official visit, Stanton, but your boy has been in a spot of bother. Nothing serious, you understand, just a scuffle. He insulted another lad, a Jewish lad from Park Mansions. You know, where all those rich Jews live who take your money.'

'What the fuck are you talking about?' said Stanton.

'I just called by to tell you that you are a piece of garbage, an anti-Semitic thug, but that is your choice, you bastard. What is unforgivable is that you have poisoned your own son's mind with your rubbish.'

'It's not against the law,' cried Stanton.

'It's against common decency,' said the constable, 'although I doubt you could even pronounce the word.'

'Just piss off, copper,' said Stanton.

'Oh, I will. Don't worry. But hear this, Stanton. I'm going to keep an eye on you, especially at your horrible rallies and meetings, and if you step out of line an inch, even half an inch, I'll nail you to the bloody wall. And give your lad a chance to grow up without that hatred in his heart; don't fill his mind with all your poisonous nonsense. We've just won a war against people who think like you. You disgust me.'

With that, the constable turned and walked away as Stanton gave a V-sign before slamming the window shut.

An hour or so later, the constable was walking slowly with measured tread along the Kilmaine Road, a slightly down-at-heel thoroughfare just off the busy Munster Road. As he reached the middle of the Kilmaine Road, he noticed a gate had been left open; one that gave onto a tiny patch of concrete at the top of some wooden stairs that led down to the small basement flat. He noticed that the window in the basement appeared to be hanging off its hinges and was swinging slightly in the light, muggy breeze.

Instinctively, the constable went through the gate and walked towards the wooden stairs. As he approached, a face appeared in the open window. A startled young face with a shock of straw-coloured hair. Then it disappeared, the window slamming shut with a sharp spluttering sound. The constable, who knew the layout of these houses, moved down the side alley that separated the house from its neighbour and arrived at the tiny back garden, no more than a scruffy patch of earth. He stood silently at the side and seconds later, there was another splintering crash and a young man, in what appeared to be overalls, burst out of the back door. He was carrying a hessian sack. The constable sighed. Why do they have to be so bloody obvious? he mused.

The burglar, sensing the constable's presence, stopped in his tracks and looked round.

'Aren't you Mrs Crabtree's lad?' the constable said.

A look of panic spread over the youth's face. 'You leave my mum out of this,' he blurted.

The constable nodded. 'Oh I intend to, lad. Make no mistake. If she knew what you were up to, it would break her heart. Now what have you got in that sack?'

'Stuff,' said the youth sullenly.

'What sort of stuff? Silver? I doubt it; there aren't many treasures in Kilmaine Road. Open it.'

The youth shook the contents of the sack onto the patch of earth and out tumbled some brass candlesticks, an old clock and a small brown wireless set.

'And how much did you think you'd get for that lot?'

The youth shrugged. 'A few quid. Down the New King's Road.'

I don't think so,' said the constable. 'If you want my opinion, young Crabtree, you'll never make it in the burglary lark. First of all, you haven't the faintest idea of what to nick. And second, you try to perform your work in broad daylight. Now I've got you red-handed. Do you think it was worth it? I mean a sack full of nothing in return for six months in clink.'

'I was going to give my mum the money.'

'Oh?' said the constable.

'Yeah, she owed on the rent. I ain't got none. Lost my job last week. Landlord says she owes three weeks. Police widow's pension ain't enough. So I thought –'

'Yes, I know your father was in the force. He will be turning in his grave, God bless him. Why didn't your mother contact Police Welfare?'

'Dunno.'

'Right, now listen, you put that stuff back in the house, put it back where you found it.'

'You gonna arrest me?'

'I will if you don't put that stuff back in the house.'

The youth went back to the door he had emerged from after replacing his loot in the sack. He re-emerged two minutes later, wiping his hands nervously on his overall trousers.

'You will now do two things, young Crabtree, and you will do them exactly as I tell you. First of all, you go home to your mother and tell her to phone this number. It's Police Welfare. Run by ex-coppers. She can phone from the public call box in the Fulham Road by Browns the tobacconist. Secondly, you will go to Sam's yard in the New King's Road; it's up by the old pottery works. Sam is looking for lads to work in his yard. I know this because he told me. Tell him I sent you. I think he'll give you a job. He's looking for somebody with a strong back. By the way, how much rent does your mother owe?'

The youth shrugged. 'Well, it's two quid a week. She owed three weeks.'

The constable put his hand inside his tunic and removed a flat purse. 'Here's two quid,' he said. 'Tell her to give it to the landlord and say the rest will follow. Who's your landlord?'

'Mr Hopkins.'

'Ah, old Hopkins,' said the constable. 'I know him. I'll have a word. Now just bugger off home and tomorrow, first thing, go to Sam's yard. I'll tell him to expect you.'

Chief Inspector Bernard Ferguson was five years younger than the constable but he had been educated at the Sloane Grammar School in Chelsea and had attended the Hendon Police College. His uniform with its silver badges of rank was immaculate, his shoes gleaming and his small, clipped moustache faintly reminiscent of Charlie Chaplin. His eyes were ice-cold, blue and penetrating. He sat behind a small desk on which there were two telephones, a large blotter, a jug of pens and a buff ring-folder.

'Well now, constable,' he said, tapping the folder with his fore knuckle. 'You've been in the force twenty-seven years, I see.'

'I have, sir. Yes.'

'And turned down the chance of promotion to station sergeant twice. Is that right?'

'Yes, sir.'

'Why was that, constable?'

'I'm a street copper, sir, like my dad before me. It's what I do. What I like. I'm not cut out to sit behind a desk shuffling paper.'

'A station sergeant's pay is a great deal more than that of a constable.'

'I know, sir. But I'm not in it for the money. I like the security. It's my life. The wages are OK. I don't want for much. My wife works part time at Shepherds in the Fulham Road. We manage.'

'Didn't think you could handle the responsibility or the pressure. Is that it, constable?'

'Pressure? I don't know what you mean, sir.'

'The pressure of responsibility. Of command.' The Chief Inspector pronounced the word "command" with some relish.

'There's a fair amount of that out on the street, sir. And responsibility.'

'Yes, yes, I know. Well, all right, you've made your point. However, looking over your record, as a "street cop" as you put it, your arrest record is pretty poor. In fact, you've hardly arrested anybody over the last few years. A few cautions, perhaps.'

'Lots of cautions, sir, not all of them recorded.'

'Didn't like the paperwork, eh?'

'Well yes, I mean no.'

'Our job, constable, yours and mine, is to prevent crime, catch criminals and wrongdoers and bring them to justice, is it not?'

'Yes, sir.'

'Well, I see precious little of it in your records, constable.'

'I disagree, sir,'

'You disagree? I've got your record in front of me. A complete dossier, if you like, of your work as a street copper.'

'Yes, I agree. Not everything I do is written down in a report. I work differently.'

'You certainly do,' said the Chief Inspector with a short laugh.

'Look, sir, I think my priority is preventing crime and gaining the confidence of the public I serve. I know most of the people in this manor; know their kids, too. They trust me. If I can turn a youngster away from crime without the hassle of an arrest, and the shame it will bring on his family, well I do.'

'Yes, that's perfectly clear. You also believe in summary justice, don't you? The short, sharp shock. A clip around the ear! Such antique clichés, constable. For God's sake, man, it's 1948! The police force has to accept the pace of change. To adapt. To gain the upper hand on a new, more sophisticated brand of criminals!'

'With respect, sir, I don't think criminals, petty criminals mostly, that's who I deal with in this manor, well I don't think they are any different from those around when I first joined the force.'

'Before the war?'

'Yes, sir. Before the war.'

'Another thing, constable, we've had a complaint that you have intimidated and harassed a local man without good reason. I hope intimidation is not part of your lexicon as street copper?'

'I assume the complaint was from Mr Ronnie Stanton?'

'It was. Why did you threaten him?'

'I warned him. That was all.'

'You warned him! Come off it, constable, you said you'd nail him to the bloody wall! You call that a warning?'

'The man's a fascist thug. He's trying to turn his son into one, too. So I warned him. Unofficially.'

The Chief Inspector turned to the station sergeant, a thin-looking officer with a bald head who had been standing silently throughout the interview. 'Fascist?' said the Chief Inspector.

The station sergeant nodded. 'Yes, sir. Stanton is a well-known rabble-rouser, one of Mosley's boys.'

The Chief Inspector sighed and tapped his fingers on the desk. 'Why didn't you tell me? Why isn't it in the report accompanying the complaint from Stanton?'

The sergeant shrugged and glanced at the constable. 'Didn't think it was relevant, sir.'

'Very well,' said the Chief Inspector, 'but it makes no odds. A citizen has made a complaint and I need some kind of answer. The Fulham nick is not the bloody Wild West, sergeant. So, constable, do you admit to threatening this person, Stanton?'

'No, sir. I was just warning him. In a friendly way. And I'd do it again if presented with the same situation.'

The Chief Inspector turned again to the station sergeant. 'Were there any witnesses to the incident, sergeant?'

The station sergeant rubbed his chin with his hand. 'I don't believe so, sir. That's right, isn't it, constable?'

The constable nodded. 'No witnesses, sir. To me, issuing an unofficial warning ...'

The Chief Inspector rearranged the file on his desk and put a pen back into the glass jar. After a long pause, he looked up at the constable and gave a theatrical sigh. 'Stone Age behaviour,' he mumbled.

'Sir?' said the constable.

'OK,' said the Chief Inspector, 'that will be all, constable.'

'Thank you, sir.'

When the constable had left the room, the Chief Inspector stood up and took his peak cap from the hat stand where it had been hanging. He put it on and adjusted it carefully.

'How old is he?' he said to the sergeant.

'Fifty-five, sir.'

'Can't we fix early retirement, is that possible?'

'I can look into it, sir. I think that would be a good solution, although I'll miss him. He's a good copper.'

'No room for sentiment, sergeant. We have discipline to maintain. I will not tolerate independent cowboys on this force. Speak to my assistant in Hammersmith. Look into the early retirement option. Let me know. Do it today.'

'Yes, sir.'

The Chief Inspector strode out of the office through a small squad room and into the street. A black Ford was waiting. He got in and slammed the door. As the car pulled away into the Fulham Road, it passed the constable on his bicycle. He was wearing a raincoat over his uniform and no helmet. He was cycling towards Putney, off duty now and going home. A cool wind had sprung up and a few drops of rain had started falling. A fairly typical finish to a July summer's day.

Pretty Well Everybody Over Fifty Knows This ...

The Rolling Stones spent the first year of their life hanging around Fulham and Chelsea, stealing food and rehearsing the obscure new music style, rock and roll.[2]

Mick Jagger, Brian Jones and Keith Richards lived at 102 Edith Grove in Fulham, just off the Fulham Road, in 1962. Scarcely a block away in Fernshaw Road, the author and his wife had their first flat in 1956 and in the upstairs flat dwelt Winifred Attwell, the famous jazz pianist.

In the early sixties, before fame swept them off to world stardom, the Rolling Stones – yes, them again – used to sit around tinkering with their guitars in the Wetherby Arms in the King's Road, Chelsea. According to Keith Richards, the boys would steal the pub's empties and then sell them back to them. They pulled in a couple of pence a bottle.

I'm not sure that today the lads would get much more than that on a returned bottle of 1960 Dom Perignon.

---

2. *Life: Keith Richards*, a rock and roll story by Keith Richards (London: Phoenix, 2011)

Jealousy, Revenge and Honour

Just behind Barons Court Underground Station is a maze of streets that lead with serpentine twists and turns to the Queens Club that later became the famous venue for the Stella Artois Annual Tennis Tournament.

On a fine May morning in 1963, however, just a block or two from Queens, a quite different form of competitive activity was taking place. In the gymnasium of a former school, two men faced each other, each holding a fencing foil. Both wore meshed metal face masks and thick white jackets buttoned up to their throats. Their hands were gloved with tough leather gauntlets, not unlike ski gloves.

The taller of the two men, who stood well over 6 feet 7 inches, was poised in the on-guard position, his right hand holding the foil extended towards the other man, his left hand curled behind his left hip. His front leg was flexed at the knee while his rear leg was straight, extended. The other man, who was poised in a similar stance, suddenly lowered his weapon and then removed his face mask. He was a foot shorter than his opponent and about twenty-five, sandy-haired, blue-eyed and sweating profusely.

He tossed the mask to one side and it clattered to the floor. Then he unbuttoned his jacket and removed it, revealing a slim, hairless torso, the belly flat and ridged with muscle.

'For real this time, professor,' he said in a soft London accent.

The giant opposite lowered his foil and from behind the mask came a throaty, guttural laugh. 'Surely you are not serious.'

The sandy-haired man nodded. 'Deadly,' he said. 'The final test of your training, professor; you always said that the ultimate judgement of a man's skill with the foil was to expose him to it as a real weapon, without that pathetic button on the tip, and without face and body protection.'

'Did I really say that?' said the fencing master.

The younger man nodded, beads of perspiration flying from his face. 'Yes. You told me that when you were a boy in Hungary, before the war, your own fencing master said much the same thing.'

'Well now,' said the fencing master, 'then it must be true!' He took off his mask and tossed it to one side. Then he removed his jacket and as he did so, steam rose from his massive barrel chest.

'And the foil button, too, professor.'

The fencing master gave a deep sigh and then smiled at his pupil. 'OK,' he said, 'button, too.'

He was unmasked as a handsome giant of a man with long sinewy arms and the tapering fingers of a pianist or violin player. While just forty-five, he was past his prime as a fencer, but his reputation as a fencing master was international.

After fleeing Hungary to escape the march of Nazism, he went at first to Hollywood, where he earned a living teaching film actors to fence. Then he came to London and set up his fencing school in Barons Court. His pupil today had made extraordinary progress in the year he had been under instruction. He had not only grown as a technically competent fencer, but his emotional and cerebral involvement was also exceptional.

Professor George Kanchek removed the rubber button from the tip of his foil and flexed the blade. 'Why are you doing this, Teddy? What are you trying to prove? That you can endure pain? Overcome fear? What?'

Teddy Peterson prised the button from the point of his foil and grinned, but it was a mirthless grin. 'Something like that,' he said.

'OK,' said Kanchek, 'but no head shots. I don't want to take your eye out.'

'Very well,' said Teddy. 'No head shots. Now can we get on?'

The two men faced each other and in the ancient tradition of the sport, saluted before both adopting the on-guard position. They extended their sword arms until both blades touched with a faint metallic kiss.

The early days of Teddy Peterson's marriage had been blissfully happy. He had met his wife, Sally, when he was still at school and they became engaged at eighteen and wed when both of them became twenty-one.

After leaving school with modest qualifications, Teddy had secured a position at one of the big five banks in Fulham Road and it was there, moving slowly up the promotion ladder, that he eventually, after spells in other London boroughs, returned to Fulham as Assistant Manager. While he, and indeed his parents, felt this was an enviable career with good, safe prospects, his wife was less enthusiastic.

On leaving her school, she had joined the staff of a glossy fashion magazine, initially as a junior, making tea and running errands. But she displayed a talent for writing and the creative arts associated with glamour publishing, and was soon working with photographers, fashion designers and advertising executives.

Where Teddy's work was routine and reasonably well remunerated, hers had become a kaleidoscope of studio shoots, expense-account lunches and trips to the Paris fashion shows, for which she was now earning double the salary of her husband. The latest cherry on the top of her cake was a smart, glossy red company car.

At first, Sally's supercharged career had been exciting for both of them and Teddy had been inordinately proud of his high-flying wife. They were buying a smart two-bedroom flat close to the river at Bishop's Park Mansions and their annual holiday was taken in the south of France. Sally would have liked to ski, but Teddy felt he couldn't get away in the new year period as it was a busy time for the bank.

One year, however, Sally's job took her to Zermatt on a fashion shoot and she managed a weekend's ski lesson after the work was completed. She came back full of enthusiasm about the thrill of skiing and the glamorous après-ski atmosphere in the hotels and nightclubs that nestled on the snowbound slopes in the shadow of the great Matterhorn.

After three years of marriage, they discussed the prospect of children. Teddy really fancied the idea of becoming a father, but was surprised at Sally's sharp rejection of the prospect of motherhood.

'Honestly, Teddy,' she had said, 'I'm just not the maternal type. The idea of sitting at home surrounded by screaming kids has zero appeal. Anyway, we can't afford it.'

So they soldiered on, childless, with Teddy quite content to confine his leisure pursuits to a little golf and walks along the riverbank on the Thames. 'So suburban,' Sally had moaned, refusing to join Teddy on the golf course. Her choice of leisure activity was tennis and now of course the ski slopes of Austria, Switzerland and Italy.

What at first was a mild difference of opinion about how they should spend their off-duty hours became a bone of contention between them. It spilled over to their differing tastes in music, restaurants and what actually constituted "having a good time". How they dressed also became a source of friction, as Sally moaned about Teddy being just another "suit".

He, in turn, was just a touch apprehensive about her penchant for very short skirts which displayed her long legs to great advantage. She also spent a great deal of money on clothes, paying more for a pair of shoes than Teddy paid for his modest two-piece suit. At lot of time was spent in the hairdressers, too. Teddy simply had a haircut, a short back and sides at the local Sweeney Todd. She languished in Mayfair salons for styling, colouring and what Teddy called "general poncing-up".

After one particularly bruising row, Teddy had accused her of living a "fantasy life" and she, in turn, had suggested he was heading in the direction of becoming a middle-aged bore.

'Why don't you take up an interesting hobby?' she said not unkindly after they had made up for the row in bed. 'You know, Teddy, golf is so predictable; it's so bank managerism.'

'Well yeah,' Teddy had said, relaxed now and in a post-coital glow. 'But you see, Sally, I am a bank manager.'

'Assistant,' said Sally and she kissed him.

'OK, OK,' he said, 'what sort of hobby would you like me to take up? I'll even go skiing with you next year if you like.'

'Well that's great,' she said, 'but that's just once every twelve months. I'm thinking of something you could do regularly, something glamorous.'

'Something glamorous,' said Teddy, 'like what?'

'Well, we did a photo shoot on the magazine recently at a fencing club in London; a bunch of actors posing as Errol Flynn, that sort of stuff. It was a fashion shoot. But wow! it's a sexy-looking sport.'

'Sexy?' said Teddy. 'Another of your buzzwords. I thought you wanted me to do something glamorous.'

'Oh, don't nit-pick,' said Sally, 'looks fun.'

Teddy sat up and rested his chin on his knees. 'OK,' he said, 'I'll do it. I'll join a fencing club. How about that?'

Sally hugged him and gave a whoop of joy. 'Teddy, that will be great. I'm sure you'll love it.'

'Will you join, too?' said Teddy.

'Darling, I've got my tennis,' she said. 'No, fencing is just for you – you could become the fourth Musketeer!'

*   *   *

And so Teddy joined the fencing club and was taken under the wing of Professor George Kanchek, in a converted schoolhouse in Barons Court. From the moment he picked up a foil, he knew this was the sport for him. It had everything, tradition, vigorous physical exercise, mental discipline, even glamour.

Professor Kanchek explained during Teddy's first half-dozen lessons that although swordplay in the modern world was now obsolete, practising the art was a path to self-knowledge as well as a way of maintaining the peak of physical excellence. He further explained that a fencing bout between men of honour under the direction of a master inspired by the same feelings was a diversion proper to good taste and fine breeding.

'Hold the foil as you would a live bird,' Kanchek had said. 'Not so loosely as to allow it to fly away, but not so tight as to kill it! Parry, engage, break, feint, avoid elaborate strokes, no showing off. Discipline, order, pace, speed.'

Professor Kanchek was ruthless in his method of instruction, making Teddy practise and repractise every single fencing stroke, the defensive moves and the myriad thrusts associated with attack. He was given "homework" which required him to practise certain moves in front of a mirror at his flat in Bishop's Park Mansions.

Sally, for her part, seemed to bask in the reflected glory of her husband being involved in such a "glamorous" sport. She told all her work colleagues about Teddy's prowess at the fencing club and they, being hyper-conscious of what was "cool and trenof the cocktail parties thrown by the glossy magazine on which she worked.

His new hobby, it seemed, had elevated and consolidated their married social life into dizzy heights hitherto unimagined. At the party where gorgeous girls and excruciatingly fashionable young men assembled like human peacocks at feeding time, Teddy was accepted, to Sally's delight, not as a dull number cruncher in a suit but as a dashing, even dangerous fellow on the very cusp of what now passed as "swinging London".

Teddy was deeply flattered to find himself surrounded by some of Sally's work colleagues, who listened to him explaining the mysteries and psychology of the fencing art. 'Fencing is more than mere sport,' he had explained. 'It is a precise mathematical science. It is a tradition that with a foil in your hand, you can feel equal or superior to any man in the world.'

'Unless he's got a gun!' said an advertising man, blowing smoke from his black Sobranie.

'The gun,' said Teddy sternly, 'is not a weapon. It is an impertinence. If two men are to kill each other, they should do so face-to-face, not from a distance like cheap criminals.' He was paraphrasing a passage from an extraordinary novel that Professor Kanchek had recommended, *El Maestro de Esgrima* by Arturo Pérez-Reverte, but the assembled throng were not to know this.

Sally was making progress in her career with an increase in benefits, which included an even glossier Italian car and signing accounts at some of London's top restaurants.

Teddy ploughed on at the bank, but they were no longer living such obviously separate lives and Sally had persuaded him to buy his suits from Huntsman in Savile Row and occasionally to accompany her to Annabel's nightclub in Berkeley Square.

Teddy's progress as a fencer was proving to be remarkable and he was now visiting the club two or three times a week. He had quickly conquered some of the most subtle and complicated moves and was pushing himself both physically and mentally to the limit.

Professor Kanchek invited fencers from other clubs for friendly bouts and watched with considerable pride as Teddy, only six months into the art, saw off much more experienced fencers.

But the lessons continued; nothing less than perfection was accepted by the professor.

On the fencing master's forty-fifth birthday, he threw a cocktail party for his friends, his pupils and a handful of Hungarian émigrés, at the club. Trestle tables were laid out and loaded with food and wine and a small jazz band played throughout the proceedings.

Among the guests were some of Professor Kanchek's other "star" pupils, including a Member of Parliament and a well-known actor. Teddy took Sally along and she was suitably impressed.

The professor, towering above his guests in a white suit, greeted them formally, even kissing Sally's hand in the style of an old Hungarian nobleman.

Just before the party ended, a late arrival was the Hungarian Ambassador to the Court of St James who, it turned out, was an old friend of the professor.

'I should have brought the magazine photographer,' said Sally. 'This party would have made a great picture feature.

A couple of months later, Teddy was promoted to Manager of his branch, much to Sally's delight, and she, too, was moving inexorably up the career ladder, now writing a solo feature article each month for one of her company's fashion magazines.

It was about this time that Teddy noticed a subtle change in Sally's behaviour. She was busier than ever, of course, but she seemed a touch distant in the evenings at home when both of them had returned from work. There were increasing trips to Europe, Paris, Rome and Berlin, and sometimes whole weekends were spent on assignments in England and abroad.

One evening, he was sipping coffee in their sitting room after dinner when he noticed something about Sally's body language. The way she sat. The odd way she curled her legs up on the sofa. These were subtle changes that intrigued Teddy. Their sex life had reached a plateau, too. They made love less frequently and when they did, it was short, almost mechanical business.

As he watched her, relaxed on the sofa, her eyes had a faraway, distant quality. It was almost as if she were sitting in the room alone.

A month later, Teddy joined Professor Kanchek's chosen team of fencers to fly to Berlin and engage in competition with a highly regarded German fencing team. The club in Potsdam was in an old barracks, which to Teddy looked suspiciously like an ex-Nazi training camp. It had cathedral ceilings and iron-barred Gothic windows and the L-shaped buildings overlooked a vast parade ground of beaten gravel. Empty flagpoles stood sentiment at one end of the parade ground and it was not difficult to imagine a black-and-red swastika flag snapping in the breeze way back in the forties.

Teddy was matched in the first bout with a tall blonde Hanoverian who was about the same age and height. He was very fast and used his foil in the classic style, forcing Teddy onto the back foot and making him parry his thrusts with that section of the blade nearest the hilt, which had a cramping effect on Teddy's movements. As he was driven back, he tried to remember everything Professor Kanchek had taught him. Tierce. Parry in tierce. Thrust in tierce over the arm. Low quarte. Semicircular parry, thrust and quarte. Lunge in seconde. Their blades rang out like tiny bells as they clashed, the German growing more aggressive with every stroke.

Eventually, the overconfident Hanoverian lowered his wrist an inch and his shoulder and the top of his chest presented a brief window of a target.

Using his forearm and wrist in a circular movement of great speed, Teddy disarmed his opponent and sent his foil clattering across the floor. His point reached high up on the Hanoverian's breast and as he thrust it home against the man's thick tunic, the blade of his foil bent in a shallow "U" shape.

In further bouts later the same day, Teddy remained unbeaten, to Kanchek's pride and delight.

Over dinner, as guests of their German opponents that evening, Teddy was seated next to the young Hanoverian he had defeated in the first bout who spoke good English, albeit with a strong German accent. The conversation over excellent food and wine ranged from the art of fencing to politics and philosophy.

The Hanoverian, whose name was Karl, revealed that he was the descendant of a military family who in the nineteenth century had fought with the British as part of George III's King's German Legion in the Peninsular War.

'Even your Duke of Wellington,' said Karl, 'described our regiments as the finest fighting men! We had our code of behaviour,' he continued, 'that meant outside of war, we could not kill a man unless it was to avenge a slur on our honour.'

'And what would constitute a slur on your honour?' asked Teddy, amused at the young Hanoverian's intensity.

Karl shrugged and took a sip of wine. 'Well, many things,' he said. 'If one's woman is unfaithful, then, well, killing becomes judicial!'

'What? You'd kill your wife or girlfriend?' said Teddy.

Karl shook his head vigorously. 'No, no, not the woman but the man who besmirched her and thus tainted your honour.'

Teddy laughed. 'Would you do that?' he asked.

Karl nodded again and took a huge gulp of wine. 'For sure I would and hang the consequences. It is my code!'

The dinner ended with brief speeches from the German fencing master and a reply from Professor Kanchek and then, full of rich meat and German wine, the parties rose from the table and headed for bed.

Back in Fulham, Teddy continued his three-times-a-week visits to the fencing club. Professor Kanchek now regarded him as his number-one star pupil and he was always included in the professor's team when they had friendly bouts with other clubs.

Sally was busier than ever, having been tasked with opening offices for the magazine on which she worked in New York and Paris.

Life was comfortable, even luxurious, but Teddy had a growing sense of unease, of separateness from his wife. There were no rows – their relationship, though distant, was perfectly tranquil. Quite why Teddy came to the conclusion that Sally was having an affair, he couldn't quite fathom. Maybe it was a combination of factors. Her faint aloofness, her work obsession, the increase in the purchase of rather sexy underwear, the twice-weekly visits to the hairdresser, the regular massage sessions at her "ladies only" club in Covent Garden and her frequent references to the magazine's new "star" photographer, whose talent was described as "awesome" and his personality "testosterone-charged".

Teddy's sense of apprehension increased as the weeks went by. His work at the bank had suddenly accelerated, too, and he would arrive home exhausted and too tired to enjoy a relaxed dinner with Sally, even through they now had an Italian woman who came in to cook each evening.

Then came the magazine's annual Christmas party, to which Teddy was invited, giving him a brief sense of relief that his fears about Sally were unfounded. Until, that is, he actually arrived at the party, which took place at Claridges, one of London's most elegant and exclusive hotels.

Sally introduced him to a whole host of magazine executives, many of whom Teddy thought were quite shallow and self-obsessed. They were all exquisitely dressed and carried about them a whiff of either aftershave lotion or in the case of the women, fragrant notes of Estée Lauder or Chanel.

Then Sally's "star" photographer strolled over to where Teddy was standing nursing a glass of champagne and extended his hand.

'I'm Rupert,' he said in what Teddy later interpreted as a faintly mocking tone.

Rupert was about 6 feet tall, just twenty and built like Michelangelo's David. He wore a denim shirt unbuttoned to the navel, exposing a set of bronzed pectoral muscles on which nestled a gold crucifix on a thick gold chain. His denim jeans were so tight they clung to his snake hips like wet wallpaper, revealing a provocatively large bulge in the crotch. His handshake was firm and Teddy could feel the pressure from the fat signet ring he wore on his middle finger.

Sally fluttered over in gushing mode. 'I see you've met Rupert,' she said, kissing the young man on his tanned, stubbled cheek.

He responded by slipping his arm around her waist in a proprietorial manner and smiling, to reveal more white teeth than seemed entirely necessary.

It was at that precise moment as Rupert's gleaming bicep flexed while his arm made the journey around his wife's waist that Teddy knew, beyond doubt, beyond any doubt whatsoever, that this grotesque young stud was sleeping with her. But not just sleeping with her, oh no, he was also rogering her with the expertise and unflagging sexual energy of a Casanova on speed.

Vile images of their coupling raced through Teddy's mind. They were doing it standing up, lying down, upside down, in the bath, in the back of her car, probably in Teddy's own car too, in the Fountains at Trafalgar Square, in the Whispering Gallery in St Paul's Cathedral. His Sally and Rupert. Rutting like beasts.

A slow, roasting anger began to rise in Teddy's chest and he felt beads of sweat breaking out on his forehead. With great exercise of self-control, he managed to subdue the emotions wracking his body and continued to smile, sip his drink and socialise.

Testosterone-charged, Rupert engaged him in a little trivial gossip about how difficult it was for freelance photographers to manage their financial affairs.

Sally hung on his every word, even suggesting that with Teddy's expertise at the bank, he might even "advise Rupert on an informal basis".

I am more likely, thought Teddy in silence, to gouge out my own eyeballs with a screwdriver.

'I'm sure Teddy's *far* too busy,' said Rupert, giving one of his blinding 100-watt smiles.

'Absolutely,' said Teddy, relieved to be off the hook.

Then Sally swept Rupert away to meet another group of people, leaving Teddy alone with his now warm champagne.

A middle-aged man in a pinstriped suit with a large polka-dot handkerchief in the breast pocket sauntered across towards Teddy. He exuded an air of executive confidence.

'Pleased to meet you,' he said, extending a hand. 'I'm Giles Freemantle, Managing Director of Harlequin Magazines. I must say, your wife is the star in our little firmament.'

Teddy shook the proffered hand and nodded politely. 'I'm so glad,' he said.

Fremantle beckoned a waiter over to recharge Teddy's glass.

'Yes,' he continued in the same ebullient tone, 'and since we coupled her writing with the genius of Rupert de la Rue's photography, we have a combination that is making our friends at *Vogue* and *Vanity Fair* absolutely livid with envy.'

Teddy nearly bit through the glass he had raised to his lips, but managed another insincere smile.

Fremantle droned on for another couple of minutes before drifting off, to be replaced by another brace of magazine employees who, like their boss, extolled the virtues of both Sally and the chemistry that had been created by combining her work with that of the grinning hyena Rupert de la Rue.

By his fifth glass of champagne, Teddy was beginning to calm down inside, curiously enough experiencing a kind of tranquillity and peace of mind. The events around him had taken on a surreal quality, all the voices blending into one, all the mouths laughing and showing identical rows of preposterously white teeth. Some of the girls from the advertising department of the magazine seemed to be bursting out of their flimsy knee-high party frocks. There was a plethora of pouting red-lipsticked mouths, cascades of shimmering blonde hair, row upon row of bulging tanned cleavage, a growing cacophony of voices and a distinct rise in temperature.

Suddenly he felt a tug at his sleeve. It was Sally. 'Are you OK?' she said, staring hard at him.

'Yeah, yes, why?' he blurted. Then he noticed she was wearing her ultra-chic blush pink raincoat. 'Are we off, then?'

Sally laughed and patted his arm. 'I think you've had a touch too much champagne,' she said.

'What?' said Teddy.

'Teddy,' she said, 'you know I'm flying to Zurich in an hour in the company jet. I told you yesterday. We've got an important interview with Trinny Norsworthy, the Swiss answer to Coco Chanel. It's a big scoop. I'll only be gone four days. Anyway, I've arranged for you to be taken home in a company car; it's outside whenever you're ready to go. Bye now, must fly.' She pecked him on the cheek and floated away, leaving him leaning against one of the elaborate Claridges' mirrors with an empty glass in his hand.

The dreadful Rupert was on the far side of the room surrounded by four girls and a skinny boy in a shiny blue suit and white shoes.

Teddy walked with a careful gait past little bunches of revellers until he was on the outskirts of the Rupert de la Rue group. 'It has been a pleasure to meet you,' he boomed.

The five people surrounding Rupert all reacted as if there had been a pistol shot; one girl spilled her drink down the front of her dress.

Rupert, to whom this very loud comment had been directed, gave an oleaginous smile and raised his glass. 'Mine too, squire. Mind how you go.'

'I will most certainly,' slurred Teddy, who then turned on his heel and walked crablike towards the door.

A black Mercedes with an even blacker chauffeur drove him back to Bishop's Park Mansions, during which time he fell into a deep sleep.

On arrival, the chauffeur had to nudge him awake after opening the rear door of the car and help him out. Once inside the flat, he took a needle-sharp shower, drank a pint of cold water, changed into his pyjamas and fell asleep on the sofa in the living room.

He awoke about three in the morning with a thumping headache, got up and made a pot of coffee. After the second cup, his head began to clear a little and he started to analyse just what had happened at the party and why he had now come to the conclusion that the grisly Rupert de la Rue was in fact sleeping with Sally.

Before he could take any action, however – any action including murder! – he would need proof. The fact that he had actually muttered the word "murder" under his breath made him laugh out loud. God, he must have been hammered last night. Maybe he would wait until Sally came back from her trip to Zurich and simply confront her with the facts.

But just what were the facts? There were none. It was all in his head. But he was sure that Rupert de la Rue was cuckolding him. To coin a disgusting phrase, "it stuck out a mile". The pomaded, arrogant bastard.

Then he remembered the phrase used by Karl the Hanoverian fencer during the fencing-club dinner in Berlin. 'We have a code. Should one's woman be unfaithful, it is not her that the wronged partner should rebuke, but the seducer. In such circumstances, even killing becomes acceptable, even judicial!'

The man was clearly insane. A foaming nutter. A Nazi throwback, a barmy Hun. Or was he?

Killing a rival in the game of love was in fact a basic animal instinct, only lightly suppressed by a thin veneer of civilisation, and Teddy was a human animal, after all, and his honour had been besmirched.

Or had it? He needed proof, God dammit. He bloody well needed proof.

Later that day, he reported for work at the bank in the usual way, even though he was feeling exceedingly fragile, and went through the motions of his daily routine. Insidious doubts and worms of jealousy still plagued him, however, and as he plunged himself into work, they still hung there at the back of his mind like spectres at a feast.

On the way home that evening, he stopped off at a bar in the Fulham Road and drank three stiff whiskies. The alcohol relaxed him a little and his dark thoughts about Sally's infidelity lightened a little.

Back at the flat, he ate the pork chop, potatoes and broccoli that their Italian lady Lisa had prepared and drank a half-bottle of Chablis. After she had washed-up and left, he sat at his desk and shuffled through the domestic post. Some of it was for Sally, a couple of letters and a postcard from her mother who lived in Gloucestershire. He picked up her post and took it over to her desk, which was much smaller than his and occupied a corner of the living room. On the leather desktop was Sally's address book and Teddy picked it up. All the entries were in Sally's neat handwriting and he flicked through the pages, slowly. There were the addresses, phone numbers and email addresses for all their friends, the doctor, the dentist, the local florist, the hairdresser, the butcher plus a few business numbers. As he turned the pages to the letter "D", he saw the entry, de la Rue, Rupert, photographer, 16A Observatory Studios, Kensington. There was no phone number.

Teddy closed the book and sat down at the desk. So the bastard lived in Kensington. A very smart address, indeed. Perhaps it was here in Observatory Studios that his disgusting acts of lechery took place with Sally.

Teddy lit a cigarette, inhaled deeply, picked up the phone and dialled the local taxi firm. 'I'd like a cab in fifteen minutes,' he said, 'to take me to Kensington.'

Observatory Studios was a row of Victorian houses built originally as artists' studios, but many of them had been converted into smart family apartments. The red-brick facades were stylish with tall sash windows on the upper floors, but on the middle floor there was a huge picture window which allowed the studios which occupied this floor to be flooded with light.

Teddy paid the taxi driver and walked across the pavement outside number 16. An iron gate with security buttons was positioned at the entrance to the four-storey building and Teddy pressed the one marked 16A. A disembodied voice, but clearly Rupert de la Rue's, said, 'Yeah, who is it?'

'Teddy Peterson,' said Teddy.

'Teddy who?'

'Peterson. Sally's husband.'

'Jesus Christ, what do you want?'

'Let me in.'

'OK, OK, hang on. We're on the third floor.'

The gate device buzzed and the gate opened. The internal hall on the ground floor was carpeted in royal blue. An elaborate Gothic mirror hung on the wall next to a tiny, old-fashioned lift with metal concertina doors. It carried Teddy, creakingly, to the third floor, where he got out and found himself in a small corridor facing a glossy black-painted door with 16A in gold letters on the front. He pressed the bell at the side of the door and it opened at once.

Rupert de la Rue stood there, a puzzled expression on his face. He was wearing what looked like a kaftan or a silk bathrobe. It was bright scarlet and decorated with stylised embroidered peacocks. The sight of him standing there, his white teeth gleaming, the "V" of his open kaftan revealing his bronzed chest with the heavy crucifix, inflamed Teddy to the point of speechlessness.

'Well come in,' said Rupert after half a minute as Teddy glowered silently.

Rupert moved to one side to allow Teddy access to the flat, but Teddy suddenly gave a yelping cry and grabbed Rupert by the loose folds of his kaftan, forcing him backwards. The impact threw both men down in the small entrance hall, with Teddy kneeling on Rupert's chest.

'What the fuck is going on?' cried Rupert, pushing Teddy to one side.

Teddy, whose face was now a mask of red fury, lunged out to grab a handful of Rupert's hair. 'You bastard,' he hissed, banging Rupert's head against the stripped pine floorboards.

Rupert wriggled free and rolled to one side. Then as Teddy reached out to seize him again, he delivered Teddy a short punch on the side of his jaw, which sent Teddy sliding against the wall.

Teddy kicked out and his foot caught Rupert in the chest and he fell backwards. Teddy was on him in an instant, his fingers closing round Rupert's throat.

'You seduced my wife,' screamed Teddy. 'I'm going to kill you!'

Rupert, who was as slippery as an eel, jerked his head free of Teddy's grip and gave Teddy another punch in the side of his face. This one stunned him and he momentarily blacked out. The next thing he knew, he was on his face with his arms pinned behind his back. Rupert had him locked in a half nelson and it felt as if his arm would be wrenched from its socket.

'Are you pissed again?' said Rupert, increasing the pressure, 'or are you just a bloody lunatic?'

'Bastard,' said Teddy into the carpet. 'For God's sake, you're going to break my arm!'

'OK, OK,' said Rupert. 'Now if I let you up, just control yourself. OK. No more rough stuff, *comprendi*?'

Rupert eased his grip and Teddy knelt up, gasping. As he raised his eyes, he saw a pair of feet directly in front of him. They weren't Rupert's. The feet were clad in monogrammed blue velvet slippers with a crown on the instep.

'What's all this?' said a voice. 'Fancy a bit of rough, do you?' This was followed by a fruity laugh.

Then Rupert's voice saying, 'Oh for God's sake, Garth, can't you see the man's a lunatic. Go and pour us all a drink.'

Teddy staggered to his feet, his head spinning. And in front of him stood a very tall, slim man wearing jeans and a T-shirt. He looked about thirty with long, very curly blonde hair and a large earring in his right ear.

'I do wish you wouldn't bring your work home with you, dear,' he said to Rupert. 'What in God's name is going on?'

A sense that Teddy was taking part in some surreal nightmare overwhelmed him and he staggered to his feet.

'OK, OK,' said Rupert, 'just come in and sit down. Garth is going to pour us a nice drink. And after your first sip, you are going to apologise to me for behaving in such a very ugly manner. I mean to say, I would have thought a bank manager would know the rights and wrongs of social intercourse.'

Teddy walked into the big studio room which was furnished only with rugs, a couple of leather-and-steel modern chairs and a vast sofa draped with goatskin rugs. Garth was re-emerging from what was obviously a kitchen with a tray of glasses and a champagne bottle.

'Oh, this is Garth, by the way,' said Rupert, adjusting his kaftan. 'Garth is my partner.'

Teddy gaped for a moment and then sank into one of the leather chairs. 'Your partner?' said Teddy woodenly.

'Yes, Teddy. Partner. As in lover. As in intimate flatmate.'

'You mean, you mean –'

'Yes, Teddy, I do.'

'So you are not, you know –'

'Fucking your Sally? Oh for God's sake, Teddy, I wouldn't know how. What on earth put such a ridiculous idea into your silly head?'

Teddy felt his cheeks glowing red and he fumbled in his pocket for a cigarette. 'Do you mind if I smoke?' he said flatly.

'My dear chap,' said Rupert, 'I don't mind if you burst into flames. Now have a glass of champagne and say you are sorry, but for Gawd's sake, make it sound sincere.'

'I feel a complete idiot,' said Teddy, taking the glass of champagne that Garth offered.

'That's a given,' said Rupert, 'now come on, say sorry, pretty please.'

'I'm sorry,' mumbled Teddy, 'I am very sorry, indeed.'

'Well that's settled, then,' said Garth. 'Oh, don't gulp it down, dear boy, sip it, it's Dom Perignon.'

Feeling increasingly small, stupid and humiliated, Teddy sipped his champagne and tried not to meet Rupert's gaze. 'Look,' he said, 'I'll pay for any damage – that lamp and, well, anything else.'

'Oh, for God's sake, don't worry about the lamp,' said Rupert, 'we hate it anyway. Present from Garth's aunty in Godalming. Silly cow has the taste of a stevedore.'

Teddy finished his champagne and stood up. 'Well I'd best be off.'

'If you must,' said Rupert. 'Garth will show you out. Do you have a car?' Teddy shook his head. 'Came by taxi.'

'Well, Garth had better phone for a cab. You can't walk back to Fulham this time of night; you'll get gang banged before you leave Kensington.'

Garth made a shrugging gesture and went gliding off into the kitchen.

'I'm really sorry,' said Teddy again. 'I was convinced Sally was having an affair. Now I feel I have let her down by barging in here with my mad accusations, and she was innocent all along.'

Rupert took a cigarette from an elaborate cigarette box on the table, extracted an oval cigarette, lit it and inhaled deeply.

'Teddy, do sit down. You were wrong about me being your wife's paramour. But, my dear fellow, she was having an affair. But not with me. You obviously don't know.'

'Know what?' yelled Teddy.

'Who her lover was or is,' said Rupert.

Teddy gazed at him blankly, his heart pounding.

'You'd better sit down and have another drink,' said Rupert. 'And promise not to have another seizure on our lovely Persian carpet.'

The sunshine filtering through the tall windows of the gymnasium made the fencing foils reflect with flashes of light. Both men were stripped to the waist and bareheaded, both men's bodies glowed with a sheen of perspiration and both had veins standing proud on their forearms and necks. Teddy could see out of the corner of his eye the images of himself multiplied many times in the mirrors that lined the walls of the gymnasium gallery.

As Professor Kanchek thrust at him, Teddy stepped back a pace, covering himself in quarte. Kanchek made a feint to the left then made a half thrust and the blades rang out as Teddy turned his foil hand into pronation. To retaliate, Teddy came in with an untidy thrust over the arm, his point missing Kanchek's exposed throat by a thousandth of an inch.

Kanchek stepped back nimbly, opposing him in quarte, and as Teddy moved forward a step with a lunging attack to Kanchek's body, he parried with an awkward turn of his blade and his front foot slipped.

With the speed of light, Teddy made a lateral slashing lunge and opened a 6-inch cut across the professor's body. It was a surface wound but oozed scarlet immediately.

'It's over, you know, with me and Sally,' said Kanchek. 'Your wife still loves you.'

Teddy lunged again, but Kanchek deflected his blade with a classic cross-body parry.

'Admitting you used my wife as a plaything doesn't get you off the hook, you bastard,' hissed Teddy.

'Don't be a damn fool,' said Kanchek, blocking another thrust from Teddy. 'You've blooded me, quit now. Honour is satisfied.'

In answer, Teddy came in with a slashing, lunging attack, driving Kanchek back towards a big mirror at the end of the gymnasium. He attacked over Kanchek's arm, aiming for his throat, but Kanchek parried again, the force of the blades sending vibrations up both men's arms.

Now the bout was becoming frenzied, with Teddy's attacks growing wilder. Each time Kanchek deflected Teddy's thrusts, he found himself inches from the mirror behind him. Teddy came in again over Kanchek's arm as Kanchek turned his wrist an inch too far and his point sliced through the professor's nipple.

The professor's back now touched the mirror, but he bent his knees and made an upward thrust that slit Teddy's hip with the point of his foil.

Teddy's sword arm dropped and Kanchek lunged, but Teddy swung his body like a matador facing a charge from a fighting bull and Kanchek's blade whistled through the air.

Teddy drew back his arm and with a massive thrust that was backed by his whole shoulder and arm, drove 6 inches of steel into Kanchek's chest, where it went clear through tissue and muscle, emerging from his back and clanging against the mirror. Kanchek's foil clattered to the floor and he vomited blood that spilled down his chin and onto his chest.

Teddy withdrew his blade as Kanchek slid down into a sitting position, leaving a smear of blood on the mirror. His eyes went wide then glazed over as he toppled sideways with a faint, gurgling groan and died.

The eighteen months after the death of Professor George Kanchek were packed with incident for Teddy Peterson. Sally had flown back from Zurich four days after the event, to find that her husband had been interviewed by the police then charged with manslaughter and released on bail.

Not a single word passed between them about her affair with the professor. As Teddy looked into the eyes of his wife he saw guilt, fear and resignation. He knew there was no need to discuss it. The sordid business was over. Short-lived and humiliating though it was, she would live with the pain of it for the rest of her life.

As to whether Teddy actually forgave her, it is hard to ascertain. That, too, was never discussed. But both of them knew with an iron certainty that they would now have to look ahead and try to bury the past once and for all.

For Teddy's trial on the charge of manslaughter, he appointed Mr Jason Pollock, QC, a brilliant "celebrity" lawyer who had for some years represented Harlequin Magazines. The trial itself was a no-brainer, as Pollock utterly destroyed the prosecution case with his forensic logic and theatrical eloquence. The death of Professor Kanchek had been no more than a tragic accident; two men, voluntarily engaging in a dangerous sport not unlike two boxers, where both participants draw blood from their opponent and then, in a regrettable accident, one of them dies. Pollock's client, Teddy, had after all called for an ambulance and the police immediately after the "unfortunate" business. This was surely not the action of a man intent on an act of homicide or even involuntary manslaughter.

'It was,' Pollock cried in his closing peroration, 'the unforeseen effect of a known cause,' or in the wise words of *Cassell's English Dictionary*, 'a mishap, a property or quality of a thing not essential to our conception of it. In short, my Lord, *an accident!*'

After he walked free from the courthouse without a stain on his character, he and Sally took a short holiday in Tenerife and on their return, set about rebuilding their lives.

Towards the end of the year, two events occurred that seemed to cement their future together. Teddy was promoted by his bank to a very senior position in the St James' branch in London's West End and Sally announced that she was pregnant.

Several People May be Faintly Aware of This, But ...

In the 1960s, there was a small cinema in the King's Road that occasionally put on low-budget musical shows. One such was *The Rocky Horror Show*, which caused something of a stir, even in bohemian Chelsea. Its theme was transvestism, homosexuality and vampirism. It became something of a cult and some years later, a film was made of the show staring Tim Curry in stockings and suspenders as the High Camp Villain in Chief who presides over a household of eccentric deviants. A couple of innocent strangers on honeymoon, whose car breaks down, stray into this crazy house where high jinks, low jinks and fabulous jazz and dancing take place.

There is a sewer deep underground that runs from Hammersmith and continues its very long and mysterious journey by passing under both Fulham and Chelsea. After being pumped through Millbank, under the Houses of Parliament, Victoria Embankment, Tower Hill and Whitechapel, it snakes on to Stepney. It has in fact, according to the great London historian Peter Ackroyd, traversed the Stygian depths of the City. Rarely, if ever, seen by members of the public, the sewer's arches are decorated in an elaborate, almost Egyptian style. It is a wonder of subterranean Victorian architecture. There is an ancient myth that in the 1860s, rats as big as dogs lived in the Fulham end of the sewer; although none have ever been seen.

Fond, Filthy Memories

Barbarian

'I remember walking down the King's Road in the 1960s. Blimey, stone the crows, I tell ya, it was a right peacock parade. No, straight up, no kidding, a right bleedin' peacock parade. All these dolly birds in their miniskirts, cor, a bit of all right they were and no mistake. Long blonde hair, shag-me shoes with the old ankle straps. Blimey.

'And the blokes, well, I tell ya, I was one of 'em. I had all the gear, the drainpipes, the flash silk jacket like what Mick Jagger wore, double cuffs, pearl buttons and a shirt with ruffles from John Lord or was it Blades? I can't remember.

'Yeah, lunch in Alvaro's, one of the Italian joints like Terrazza and Tiberio. Great scoff; your T-bone steaks and your pasta and that. And wine, Orvieto thingy or the Pinot Grigglio or that Frascati. I tell you, and you know what, you could smoke in restaurants then. Too bleedin' true. Castella cigars.

'And down at the far end of the King's Road, down by the bleedin' World's End pub, that great restaurant, La Famiglia. Bloody good. Great wop food – sorry, just slipped out – great Italian scoff. Sorry, Mario, no offence intended.

'I tell you, of a Saturday morning, you stroll down the King's Road in all your gear, your barnet well Brylcreemed, a smart, well-cut whistle and a fancy Peckham, you'd have the dolly birds falling over each other to get a piece of you. No kidding. Straight up. Damp gussets all round. Blimey, they were the days.

'All gone for a shit now, of course. Just tourists and bleedin' chain stores. Alvaro's gone. Yeah. The sixties. Chelsea. Swinging London. Mind you, I lived in Fulham. Bit dull compared to Chelsea then. Chelsea was for toffs. Fulham, well, Fulham was for the lads like me. But I fitted in. No question. I took no shit from those toffee-nosed wankers who lived in the big houses off the King's Road. Oh no. No bleeding way, Jose.

'We was all equal. All those class divisions smashed up. I mean, bloody hairdressers were part of the aristocracy. And David Bailey, a bit of rough if ever there was, the top photographer of his day. Too bleedin' true. Straight up, no kidding.

'You know what pisses me off now I'm 77 years old? What pisses me off is that I didn't realise how lucky I was back in the bleeding sixties. If I knew *then* what I know now, I would have shagged a thousand birds a month. No kidding. I was good with the birds. Know what I mean? Yeah, always had a tan. Great sideburns. I was hung like a bleeding donkey. Hard to believe I know. Yeah, now I'm hung like a bleedin' prawn.

'Oh well, happy days. No good crying over spilt milk.

''ere, have another beer, Mario, I feel like getting pissed.'

Toffs

Yes, I did find the King's Road a trifle brash in the sixties. A huge explosion of clothing shops, a sort of spillover from Carnaby Street, mostly very flash, not particularly well made, either. Although I bought shirts there, very colourful, long, spear-point collars which oddly enough looked quite OK worn with the old Henley blazer.

Lots of pretty girls, Eliza Doolittle to the life, but common as muck. Came in on the bus from places like Peckham and Bermondsey or on the Tube from Essex to Sloane Square. There was still the occasional oasis of class like The Pheasantry or 30 Pavilion Road where decent, OK chaps could throw a party.

Fabulous eighteenth-century houses could still be bought just off the King's Road for fifteen grand and many had been in the same family for generations.

Gone a bit pear-shaped now in the twenty-first century. Coarse City types or Russian oligarchs are buying them up. Alvaro's gone and the Pheasantry's a pizza place.

In those days, a chap could park his E-Type Jag or Bentley Flying Spur outside his house. No wretched traffic wardens then.

La Familigia is still there, opposite the World's End pub. Still excellent. Mixed clientele, of course. Just like the sixties. Pop stars and aristos mixed together in a very bubbly, social cocktail.

Anyhow, Mario, my dear chap, I mustn't bore you with my reminiscences. Now I'm seventy-seven, I incline to dwell too much on the past. It's funny though, as I mourned the popularisation of Chelsea, turning the King's Road into a rather common tourist attraction, I was offered a king's ransom for my little cottage in Anderson Street just off the King's Road. By a Russian oligarch, no less. Well, of course I had to sell. So many noughts on the end of the price. Now I live in Fulham, off the North End Road, in a splendid bijou house. Used to be three flats; and the North End Road was quite awful. Like all of Fulham. A working-class hellhole. Now it's as good as Chelsea. Maybe better. How things have changed.

Another glass of champagne, Mario? I feel like getting smashed.

Last Words

During the Second World War, a number of octogenarian Chelsea pensioners offered to "join up" and help the Allied war effort. Of course their noble offer was not accepted, but they did receive a letter from Winston Churchill, thanking them for their patriotism.

In 1715, on the site that is now the North End Road Market in Fulham, a huge, double-fronted villa was erected. The famous novelist Samuel Richardson lived there, then in 1867 the pre-Raphaelite artist Edward Burne-Jones.

A regular visitor was Rudyard Kipling, who spent his youthful holidays there. Kipling's Aunt Georgina was Burne-Jones' wife. So Fulham can lay claim to being a breeding ground for literary giants!